The past claimed her when it chose and she was a victim. She was looking at one of the most impressive sites in the world and yet she saw a wall painted orange. And there was a painting on an easel to the left side. She could see the scarlet paint was still wet, and the corner of a thick, old, wooden table, scarred and cut. To her right, there was a window. She felt hot, unable to breathe, and she opened the window which looked onto a courtyard. Opposite, all the windows were open. And the air outside was the same as the air inside. There was no difference. In the air was a heaviness, a darkness, a certain perfume that was undeniably Paris, and she was not Vicky but someone who so appreciated the difference between colour and texture, that the scarlet of the paint in contrast to the roughness of the bread crust on the table gave her an exultant sensation. She felt so alive and so hungry for colour and textures, they fed her, as food did Vicky. The luscious yellow petals of the summer plant gave her joy. And the table, she saw, was scattered with painting tools and bottles and the floor was wooden with painted, uneven boards. She felt heavy, as though her abdomen was pressing her stomach upwards – she knew it would be a case of having to squeeze past the table-corner to leave the room.

Now she was full of apprehension. Should she go out into the street and look for something to make her apprehension lift, or stay where she was? The cause of the unease, she was sure, was a man. And then came fast footsteps, quite heavy, up flights of stairs, undeniably his, and she heard him singing and whistling, heard it in her mind – there was no sound. Her heart soared because the door would open and he would give her the unimaginable. He so charged her, he filled her with light, like a carousel, when he was there, when he was absent. The light, the dark, the absence was unendurable.

Also by Patrice Chaplin
**available from Mandarin Paperbacks*

Having It Away
The Unforgotten
Siesta
Harriet Hunter
Don Salino's Wife
Albany Park
Another City
*By Flower and Dean Street
*The Fame People

PATRICE CHAPLIN

· *Forget Me Not* ·

Mandarin

A Mandarin Paperback

FORGET ME NOT

First published in Great Britain 1989
by Methuen London
This edition published 1990
by Mandarin Paperbacks
Michelin House, 81 Fulham Road, London SW3 6RB

Mandarin is an imprint of the Octopus Publishing Group

A CIP catalogue record for this book
is available from the British Library
ISBN 0 7493 0256 9

Printed in Great Britain
by Cox & Wyman Ltd, Reading

· *One* ·

Vicky saw him by chance because the television remote control button still was not fixed. She pressed BBC1 for the American soap and got Serge Marais conducting an exotic Russian work on BBC2. His eyes were mesmerizing, filled with light. His expression constantly changed, deepening with sorrow, ecstasy, even joy. The face was lined and fine with a hard, sensuous mouth, the famous hair was swept back, long and silver-streaked, almost to his shoulders. His hands were fitted to receive and purvey life's higher states of being. He produced music as a priest gives mass.

For a moment his face lost control, was given over to passion, and she could see how he would look while making love, and a trumpet soared as though announcing alarm. The huge German audience rose with a roar of approval. He bowed deeply, swiftly and left the podium wiping sweat from his face. The audience shouted his name. Vicky waited to see if he would come back, before switching to the soap. She had never seen anyone inspire such adulation. Popstars received something less respectful. He came out of the darkness, hands above his head, applauding his orchestra and the camera closed up on his face. Then he smiled and laughed – he was magical. And Vicky said, 'I'll see him. Somehow I will get to him.' It was her birthday and she was alone. The decision to meet the most famous conductor in the world was her present to herself. It dealt with the loneliness.

The room was dusty. Even the pile of new radio drama scripts had a coating of dust. Her make-up and shoes were gathered in one corner, still not put away in a cupboard. The white curtains needed washing and were shown to disadvantage in the June evening light. She never was exactly ahead with the housework. In contrast Jay's desk was neat and dust-free. She noticed there were several messages on it to Jay from her friend Lorraine. Ostensibly, they were concerning his writing career.

The flat was near Hampstead Heath in an enviable street. The hallway needed paint, the fireplace new bricks, but her trunk stood in the same corner, still packed. The flat may be hers but she still could not settle. At twenty-seven, she had not found the place, the one where she should be.

Jay came in as the sun was rising. She heard him say 'Shit'. Several things could have caused that – her dinner plate left on a sofa, the scattering of unpaid bills and messages by the bed. Jay was immaculate. It did not mean he was not unfaithful.

She said, 'Your L.A. agent called.'

'Which one?' He came from Brooklyn and his voice was sharp, dry and always attractive. He said exactly what he meant to say. No more, no less. He could be acerbic and occasionally very seductive.

'I don't know which one. I think it was William Morris.'

He started to take off his clothes, indisputably clean, unchallenged by city dirt. 'The meeting went on longer than I thought.' He hung up the shirt and trousers. 'We got a budget agreed but he's a tough bastard.'

'Is he a cannibal as well? You've got teethmarks and scratches all over your back.'

'Vicky, I'm allergic to the dust in here.' His tone implied it was no time for a fight. He lay down swiftly, out of sight, hiding his marks of sin. The duvet was generous enough to keep them both covered and separate.

'I work too, pal.' Her voice had the same edge as his when angry. 'You're here in the day. You can switch on a Hoover. No one will see you.' She was deeply jealous, worse, rejected.

'Of course you do, babe. So get a woman to sweep up a bit. Maybe London's a dusty place. It sure makes me scratch.'

'And lie,' she whispered.

They lay, not touching.

'Go to sleep, Vicky.' He patted her part of the duvet with a small brown hand. 'By the way, I didn't forget your birthday. We'll go out and do some things around noon.'

'Oh, don't worry,' she said. 'I had a good time.'

'Yeah?' He was surprised.

'I went out with some people from the BBC. In fact, it was great.'

'What, to Groucho's?'

He might have been there, so she said somewhere unfashionable. By the look of his back he had not spent the evening in public.

She wondered why she had to lie. Sometimes she had such a bad time she felt almost ashamed.

After Jay Landis got the Pulitzer prize he had come to London to stage his latest play, 'Scam', and met Vicky in Fortnum and Mason's tea room. He was thirty-nine, small, dark, with a good, well-toned, compact body, black piercing eyes and sex appeal so obvious it had all the immediacy of cheap scent. He did not lie but he left a lot out.

He had dragged himself up from the lowest classes – his parents, separated, could not read. He had got himself educated, to university, and had managed a good degree and won a research fellowship. He knew all about winning against the odds. Now a successful, respected playwright, he had not forgotten the rules of the street. Don't trust anybody except the dead ones. Hit first, to kill. Be soft and you get no mercy. Women are mothers or whores and they have their own rules. Nothing less than a one hundred percent attitude brings change. God exists only in literature. Jay could only ever be on the side of the underdog after what he had seen. He mixed with rich people if they were bright and he played their game, to win. But he would never be one of them.

He told Vicky he had been married twice and was now between marriages but Vicky thought wife number two was still legally attached. And he had a lot of children. Alimony was a serious thing in the States. It was the dread of his life. 'Ali knocks every month and if I don't pay, I go inside. I'm going to have to write crap for Tinsel Town to keep those wives off my back. I pray every night some guy will marry them and take the problem away. This way, I'll have to work till I'm ninety.'

He had moved into Vicky's flat with the understanding they were free people. 'We have it good in bed because we don't try to put anything on it, OK? Nothing that isn't there.' While Vicky produced radio drama at the BBC he sat in the kitchen and turned his play, 'Scam', into a filmscript.

He ran on the Heath, worked-out in a gym, took steambaths, had massages and aromatherapy. He had borrowed a car but liked to walk everywhere. He did meditation and t'ai chi. He needed to be on peak form at all times and liked his clothes to look alive and have good colour. He hated the drab, the lifeless, the creased. His suits, well-cut and elegant, were made for him from quality material and he only wore good shoes. The desire to feel and look at his best came from a childhood where everything had been at its worst. He had worn handed-down clothes and washed at a cold tap in the yard.

They had been together three months but Vicky knew not to depend on him. London was too slow, the atmosphere too neutral, and he could never work out the class system. He would go back to New York on impulse and she dreaded his going. How lucky she was not to be in love with him.

She thought, it was not often she was lucky.

· *Two* ·

They said her mother was in a side ward and left her to find the way. Like most National Health hospitals there were not enough staff. A woman in a grey nightdress ran at Vicky, caught at her dress and wanted a knife. Her eyes were sly and sideways-looking and she kept trying to pull at Vicky's bag, her fingers covered with half-healed cuts. A man was peeing at the end of the ward. Vicky felt terrified but hoped it did not show. The others asked for cigarettes. She moved purposefully on and refused to let the mentally ill stop her.

'Are you a visitor or one of us?' asked a young, curly-haired man.

'I'll let you know when I leave,' said Vicky.

By her mother's door a woman cringed, terrified. Her stockings were around her ankles and her legs blue-veined and bruised. 'Let me come with you, love. Please let me come back with you.' Her voice was rough with panic.

There was so much fear in the air Vicky wanted to shout for help.

'I'll be no trouble. Please, dear, help me.'

With effort, Vicky recognized her mother. One eye was black, her front teeth broken.

'Please get me out of here. I don't belong here.'

The ward was full of screams and cries.

'It's all right,' said Vicky steadily. 'I'll go and get some help.'

Appalled by the sight of her mother, she went to the nurses' office. It was empty. A sectioned patient had tried to break out and the attempt to dissuade him was only just successful. The crisis had all the nurses' attention. Vicky had to wait for a male nurse to re-lock the medicine room. He was unimpressed by her mother's condition.

'She was brought in last night, love. She has to be seen by the ward round.'

'Can't you give her something? She's in a terrible state.'

'Please don't go around diagnosing the patients.'

'But she's in hell. Can't you give her something for the panic?'

The nurse looked at Vicky as though she was the one in need of sedation.

'Can I speak to a doctor? Who's in charge?'

'Your mother's being given the treatment that the admitting doctor thinks necessary.'

'Well what is it?'

'That's for the doctor to say.'

'It's not working. Can I see the doctor?'

'Your mother's now in the care of the registrar.'

'Well, I'll see him.'

'He's only here Wednesdays.'

'Can't you give my mother something?' Vicky's voice rose towards hysteria. The male nurse, after some persuasion, accompanied Vicky to her mother's room.

'Now what's all this, darling?' He took her mother's arm and led her back into the cubicle. 'Your daughter thinks you're upset. Why don't you pull up your stockings and we'll get you a nice cup of tea.'

'My daughter's dead, you fucker!' And her mother suddenly screamed and grabbed Vicky violently. 'Save me!' And the woman's face was inhuman with madness. She slid away from the nurse's grasp and reared up at Vicky, all pale and splotched and injured. Vicky could smell the stale whisky on her breath. Her mother, as she had been previously, no longer existed. Instead, this violent creature wished her harm.

Vicky said, 'I can't stand it. I'll have to go, I'm sorry,' and she started to sprint away down the corridor.

'I don't blame you,' said the nurse.

Vicky was reminded of Serge Marais. He had the same degree of intensity of expression as her mother. But how different it was, coming from a disturbed person.

*

Vicky sat on the pavement outside the hospital and, as always when her mother was ill, she believed it was her fault. She linked her mother's bad times with some lack of faith in herself. She was cold, sweating and, as usual during the worst moments, alone. Why did she always have the responsibility? And what help was she? Vicky could only witness the pain. She could do nothing to alleviate it.

St James, an old-fashioned mental hospital, was due to be closed because of the National Health cuts. Vicky knew from other occasions that the receiving ward was always turbulent. Once her mother had been diagnosed she would be moved to a less chaotic ward. Her illness was usually labelled as depression. Vicky had come from London, at least seventy miles on the train, to be scared by her mother. She must do something other than run away.

The administrator was not available. No doctors were, either. She got a secretary, who gave her a cup of tea and read her mother's notes. 'She was admitted as an emergency. She's receiving medication. Sometimes it takes a little while to work.'

'But she's in a terrible state and –'

'Well, there's bound to be something wrong or she wouldn't be in here.'

Vicky wanted to say that her mother was not being helped, left to stand in deep horror in a gloomy corridor. But she knew the hospital was dramatically under-staffed. She had just finished a documentary on the NHS cuts for the BBC. She explained she lived in London and could not visit every day.

'Her teeth are broken and there are cuts under her eye.'

'She was admitted with those.'

Vicky knew her mother had received the injuries bashing her head against the hospital dormitory wall. Why did she have to have such a mother? How often had she wondered that? The woman should never have had a child. In the old days Vicky had tried to show love but her mother remained withdrawn. Vicky thought it might be her fault; perhaps she was not exactly lovable. Her mother seemed affectionate enough to other people's children and animals.

Lately, Vicky had stopped trying to conduct an emotional relationship with her mother. She simply did what she was asked and kept the visits short. She felt very sorry for her father but did not dare show it. He was one of the trigger points of her mother's madness. Since retiring, he had become a grey stranger, trying to keep his wife's behaviour a secret from the neighbours. He was middle-class, a professional man, and her mother, Ruby, one of eight from a working-class family. She was twenty-six years younger than him and at some time, early in the marriage, had been made to feel inferior. Whenever a hospital doctor asked about her marriage, Ruby always said, 'Fine. We're happy.' But then, she wanted to go home.

As always, Vicky would do her best. She took one of her own emergency tranquillizers and went back to the receiving ward.

Ruby was still standing pressed against the corridor wall in wild terror. Vicky extended a hand to try and touch her. Ruby shuddered and pulled back.

'I'll help you, Mum. Just come in to your room. I'll sort things out.'

Vicky found the nurse in charge and asked if being with her mother helped.

'Help who?'

'Will it make her better?'

She got the answer she wanted and left immediately. Once in the sanity of the suburban streets, she remembered her mother as she was when sane. 'I'll look after Dad, don't worry.' She felt seared with grief but would not allow herself one tear.

Her father was standing at the door of the three-room flat on the border of Hampshire and Surrey. He had sold the house because he couldn't keep it up. Ruby was too much trouble and often not well enough to do any housework. The flat was easy and he could manage it himself. He was a stubborn, proud man and at all times refused help.

Now he said, 'Why don't you mind your own business, Victoria? I'm not having a home-help or anyone else. I can look after myself.'

She said she would pay for a local girl to come in and cook him a meal. He was over eighty.

'And have her tell the whole village about your mother?'

He did not look well but he would not do anything about it. Advice he saw as interference. Vicky said, 'Do you need anything? You can come and stay with me, Dad, if you like.'

'Thank you, but I want to visit her. I don't know what makes her like it, I really don't. They can put men on the moon but can't get human beings straightened out.'

So she left him some fresh fruit, cheese and biscuits and asked what he would do that evening. He didn't know.

'There's no point visiting her, Dad. It's too far and she's out of it. She's fine, really.'

'She was doing one thing one minute and the next she was screaming the place down. What had she seen? It took three of them to hold her down. She can't go on like this. The neighbours. I have to live here.'

She wanted to say, stuff them, worry about yourself. She said, 'D'you want me to stay?'

He did not, so she turned and left. And she thought, I keep trying because I think I need parents. Do they need me? Once, when they asked her at school what she wanted to be, she had said, an orphan.

· *Three* ·

She got home after eight and Jay was typing in the kitchen. 'I hope they pay you overtime.'

She did not answer.

'What was it? Difficult actors?' He knew it was not. He just thought that because he played around, everyone else did too.

'I taped some interviews with the alternative comedy show. There's always room for satire in this world.'

'There sure is.' He went on typing. 'So you had a good day.' He sounded almost bitter. He loathed unfaithful women.

She put a Marks and Spencer's quick-bake in the oven. 'Absolutely.' She almost choked on the wildness of the lie. But she could not tell Jay about her mother's illness or her own suffering. She had learned some time ago to keep family horror stories to herself.

Jay said, 'I press BBC1 and I get BBC2. It makes life kind of confusing.'

She could see how it might. But if the world worked perfectly she would have turned on 'Dynasty' and never seen Serge Marais.

As she was going to bed, Lorraine phoned. Vicky felt she really wanted to speak to Jay.

'I put you up for a film. Don't get excited, but it could happen.'

Originally, a long, hard time ago, Vicky had wanted to be a film director. She had made a short. It was the thing she most wanted to do in the world. But as she needed to make money to keep herself, she did a regular job. Radio producing kept her in touch with actors and drama. Lorraine was a top agent with one of the big American conglomerates so her offer was not just empty talk.

'Look, it's nice of you, Lo, but I don't think it'll go any further. There are five women directors who'll get in ahead of me.' She sounded dispirited.

'No, you have your own voice and your own way of seeing things. Five other women directors do not see life exactly as you do. You've just had a run of bad luck.'

'What, twenty-seven years?' Vicky almost laughed.

'Things will change for you. You've just got to want it enough.' Lorraine's voice was steady and serene and blotted up other people's distress. It made her a great agent.

Before she went to sleep, Vicky said a prayer for her mother. It was very hard to get the image of her, crouching terrified in the doorway, stockings around her ankles, out of her mind.

She lay sleepless beside Jay and thought she would have to change it; her life, herself. Not just wait for something lucky to come along.

What are my virtues? I'm patient. And I'll put myself out for someone in trouble. I want to make films because I need another reality, something I can control. The only remedy for all this bad luck is to be in the fast lane. I'll do practically anything to get what I want.

The BBC studio below Broadcasting House was too cold. The boy on grams, Micky Duke, wanted it even colder because the studio manager smoked non-stop and smoke made Micky cough. Vicky was used to environmental squabbles and marked up the Saturday Night Theatre script in the order of rehearse record. The actors sat in a circle in the studio, drinking coffee out of plastic beakers. The playwright sat moping behind Vicky. It was her first play for radio and Vicky had just finished explaining why the most glamorous scenes had to be cut.

'Listeners out there are not going to understand, or identify with, this jetset life. So it has to go. We put on plays they can understand and feel comfortable with.'

'That's ridiculous. Why not take them out of their ordinary lives?' The writer had had several successes on the stage and was now vowing never again to work for radio.

'They haven't got the concentration span. Radio goes very fast and if they miss a plot point they lose interest. They can't roll it back. Keep it simple and well-crafted and don't give them problems about things they don't know about.'

The writer would not agree.

'Then go and write for Radio 3. On this show, you're dealing with mass audience.'

'That's so damned safe.'

'Sure,' said Vicky. 'But we keep our audience. The high life is out. Sorry.' Sometimes, when being firm, she sounded like Jay.

She flicked a switch, so putting herself on the studio mike. 'OK, people, let's have some fun.'

'Is this for real?' asked the studio manager. He meant, should he tape the scene?

'It's all real.' And she left the recording cubicle to talk to the actors. She looked cool and clear. There was no suggestion of the havoc around her or the fact she was desperately waiting for a phone call from Lorraine to say she had got the feature film. The way she felt, she would direct it for nothing, take her money on deferred, trim half-a-million dollars off the budget and bring it in under six weeks.

At twenty-seven, Vicky was one of the BBC's youngest radio producers. Apart from plays, she did documentaries on topical subjects she cared about. She was considered too ambitious to stay in radio. She was well-read, loved literature and poetry. She had a quiet authority and turned in her productions on time, within the budget. The fact she lived with Jay Landis, the Pulitzer prize-winning playwright, gave her a certain status with colleagues and actors. 'Scam' was a West End hit. But nobody really knew her. She was considered too cool. Her long auburn hair was her best feature. Her eyes were slightly slanted, hazel-green with long lashes, her skin was pale and she had freckles on her nose. Her face was oval. She looked dreamy, as though in another world. People who knew about these things said she had an old soul. She thought they were really saying she had had a hard life. She preferred individual, arty clothes but usually wore chic outfits and elegant high-heeled shoes because they gave her more impact. In a quiet way she wanted power.

In the break, while the props were being set up, she asked Micky Duke what he knew about Serge Marais. Micky loved music and went to every major concert.

'When he was in London last year I couldn't get a ticket. They were going for crazy prices – the cheapest was ninety pounds. So I watched it on the box. He did a concert in Munich a few days ago. We got that live.'

Vicky had seen it. 'Does he come to London often?' she asked.

'No,' said Micky.

'People are crazy to pay ninety pounds,' said the playwright.

'They're crazy about *him* and they'll pay anything,' said Micky. 'He's not French. He's Romanian, was born in Romania. Maybe his father was French.'

'Is he married?'

'Bound to be, Vicky. I should think several times.'

Lorraine picked Vicky up in the Maserati and they went to Groucho's, then L'Escargot for an early dinner. Lorraine was wearing a power outfit and make-up that took five years off her age. She admitted to being thirty-six. Vicky had not got the movie.

'I'm sorry, love. I really went in to bat for you. I showed them your horse film but it just happened the financier hates horses. So we started off wrong.'

Vicky sighed, letting out the disappointment. 'Thank you for trying.'

Lorraine told her a dozen good things they had said about her film. Vicky was thinking, I need a real piece of luck. I know Jay is going to leave. I feel it in my bones. I've got to be deeply involved in something good to get me through that.

Lorraine was warm-hearted with a sincere smile, and when she came into a room everyone looked up as though something was happening. She adopted a motherly manner that clients and friends appreciated. Vicky was different. She did not like too much motherliness.

Lorraine had been very supportive in the old days when Vicky had been trying to get money to make her film. They helped each other professionally. Vicky used her clients for radio plays.

Actors engaged in a long West End run were often pleased to do radio during the day. And Lorraine occasionally got Vicky a job directing low-budget commercials. Their friendship stopped there. They rarely visited each other's homes and Vicky never spoke about her past or her parents. Lorraine assumed she came from a county family in Hampshire and Vicky let her go on thinking it. She knew Lorraine, at thirty-six, was anxious to find a husband and have a child. Sometimes Vicky actually met an attractive, unattached man and if she did not want him herself, sent him immediately to Lorraine. Vicky was sure, however, that the one she had not sent, Jay, was the one that Lorraine wanted.

'Order what you like,' said Lorraine and flipped over the menu. 'It's on me. I'm going to take L and C Entertainments for all they've got. They're going to have to pay me to breathe from now on.' And she ordered the most expensive starters. Vicky was surprised. Lorraine always seemed secure in her job.

'The old man has handed out raises and promotions like it's Christmas, but not to me. My assistant is allowed to go to the New York office and L.A., for what he calls a training programme. And I bring him every damn mini-series before they even write it. So now I go to the health club, the hairdresser, health farms and charge it to L and C. I even charge my cat food. How's Jay?'

'The same as he was when you rang this morning.'

Lorraine ignored the sharp tone. 'I've done everything to persuade him to be on my client list.'

Vicky, looking at her long nails painted red, remembered his scratched back and thought, yes, I'm sure you have. Vicky talked about the new play Jay was writing with one eye on film sales.

Lorraine's eyes flicked over the abundance of food. She was not in the mood for eating. 'It's a dog-eat-dog world.'

'So, what's new?' said Vicky. 'When are you going to L.A.?'

Lorraine felt the queasiness that came on at the same time every evening. Was she, at last, pregnant?

The *maitre d'* brought Vicky her favourite pudding although it was not on the menu and said he had seen Jay's play at last. 'I had to wait three weeks for a ticket.'

'But you should have asked me to get tickets from Jay,' said Lorraine. Then, realizing she was sitting opposite the playwright's girlfriend, said, 'I can get you into anything.'

Vicky knew she was looking good. Her hair was piled up high, with ringlets dangling at the sides. A leather choker emphasized her neck's shapeliness and her breasts were firm and swooped forward in the blue silk shirt. She had a wide, beautifully shaped mouth that was rarely in repose. It turned down at the sides sardonically, twitched, half-smiled. The mouth relieved the tension her eyes did not show. They seemed calm. She got the attention of several men, including a film actor. She liked to be noticed, approved of, it made her feel special. Tonight she felt at her best. She was taken aback when Lorraine said, 'We've got to do something about you.' Her voice was warm.

'Do?'

'You are so unlucky, you really are. We've got to find out why.'

Unlucky? Occasionally unlucky, yes. But Vicky did not like the 'so'; and how did Lorraine know? Vicky said very little about her problems. She could put a good face on anything.

'Sometimes it's Karma. You know; the result of past actions. Cause and effect; what you've done you have to pay for. Even from another life. I was thinking, your being unlucky has a pattern.'

Vicky laughed caustically. 'Spell it out for me.' On the spot, again, she sounded slightly like Jay.

'That's not important. Let's change the pattern. You try very, very hard, Vicky. I'll give you that. But something's blocking you. I go to a healer who helps me. He works directly from the spirit.'

'Healer?'

'He puts his hands on you and you feel better.'

'Like Jesus,' said Vicky.

'OK, like Jesus. Why not? And he's in contact with the spirit world and can get messages to help speed up a black time of adversity. Spirits direct you to the right areas, put you on the right road.'

'Did they help you pick out Jay?' It was a rash accusation.

Lorraine looked perplexed.

Vicky said, 'I thought this conversation was leading up to you telling me that you and Jay have got something going and he's leaving me. Now that would be a stroke of luck. Trust me, Lo. He's hell to live with.'

Lorraine tried to laugh. 'Kiddo, I was thinking more about your work. But if things between you and Jay are difficult –'

Vicky was now sure Lorraine had seriously wanted him, not just for the client list. 'I don't want to quarrel with you, Lo. We've always got on.'

'Yes,' said Lorraine. 'From the first time we met. We go back a long way. We laugh together, that's really valuable. How could I be disloyal to someone I laugh with?' Lorraine's voice was steady. 'I talked to the healer about you. What you do is ill-starred. You are talented enough to make movies but you end up doing radio drama. You want to record the classics but you end up producing afternoon playhouse for housewives. And now they're putting that snotty little bitch from TV drama doc over to radio so she can have a quick rest instead of a nervous breakdown. She's been given *carte blanche* to produce what she likes and she thinks she likes classics. Vicky, she'll do the big stuff and she'll take your slots. Come with me to the healer. He lives in Stoke Newington.'

'Not a chance.' Vicky did not approve or disapprove. She knew nothing about the occult. It just was not part of her life.

· *Four* ·

Two years before, in 1986, Vicky had finally got tired of the negative answers from TV and film companies and, using a bank loan and a second mortgage on her flat, had shot eight minutes of film about a day on a racecourse from the horse's point of view. She sold it immediately to a TV company and was invited to show it at film festivals in Berlin and Deauville. She stopped off briefly in Paris to try and get a French cinema sale and, to give herself promotion, appeared on a French TV chat show. A racehorse owner in Normandy promptly injuncted the film; she said it was about her. Vicky's protests that the film was shot from the point of view of an animal achieved nothing in the French courts. The racehorse owner had property, power and connections. She squashed Vicky's career as she would a cockroach and Vicky slunk back to England. It took a year to pay off the court costs and she decided next time she shot a film it would be from the point of view of a killer.

In the winter of '87 the French racehorse owner was discredited in a scandal involving works of art. For one wild, happy moment Vicky thought her film could now be released. But her request to lift the injunction was refused. Vicky tried to meet the hidden enemy, Madame de Fleury, who was considered eccentric, rather arty for the racetrack, and was over-indulged, with a wealthy husband to back every whim. The woman would not even speak to her on the phone. The film had received good reviews in England and won a minor prize at Berlin. Vicky made enough to pay her camera man and crew. After that experience she decided the French had special views about things and should be avoided and she should get herself a three-year course at the Beaconsfield film school.

But then her mother became ill and Vicky spent three evenings a week taking the train to the hospital. Weekends were spent helping her father move from the large house into the small apartment. She decided to stay at the BBC which gave her security and money. She never found out the reason why Madame de Fleury had been so appalled by her film. The implication of doping? The mean tricks played to get the animal to jump higher, faster? The fact the owner depicted had a huge fat arse and dyed hair?

It was a drama that appealed immediately to Jay Landis; 'It has nothing to do with the footage you shot. You went on television and spoke prettily and her husband fancied you; simple as that.' Jay thought she should get her own back, seek out the husband who had enough petty cash for fifty films.

Vicky wanted to move her mother out of the public mental hospital into a private clinic immediately, even though her mother was not insured and the fees were astronomical. It was too painful for her father to visit the public ward. In ten days he would be eighty-one and Ruby's last illness had broken him. Vicky waited for Jay to get dressed and leave so she could arrange a bank loan. Her mother's condition was labelled psychotic. Apparently, this particular crisis had resulted from a shock followed by lots of drinking. In the hours between the first scream and the arrival of the ambulance there had been some fighting. Quite often, Ruby came near to hating the old man who had married her; Vicky could see he was wrecked too, but thought she should deal with one catastrophe at a time.

The hospital had said her mother was settling down. Vicky saw she was deteriorating into a panicky place that words could not reach. The fact she believed her daughter was dead did not help.

Jay buttoned his ice-white shirt and knotted a woollen tie. 'I came across a good writer the other day, from my neck of the woods. I've told him to call you. He's prepared to do radio. Before you say you're full up, he looks like Sam.' He meant Sam Sheppard. Vicky did not like the 'prepared' to do radio. Too condescending.

'Come on, Babe, who listens to it? You'll end up mangling out those murder plays no one cares about, and you'll stop caring, and you'll die a little and get old. It's time to take a dive off a high board. Get behind a camera. It's what you need to do; and if you need something enough, do it; I know. A hospital called.' He tried to remember its name; 'They wanted to put your mother on the line.'

Vicky told him the first lie that occurred to her. 'Possibly one of my aunts is ill and my mother's visiting.'

'I don't think so; this was a mental hospital. I said you were out and to call back before nine in the morning or after six.' He looked at her, expecting an explanation, something.

Vicky said, 'I've been interviewing patients about the NHS cuts programme. I told you about that. I guess one of the patients thought she was my mother.'

It all sounded too glacial for Jay. The English were an odd race. There was some truth in the saying, all the Americans and the English shared was a common language.

'Well, if there's anything I can do. I –'

She was already shaking her head.

'I'm tough, Vicky.'

'So am I, Jay. Just as tough as you.' And she went on to the patio, hoping he would leave.

She was not secretive. Neither was it pride that made her keep her mother's illness to herself. What she hid was the degree of her vulnerability. She would never let Jay near her mother or he might think she would end up the same. Hadn't her husband said that, when they used to quarrel; 'That's it, Vicky. Keep shouting the odds. You sound just like your mother. You even look like your mother.' That was enough to stop any argument.

She had let her husband see the family face, full-frontal, because in those days she did not think adults were cruel. These days she did not shout. She kept within herself, centred, searching for harmony.

She stood in the weak sun, a cold east wind blowing across the Heath and she saw so clearly Serge Marais' face, the way it gave in to passion. In front of thousands of people, he let himself go completely.

· *Five* ·

Micky Duke rewound the tapes. 'Another one in the can.'

'Shall we let them free?' The studio manager meant the actors standing by the studio mikes.

'I want to run the end again,' said Vicky. 'One last time; won't do any harm. There were some ps popping and script-rustle. Then I'll take them, and you, for a drink.'

'Always the perfectionist,' sighed the studio manager.

Vicky laughed; 'You should see me when I really try.'

Micky Duke gestured with his eyes. 'And here comes another one.'

The heavy door opened softly and swooshed shut; strangers were in the room and Vicky did not like that when she was working. Then the head of Radio 4 made an entrance and introduced Vicky and the operators to the woman with him. 'This is Kirsty Cobb. She's come over from the visual side to see how we do things.'

Vicky shook Kirsty's hand.

The controller said, 'Let's give Kirsty all the help she needs.'

Vicky, looking into her eyes, thought the help this woman needed did not exist at the BBC. Her china-blue eyes were stricken. A lot of make-up nearly covered the signs of sleeplessness underneath. The yellow curls would suit a milkmaid, the cheeks were too rouged. Kirsty had made up her face as though she had forgotten what she looked like. The glitter in her eyes showed she drank. Her voice was used to giving orders but on this strange territory she tried a softer tone. She had summed up the operators, could handle them. She gave Vicky another assessing glare, not sure about her. The stricken look was gone but she looked in pain, as though injured.

The head of the department took Kirsty away and it was now after official working hours. Vicky still insisted on re-touching the last scene.

'She's starting at the top. Will Shakespeare, no less,' said Micky. Vicky felt cold, dejected, all liveliness gone. How she had longed for a prestigious production.

'She'll need watching,' said the studio manager. 'She's got her own ideas and they won't fit in with me, I can tell you.'

'Is she good with actors?' asked Vicky suddenly. The woman had a weakness, perhaps because she came over too strong. You had to be able to fuse with people, not dominate them, to get the best result in a short time.

'I wouldn't think so,' said Micky. 'She's keen on new technology. That's what she specializes in. Mono, stereo, CD, video, film, digital. She's into cable TV, new high-frequency signal, satellite – and drink.'

Jay came back from Stonehenge outraged because the police would not let anyone near the place. 'The Druids did their ceremony, but so far away it was like sitting in the gods; we got some of it on film.'

He wiped the kitchen stove. A piece of fried courgette had got lodged in the gas ring. He shuddered. Moving the courgette revealed earlier dirt. 'This needs cleaning, Vick.'

'Do it yourself, Jay.'

'You just don't keep a tidy place. It can't be good for you to be in –' he used a big word – 'squalor. Seriously, now. Have you always lived like this? Even with Dean?'

Dean Tyrell, her ex-husband, came from a Bostonian family. Their name was on real estate across America and they were super-rich. Jay just could not understand why Vicky let Dean have a divorce, as meek as a lamb. Why the hell had she not got a settlement? It maddened him just to think about it. Here he was, a guy from nowhere who had found he had a writing talent and had been taken on by serious people. And yet he had to pay women and children and the tax man, so whatever he earned was not real. He did not even get to hold it in his hand. Yet Dean

Tyrell, who had never done a day's work in his life and lavished money on any poetic flake who did not rhyme cat with mat, walked away from his wife, who knew his darkest secrets, assets untouched. He had just about left her the Hampstead flat, but with a mortgage outstanding.

'You always live so down. You don't have to.'

She was not answering.

'I don't understand you, Vicky. You could live well; why don't you give comfort a try? It won't bite.' He cleaned the stove.

Did she live down? She felt comfortable when her style was frugal, the surroundings set like a stage, with all the props and scenery, but not ready for a production.

'You don't seem settled because you're not in the right place.'

She had to agree with that. It was all temporary and she was just passing through. 'I feel as though my life hasn't begun.'

'But it has, sweetheart. Thirty's knocking on the door. Get a cleaner. How was it when you were married?'

'We kept moving. He liked hotels. So do I.'

'He had plenty of scratch?'

She shrugged. Dean had been one of the fifties' beat poets. He still lived on the road. Yes, he had plenty of scratch. She seemed to have a rapport with American men. It did not mean they did not quarrel.

'The lavatory is always clean.' She sounded defensive. 'So is the bath. And the food. And the plates, the bed; so are my habits. I don't sleep around.'

He let that one pass. The two days in Druid country with his secret mistress had been exhausting and he was in no state for an interrogation. 'I just think a cleaner, more orderly set-up would be better for you, that's all.'

'I work and I look after myself. I just don't have time to dust the frigging ornaments.'

'Get someone in!' He sounded savage.

She did not explain that she needed her money to help her mother. There were a lot of things he did not know – most things. He did not know that she had never ever found the right man. It was as though she was already linked to him, he was there, yet she could not see him. She had known him all her life. Every other man seemed foreign, of the wrong blood.

'You should get a kindly, retired woman to run things, who'd be glad of the money.'

'Jay, is this some kind of obsession?'

When he had finished describing the kind of person he meant, he said, 'I can't help you. I'm off.'

'Off?'

'To L.A. I've got to get "Scam" on to celluloid.' He tapped the freshly-typed script. 'So, you come out in a week or so and look around and –'

'Won't three be a crowd? Come on, Jay. I know there's someone else.'

'Sure, but she's not important. This is important.' He tapped the script.

'Who is she?'

For once he did not have an answer.

'Is she actually going with you?'

He sighed. 'Yeah. I'm taking Lorraine to L.A.'

Jay moved out quicker than he had moved in, but he had had a lot of practice. Before he left, he said, 'Vicky, you never get what you want. You don't even get near it. I see you try. Lorraine says your path's blocked. Maybe she's got something.'

'Jay!' She felt murderous. 'Leave my one-time, so-called friend out of it. I don't think I want her advice right now.'

He put a pile of English currency on the table.

'What's that? A tip?'

'Don't make a fuss and I'll dedicate the new play to you.'

She did not make a fuss. When he had gone she stayed very still. It was odd, but something was pleased he had left. Was it part of her? That did not feel right. There was a pleasure around because Jay had gone and she was alone. She closed her eyes and was sure someone, some presence, was actually in the room. And there was such sweetness. She stayed still, expecting to be embraced. It was better than that; she felt loved. Then she opened her eyes and there was just the room. 'Don't question it,' she said; 'if something lovely comes, be glad. Whatever it is.'

The kitchen felt light although the day was grey. The presence had a distinct perfume. She sniffed for it, deeply. It was like old paint. Then she took hold of the broom and started sweeping the floor.

· *Six* ·

The third night after Jay had left, Vicky was glad Channel 4 showed late-night films. It was as much as she could do to stop herself running to the neighbours, whom she rarely saw, and shouting, help me. She was lonely and she had failed again. What did it matter that she had a good body and face? She, the person inside the trappings, could not keep anything, not a husband, lover, friend. It was as though the people she chose were always taken from her. She gasped at the full sorrow of her situation. It was worse than she would ever admit. The room, in spite of the television, was silent.

Out of the blackness she carved the figure of Serge Marais – she would get him. Things were so bad, only something wonderful would do.

Vicky's first conscious impulse had been to try and cheer up her mother and help her father. They were locked into each other's tragedy like sparring deer with their antlers caught, and Vicky was ignored. She was never shown any affection. She did not even know it existed. She had never seen a caress. Once, when she was four or five, she had been in a neighbour's house and seen the mother stroke the daughter's hair. Vicky had been amazed. 'What are you doing to her?'

On one occasion, after getting her mother yet again into hospital, she asked her father, 'Why the hell did you have me?'

He did not know what she meant.

'Couldn't you see she was a sick woman?'

'Oh, Victoria, it was so long ago. How do I know?' He looked upset. Life was bad enough without bringing in a bad past. In the end, Vicky saw that people just got born. There was no logic to it.

Vicky's earliest memories were of the Hampshire garden in summer. She loved flowers and shrubs, the difference in colours, shapes and textures. She loved their scent and tried to remember their names. There were times when she felt too sad to cry. Her father would rush off somewhere to attend to Ruby, and Vicky would be left alone. A neighbour would usually look over the wall and try to pretend everything was alright. Something bad would have happened. Vicky knew bad alright. Everyone smiled too much and Vicky's legs would tingle with fright.

And then he came to be with her and quickly cheered her up. He was like a film star, glamorous, enviable and hers. His sleeves were soft like the petals of flowers, velvety. She told her parents about him, asked his name. They said she had made him up. She thought of him now. Had she actually seen him? He used to give her ideas. That is how she had known he was around. Later, she dismissed him as a childhood fantasy friend. But now she thought it might have been him in the kitchen when Jay had gone.

Vicky watched the film without seeing it, had another drink, ate some fruit. It was 3.30 am and would soon be dawn. Should she call Jay? It was strange how she had never been able to keep anyone.

· *Seven* ·

Vicky persuaded Micky Duke to run all the visual material the BBC had on Serge Marais. Alone in the viewing room, she watched the climax of his concerts, the jubilant audience, his departure from the podium. There was one rare ten-minute interview, but no footage on his personal life. Over the years he had not changed. Apparently he did yoga and meditation and lived a frugal, spiritual life. He did seem joyous and full of a refined energy. He seemed to fit the music. By just standing still on a platform he held thousands of people captive. She supposed it was because he was a great man. She got nothing from seeing the reels of film except heartache. She suggested doing a documentary on his life. The controller replied, 'Think of someone really difficult to get to.'

Vicky said, 'The Queen?'

'He's harder. Sorry. Everyone's tried.'

On the way back to the editing room she met Micky carrying a huge pile of records. 'The Empress wants to select something grand for her first production. Will Beethoven's Ninth do?' By the Empress he meant Kirsty Cobb. He showed Vicky the record sleeves. On one she saw Serge Marais.

'Has he ever given a personal interview?'

The boy shook his head.

'Why not?'

'He hasn't time? The music speaks for him? Maybe he's boring?'

She doubted that.

'What do you know about him?' Micky had friends at Decca.

'He's not afraid to be a perfectionist. Very concerned about the development of compact discs, all the technological side. He's got great charm and everyone falls in love with him. I'm sure there's a wife and family but he's a very private person.'

'Doesn't he want anything from the outside world, Micky?'

'Why should he? It all comes to him. Before he even asks he gets everything. But he's a fanatic about the new high tech research.'

'What's that?'

'The stuff Kirsty Cobb knows about; CD videos. He's an avid reader of the science mags and tries to find out about every development ahead of the major companies, which suggests he wants to market his own discs and videos. I'd say he wants to be first in the high-quality field.'

'Doesn't he believe in live audiences?'

'He believes in reproduction of the glorious original. It will make him rich, richer, given luck.'

Given luck, she repeated. And then she saw her way in. Kirsty was the specialist. All Vicky had to do was pretend to be her.

At lunch in the George Hotel near Broadcasting House, Kirsty put away a bottle of Beaujolais before the food even arrived. It stopped her hands shaking. The second bottle turned her into a normal person. Vicky knew she was looking at an alcoholic. She talked about Kirsty's Shakespeare series and how well she had fitted in. Sometime after her last visit to her father Vicky had turned into a tough person. She could no longer be receptive in a dangerous world. She was building some muscles for those odd moments of adversity.

Kirsty said, 'They told me you'd be the one to watch out for. You'd block every move I made. Or try to.'

Vicky gave a generous shrug. 'I think you're good. I'm not being patronizing. Good is what I like, as it happens.'

The Empress was far from good. She had not found the right way to deal with the technical crew. That they all needed acknowledgement, were not just extensions of the machines. And she was lousy with the actors. She was not used to quick rehearsal. Television had allowed her three weeks and more. In radio, she got three days. And worse, she was brilliant with the machines. That is what interested her. Vicky spoke about that side of the work and got plenty of tips on new sound. There was laser technology, reels of tough celluloid that would never disintegrate. Long sentences occurred, containing memorable phrases – 'precision discs, high-speed rotate', 'disc-unit power supply, logical band'. She even wrote them down. In return, Vicky made sure Kirsty had plenty to drink.

'Now this is all for the future. They're all after it – the recording companies, video industry –'

'So who actually knows it all?'

'Those who do the research.' And Kirsty even knew names. The big one was a postgraduate at Cambridge. 'He'll be shit hot in about six months. The recording firms will be crazy they didn't grab him. I told him, sign nothing now. Your price can only go up.'

Kirsty had a problem, apart from the obvious one. Bottle three and she was pals enough with Vicky to hint at a love affair in the TV world which had gone badly wrong. She was the victim. That was why she had moved to radio. Vicky guessed it was a married guy. That was one entanglement she had not yet encountered.

'I like talking to you,' said Kirsty. 'You're easy to be with. You'll make some guy happy.' She had obviously heard about Jay's untidy flight with the hot-shot agent.

Vicky walked Kirsty around the back streets to sober her up enough to go back into the world of Shakespeare. She gave her black coffee before letting her loose on 'Macbeth'. Then she picked up a phone to France and said she was Kirsty Cobb and she had some CD video developments that would interest the Maestro. She invited his people to check her out. She was a big enough name in TV and her connection in the science world was good enough for them to call back on the extension Vicky had given.

'So, you have information on new technology that might possibly interest the Maestro. Are you marketing this material?'

'No,' said Vicky.

'Then why does he see it first and for free?' The woman was Canadian.

'Because he deserves it.'

The Canadian understood. Another fan. 'So you'll bring samples and data of what's in progress, right? You're taking a risk, Miss Cobb. If the research graduate or your employer found out, you could be in trouble.' She arranged the meeting for the following Monday. It would take place in Paris. That was neutral ground.

Lorraine sent Vicky a letter from Los Angeles in which she tried to explain that her infatuation for Jay did not diminish her friendship for Vicky. If Vicky could see a way to understand what had happened and get over her hurt, Lorraine would love to hear from her. At the end of the letter she wrote, 'Jay is not what he seems. Love, Lo.'

That figures, thought Vicky. She has obviously run up against the wives.

She packed for the Paris trip, told the BBC she needed sick leave and arranged for her mother to be moved to the private clinic. She had given the Canadian assistant her home number but there had been no further enquiries. It was, after all, a delicate business. She was dishonest, they were careful.

She now chose to view what had seemed like disasters as positive acts. Jay leaving, Lorraine leaving, Kirsty getting too much work. This was all good because it meant change. From this unexpected space she was now forced to take active steps and make a new life. She was reaching out for what she wanted. The fact that Serge was the fantasy of thousands was a slight drawback. A wife would be another. But something good would come from it. Good things happened all over the place. Vicky's first secretary at the BBC, a very nice, ordinary girl, had spent her nights writing a love saga. And the first American publisher who saw it, bought it for a quarter-of-a-million dollars. You just never knew your luck.

*

At that moment, Jay, choosing groceries at the local Zuma Beach supermarket, felt panic. He put down the carton of Haagan Daaz ice-cream he was holding and ran out to his Porsche. She was in danger – Vicky. He broke the speed limit driving to his house on the beach. He was still breathless when he got through to her in London. It was nine o'clock in the morning where he was. She had just finished her afternoon.

'Vicky, are you alright?'

'Absolutely.'

'Oh, don't keep putting a good face on it. I know all about you. You lived with two girls who went to smart places and had a good time, you didn't want to play Cinderella, so you put on your party frock and pretended to go somewhere enviable. And you stepped out and spent three hours sitting in the local laundrette. You did it with me, too. You weren't having such a good time as you made out. Why do you do it?'

'I see Lo has been gabbing. Are you so bored with each other already you have to talk about me?'

'Why did you do it – sit in the laundrette?'

'Because they were two ritzy debs and I couldn't stand just sitting around so I invented places to go and dressed up for them. Then I went back with some fairytale. I didn't do it with you, Jay. I was very young then. It was before I married Dean.'

'So you're alright? It's like I heard you call me and you seemed to be in real trouble. Like something was all stirred up and coming after you. So I rushed back here.'

'I couldn't be better. I'm off to Paris.'

'Paris.' He made it sound dead and flat. 'Have you got another guy then?'

'I'm doing a documentary.' She did sound excited.

'On what?'

'On whether you are responsible for getting your own happiness or whether it just comes along.'

He could not believe he had felt all that panic in the supermarket. Was it a sign of being irrational? Was the pressure of the alimony payments finally catching up? For something to say, he asked if she liked Paris.

'Of course. I love it.' And then she thought, do I? She had gone there for her honeymoon. There was something about the city she could not quite locate, but it made her uneasy.

Jay asked what the documentary was really about.

'Serge Marais.'

'Make sure you keep the rights and sell it worldwide. No one has ever got his story.'

'Have you ever met him?'

'No,' he said swiftly. 'He was out here in Los Angeles for a while with the symphony orchestra. Your ex-husband's family, the Jason Tyrells, sponsor his concerts.'

'Really?'

'But I don't think they have any pull with him. I think he just about makes it to the gala dinners. Why are you interested in him? He's not exactly a Thatcher victim. Where's his social problem?'

'He's the exact opposite of me. And he's unique.'

'Oh yeah?' Jay loved that one. When a woman said unique it meant sex came into it somewhere. 'Have you actually seen him yet?'

'Tomorrow.' And for once, she used Jay. 'What sort of things would you ask him?'

'How does he feel music is portrayed in literature. For example, Vinteille in Proust. Why isn't there any good music being composed today? Why is he daunted by Mozart? And, Vicky, he's not what he seems. The charisma has impressed you, but it's all show. He's in it for the money. He commands outsize fees and he's got more real estate than a movie superstar. He's paranoid about his privacy. There he is, living in terror with his art collection on East 72nd and there they are, the proletariat on West 42nd, wanting revenge.'

She did not believe him, about the showmanship.

'He's a sham,' Jay insisted. 'And manipulative. Women and guys fantasize about him. He's their fix.'

'Jay, you sound jealous.'

'Take care.' He hung up.

She wondered idly whether or not to get her TV remote control button fixed. Because of her scrappy life, she had fallen in love.

· *Eight* ·

First of all they checked her out, the Canadian woman, all high gloss and hard eyes, doing the talking and a young, thin man with long fair hair, who was an assistant to the impresario. The office was in the smart area, the sixteenth arrondissement, near the Trocadero. There was a lot of glass in the room, ornaments, shelves, mirrors, low tables. Phones rang melodiously and were picked up in an adjoining room where slim girls took messages and did a little non-exacting office work. Vicky sat beside a glass sculpture which reflected the radiant blue of the carpet and the paler shades of the walls. There were a lot of paintings, probably originals. This was the informal office, for comfortable discussion.

They wanted to make sure she was not going to unload a new dramatic discovery on them and then weigh in with some heavy blackmail. Vicky repeated her original story – she admired Serge Marais – and stuck to it. She wanted the breakthrough information to go to him. Her condition? That she give it to him personally.

'Why?' asked the Canadian.

'Because I'm taking a serious risk. His hearing it directly gives validity to what I'm doing.' She could hardly tell the truth – that she had been having a bad time recently and needed to reach out for something dazzling.

So what did she have to offer? they asked. She spelled out Kirsty Cobb's insight into new developments and the particular Cambridge research graduate, who could be approached now and picked up before a major recording company bought him. She came out with the 'precision-disc high-speed rotate' talk, incomprehensible to her and possibly to them. Then she mentioned the BBC's new activity, both in mono and stereo sound. She refused to show samples of work or data because she didn't have them. 'The material I have is in the hotel. Only the Maestro sees that. He will also be given the name of the Cambridge graduate.'

'Aren't you happy in your job, Miss Cobb?' asked the young man.

Vicky nodded.

'But you recently moved from television to radio? Was that your choice?'

So they had researched her. They obviously knew about the married man. They would have a photograph of Kirsty Cobb next.

'You produced some critically acclaimed television, Miss Cobb. If you feel this is underhand, walk away. We're not morally bound. We did not solicit you.' The young man had a mid-European accent. Was he Romanian too?

Vicky said she would go on with it. They asked again what financial remuneration she was looking for. She said none.

'You may or may not see the Maestro. We will inform him about the substance of this meeting. He will decide if he wants what you are offering.'

'He won't get it any other way. I know he is eager to get the best, the most advanced equipment. Apart from being a brilliant conductor, I'm sure if he's a businessman he wants to lead the market. One of the commercial companies is on the point of approaching this unknown Cambridge graduate, working humbly –'

'We get the point, Miss Cobb,' said the young man.

The Canadian asked if Vicky would speak to the Maestro by phone.

'Absolutely not.'

The man handed her a typed sheet to sign which said Miss Cobb was introducing un-marketed material solely at her own request and that the source of the material had not been informed of her visit. There was a long paragraph about money and how she did not want any.

'I'll only sign it if I see him.'

'We'll come back to you.' The man took the paper away. The Canadian wrote down the number of Vicky's hotel and Vicky stood up, prepared to leave. 'I'm going back to London tomorrow morning.'

The Canadian gave a huge, complicated shrug. 'The Maestro is never pressurized, Miss Cobb.'

Vicky had sat in too many mental hospitals, had been too scared, too lonely, to have to put up with a mediocre bad time. The experiences, in spite of everything, stood her in good stead. She had the pride of the desolate. 'Let me hear from you before this evening. I'm busy too.'

They watched as she went out. They did not like her.

One of the slim girls in the adjoining office handed her an envelope. Inside was a house seat for the Serge Marais concert that evening at the Paris Opera.

Vicky walked along the river towards Montparnasse. She could not get his face out of her mind. He had an aristocratic look. He was charged with energy and power and so desirable. As Jay said, he was everyone's fix. He could not be further from her way of life.

She crossed to the Left Bank and sat at a café terrace in the sun. It was 2.00 pm French time, and the sun was hot. She did not feel any guilt about her actions. She was not going to sell anything because she had nothing to sell, but only Serge Marais would know that. All she wanted was to see him in the flesh and let him see her; to register in his life, to be part of his present and share his past. For her part, she would look as fabulous as she could and try and arouse his interest in her. If it went wrong and the BBC found out, maybe they would think she had gone mad and send her over to television. Kirsty might retaliate, but Vicky did not feel bad about her either. Kirsty had taken her coveted productions. Life had been black and Marais was the one shaft of brightness. She deserved it.

· Nine ·

As always, she found Paris beautiful but not easy to penetrate. It kept its secrets and its real life away from visitors. She thought places were what you made them. Some cities could give you a bad time because you were poor, a woman, or English. She felt it was always to do with the present. But Paris had an absolute and undeniable atmosphere which affected moods and responses. She always forgot about it the instant she left. Now, she was not altogether sure it was pleasant. For a start, the atmosphere stirred all her emotions until she was moved and heightened and near to tears. There was no reason for it. Most people who came to Paris felt great, or so they said. She certainly did not think it was a city you could lose yourself in. It was without kindness. She decided she would not like to be in trouble in Paris. It would throw up your shame onto the boulevards for everyone to see and disapprove of.

She walked for hours along the streets of Montparnasse. There was not quite enough air and there was a draught on the back of her legs like a dog's breath. That was all. But these physical signs heralded panic. Was it because the streets were too familiar? Her throat felt tight. Her thoughts had been passing one after another, aimlessly, without focus, and on their own they were getting into trouble. The sight of the Panthéon terrified her. It seemed to loom up and she averted her eyes and walked quickly in the other direction. Her heart, now involved, was jumping and noisy in her ears. Her thoughts had led her to a strange state.

She realized she had been thinking about the colour red, and it started to worry her. It had too much importance. She went speedily into the nearest brasserie and ordered a double brandy at the bar. Then she sat on the terrace and ordered another. It all felt wrong, as though the town was working on a degree too far to the left or right. It did not feel like England or Normandy or anywhere else she had known. She sat amongst the closely-arranged, overcrowded tables, facing the pavement. She was waiting for someone to come in. She had the absolute certainty that someone familiar and wanted would push open the glass door and join her. She leapt up, sweating, and left, running. The bar was called the Rotonde.

Back at the hotel in Montmartre, she prepared for the concert. She wore a long white dress with a single silver strap, that showed her body off to advantage. The room was like every other modern hotel room in the world, but even this seemed disquieting. It made itself too known. It was as though the room, like the Rotonde, was inhabited by some source or energy which was imposing itself on her thoughts. The room was too quiet. She sighed loudly to give it noise and opened the window to look down into the courtyard. 'It's so beautiful, Paris,' she said aloud, as though to placate it.

She remembered her honeymoon with Dean. On their first night he had accepted he was gay. For forty-seven years he had tried hard to convince himself that he was heterosexual. She laughed, thinking of him, good-looking with his spoilt face. He liked her because she was passive and very young and did not threaten him. She did not demand a superlative sexual performance. Also, she was not socially ambitious and hard like his mother.

Memories of Dean made it bearable, sitting on the bed, her hands in her lap, quite still, just sitting. It was most unlike her. She normally liked to be doing something. Her breathing was noticeable. There seemed to be more than one person breathing. She heard the deeper, louder breathing of another person. Were the walls that thin? She hoped so and stood up. If a hotel room could turn against you, this one had. She could not even bear to look in the mirror. She was not sure if any of the furnishings were reliable. She left the room hurriedly and finished her make-up in the powder room of the Opera House. At the bar, she ordered

Dean's favourite drink, grapefruit juice with gin and soda, and wished him well, wherever he was.

As soon as she got to her seat, the Canadian joined her. Her hair had been freshly tinted and had come out a greenish, mean yellow. She wore a black silk suit with silver trimmings. On one side the skirt was split to the knee. It looked as though it belonged on a prettier woman. Her perfume was strong and sweet. It had plenty of rivalry from the women quickly filling the seats around them. Everyone was highly-scented, immaculate, determined to squeeze every drop of pleasure out of the evening. After all, they were the privileged ones, they could afford the tickets. The Canadian felt in her flat bag for the sheet of typed paper. 'Sign!' She handed Vicky a pen.

'When I speak to him. I've already made that clear.'

'You'll be introduced to the Maestro after the concert. He may or may not decide to talk to you. It's up to him.' She pushed the paper into Vicky's lap.

'I'm not having my name on an incriminating document.'

The Canadian put the paper back in her bag. 'He may well not talk to you.' She stood up.

'Have you asked him?'

'He decides these things, Miss Cobb.' And she moved off to the house seats on the other side of the aisle. The orchestra took their places. The applause began. Then Serge Marais walked briskly up to the podium and gave everyone a night of Beethoven they would not forget. The music flowed through him, to the orchestra, out to the audience. He set the spiral in motion. His energy was endless. It all came out as he wished. He was beyond adulation, in touch with perfection. The woman next to Vicky cried. At the end, the applause lasted for twenty minutes. The audience, as though hypnotized, kept calling for an encore. For once, he gave in and conducted a brief piece of triumphant music – Vicky thought it was Bach. The audience rose to its feet. Never had she seen one man receive such adoration. Over-emotional, she was on her feet, shouting his name. Flowers were thrown. One last smile, a wide gesture of embrace, then he left the stage. After an experience like that Vicky hardly expected him to be rational enough to discuss high tech. The Canadian found her as the applause was dwindling.

'Something magical happened tonight,' she said. 'I've never known applause like it.'

For Vicky, the occasion was beyond words. What could she say to Serge Marais? There did not seem to be any syllables to do it justice. She wanted to redo her make-up and hair but the Canadian said there was not time. The super-smart groupies would be in line as far as the exit door.

'What? People just go back to the dressing room?'

'Not people. The rich and well-known.'

Backstage, the queue was enormous, and patient in the heat.

'Do they all know him?' asked Vicky.

'Of course not. They might have said hello somewhere.'

The queue shifted slowly, women fanning their make-up with programmes and record sleeves.

'A lot of them support the Opera House or sponsor his concerts, so they want their programmes signed at least. He plays the game.'

And then she saw him, covered with sweat, wiping the hair out of his eyes, smiling, talking. One after another, as though visiting a guru, the devoted kissed his hand.

'Isn't he exhausted?' asked Vicky.

'High,' said the Canadian. 'He's still full of adrenalin.'

And Vicky wondered what she would say to a high superstar.

A fat, bearded man hung a long black cloak over the Maestro's shoulders.

'Have you got the specifications and details of the technical side? The information you mentioned this morning?'

Vicky nodded. They shifted forward. The queue moved more quickly now. He bestowed a gracious thank you, I am so pleased, on each admirer.

Close to him, she saw the lines on his face, the shadowed eyes. The queue held photographs, his albums, programmes, all to be signed. Some brought gifts and invitations to dine, to appear on television, to visit a country estate. The progress of the queue was halted when a man in a grey suit was escorted through the crowd. He was allowed several minutes with the Maestro and did not kiss his hand.

'The French president,' whispered the Canadian.

Flashbulbs popped. Then, that ceremony over, the queue inched forward again. How nervous she was. Her reasons for meeting him made sense to her, but her supposed reasons became hardly logical. His eyes saw hers. They paused. It was a cool look but his eyes had lingered. Now they were back on the person in front of him. She had been standing for over forty minutes. The bearded man gave the Maestro a glass of mineral water.

'Who's he?'

'The impresario.'

'Does it always take so long?'

'Oh yes,' said the Canadian. 'Especially in Paris. He's very popular here.'

'But you have the right to go to the front of the queue?'

'Miss Cobb, you're only one of six people I have to introduce tonight.'

He was looking at Vicky again. Was it the CD video spy deal that interested him or the fact she was attractive?

'You've got your speech prepared, Miss Cobb? Because you only get one-and-a-half minutes.'

She could hear his voice now, mid-European, deep. He sounded very sane. 'Wait for me, François,' he called. 'Come and eat with us.' He spoke perfect French to François, German to a director of his recording company. He looked at Vicky again, an assessing look. She reminded him of someone. She was standing with his employee? Perhaps it was the employee he was eyeing. Or someone behind them. His eyes were like no others she had seen. Intense, intelligent. Then she was in front of him and the Canadian was doing the talking. He listened and breathed in deeply, then he yawned. The gesture implied he had few inhibitions.

'Well, Miss Cobb,' he said in English. 'I have no time, you understand.'

She quickly listed some of the specifications she had memorized.

'I hear you make very good television documentaries.'

He was looking deeply into her eyes and her face flushed, responding too much. In spite of the heat, she shivered.

'Perhaps we could have something? A coffee? A drink? Let's say ten o'clock at my hotel.'

'Tonight?' she said.

'Tonight? My dear, it is already nearly eleven-thirty. Tomorrow morning at The Élysées near Rond Point. You bring her,' he said to the Canadian. Then he looked again at Vicky and suddenly smiled. The smile was amused. He knew her game. She knew his. The familiarity was disconcerting. But they did not have to go through the process of getting to know each other. She told him how marvellous the concert was. How sick he must be of hearing that.

He thanked her gracefully. 'Until tomorrow. I look forward to that.' And he greeted the next in line, full of charm and patience but always controlling how long they spoke, he spoke. The Canadian had to stay. Five others had something to offer him personally.

Vicky left the theatre, her body light, joyful. She was reborn.

· *Ten* ·

She remembered that Paris with Dean had seemed slightly unstable. Its atmospheres were too much for her and seemed to change her. Like a weather-vane, she pointed west and Paris wanted her swung round to east. She had assumed it was because Dean and the honeymoon were stressful. When she was not actually in Paris she remembered its trees, its buildings, with gratitude. At least one city stayed beautiful.

Dean had despised money but certainly liked spending it. The honeymoon was a de luxe affair in a top hotel. Only the right credentials assured you a booking. The lobby was packed with the élite of New York and Hollywood. She did not remember much about it except that Dean had behaved like a man in a prison cell about to be executed. His face was actually beautiful and she thought it a shame it was so spoilt. He was finely attuned, intelligent, articulate, witty and it made speaking with him, for her, difficult. His family lived in Boston in grand style and their real estate company seemed to own half America. The family name, Jason Tyrell, was everywhere. Dean was the only heir and the family wanted him settled, with children. Vicky was his last attempt at normality. She was receptive and gentle enough not to cause trouble. Aesthetically, he found her beautiful and was always grateful that in her body he managed an erection and experienced a climax, its pleasure slightly reduced by the picture in his mind of the hard, brown buttocks of the Greek boy he was in love with. Dean tried very hard to be straight. But on honeymoon he could no longer deny that he wanted the languorous brown boy with the tight arse, however dangerous it turned out to be. He gave in to the desire. The marriage was over.

After he had made love to Vicky, he said, 'I think I love a boy.'

At the time, she had been looking out through the window, right on to the legs of the Eiffel Tower. She had difficulty with his confusion because he did not seem gay. 'What does that mean to us?' she had asked.

'Help me, Vicky.'

And she tried. She let him play out all his fantasies. She gave him more. And between them there was a definite attraction which they believed would overcome anything and they had more sex than a straight couple. He had taken her to the clubs, restaurants, galleries, museums and concerts he had enjoyed with the poets in his youth. She had had moments of depression which she put down to the Parisian atmosphere, which was too evocative – she could not live up to it.

And then he had fallen ill on the last night and thought he was dying. A private ambulance had taken him from the hotel and he had flown himself to Greece where he experienced a sexual revelation and decided to live. He left Vicky the Hampstead flat, due to his controlled allowance still on a mortgage, and offered her the use of his Greek island retreat. He was willing to give her alimony if, in return, she did not mention his sexual predilections. She said, 'Why pay for what doesn't work?'

She cleansed her face and got into the bath, a shell-pink affair with gilt taps. Then she took the usual cold shower to tone her circulation and did a short session of floor exercises. After cleaning her teeth she meditated for several minutes.

She opened the window. Paris was noisy. Wide awake, she sat in bed and read a biography on Serge Marais. His career was one long leap-frog into success. It all seemed so smooth. All he had done was find his rightful position. Then she turned out the light and decided to sleep. That was what was wrong in the room. In London everything flowed effortlessly but here she made decisions. Clean face, wash teeth, sleep. She turned about in the narrow sheets which were dry and rasping and made her body too hot. The pillow was a stubborn, hard oblong. She sat up, turned on the light. There was too much in the room, it was too busy. Her legs were suddenly chilled, the dog-breath feeling on the back of them which she had experienced in the afternoon had returned. And then she started to shake. All the strain of the day, the panic, leapt out of her as she tried to hang on to something. Serge Marais's face? She could not see it. She tried prayer. Her mouth was dry and she gulped water from the Perrier bottle. It was one of the worst nights she had ever experienced.

Breakfast was brought in at 8.30 am and still she had not slept. She had one-and-a-half hours to perform a cosmetic miracle. Her face was a grey smear with dark circles under her eyes. She turned on the shower but could not get under it. She drank some coffee, attempted the croissant. She believed she had a virus. She could pass through towns seething with germs and catch nothing, but here she was in a three star hotel and she was sick. The Canadian rang and arranged to meet her in Serge Marais' hotel foyer.

Vicky did make an effort to leave. But when the lift doors opened, her legs would not move. She went back into her room and ordered peppermint tea with honey. There was no honey. Her body felt unstable and she was far from sure that, if she did meet the Maestro, she would not throw up over him. She called his hotel and was put through to his room. A woman answered. Vicky asked for the Maestro and gave her name. A small pause and he was on the line.

'I was supposed to see you this morning.'

'Yes, I am expecting you.' He sounded matter of fact.

'Naturally, I will come, but I should say first that I may have a virus.'

'A virus?' He sounded calm about that. 'What sort of virus?'

She listed the symptoms. 'I don't want to give it to you. After all, you have to perform and –'

'You mean you have a cold?'

She felt considerably worse than that. This could be a serious illness but she wanted to see him. She made it sound like a very bad cold.

'Come if you want to,' he said. 'Don't worry on my behalf.'

'Alright. Thank you.' She would go if it killed her.

In the background the woman spoke.

'No, listen, Miss Cobb,' he said. 'I have a better idea. I'll come to you. Because we have the children here and my wife doesn't want them to catch anything. We're off on a long tour. Give me the address of your hotel.'

She could not believe it. 'It's only modest.'

'Expect me in ten minutes.'

She went down into the street, to the nearest pharmacy, to buy pills over the counter. Even with make-up she looked ill. For a couple of minutes she stood with her face in the sun, then went back into the dark foyer. She could not decide where to sit. She felt it should all be kept in shadow, this ludicrous tryst. She sat, hands in her lap, almost demure, waiting. Her strongest impulse was to topple sideways and lie flat on the mock-leather sofa and groan.

He came in swiftly wearing dark glasses. He looked quite different and his light jacket did not entirely suit him. His hair flopped over one eye. He moved with confidence. Life was almost too easy for him. He took off his glasses when he saw her. His eyes were so strange that, in the daylight, it looked as though there was something wrong with them. She almost rose to greet him.

'No, don't get up,' he said, almost irritated. 'You look so – unusual sitting like that. As though you're posing for someone. There's that kind of tension about you. Do you model?' He chose the armchair opposite. 'You look young, Miss Cobb.'

She smiled, almost provocatively. 'Thank you.' She behaved as though it was a compliment.

'For thirty-six.' He lifted his arms over his head and stretched. He was perfectly at ease; his movements were almost rough, he was so certain of himself. And her. She looked at his hands. In the hotel foyer they looked normal enough.

'So, do you model?'

'No I don't. And I'm not Miss Cobb either.'

'Of course you're not.'

There was a pause in honour of that fact. She had thought his hands would be protected, in gloves, perhaps, or lying quiet on his lap. Yet they hung over the back of his seat or gestured casually to emphasize a remark, and life was a dangerous business. She wondered how much he had insured them for.

'But I was a journalist and worked for several English papers. And now I'm at the BBC. I do documentaries and drama and I'd love to do an interview with you.'

He nodded, still looking at her, taking his time as though she pleased him. He said, 'You make my day. It started off not so well. And now I feel quite turned around.'

'I really hope you don't catch my illness.'

'I don't catch things.' He turned and a waiter stood, prompt, beside him. In French, he said, 'Bring me lemon tea with lots of lemon and some honey. Also, I would like whole-apple cider vinegar. Make sure it's whole-apple. If not, send out for it. Bring me the bottle. And a jug of boiling water. And an extra cup.' He did not ask what she wanted.

His eyes were grey-blue, penetrating, stirring her blood. Breathless, she said the first thing that occurred to her. 'But I do have information from Miss Cobb.'

He was now looking at her in a way that was undeniably sexual. At first she could not believe it. She looked at him again to make sure. What she saw made her forget all about being ill.

'So what does Miss Cobb have to say that's so important?'

'There's a postgraduate at Cambridge. This is important, if you want it –'

'You tell me.' His voice was caressing, thrilling. She was about to speak, could not say a word. 'Do I want it?'

And then it occurred to her that he liked fans and, if one caught his eye, he slept with her. There was no other explanation. This man was highly promiscuous.

'Come on. Tell me if I want it.'

'I'm sure you know.' She tried to free herself from his – was it a spell?

'I'm sure I don't.' He sounded as though he was making love to her. Everything around seemed to cease, to fade: Paris, her past, her obligations. The boy bringing the drinks was an intrusion.

Serge Marais spooned the honey into the lemon tea and stirred it. Then he checked the cider vinegar bottle was the one he had asked for. He poured a teaspoon of vinegar into the cup of boiled water. 'Drink this fast, while it's hot. Then that.' He pushed across the vinegar water, then the lemon tea. 'It's what my mother always gave us. It cleanses the system.' He rubbed his hands together as though washing them at the end of a ritual.

'Do you want anything else, sir?' The waiter had recognized him and was prepared to give him the entire contents of the kitchen store cupboard if he so desired. His admiration was such, he would have brought a hive of bees, a vat of cider. Tray in hand, he suggested a coffee for the Maestro, or a cigar. Everything was on the house, naturally.

Serge Marais stopped the lovesong with a simple, 'Nothing, thank you.' Then he turned to Vicky and the boy went away.

Something chemical and obvious had happened between them. It surprised them both. Almost shyly he said, 'You didn't tell me.'

'What?' Her voice was almost inaudible.

He leaned towards her. 'What I should find important. Tell me.'

She started to tell him about the research. He cut through that with, 'The important things. Tell me those.'

She paused, then continued about the Cambridge graduate.

'Then I will try and help him, if you want me to. I'm always looking for exceptionally talented people.'

She noticed he had turned it all round to suit himself. He could not be described as a receiver of technological secrets that way.

She watched, absorbed every nuance, each change of expression, greedily, like watching a film that would never be shown again.

'D'you want his name?' she said.

'I want yours.' He was thinking about something else altogether.

'Vicky Graham.'

'So what do you really do? Apart from the radio productions and journalism.'

The love affair was sudden and as out of control as a fire. She thought that fire was what it was, all consuming, hot, dangerous, with its own rules. Who would put it out? Her? Him? Or the wife? She had the distinct impression now that it was real for him too, and that it was not something that had happened to him before. He did not seem to know the rules any more than she did. For all his tantalizing looks and gestures, he was awkward.

She talked about the film she had made. She kept it short. He reached across and felt her head. 'It's nothing. You haven't got a temperature.' He took his time removing his hand. 'It's possibly something you ate yesterday. You must be careful, you know. Paris is like any other city. Where did you eat?'

It could not possibly interest him, her two sandwiches and few drinks. But he wanted to know, as though every detail about her was important.

'Aren't you ever ill?' she asked.

'Not at all.' He drank some of her lemon tea.

'But it's a sick world.' She felt very close and safe with him.

'If something starts, a flu, a cold, I just work through it. Music is the best cure, I think.' There seemed to be such a small space between them. Moment by moment, she was aware of it, the event, as it happened, the falling in love. Their hands met as he reached again for the tea glass.

'So, Vicky, what do you think?' He moved his hand away, 'For instance, about modern technology?'

'Me? What do you care what I think?'

'I asked you. You tell me.' He sounded challenging. She sat straighter on the sofa but felt as though they were already in bed.

'What do you think about modern music?' She remembered Jay's questions.

'It's non-existent today, isn't it. Worthless. Don't you think so, Vicky?'

'Well, it's not for me to say.' She did not know what to call him.

'Oh, but it is. You must tell me what you think.'

'You must feel very restricted by your profession. Rather, vocation.'

'It's my life.'

'Don't you ever long to do something free, outside of yourself?'

'Music is free.'

'No, something out of the ordinary.'

'Like?'

'Taking the subway in New York. I bet you've never done that.'

'Have you?'

'No.'

'That sort of freedom has no place in my life. To be like the ordinary man. No, I can't be that.'

'But you'd like to?'

He shrugged. 'Like to? What's the point?' He stirred on his chair and the mood was broken. He was back in his space, a famous stranger. How dare she challenge him with the ordinary, accuse him of longing for anonymous, mundane pursuits.

'Do I seem as though I'm missing something, Vicky? Is that what you're saying?'

'It occurred to me that if you're celebrated and very public you lose the chance of being anonymous.'

'You're right. I do miss that. So, do you take the subway?'

'I'm nervous of it.'

'Then let's do it together. We'll go from Times Square, north for twenty minutes. How's that?'

She could hardly believe what was happening. She had challenged him with ordinary needs and she had won. She had coerced him into suggesting a meeting.

'Give me your phone number and address.' He wrote it in a small, ordinary notebook. 'Do you like red roses? Look out for them!' He got up, prepared to leave. His eyes stayed on hers, a caress, and she burned with pleasure. Then he looked at his watch. 'My plane! My God!'

At that moment the Canadian skidded into the foyer. She was flapping the disputed sheet of paper.

'I'm just leaving. Tell them to hold the plane a few minutes,' he said.

The Canadian did not know what to do with the paper. He had seen it.

Serge turned to Vicky. 'Tell this prodigy in Cambridge I will try to help him. Miss Cobb finds things for me. If you find any singers, bring them too.' His eyes widened playfully.

She sat, stunned. They were gone. He would contact her. She had never been more sure of anything. She was glad her life had been dark and lived under a stormy sky because it made her début into happiness all the more dazzling. The illness had quite gone, cured by the Maestro's mother's remedy, or love. She felt light and so happy she wanted to share it with everyone she saw. Happiness made her generous.

· *Eleven* ·

Micky Duke called at Vicky's flat with a pile of scripts. He was amazed at the change in her. She looked quite different, as though something had happened. The excitement was never absent from her body for long. She only had to think of the Maestro's eyes. He was a mixture of casual behaviour and complete unavailability. It had not occurred to her he could become so intimate so quickly. And a subway journey in New York had to be a sexual metaphor. This was a courtship, and daily she waited for red roses. They did not come.

It took three days for the euphoria to subside. She imagined him in America. She knew absolutely that the love between them had been real. But he was also manipulative. She remembered the way he had turned her information around so that he became the benefactor and she, picking around for help. Also, he was married.

Jay woke, sweating and terrified. He had had that dream again. He did not know where he was. He knew where he had been: in some dusty, oddly-shaped room. When you walked, the wooden floorboards were noisy, a couple broken, painted red. He had seen an empty bottle roll towards him. The dust and cigarette ash everywhere bothered him. The walls were orange, another red. And the feeling was terrible, verging on overwhelmingly terrible. There was a splash of thick scarlet on the floor which he did not think was blood. It looked fresh and could be paint. Then he heard the sea and realized he was in his Los Angeles house on the shore. He turned on the light and reached for a cigarette, so waking Lorraine. He had forgotten she existed.

'Babe, go back to sleep.'

Lorraine was awake enough to be worried. Why, every night, did he get up, obviously anxious? Was he tired of her? The original sin in the relationship had all leaked out and responsibility had set in. She was far from sure it was what he wanted. The physical act was tremendous still, but he was not as he used to be. Before, he would say, 'I've never ever had anything like this.' He would come again immediately, would shout out with the excitement, and she would claw him, leaving her mark, and get more of him into her. Their sexual performance was an orgy of greed. It depended on illicit meetings and novelty to bring out the best in it.

Now, she said, 'Is there anything I can do?'

'Yes, sleep.' He was unapproachable, hunched forward, his brown back smooth, unscratched.

'Is it me?' she dared to ask.

He walked to the open window, his penis flapping showily. She thought better of reaching out for it. His eyes were black, opaque. He threw the cigarette, still burning, into the sand.

She sat up, prepared to meet bad news half way. 'Do you want me living with you? I'll move into the company flat in Beverly Hills.'

He turned and looked at her and prayed that this was one that would not cost any alimony. There always came a point, a few weeks after the conquest, when he would pay for his carelessness. He had assumed every female over sixteen used protection. He never checked. It was their business. Then, suddenly, it was his business. God said, take what you want, then pay for it. Vicky had told him that.

'So, do you want me to go?' she said again and crossed her arms over her breasts. The way he was looking made her feel naked, not pleasantly.

'It's Vicky.'

'So you haven't got over her.' Lorraine's throat tightened with pain.

'I keep dreaming the same dream.'

'So you want to go back to her? I'll move out, Jay.'

He ignored what could turn into hysteria and said, 'It's not a dream. It's a fucking nightmare. I'm dying in there.'

'You want her back?'

'No, Lorraine. She's in danger.'

Ten days passed and Vicky was suddenly scared. What if the Maestro was unreliable? For the first time, her perceptions might have let her down. What if he did go after women, liked to tease and play around, even have quick affairs? And then, so easily, he could say that she had brought it on herself, coming to Paris, pretending to be someone else. He could even boast of her extraordinary behaviour over a drink with friends. The things fans do. Even bright ones. Or perhaps he had had second thoughts, third thoughts, about getting involved with her. And he would worry that she knew too much. She had seen him in an amorous mood. He would tell the Canadian about her deceit: 'Get her fired!'

Vicky turned for help to Micky Duke. He was a young kid, a loner, probably unhappy but trying to do a good job. He loved, adored music. It justified everything else. She took him across to the club for a drink.

'What do you know about Serge Marais' character?'

'Only what I see in the concert hall. I'd say music came first, second, third . . .'

'There's a wife.'

'That's right. She's much younger than him. Quite beautiful. Comes from Estonia or Latvia, behind the Iron Curtain. Are you in some kind of trouble?'

'No. Why?'

'Last week you looked happy and now you don't.' He did not want to sound rude.

'Yes, I'm in trouble.' And she told him all of it.

'The worst part is Kirsty. If she gets to hear about it she'll go to the Controller. Definitely. Your being infatuated with him –'

She wondered why he had changed love to something slighter.

'– is bad luck. I think he's busy in the States and –'

'Forgotten all about it,' she said quickly, before he did.

'Maybe he's run into a problem. I did hear on the grapevine

that he was having trouble. He walked out of a concert recently because it wasn't a good enough performance. He wasn't getting it right. He's never done that before.'

The news surprised her. He seemed far too stable.

'He said it was because it had gone stale. He won't touch Mozart because his first concerts weren't a success. But he was very young then. And now this new Russian prodigy has excelled in Mozart. He could be jealous. You see it's not easy being a great conductor. You must always keep stimulated. If you get into a rut, you've had it.'

And she saw why he wanted to take the subway in New York.

'What shall I do, Micky? About the Empress?'

'I'd contact Marais and make sure he realizes what you did is serious. Find out which city he's playing in and phone him at the concert hall. Leave a message. Or get the sponsors to give him a message.'

That was easy. His sponsors in America were the Jason Tyrells of Boston.

She had to phone around the world to get Dean. At his Greek house, they said he was in Rome. Then she tried Boston. He was at the family house in the country and pleased to hear from her. His new volume of poetry was coming out in the fall and he had already had a two-page interview in the *New York Review of Books*. He was giving a series of seminars at Harvard. He told her about the Greek festival he hosted on his island. She was welcome. He often thought of her, because she pleased him aesthetically. Her shape, colouring and the way she held herself, reminded him of several works of art.

'Vicky, I always think of you as other-worldly.'

'What does that mean?'

'Don't rely too much on this one. What you're looking for, you'll find. Because you're definitely looking. Even in the photos of you as a kid I can see it: you had a quest. It's in your eyes.'

She remembered this was her call and she was paying for it and asked if he could get a message to Serge Marais.

'Oh, do I have to?' He sounded irritated.

'Can you ask him to phone me at home? It's very important, Dean. Could you see he does it?'

'I don't draw water with him.'

'Your family pay his wages. Let him know I mean something to you. Say your family value me.'

'You sound imperious. I hope you haven't changed too much.'

'Will you call him now?'

A thoughtful pause.

'Dean, don't you like him?'

'It's not a question of whether I like him. He's just incredibly difficult.'

'In what way?'

'He's got a lot of real estate and he's quarrelling with my father about the terms of buying into the cartel, and all the while he's losing profit and –'

This surprised her. He did not seem to be a businessman at all.

'And that wife is always so intrusive. The why, the how of everything.'

'Is the wife the one who's into real estate?'

'Possibly. Yes, it's probably her. She handles everything, anyway. But I'll do it. I'll ring him. I'll make someone happy tonight.'

'What's Serge Marais' wife like, Dean?' she said casually.

'A madonna. Don't touch; just worship. I suppose she occasionally falls from grace. Wouldn't we all, with him in the bed?'

Vicky put on Mozart and waited for a call which might or might not come, depending on the Tyrell company's influence on the world's greatest conductor, who lived for music but had a greedy wife.

The phone rang and she waited gracefully a few seconds before lifting the receiver. Her voice was at its best, low and calm.

Her mother said, 'Get me out of here. Do you hear? This is a mental hospital. I'll go mad if I stay here.'

The phone was snatched away by a nurse. The private clinic did not seem to help anymore than the NHS hospital had. What was the good of nice surroundings and a room to yourself, if you were in hell? And Ruby was in a bad place. But at least she was aware her daughter lived. Was that a sign of returning health?

The nurse told her that her mother was not on section but free, by the law of the land, to leave whenever she chose.

'But my dad can't take it. He's over eighty. He's had enough.'

The nurse said the medical staff would do everything they could to persuade her to stay.

'Use a syringe,' said Vicky, impatient with it all. The sort of money she was paying would sedate a whole town.

And all the time Serge Marais could be dialling her number.

She blamed herself for her mother's illness. She had not been able to persuade her to stay sane, even to enjoy life. Sometimes she felt hurt that she was so cut off from her mother. Why couldn't she show her love and affection? Then she thought of her mother, all soiled, damaged and angry, bitter, frightening. How could she embrace that? But, then, Ruby had not gone in for too much affection either. Had she ever held Vicky? Cuddled her? If she had, it was before memory came into question.

And then she realized it was not she, Vicky, who could not love her mother. Her mother did not love her. She thought it laughable that it had taken twenty-seven years to work that out. Her mother had never wanted her. That was why she had taken a dive down the stairs at seven months, and she could not be bothered with her when she was young. Not because she was sick. However sick, she could always stroke a cat. Vicky sat, rebuffed and angry, not with Serge but with her mother. She had been denied the common experience of motherly contact and love.

She took a mirror into the brightest light. Who did she look like? Ruby? Her father? She had a good nose like her mother's and the mouth was similar. Same skin. But the hair and eyes were what you noticed and they did not come from either parent. The eyes, long, slightly oval, extraordinary eyes, were passed down, perhaps from a great-grandmother, too good to be lost in the genetic gamble. Was she, too, violent, bad-tempered, savage, irritable? She had spent most of the time having to fit in around difficult people.

Still looking in the mirror, Vicky started to plait her hair and coiled it around her head as though it was an ordinary thing to do. The restlessness in the room immediately faded and there was a particular attentiveness, as though something unusual and concentrated was happening. She put on the first record that she touched; it was a little-played violin concerto and the sweet, rasping music fitted the atmosphere exactly.

The phone rang again. It was a long-distance call and her body, how it jumped with joy. Then Jay's voice said, 'Vick, I'm worried about you.'

'Oh, Jay, for heavens' sake.'

'Don't give me any of that "I'm alright" shit. I keep dreaming about you. The dreams are in colour and you're in purgatory. It's that bad. The dream stays with me all day.'

'Guilt, Jay. Good old-fashioned guilt.' As she listened she let her hair down out from the braids and the special atmosphere in the room was quite gone. How it had approved of her.

'It's always the same place. I reckon I'd know it if I saw it. It's not English. More European. You won't admit your misery, you always block off from the horror stuff. So I'm picking it up in my subconscious.'

'I'm not miserable. I'm in love with someone.'

'Yeah?' He sounded cautious. 'That's quick.'

'Not quick, not slow. It just happened.'

'While I was still with you or –'

'Oh, Jay. Give your vanity a rest.'

'Well, I just wanted to say, I feel you're in trouble. I can't give you the reason. Lorraine says you're inclined to block off what doesn't suit you.'

'What's up with you two? Love gone stale so soon? So you've got to talk about me, for heaven's sake?'

'We do all the usual things, don't worry. I'm just talking about my sleep.'

'Take pills.' And she hung up.

Half-past-one in the morning. Six or seven hours later than American time, depending on where he was. He would not ring now. He had obviously thought better of it. But it *had* been real.

She brushed out her long auburn hair, now crinkled by the plaits she had made. She did her other rituals before sleep. She prayed for her mother and father. She set the alarm clock, turned out the bedside light. Then the doorbell rang.

Serge Marais said, 'Come on, open up. I've had to come here because Miss Cobb would not let me in.'

Laughing, she opened the door. Without hesitation he walked straight up to her body, his arms already lifted to embrace her.

· *Twelve* ·

Lorraine caught up with Jay on Zuma beach as the sun was setting. He had been swimming and she dried his body with her skirt. She told him about a deal she had just set up for one of her London clients. It sounded too impressive to be true. 'So you see, it was worth coming here.'

He still did not answer.

'That's why I came, didn't I? To see clients in Los Angeles.'

There was a period in his relationship with women that he dreaded, even more than announcements of pregnancy, and that was the one when he had satisfied his desire for novelty. Then they became just female, yielding, cunning, fleshy strangers. It was a terrible moment and he blamed it on the fact he had never been close to his mother. Lorraine was now an exhausting intrusion and he wanted her out of his house. He felt disloyal, so he could not actually tell her to go. Therefore, he had become resentful and the rows had begun. It was always the same pattern.

'You know, Lorraine, I'm no good. I said that way back in London. Because you're really bright' – a lie – 'I'm going to tell you the truth. For me, sex is on the wing. When it slows down I've had my fill. Like at the table, I can only eat so much.'

'So, it's been a nice meal but if you go on with it you'll throw up.'

Foolishly, he said yes.

She slapped him ferociously across the face. It almost broke his nose. 'See a shrink!'

'Why?' He held his nose. 'They've got more problems than I have.'

'You're still in love with Vicky.' She hit out again but he managed to dodge the blow.

'What woman's logic you do pull. I was never in love with Vicky.' He changed position again – you never knew from where violence could come. She kicked back like a horse. 'Just save face, Lorraine, and say you came to do deals in L.A.'

'And I've lost her, my best friend. She hates me.'

'I doubt it. She didn't love me. At least, she didn't act as though she did.' He skimmed a flat stone across the still water with its reflected sun, full to bursting like a blood orange. 'So you can go back to London and she'll still be pals. Don't worry on that score. You might even find her happy.' He slipped another stone.

She told him how cold he was, how she hated him, and then she cried and really lost her temper. How he wished Vicky had shown more of this. Her reaction had been dull. It was strange, because she was not a listless kind of chick.

He said he would buy Lorraine a ticket to London and take her to the airport. Furious, she ran back to the house on the beach and he walked on into the sun. And then he saw it, the room with the dust on the wooden floor. It filled his mind like an actual reality in front of him.

'Oh, shit!' He had hoped it would go away. His body did not like it and his heart started pounding. He talked to himself gently as though he was someone else. 'Don't panic. Just let it happen. It's come up from your subconscious. Watch it, detached, like it's a movie.'

He could see a stove with a pipe going into the wall and coal all over the floor. He could hear the swish of her skirt. She was in the room. Put it this way, she shouldn't be. He looked at the sun. The room was still in his mind but fading now. She's in danger. He turned and ran to the house and shouted to Lorraine, 'I'm coming to London with you.'

She was so relieved. He let her stay that way.

He had eleven hours' flight time to keep working on his play, eat, watch movies and sleep. Instead, he tried to concentrate on Vicky. If he held her in his mind he would protect her. He had been trying to write about a victim in his last play, 'Scam'. The critics and audiences thought he had succeeded. The part was a minor one and suggested the signal a victim put out attracted the correct attacker. It was a very particular business, like good sex. He thought deliberately about the room that had so scared him, a room he had known in a dream and then in his waking mind. He had established she was there. The noise of her skirt suggested it was a voluminous one. So what had happened? Had someone come in? Was she raped? Chopped up? He knew that that was wrong. It was all too modern. 1980's snuff movie video violence shit. This was worse because it was not physical. The room was mean and without hope. It was the last room in the world. It was endless. It was the unthinkable. He felt frozen and shifted in his seat. Lorraine tried to sleep. Now he knew what they meant when they said physical pain was bad but spiritual pain – that was torture. That room was the place where real suffering began. It was the back door to purgatory.

At Heathrow, he put Lorraine in a taxi and said he would call her. Jay had thought she had something but she did not. It was just a trick of his eyes. She looked motherly and warm. That was her front. She was fuelled by an ambition that was almost indecent. He took the tube because it was quicker.

He did not know what to expect when he saw Vicky. Would she need medical assistance? A priest? He certainly was not prepared for what he saw. She was happy.

· Thirteen ·

Serge wanted to keep making love with her all the next day. With this girl, he could go on and on, all his pent-up, lustful ideas finally finding expression and a response. About most things Vicky knew nothing. About the sexual act, everything. She gave herself to it heart and soul. She induced him to acts he could not believe lovers performed. She found his hottest spot and played on that, the forbidden. She let him loose with his fantasies, then gave him more. She taught him how not to come, to hold it at the best moment and make it last. It even surprised her, how good she was. She did things she had not known before. She sat straddled across him, his penis still hard inside her and, talking to him, started to move, to ride him, her breasts moving, hair wild. And what she said, he would have found obscene, if he had not been desperately aroused by her. How could she know this was the position he had longed for, that Anna could just never manage? The final thing she did was more a submission, and he loved that too. That was something he had never dreamed of, even as a youth with quite a range of sexual ideas. He had made the mistake of thinking them infantile.

Then he lay back, reaching for her, pulling her on top of him. He said, 'I owe you everything.'

She was not sure about the 'owe'.

After they had eaten a plate of spaghetti and tinned sauce, he pulled her onto his lap' 'Have you done all that before?'

She shook her head. He did not believe it. He was already getting into a possessive state. She felt completely changed, rinsed out of all sadness. Her life was now beginning.

'Tell me about the men, Vicky.'

And her story came out in bursts, the good stuff, winner's talk. She did not mention her mother. She gave her parents the kind of life they would like to have had. He held her, his hands really held her body.

'So you've never even thought about these things we did? I brought them out of you?'

She agreed with that. It happened to be the truth. She did not ask about his wife, but she tried to find out if he had had other women. 'You're away so much on tour.'

'She comes with me.'

'Isn't that imprisoning?'

'It's the way I wanted it.'

She did not miss the past tense. 'So you didn't have anyone else?'

'You know the answer to that. Come on.'

She did not answer.

'If you don't know it, words won't help.'

He loved her without make-up but he did not want anyone else to see it, her vulnerability. He wanted to keep secret, away from others, what he enjoyed in private.

'So, how many men have you had?' His intense enjoyment had made him unusually jealous and possessive. She was glad she had only had Dean, Jay Landis and a couple of minor dalliances. Men had wanted her but she had never found what she wanted. He was what she wanted.

'So you didn't make love a lot with Dean?'

'He wasn't into it particularly, after the beginning.'

'But, with me, you couldn't get enough of it.'

'It must be you.'

They did not leave the flat all day and, in the evening, sat on the patio, entwined in each other's arms. There was no need to speak. The harmony was something she had never supposed existed.

Then he stroked her hand softly and freed himself. 'I have to make a phone call.' He went into the bedroom and shut the door. She made coffee and stood on the patio, looking out at the Heath. After twenty minutes he came out of the bedroom and put on his jacket, reached for his briefcase. She waited, as though expecting a death sentence.

'I have to go and talk with my business people. You see, I walked out of my concert tour. I just cancelled.'

'Why?'

'I thought it was better I do that because I wasn't giving my best. I was not even half good. Everything was a repetition. So I think I'd better go and settle this.'

'Where are they? Your business people?'

'I'll meet them at Claridges.'

'And your wife, presumably?' She did not like the sound of her voice and cleared her throat. 'I'm sure my ex-husband, Dean, could get you released from any contractual situation you have in America. After all, his family sponsor you –'

He held up a hand. 'Darling, I know how to do business. Please.'

And, for a moment, she did not like him. The 'darling' was commonplace. Sometimes he sounded less European than others. His arrival at her door had not been prompted by any call of Dean's. He had taken Concorde, on impulse, to come and see her because he felt very drawn to her. He had tried to resist for at least a week. He had given in, and now his life, and hers, would be different.

She waited for him to pronounce the next step, if he knew it.

'Will you trust me to get in touch?' Then he held her, really held her. 'You trust me enough that I'll do that?'

'Do I?'

'I always get what I want.' And he looked at her, his eyes full of sinful pleasures. Then he left. She sat on the patio, on the cold stones. Her body was ransacked, sore, bruised, aching. They had fallen in love. There was no sense to it. No choice, either. Except to walk away, which might seem like a choice. They would still be in love if they never saw each other again.

She looked up at the sky. 'I never thought I'd be so happy. Thank you.'

· *Fourteen* ·

Jay, his face pale and pinched with jet-lag, made a meal of eggs, bacon and baked beans. 'I hate the bacon in L.A. It's too burnt. Come on, you've had those burned strips on Cobb salads.'

The name Cobb did not please Vicky. She still had not got Serge to suppress her earlier lie. Somehow, with him, little details like lies ceased to exist.

'You know those salads. Lettuce, avocado, tuna, burned bacon.'

'Jay, how are things with Lorraine?'

'Fine.'

'Because I notice you're eating here and not at her luxury Belgravia apartment.'

'Who's the guy? The one you're happy about. Is he real? Why don't you just admit you're on your own and not making it socially?'

She sighed. 'You cling on to all my little weaknesses as though they're crimes, Jay. It was years ago that I sat in that laundrette.'

'You don't admit much. Only what you choose.'

'Is that a crime?'

'What's crime got to do with it? It just means you're not fully alive. So much of you is in shadow.'

'Is it?'

Jay was irritated because he had crossed the Atlantic to save her and she turned out to be happy. 'You're sure nothing's happened to you? Like trouble or –' He did not want to tell her about the room in the dream. 'Do you want to talk about this new lover?'

'Absolutely not.'

She looked better than he had ever seen her, as though she had fallen into place. Before, she had been not quite right, as though her mind and body were not synchronized.

Lorraine rang and wanted to know if Jay was there. He waved his fork desperately so Vicky said no.

Lorraine spoke quickly. 'You've got every right to hate me for what I did, but you must hear me out. No, don't speak.'

This would be the moment that Serge would choose to ring. Vicky hung up.

Jay said, 'Get her off my back.'

The phone rang and Lorraine said, 'I did what I did because I was in love. Mere sexual attraction could not have –'

'Lorraine, I've got to go.'

'I went with him for the best reasons.' Her voice was rough and desperate. 'But he's still involved with you, Vicky. Please put him on –'

'Goodbye.' Vicky hung up.

'Your friends are so boring,' said Jay.

'Why pick them up, then?'

Jay finished his meal and she poured him some coffee. He had arrived with a small travel bag. She could never tell by his luggage whether he was staying an afternoon or a month.

'You can't stay here, Jay. I'm with someone.'

'Is he likely to come here in the next four hours?'

She shrugged. How did she know?

'Just let me get some sleep.' He went into the bathroom, quite familiar with everything, and cleaned his teeth. He would take the plane the next day, back to Los Angeles. There was more danger coming from Lorraine towards him than around this quiet, secretive, composed girl. He took his clothes off and got into bed.

Vicky would not have that. He had to lie on the futon in the spare room. She made it clear that when he woke, he must leave, and on no condition answer the phone.

He sat up, head resting against the wall. 'Vicky, it's crazy us having this kind of conversation. Leave in four hours? We've got better going for us than that. I'm in your life.'

'It's over, Jay.'

'Sure. The sex stuff's out. I'm talking about caring for you. Now all the fucking is out of the way, I can be friends with you. No one looks after you.'

'Someone does.'

'Come on, Babe. You've only known him ten minutes.'

'I mean me. I look after me.'

The next day Vicky was sure she would hear from Serge. By eleven o'clock she was distressed. She could not stay away from work day after day on weak medical excuses. The wife had got him back. It was obvious. It was the first time Jay had seen her in a bad mood. She clattered the pans about and swiped at a crumb on the kitchen table. Jay moved his newspaper about a quarter-of-an-inch.

'Move!' she said.

'Why don't you call him?'

'Why don't you give your fat mistress some time?'

'I'd rather be with you.'

'I don't give a flying fuck, Jay. Your plane leaves at midday, you said. How are you going to be on it? It's now after eleven.'

'You can't call him because you don't know where he is and who he's with. I bet he's married. If he was serious he'd have given you a number.'

'Jay, I'm not talking about some showy, Tinsel Town party pick-up where you both exchange numbers, screw for fourteen hours on an ecstasy pill and never see each other again.'

'Is that what you did? Banged the guy for fourteen hours? Blew him out of his mind? Blew the cobwebs off his marriage and sent him back all new and interested, with some techniques to teach the old woman? You'll never see him again.' He laughed sardonically.

'It might be true, but you've left out love.'

'You just left clever-land, Vicky. You've joined the dumb herd along with Lorraine. Love?' He shook his head sadly. 'You're off the air, Vicky. And I thought you were smart. Love does not exist. It's the meanest snort, the worst shot. You just think it's there. A swift virus that doesn't even leave its tracks. Love!' He loved it. 'Perhaps he's rung you at work. You never seem to do any.'

'When are you leaving?'

'I'll go tomorrow.'

In the afternoon she went to a casting session for the BBC rep. She was short-tempered but tried to give her best. Why should someone be out of a job because she could not choose the right man for herself?

Micky Duke was in the record library selecting background for Kirsty's next epic.

'I want to know where the Maestro is,' Vicky said immediately she saw him. 'Ring his London impresario. Find out where he is, right now.'

Micky showed her an item in *The Times* stating his American tour had been cancelled due to illness. Then he rang the impresario's office and asked for the Maestro's next concert dates. He said he was from Radio 3 and needed to book a recording team. He was told there would be no concerts because the Maestro was away on an extended holiday with his wife and family.

Vicky was stunned but she had learned a long time ago to hold herself together.

Jay had done a PhD on theoretical physics at Princeton. He had switched to writing in his thirties because people's tragedies interested him a lot more than structures and organization, which you observed with all your skill and intelligence and gave a sound ending. People were better because they were messy and so much was unpredictable, and he found his best way of expressing his obsession was by writing. But he could not stand the market place. He could no more pitch an idea in Hollywood and wait for a lot of steaky guys, with blood pressure and IQs just slightly higher than room temperature, to throw it out than he could go back to the streets of Brooklyn. He could not rent out his mind to those Tinsel Town lowlifes with their interchangeable cars and wives. People fascinated him when they got the names all wrong. Anguished states of being, they called love. Not facing death, they described as security. As far as he was concerned, none of the human states had the correct labels.

Lorraine, her face streaked with tears, coloured by several cosmetics, asked again if he loved her. He had tried to placate her by having sex, fighting, giving her money, more sex, a meal. When she got in a certain position, with those huge breasts hanging down, he was caught. It was a muscular reaction, involuntary, and nothing to do with her as a person.

He watched her moving around, making supper. Her body looked good under the silk. He liked knowing she wore nothing underneath. He was seriously considering giving up sex and using porn mags instead. You could get a lot from a picture. He thought of Van Dongen's nudes, those of Pascin and the ones of Modigliani, the voluptuous women stretched out, waiting for it. It was in their eyes. How he had caught that. And their pubic hair, so shocking in those days. Some of the Modigliani nudes looked as though they were at the point of climax, twisting, writhing. And the painter concentrated on the breasts, pubic area and face, just like the centrefold of *Playboy*. Did Modigliani lust for women and get trapped by them, or free himself by painting? Jay thought he had sex with them first. That look in their eyes did not get there by itself.

'What are you thinking about?' she asked.

That was not his favourite question. He helped put the supper on the table, and did not answer. Before he left he said, 'I won't do one more performance in Hollywood, Lorraine, in those goddam magnets' offices. Artificial Intelligence is big now and there's money in that.'

Lorraine was not keen because she was not involved in that and she wanted control.

But what he really wanted, he decided, was to write about Vicky Graham. And he could not say why. She seemed pliant, mute sometimes, but around her the air was charged with high drama. His intuition licked its lips because it knew she was the stuff victims were made of. They came, not ashamed and ready for blows, but trying to shout the odds. She came haughty.

· *Fifteen* ·

Vicky recorded four plays back-to-back and prepared a drama documentary on Katherine Mansfield. The budget was cut again and again, partly because Kirsty was costing so much with her Shakespeare casting. She tried to hide her drinking but her walk was too careful, her speech over-pronounced. Vicky felt sorry for her but kept it to herself. If it ever got out, what she had done in Kirsty's name, she would simply say, 'But, Kirsty, you gave your permission. Don't you remember? You must have been a little drunk.'

She visited her mother in the clinic. She had thought up a set of questions designed to try and help the panic but when she looked at her mother's eyes she decided it better not to ask them. She wondered if it was fury that made you try to kill yourself.

Her mother said only one thing: 'Help me. Get me out of here.' Vicky saw no point in making herself more upset. Before she left she asked the chief nurse what could be expected.

'Some days she's worse than others. I wouldn't bother coming all this way. She doesn't know you've been.'

'It seems she's stuck in some unending panic attack.'

'She's had a shock. We're trying to get her to bring it to the surface. And we're trying to get her interested in other things.'

They asked Vicky to settle the bill and put down a deposit for the following month. She looked too young and alone to be very solvent.

Then she went to see her father. He was too depressed to eat, said life was not worth going on with. He had pains in his chest so she said she would fetch a doctor.

'Don't do that. They'll only put me away and then who'll look after her? It's my age.'

She still called the GP. Vicky thought things would have to get better. That is, if she was going to keep on doing them. In front of the doctor, her father refused all offers of help. Immediately, Vicky got the train back to London and thought of the desert, the endless, dry, healing, ruthless, pure state. It seemed the only place for her. It was absolute, mystical and there were no people.

Jay called her twice. Reluctantly, she turned off the pan of fried vegetables and went into the living room.

'Isn't this the guy you interviewed? Serge Marais?'

She sank to her knees. He was sitting in an airport lounge, a blonde woman beside him, with slanting eyes, high cheekbones and an enviable bone structure. The wife from Estonia. They were holding hands. Vicky got over the shock of that and listened to what his liar's lips were saying. 'We will stay in Greece for some time.'

'How long do we have to wait, Maestro, before you return to the concert hall?'

'How can I say? A week? A year? I am not finding in myself the standards of excellence that I expect. So a time of replenishment is necessary. A time to do ordinary, everyday things.' He looked at his wife warmly. How well Vicky knew that look! She gave the smallest sob in the world.

Marais said, 'I am very lucky because I have such an incredibly happy marriage.'

'Does he know he's breaking hearts out here?' said Jay.

'So for us,' said Marais, 'the absence from music will not be so terrible.'

'Yes,' said Vicky sharply. 'Cowards always have such happy times!' Dean was right. The blonde from Estonia was like a madonna.

The announcer made a short summary of the news piece: Serge Marais had retired from the concert hall. Jay was still watching Vicky. She looked back with a level stare but her breathing gave her away.

'Why don't you smash the set or go and tell his fucking wife?

Put him in the tabloids. Don't just put a lid on it like it never happened. Come on, Vicky! A guy cliffs you and you have to hear it on TV?'

Coldly she said, 'So, how's Lorraine?' She looked at the abundance of lovebites on his neck. 'I see we're all pals again.'

'I'd hit him. Give him a good spanking.' He waved a finger at the set, excited now because this must have been the purpose of his dream. The room, so real with the sloping, noisy wooden floorboards was just symbolism. 'He comes in, promises you everything you've ever wanted, then, contemptuous as you like, goes back to his wife. And gets an even better deal from her, because there's nothing like a spot of rivalry. Some guys are too lucky.'

'I bet Lorraine thinks that. You want to watch her. She's got a lot of friends in high places in Hollywood. Hurt her and they'll hang you out to dry. They'll keep you sitting in some little office on a paltry development deal that goes on forever and you'll never ever get your play on celluloid. She's your worst nightmare. She's worse than alimony. What do you mean, he gets an even better deal from his wife?'

'It's an old one. Your wife is giving you a bad time so you go off with someone else, then you let her know about it. You let her know indirectly, she's threatened because you're hooked. It's surprising how many somersaults she'll do to keep you. She'll bang you to death to keep the rival away. There's nothing better for a marriage. I know.'

Oddly, she said, 'Well, that fits. I think I was born to make other people better.'

Lorraine felt the healer's hands just above her head. An assistant worked on her ankles and she felt the heat soothe her body, pass through her like hot milk, easing the pain.

'He'll only bring you unhappiness, dear,' said the healer. 'This one lives out of a suitcase. He's always running. You can't keep him. I don't think a woman could. He's got a very full life, this man. He's not the one we see for you.'

'But why is he so restless?'

'Greedy. He wants every attractive girl he sees. No one keeps him.'

And Lorraine sighed, because it was true. 'But why is he like this? It isn't natural.'

'In his previous life he did not have any women. He elected to do without.'

'Why?'

'Because he was a priest. So this time he's making up for it.'

'A priest?' Lorraine was not keen on past lives. How did you prove them?

The healer moved his hand to her solar plexus and she felt easier and breathed deeper.

'But you've got a friend who's in great distress. We've talked about her before.'

'The one who's always unlucky? Vicky?'

'She'll be alright as long as she stays unlucky. It's a strange thing to say, but I wouldn't want that one covered in jewels.'

Lorraine laughed. Some chance!

· *Sixteen* ·

Lorraine turned up at Vicky's studio. She had been to a meeting upstairs with important, un-named people and now she was in the bowels of Broadcasting House trying to do another deal, getting back a friend. She loved Vicky and said she missed her. Couldn't they talk? Vicky did not like what her one-time friend had done but she missed the warmth and companionship. It was not as though she had done anything serious, like run off with Serge Marais.

'I'm really sorry, kid.' Lorraine hugged her. 'It was a rotten thing to do, but –' Vicky gestured silence and checked they were not on studio mike. 'I didn't see how else to do it. If I had told you, Vicky, you'd have been upset and he wouldn't have wanted to leave you. You know how he is about guilt.'

Vicky did not want to share experiences or talk about the affairs – hers or Lorraine's. She was glad when Kirsty Cobb pushed open the studio door and put her script and notebook on the director's table. 'I'm in here at two o'clock sharp.'

Vicky said there was no problem, she was finished for the day. She introduced the two women. They had already met a thousand times in the corridors of television.

Lorraine said firmly, 'Let's have lunch.' She meant she and Vicky.

Vicky said that was fine and included Kirsty.

They went to the George Hotel and Vicky ordered a three-course meal which she could eat in peace. Kirsty and Lorraine did the talking. Career moves, finance, production schedules. Who was in this month and for how long. Was it worth the effort and insecurity of moving to New York if that was where the juice was? Kirsty did not eat but she only drank one glass of wine. The effort could kill her but she was not going to reveal herself, to disadvantage, in front of a shark like Lorraine. Then Kirsty mentioned Serge Marais retiring. How glad Vicky was that she had left that to the final course.

'It's a defection. Of course, he won't stick to it. You can see he's terribly unhappy.'

'Unhappy?' Vicky was shaken.

'It's in his face,' said Kirsty rationally. 'And the way he held his wife's hand.' She shook her head disparagingly. 'Haven't I seen that act! It makes me sick.'

Lorraine started to speak but Vicky cut in.

'You're saying what, exactly?'

'That the greatest conductor of all time has marital problems.' She wiped her smudged lipstick and poked her smoked salmon sandwich around on her plate. Then she remembered she had an early recording and got up. 'See you in the fast lane, Lorraine.'

When she'd gone Lorraine whispered, 'She's got a problem.'

'We know.' Vicky thought she meant drink.

'She's washed up in television because of her obsessional behaviour towards a certain studio boss. She'd follow him home, phone his house, hang up when she got his wife. Haven't we all done it? Once?'

Vicky had not, yet.

'So he changed his number. She got good and mad, and broke into his house. I think drink played a part in that. And the wife threw in her share.'

Vicky could not even have imagined behaving that way two weeks ago. Before she met the Maestro.

'When does it become obsessional, Lorraine?'

'When the man withdraws.'

Would Vicky do that to Marais? She still wanted him. She thought of the sexual act, it played on her nerves, her heart was like an African disaster drum. If only she had got pregnant.

'And then Kirsty told him she was pregnant. He insisted she get it terminated and then he'd go on seeing her. So she did and she's still waiting for joy in the afternoons and it's made her like this.' Lorraine made screw signs on her head. 'And she drinks, medically, to cut out the rejection. She's out of her job in television and she'll be out of this one if she doesn't watch it. They're not in the business of paying casualties.'

'We're all so cruel to each other. Who needs wars?' Vicky poured a drink. 'He must have put out to her. It's a two-way road.'

'Who knows? He chose to stay with his wife and she should have backed off.'

'You know a lot about it.'

'I know a lot about it because I wrote it, an outline of her story, The Kirsty Triangle, for a TV movie. Everyone said, too "everyday". I think Kirsty's ex even read it and didn't recognize a thing. And now what do you think? Hollywood's bought it. You don't call me "Lo" anymore.'

'No, Lo.'

'I'll give you a tip, a sort of favour. Her ex-lover would pay anything if Jay would do a TV film for him. I was going to suggest it but you can.'

'You do it,' said Vicky. 'It would only irritate him because he would never do television. I think Kirsty is a lesson to us all.' Then she laughed. 'Why don't you introduce her to Jay? That'll make yesterday's little rejection seem like not such a bad time.' Vicky got up.

'By the way, Vicky, I spoke to the healer about you. And he said you need help. You're in need. Lonely.'

Vicky turned. 'That's rather a lot for one of your sessions. Surely you wouldn't let another person get all that attention?'

Coldly, Lorraine told her the truth.

'Well, you've got other friends. I think the healer muddled me with Kirsty Cobb. Take her.'

Vicky hurried to the lift, punched the button hard and the doors swished shut against Lorraine. Vicky was furious suddenly. Women could never, should never be trusted. They were worse than men. They truly violated. Women were so faithless. Angrily she drew with her finger, on the wall of the lift, a coiled thing. Without thinking, she marked its tongue, lashing, about to strike.

And then she looked at it. Because it was familiar. The doors had opened and people were waiting to enter the lift, but she stayed still in front of her doodle and as it faded she saw a word: LUNIA.

Her secretary brought in the list of calls. She rang the clinic first. Her mother needed long-term care. As there was no insurance, could Vicky go on paying?

'Yes, I'll pay.' She was in a poor temper.

'Or we could consider moving her into a less expensive home designed for long-term patients.'

It was her father Vicky worried about. Her mother may or may not be oblivious to surroundings. 'Keep it as it is for now.'

On her pad she had drawn the coiled snake, striking, jealous. And the word LUNIA. Her mind raced. She would get Serge Marais to pay, oh, so easily. Not by asking him. By displaying their night and day of love in the tabloids. Oh, yes. He would pay. Her secretary was in the room with more messages. She saw the snake which Vicky tried to cover with a script.

'What's that?'

'A doodle. What does Lunia mean?'

The girl said, moon.

Vicky's mood in the lift had been stranger than she had realized. It was not anger but fury that made her mark out the uncoiling snake on the lift wall. Her face had been filled with bloodied rage. She would have savaged the nearest woman. Why? Because she had been deceived? Because her friend had taken away a man she had not loved? Or because the so-called friend talked so mockingly of obsessional love and then made money out of it. It was possibly none of these things, but it had something to do with women.

Micky Duke phoned her office and said, 'He's back in Paris. He's doing a charity concert there. Tonight. It could mean retirement doesn't suit him.'

Everything Vicky had wanted had always been taken away, certainly in her adult years. She decided Serge Marais would not be one of them. People were always interfering, coming between her and the object of her desire, but not this time. She put on a tape of Mozart, the one composer he did not feel adequate to conduct and phoned the Paris Opera. There had been a swift switch in the current programme to accommodate his sudden change of heart. The impresario's assistant said the Maestro was unavailable, he was rehearsing. She told him to go and find the Maestro and say she was calling.

'About what?'

'A high tech hitch.' Then she turned up the tape.

A lot of time passed. The music, so beautiful, lifted her. It would soothe anything. Her secretary came into the room because the controller wanted to speak to her urgently. Vicky waved the girl away.

More time passed, then Serge Marais said, 'Yes, Vicky?' He sounded tired.

'I know you like to keep aloof but haven't you something to say?'

'To whom?' He sounded cold.

'The world. Or is your greatness a secret?'

'Doesn't the music say it?' He was formal. Was his wife beside him?

'Not enough. You must have views on things besides music. Let us know. After all, you are a great man.'

'Oh, no. I am like you, the next person, everybody. I'm not special. We're all the same, aren't we?'

'No.'

'No? In what way no?'

'You're quite a different person, on a different level of experience from probably the majority of those around you.'

'I didn't stop my rehearsal to come urgently to the phone to listen to compliments.'

'It wasn't one.' She was doodling on the front of her note-book.

He laughed bitterly. So she was not ingratiating herself.

'So you like Mozart, Vicky? Concerto in B flat major.'

'One thing about Mozart. He's always reliable.' She had drawn a window, open, and below, a wooden floor with noticeable boards and part of a wooden table, a violin, the beginning of a stove.

'So you want to record an interview with me? Is that right?'

'Not particularly.' She sounded absent-minded.

'I'll give you the exclusive. You can sell it worldwide. You'll be rich.'

'Is this a pay-off?' She guessed he was now alone.

'For what should I pay?' He sounded very smooth and very dangerous.

'There's a lot of money in the air suddenly. How about for failing to honour your promise?' Her reply was quick and sharp.

'Do you always do what you say? Yes, I think you do. Come to Paris and do the interview, Miss Cobb. But I'm leaving tomorrow.'

And she knew his wife was back in the room. He hung up.

She replaced the receiver and continued drawing. Along one side of the room she sketched six or seven large rectangles. Were they windows? Her pencil skidded downwards across the wooden floor and dizzily she drew a door and then another room began.

The controller said, 'So I have to come and find you. You know the rule about long-distance phone calls.'

'You'll get the phone bill paid. I just got Serge Marais. An exclusive.'

The woman was pleased and not pleased. She had never heard Vicky Graham sound so hard.

Vicky packed her very best clothes, then took them out and chose, instead, a simple yellow silk suit. Jay made her coffee and hung around while she filled a bag with make-up.

'Try and see some stuff in Paris. There's a Bonnard exhibition. Don't miss that. And I can give you a couple of introductions. One with the minister for arts.'

'Jay, I'm going to spend half-an-hour in Paris. I'll be back first thing tomorrow.' She still had to collect the direct-record equipment from the BBC. She would get a ticket at the airport.

'Do you like exhibitions?' he asked.

‘Of course.’

‘You never go to any.’

She admitted that was true. She knew people from all groups and classes, but no artists. There was something about the art world that depressed her. It felt old-fashioned, as though it could only be a repetition. That was why she loved film.

‘Paris is OK, this time of year. No one’s about,’ he said.

Paris is lovely, this time of year. It reverberated in her mind. Was Paris lovely? She felt cold. Now she did not even know if she liked it.

‘I’ll stay till you come back and water the plants. But I think I’ve had English life for a while. When I first came, I couldn’t get enough of high teas and London hotels and country houses. I bet I’ve seen more of smart England than you have.’ He carried her small bag down to the taxi.

‘Don’t answer the phone, Jay. I mean it. I’ve put the machine on so if it’s for you you’ll hear and –’

‘Babe, you’ve told me not to answer it. I don’t.’

Before, she had not wanted him to speak in case Serge rang. Now, it was her mother.

‘I think I know this country and its customs better than you, even though you come from the county set, an estate and all.’

She almost reeled at that one. Who had told him that fairytale? Lorraine, obviously supplying the Hollywood treatment so her friends would reflect well on her.

‘But I like you because you’re classless,’ he said.

‘That’s right,’ she said.

· *Seventeen* ·

She took a taxi from Charles de Gaulle airport to the stage door of the Opera House. She was far from sure he would still be there. They had made no firm arrangement. The concert had finished nearly an hour before but the applause had been endless, gratitude from his worshippers that he had returned to them. And the queue of society fans paying their respects was still shuffling slowly forward. The non-famous, hundreds of them, were held back by a security cordon beyond the stage-door. She had not travelled all this way at his invitation, carrying a recording machine, to stand in line. She pushed past the elegant, patient people, much as the French president had done weeks before. And Serge Marais saw her approach. But unlike the first time, there was no snap in the air, no chemical acknowledgement that she had something to do with his life. His eyes were flat. She pushed her way to the front. He did not speak and she felt awkward, then angry.

She said, 'I've brought the Nagra machine for a direct recording. That's what you asked for, isn't it?' She absolutely refused to call him Maestro. She was aware of the blonde woman at his side but did not look at her. She could smell her perfume, a little tart, nothing cloying, chosen by him.

He still did not speak. Was Vicky supposed to stand like a disgraced schoolgirl, carrying a substantial machine, while he made up his mind whether he knew her or not? Behind her, the line hissed and swayed like an angry reptile.

His voice, when he finally spoke, sounded spoilt. 'So you think we should do this? What good would it do? I don't know.' He gave a sarcastic shrug.

'Just let's talk about the part that *will* do some good,' she said sharply. 'I have very little time.' She looked into his eyes. Yes, they were depressed. His own state absorbed him to the exclusion of everyone else. He wore it, his unhappiness, like a robe of state, in front of everyone. Thinking it was temperament, they could only applaud the more.

'This is my wife, Anna.'

She was almost too beautiful. Her looks were unreal, as though the creation of a man's fantasy. Her hair, shining like a lamp, hung down one side. And she was cold. Anna had recently been to the jewellers and the results were festooned about her person in gold and rubies. Her black fur hung, long and sleek, to her ankles. She wore too many rings perhaps but Vicky thought she might just be envious. Anna Marais wore the trophies of her marriage almost insolently.

'This is Miss Cobb.'

Anna gave the faintest smile, as though she knew all about Miss Cobb and her misfortunes. There was no greeting in her face. She did not shake Vicky's hand or speak. The queue was hardly breathing, sensing trouble. Vicky thought maybe Jay Landis had touched on something when he said she was in danger. It was just possible violence might occur. The blonde icicle stood solidly beside Vicky's one-time lover. These days, violence was no stranger to Vicky's everyday thoughts. She handled the scene as she would if performed by a couple of rebellious actors.

'Shall I set up the machine in a dressing room, or do you want to do it against the background congratulations of your fans?'

He made a noise like a low growl. Rudeness was not something he often came across. His staff dealt with that. 'Put it in the dressing room and we'll do something if I have a moment.' The tone of his voice made her hate herself for giving herself to this spoilt superstar who was rumoured to be a great man. He, like so many lesser stars, had been ruined by fame. He could not handle the adulation any more than the newest popstar. The Canadian was now beside her, leading the way to a dressing room.

Vicky did not even observe what the room was like. She put the machine on the nearest surface, opened the lid, wound in a reel of tape, plugged in a microphone, did a test for sound. 'So, how long will he be?' She looked at the Canadian, who was surprised to see such authority in Vicky's face. It came from the fact that Vicky was no technological parts salesgirl but a woman who had been crushed for hours in the Maestro's arms.

The Canadian, therefore, made her reply more courteous than it might otherwise have been. 'Not long. The Maestro has to attend a reception in fifteen minutes. You can't do anything afterwards, I'm afraid, because they're flying off early tomorrow.'

'Where?'

'For a holiday with the children. So get your questions ready, Miss Cobb. And always refer to him as Maestro.'

He was in the doorway. 'Excuse me if I change but I have to be out of here in a few minutes.' He took off his shirt and trousers, still damp with sweat from the performance. He threw them in a corner and rubbed himself with a towel. He splashed cologne around and said, 'Well, Miss Cobb, you never really answered my question. Last time, I asked what you thought of modern music. It's non-existent today, isn't it? Worthless? Don't you think so?'

'Well, it's not for me to say,' she said quickly.

'But it is.' His voice was honey-smooth. 'You must say what you think.'

'Who cares what I say?' She was angry.

'I do. What do you think?' He brushed his hair and clipped on a watch.

She had forgotten what she was supposed to think about. He reached for a shirt. How well-toned his body was. She tried not to look at it. He wore a gold cross and chain, big enough to keep a vampire away. She had not noticed it before. Did he remove it before slipping into sin?

'You see! She doesn't answer my questions.' He laughed.

'Maestro, you're on tape,' whispered the Canadian.

'Modern music, Miss Cobb. Come on. Tell me about it.'

'How can I condemn the whole of it? It's like standing beside the Chrysler building and saying it's worthless.'

'Ask your questions.' The Canadian nudged her.

The Maestro was winding a silk scarf around his neck, ready to go.

'How does it feel to be famous, Serge Marais? Is it an advantage or otherwise?'

'Of course it isn't an advantage.' He sounded hostile. 'I am a person of simple ways.'

'I doubt it.' Vicky sounded so unusual, she aroused the Canadian's interest. The Maestro stepped into some shoes and told the Canadian to go and get the car.

'Tell my wife I'll be a couple of minutes.'

The Canadian left with reluctance. He kicked shut the door.

'You fool!' His voice was quite changed, desperate. His eyes shone with a yellow fire like a dangerous animal. 'How could you do this! You are so –' He could not think of anything which would do his panic justice.

She snapped back, 'You told me to come! "Do what I say." That's what you said in London. Trust me. Well, here I am. Docile as a little lamb.'

'But not here. I did not expect you to walk in here.' He gestured to where his wife waited. 'What are you thinking of?'

'Well, where am I supposed to meet you? Paris is a very big place.'

'My life is impossible at this moment. I thought, naturally, you would go to your hotel.'

'You're not clever with your arrangements, then. You didn't give me a clear message.'

'I don't normally make my arrangements. But why did you not go to your hotel? The one where you stay. And wait for me there. That's what women do, don't they? When they have affairs. They're discreet.'

'I don't know, Serge. I don't have affairs. Not with married men.'

'Well, nor do I.' He saw the other side of that and burst out laughing.

And she realized the machine was still recording. This was one interview that would not be slotted into a music programme.

'Go there now,' he said.

'I haven't booked anything. I didn't know what you wanted.'

Footsteps approached, a slow, contained sound with perhaps a hint of a jangle of jewels.

Serge threw Vicky a key. 'The Elysées by Rond Point. Suite 309. I'll come later.'

The door opened, a flash of blonde hair.

Serge gestured to Vicky that she hide the key. He said, 'Thank you, Miss Cobb. I have to leave now.' He grabbed a dinner jacket and whisked his wife off along the corridor, leaving Vicky to find her way out of the backstage area and into a taxi.

What the hell was she doing, pursuing another woman's man? Vicky asked herself. Why had she so eagerly believed Kirsty Cobb when she said the Maestro's marriage was on the rocks? Because she wanted to believe it. Then she realized the tape was still running and switched it off. What an interview she had, after all. Not quite the average musical discussion, but it had plenty of light, dark and tension. She phoned the airport. No planes to London until six-thirty in the morning. She did not have to keep the appointment. She could book into the nearest hotel and spend the night praying that the right man would one day come into her life. Serge Marais was turning out to be a highway to nowhere. Little things, like arrangements to meet a mistress, were not his forte. His wife and the Canadian took care of everything. If her past had been brighter she would not have gone anywhere near him. She decided to go to the meeting in suite 309 because she had had enough of the down-side of life.

The Élysées was a luxury hotel of private suites with room service, an excellent dining room, a boutique, beauty salon, health club, flower shop. She almost got to the lift, but the security guard called out, 'You have to check in at the desk, Madame.'

She crossed to the desk and showed the porter the key and the machine. 'It's for the Maestro.' Her voice was quiet.

There was only one key and the Maestro kept it himself. He

even kept the pass-key when staying in Paris. That made her story acceptable, and the familiar BBC name on the machine case gave a feeling of security. The security guard asked for identification. She showed him her BBC pass.

She swished up three low floors and walked along a wide green carpeted corridor. Room 309 was at the end, large, soundproofed and used for one sole purpose: private rehearsal. A grand piano in one corner was open, its top cluttered with written notes and cassettes. Recording machines lined a wall. Piles of music scores littered the tables and chairs. At the far end, by a fake log fire, two large sofas were covered with newspapers and magazines. The luxury bathroom contained soap, shaving products, cologne, a wrap. She took a bath and the blue and gold tiles calmed her, until she thought about the wife. Did she have a key? What if the porter alerted her to the fact a visitor was waiting in suite 309? Vicky leapt out of the bath and dressed. One o'clock, French time. She could see the bedroom was not used. There was a television and drinks cabinet, a painting over the bed, empty cupboards and drawers. She looked for something to eat, did not dare phone the twenty-four hour room service. She took a bottle of mineral water from the fridge, opened a window and looked out at Paris. Just across the river, Montparnasse and its cafés were still lively. Up came the atmosphere of the city in a rush and it was full of distress, of bitter sadness. Her throat tightened. She thought her heart would break. The Maestro chose that moment to come in. He looked older and more tired than she had seen him before. 'I thought you might be sleeping.' Seeing her face, he said, 'Of course, you're sad.'

But it was not to do with him, the feeling. It was out there on the boulevards. She knew its name: anguish. It was in the smell of the Parisian air, in and out of the rooms, the names of the streets, their shapes, even the trees were full of it. Was it a sadness she had experienced? It was more a heartbreak, because someone expected and beautiful was no longer there. That was an odd, disquieting thought. The someone could hardly be Dean.

Serge was talking but she was not listening. She had sniffed out a joy, half-remembered. Not with Dean, but further back. On her trips with the school to the museums and historical sites? Or the wicked teenage excursions, for the clubs and the men? Passing through from other towns?

It was there, the name on the tip of her tongue. She could feel its syllables and weight. And like a flame, happiness leapt and died inside her. She turned and looked at the man in the doorway. For a moment he was a stranger. He had come to the end of an explanation.

She said, 'Does your wife have a key?'

'I have the only keys.' He threw them into the air. 'The pass-keys. Because I mustn't, even for an emergency, be disturbed. The place would have to burn down. I can't bear anyone cleaning in here or moving things. And the phone is disconnected.'

'I phoned you, Serge, because I believed you were unhappy. I was unhappy. I didn't want to intrude, but it seemed we had unfinished business.'

'I've just told you. My God, you don't listen to anything! I would have called, but I didn't know from one minute to the next what I wanted to say. So I never made the call. If I muddle our arrangements it's because I don't know what I'm doing. But I've just said that. You seemed to be listening. You sit as though you're waiting for someone. No, posing for them. In Paris, that is. Not in London. You're different there. Why is that?'

She was not aware of it so how could she say? 'I was ill, the last time in Paris.'

'How lucky you had a virus or we'd never have properly met.'

'Am I supposed to stay the night here? I'd hate to cause embarrassment, more embarrassment.'

'Of course you stay.'

'I don't want to sound over-cautious but where is your wife?'

He did not answer.

'You see, your arrangements aren't too well-planned, Serge. I like to look after myself.'

He flopped, exhausted, onto a sofa. 'I'm not in a state of mind to know what I'm doing. I have five, no six, solutions within one hour.'

'Where is she?'

'She! She's in our suite with the children, packing for our holiday. It's on the first floor. I told you, I have the pass-key, so she cannot possibly come here. She knows never to come here. Give me that key.' He held out his hand. She got it from the bag and threw it. He caught it skilfully, without even seeming to look. It was now two o'clock. 'I have to have one place in the world where no one can get to me.'

'While we're tidying things up, could you please stop calling me Miss Cobb. The actual lady may not like it.'

'She won't know.' He laughed drily. 'I can't have two Miss Cobbs in my life.'

'How did you know, the first day, I was someone else?'

'Because you looked at me with eyes full of desire. Your eyes were full of beginnings. It was a game between us. I saw, then you saw, then I saw the next thing. You did not have the eyes of a corporation producer. You didn't look tough enough.'

'So why did you suggest seeing me the following morning?'

'Oh, Vicky. Come on! You know that. I wanted you.'

'Past tense.'

'It doesn't have to be.'

'But your wife could have been present at that interview, and the Canadian.'

'Vicky, I make no plans. I wanted to see you again. That was as far as I knew.'

'And the Canadian knew I was someone else?'

'When she described Miss Cobb she thought you'd worn well for your age. You didn't look thirty-six.' He held out his hand to her. 'Come on. Sit on my lap.'

'No. You're married.'

'I was married in London.'

'I've seen your wife. It's different now.'

He let his hand drop to the carpet. 'Perhaps, then, it should be past tense, our affair. I wish it was. I wanted it to be. It doesn't bring out the best in me. I can't manage deceit.'

She had heard from Kirsty that married men indulged in long, guilty monologues about their wives. It usually happened after the sexual act.

He said, 'My work is not quite right and my wife senses something is different. We have always been very close. I am going to stay with her because she gives me security. She's been a marvellous companion and support – she's given me constant attention. We've been together for eighteen years.'

'She looks well on it.' Vicky looked out at Paris, away from him. She did not think she could take any more bad news. Her mind was on the Luxembourg Gardens, just down the road. In her mind she followed the railings to the crossroads and two cafés. As though there in person, she crossed the road and went along a narrow street and she knew at the top, on the right, the Panthéon waited. And she would do anything to avoid that building. It brought the most sinister feelings down on her. She thought of the roads she could take, avoiding the Panthéon, to get to the Gare d'Austerlitz and get away. The streets of Paris all indicated flight. But why was she thinking of this, when she could walk out of this modern suite and take a taxi to the airport?

'What do you think? What should we do, Vicky?'

'I think if it goes on like it did tonight, there won't be anything to do. It'll be over.'

Escaping from Paris felt right. Hadn't she always wanted to get out? Yet nothing particularly bad had happened. She could be looking at the most beautiful site or monument and her legs would stiffen and tingle, wanting flight. She heard herself say, 'If I don't get out of here, I'll die.' She could not pinpoint her distress, except to say her escape seemed linked to another escape. None of it had anything whatsoever to do with the man in the room.

'Talk to me, Vicky.'

'I think it's a terrible mistake to get involved with a married man. I've seen the real Miss Cobb at the wrong end of that.'

'So it's all decided, then.' He sat up, relieved. 'I may miss out on a lot of happiness and the freedom I need, that you sense so correctly. But I will continue as I am. I will get back my discipline and heal myself with music. Maybe I needed the experience – the lapse from discipline. Who knows?'

It did seem to be about him, all of it. She stood and waited like a serving maid. In for the night or outside with the others?

She said, 'I'm going now. I'm sorry you're in a confused state. But I don't think it's about me. I just came along at the wrong time. Or the same time.' She got her bag and started for the door. She came back because she had forgotten the BBC machine. He thought she had given him a reprieve and gratefully reached for her hand. It was not there. She reached for the machine and turned back to the door again.

'Vicky, do you find me selfish?'

'I expect you have to be.'

He stayed, relaxed, on the sofa: she would not be going anywhere. The door was always double-locked. 'I've never had to deal with a real life crisis before.'

'Well, I'll go and take the crisis away.' She could catch the first available plane.

'Vicky, I wish you would understand. I've had personal loss, my children have been ill, the usual things. But I've never had to make a choice. Not an emotional one.' He wanted to say, my wife always makes decisions for me, so you see, I'm out of practice, but he thought he should avoid that. He had talked too much about his wife. 'D'you want anything, Vicky? I mean, is there anything I can do for you?'

'I just told you: don't keep calling me Miss Cobb.'

He laughed, although without humour. 'So, you knew I was unhappy? That's what you said.'

'Miss Cobb noticed it in your face. You were on British television.'

'She's right. So it shows. My God!' Then he realized she was still waiting at the door. Had his personal tumult deprived him of all manners? He jumped up and took her bag and tape recorder. 'You sleep here. I'll go to the family suite. And tomorrow we'll do a proper interview, I promise. Now I will make you a hot drink and you will sleep well.'

He went into the bedroom and turned back the coverlet. He watched her brush her hair. He found a kind of grace in her. Paris gave her a stillness. Whereas in London she moved about, was vibrant. His mind was made up. He had done the right thing, but he was still looking at her calves, then her thighs, then her lips, then her breasts. His eyes stayed there and he longed for her to take off the yellow silk. He turned off the kettle and put his hand up under her skirt.

She felt an intense spasm of pleasure, a shivering joy. She said, 'I'm not getting involved with a married man. Don't touch me.'

'But I want you.' He sounded wilful, not used to being opposed.

She laughed briefly. 'Want something you can have.'

His mouth was against her ear. He kissed her neck. 'Let's make love just once more. It won't make any difference. Why not have pleasure when it's this good?' His eyes looked into hers, holding her captive. She could so easily give in to that fabulous sexual caress, but her mind kept seeing Kirsty Cobb with the stricken expression, the too-blonde hair and the drinking problem. Not you, said her wise heart.

He pulled at her. She would not move. 'If you don't do exactly as you did in London, I will tell the world you are not Miss Cobb and you will lose your job.'

'I'll put you through the tabloids.' Her voice was harsh.

He touched her breast and that was her downfall. He felt the hardened reaction of her nipple. 'You want me. Oh, yes.'

Her body leapt to his, tongue to tongue, and in his eagerness he tore off her silk knickers, ripping them, and later kept them as a private memento. The yellow suit got slightly better treatment. And she thought, we do have something unusual. A fusion, several minutes before the climax, was out of this world. He said so, too.

Afterwards, she lay in his arms and thought how weak she was when pleasure was there. All her best resolutions ruined by seduction. Do I love him? She shrugged as though there might be a choice. She thought of the expression on his face at the height of his pleasure. She had no choice. Now it was to be all compromise and possibly pain, because she would do almost anything to stay near him.

· *Eighteen* ·

Quite by chance, she came face-to-face with Anna Marais in the hotel boutique. Wearing dark glasses, Vicky had hurriedly made the necessary purchase of a pair of knickers before leaving for London. On entering the shop, she had supposed Serge Marais and his family were well on the way to Greece. Vicky was holding a pair of silk and lace knickers and an erase-stick to cover the lovebites on her neck, when the exquisitely groomed wife strolled up to the counter. She recognized Vicky immediately.

'I didn't know you shopped here, Miss Cobb.'

'I'm on my way to the airport.' She handed over the first money she came across but a fifty-franc note was not enough. The knickers alone cost two hundred francs. While she fumbled for some more money, Anna selected magazines and several bars of chocolate.

'So, how was your interview with my husband?'

'Short.'

'I'd like to hear it.'

Deeply alarmed, Vicky said, 'I thought you were going on holiday.' She did not bother with a bag or the change the saleswoman was trying to hand her. She started towards the door but Anna blocked her way.

'Let me hear the interview. I suppose you're staying very near here?'

'Fairly near. But I'm desperately late. My plane –' And with the knickers dangling from one hand, she pushed past Anna to the door. Anna followed. So did the salesgirl, sensing trouble.

'Miss Cobb, my husband does not normally do this sort of thing.'

Vicky turned into the corridor where a blaze of sunlight made it obvious she was naked under the silk skirt. Should she run for it? She still had her small case and the recording machine in the rehearsal suite.

'Madame Marais, you must ask your husband. I can't just play an interview he's given for the BBC and have it rejected by a member of the family.' Vicky hoped she looked better than she felt. The bruises were obvious on her neck. Both Anna Marais and the salesgirl were looking. She turned towards the main exit and the two women followed. Should she run into the street? But she would have to leave the key to the suite in the place he had suggested. The salesgirl was already making signs to the doorman: Vicky would not get out. 'Naturally, if the Maestro wants to change his mind, I'll erase the tape. I'm not a journalist, after all.'

'Aren't you?' Anna had a terrible voice that turned Vicky's blood cold. 'I think you are a journalist and you're going to sell the interview. You used my husband's interest in technology to inveigle your way past security.'

Vicky moved quickly, turning not to the main door but in the other direction, up the stairs beside the lift. It was a very fast departure. Anna might have attempted to follow but her shoes were too high, her legs not as long and she was not as young. And it would be undignified.

The boutique owner suggested getting hotel security to apprehend the English girl. Then Anna realized her behaviour was lunatic. What would Serge say if she was caught pursuing a radio employee he had actually asked to interview him? It was just something about the look of the girl that had made Anna behave irrationally. She looked as though she had just got out of bed.

'Leave it,' said Anna. 'My husband will deal with her. And don't say anything to anyone about the incident. Certainly not my husband, he's extremely busy.' And she took the lift to the family suite, feeling odd and disorientated.

Vicky ran along the green carpet and wished to hell she had made the journey to London without underwear. Why had she bothered buying an erase-stick? Wisely, Serge had given her back the key. He had told her to rest up, then order a good breakfast, while he left for the family holiday. The plane took off mid-morning. When she left she was to double-lock the door from the outside and give the key to the head waiter, no one else.

Now she jingled the key in the lock and pushed open the heavy door. Inside the room, she slammed it, waited to get her breath, then locked it. Serge sat, very still, against the piano.

'She knows.' He made an overly-casual gesture, hiding a great deal of upset.

Vicky, still breathless, said, 'Knows? Knows what?'

'That I am changed. I can't go with her to Greece because I can't be separated from you.'

Very carefully, she said, 'So your wife knows about me?'

'Of course not.'

Vicky was not so sure. He changed with the hour and was so ambivalent he could not even finish a sentence. At one point he had even called her Anna. What did he call his wife these days? And there had been the nasty scene in the boutique, the sudden dash up the stairs. It was hardly the exit of a professional woman who was staying, supposedly, nearby.

'I don't want to cause your wife any more upset.' She quickly put on the offending knickers. 'So I'm going back to London now.'

He looked more unhappy.

She had no place here and said so. 'I can't be in all this trouble, Serge. I didn't start it. It's between you and her. When you know what's happening with your wife, call me.' She knew she had to be strong, yet she could not bear to see him so down. 'You may think I'm the cause of it, but I'm not.'

He straightened up and held out his arms. 'Come on. Don't hang back. Let me hold you. I'm not going to put all this on you. I'm big enough to sort out my own mess.'

Was he? People always confused him. They were so strident and ruinous of anything nearing perfection. It amazed him that the earth had survived as long as it had. He wanted peace, control, a world that was safe. He was not in music for nothing. It was when it came to people that life got screwed up.

And he held her, this person receptive to all his energies. She who had what he now needed. How he wished his wife had the same. How he wished his life was simple and he, a simple man.

When Anna next saw her husband he was slumped in front of a new digital machine which proved that every colour had its own sound. Anna put down the bags of salon clothes – she had been doing some serious comfort shopping – and poured herself a large drink. They were still in Paris but they could be anywhere in the world. Everywhere was becoming the same these days; it happened, once you reached a certain level of wealth.

'You can go with the children, Anna, if you want.'

'Go?' She did not like the sound of that.

'To the island. Or go to the mountains. Whatever.' It was the third time in a week she had had to cancel the holiday. He had always been a difficult man but nothing so far had approached this switchback of emotion. He often responded irrationally to what he considered a bad recording of his work or an indifferent orchestra, but was always stable, even serene, where people he loved were concerned. For the first time, he was ignoring his children. Could a crisis in music make every damn person in the family unhappy? The impresario believed it was the male menopause; Serge was forty-eight.

'If you don't want to go on conducting, give up,' she said. 'You said if it started to go wrong you'd be the first to see it and you'd give up rather than be pitied.'

'Go on holiday, Anna.'

And she realized she did not know where he had been all day. Usually, she knew his movements by the hour. The Canadian had said one thing, the chauffeur another. The rehearsal suite was out-of-bounds but she had tried the private line. It was disconnected.

And then she recalled the odd English girl with the knickers hanging from one finger in the morning light. 'Did you give the English girl an interview here?'

'Of course not.'

'But she was here this morning.'

He looked up and she could see he had not slept.

'I saw her in the shop.'

He shrugged. He was good at those. 'Well, it's a free country. Why shouldn't she shop here if she can afford it.'

'I got her checked out. She took a sideways move, not advantageous, because she had been sleeping with her employer and tried to break up his marriage. She drinks. I don't trust her. I asked her for the tape and she bolted. Upstairs!'

He slammed a fist on the desk. 'Did I ask you to check her out? Well, did I?'

She backed away slightly and became less aggressive. 'I thought I should. You've other things on your mind. You have to be careful of these desperate women because –'

'Desperate!' It made him more angry.

'Well if she's gone through all that she can't be – at her best. The way she ran up the stairs.' She made a gesture for eccentric. 'And she bought some quite expensive white lace bikini pants.'

She would have had to, he thought. In the violence of his lovemaking he had ripped apart the original pair. What he had done with them afterwards! He tried not to think about it. In spite of hours of sexuality, he still felt an erection beginning.

Anna was asking for details like a detective. Why would the eccentric girl shop in his hotel? 'Did she follow you? Did you tell her you sometimes stay here? Was she the one you were going to meet here a couple of weeks ago? The one who had a health problem? I see now. She was offering you technological secrets and now wangles herself an exclusive interview. You must have done it here. It's crazy, Serge. She'll take it to the highest bidder. It's against all the arrangements we've made with the PR people who –'

'I did not do the interview here!' he shouted.

And then she saw it. It had taken her long enough. She could not believe it. She was sure, now she thought about it, he had not come to bed last night, but that was not unusual because sometimes he would work through the night.

Anna made a quick decision, vital if she wanted to save her marriage. She would say nothing. She would fight to keep him with everything she had. And that included years of intimacy they had shared. How could some new sexual twist compare with that?

'I love you, Serge.' And she put her arms around his shoulders and kissed him.

He said, 'It will pass. It's just a phase or something.' They both pretended he was talking about music.

· *Nineteen* ·

They spent the day in the country by a river. Vicky thought it was on the way to Versailles. Like a musical instrument, she felt herself going up a scale of happiness through to joy. Walking along the meadow bank, arms around each other, was ecstasy.

He said, 'In most ways I am a pessimist. So tell me about you. That is more interesting.'

'I love music.'

'Then we have a good start,' he said.

'But you're a great man and I'm just part of an audience.'

'So, what is the difference? I am the instigator and you the receiver. It is the same experience for both of us. You share in it.'

Again, she asked about him.

'I have enemies who don't approve of home videos because they think they minimize the music, make it a visual thing. And it threatens the future of the concert hall. Will there still be live audiences if people can see a concert at home? That's what they say, but it's unjust. I want to produce a distinctive series of CD videos of my concerts because I believe people concentrate better in the home. The experience is from the best angle and the sound is uniform. They can use it as a learning experience.'

'Serge, you just want to be immortal.'

He did not like that. After a haughty silence he said, 'Now tell me about you. Anything. Your first memory.'

'I suddenly blinked and there I was, totally grown, an experienced person in a child's body. I was maybe two, or less. I always had awareness. My emotions were big. And I think I experienced too much. A smaller area of awareness would have been easier to live with.'

'You sound just like any artist.'

'But I'm not.'

'Oh, I'm sure you are.'

And he told her again that he had an ordinary life. Their eyes were having another conversation.

It was towards evening, when they started back to Paris, that she felt uneasy. He noticed she did not say much. She felt, in fact, a glowering depression which she kept to herself. They entered Paris from the south. He drove smoothly, without much effort. He did not once talk about his wife or his problems.

'Do you want to fly back tonight?' he said. 'Or shall I put you in a hotel?'

That sounded as though he would not be in it with her.

'Do you have things to do?'

He nodded once. It was time to say goodbye, perhaps for good. They both felt sad.

'If I drop you near the Luxembourg Gardens you can get a cab there. If I had time, I'd take you to the airport.'

She waved a hand, dismissing that. He got out of the car to lift her bag and recording machine from the boot. He did not kiss her. He was too well-known. A quiet grasp of her hand, his eyes lingered. Then he got back into the car and was gone.

She decided she felt shaky and should get a drink before going to the airport. She went into a café opposite the Luxembourg Gardens and sat on the terrace. She could not bear the noise or the crowded tables. She changed the order for coffee to a double brandy. And then it started again, as though her brain went into a different rhythm. She felt unlike herself – she was a wanting person, in pain. The things that happened around her seemed wrong. They took too long and were distorted. It was because she was full of grief. It came down like a hand and closed tightly over her head. Yet she had spent the day with a man she adored and the future had to be bright. There was a poster of him just opposite the café. She tried to concentrate on that, the beautiful face, but the hand, like a vice, tightened. Desolate, she got up and, without paying, went outside to find a taxi but there were none free. She crossed the road and a man tried to snatch the recording machine. Then the waiter from the café ran after her and demanded payment. With Serge, the time had been harmony. Without him, chaos. She took the métro to Porte Maillot where she believed she could get the airport bus. It started to rain and there were no taxis. Her yellow silk suit was soiled, her shoe-strap broken. She started to feel seriously forlorn and frightened and every sound scorched her nerves, every approaching person threatened her life. She could not think of one friend she knew in Paris. She felt, for a while, as though her life was over. She could be any age but it was all downhill. Time was running out. Jesus Christ, if this was love . . . She sat in the rain on the pavement, with her possessions around her, and just gave up. After a while someone, thinking she was a beggar, threw her a coin. Did she look in such bad shape? She moved her possessions along so she was under the shelter of a tree, and was reminded of the bag woman in Camden Town who lived in the street. She did not even think of Marais. It was odd that he did not once come into her mind. All that was not even real. She was somewhere very real now. She stopped a woman and tried to ask if there were any minicabs. The woman could not be bothered with her Anglicized French and walked on. She tried hitching. Then, when it was too late to get a plane, she got a cab. 'Airport.'

Relieved, she combed her hair and wiped her face. When she got to Charles de Gaulle airport she felt more normal, more herself. She was now out of the grip of Paris. The last flight had not left, but it was closed. She was desperate, but it did not mean she would be allowed on the plane. There was nothing until tomorrow.

'But I've only got hand luggage.'

'Madame, the flight closes half-an-hour before departure. The doors are already closed.'

Face stinging with rage and shame, she left the insulting Air France operator and went to a phone. Who would understand her predicament? Kirsty Cobb? She phoned Jay.

'How's it going?' He sounded cool and sane.

She said she was in trouble and could not get home.

'Just leave. You can leave.'

'No, I mean there are no planes until tomorrow. They won't let me on, although it's still standing there. The French are so obstructive, Jay.'

'Go to a hotel near the airport and get a room and have some nice room-service and a big drink. What do you like? Wine? Pernod?'

And she saw Pernod, an advertisement on a wall in the sun. Not a modern picture. And she was standing hot and vibrant opposite the poster. She felt very young, and there was a French song coming out of the café next door. She was waiting for the bead curtains to move, waiting for someone to come out. She was full to the brim with anticipation.

'And take a long bath, OK? Choose the first plane out you feel comfortable with.'

'It's not that kind of thing at all. I feel I can't get out. I feel sort of panicky – it seems against me. All of it.'

'What?'

'This city. I always thought it was alright.' She now thought she had never felt alright there. 'I'm scared to stay here.'

'Vicky, do what I say. Get into a hotel, the nearest one, and ring me. OK?'

The nearest one was full and the next would not take the credit card she was carrying, so they said. So back she went into Paris, her instincts urging her to go to the Gare d'Austerlitz and head south. She did not know where to stay but thought it should be somewhere safe and comforting. It was now midnight. She decided to try a hotel on the Quai Voltaire because Dean had liked it.

Her breathing was difficult. She could not get enough air. She asked for a peaceful room and some food to be sent up. She opened the windows and it was too hot. She closed them and the air-conditioning gave out a false, cold air. She moved restlessly from the bed to the bath. The food still did not arrive. She phoned reception and they said the kitchen was closed. She became argumentative, but it remained closed. No, they did not have food sent in; this was not New York. The creepy feeling was back as she sat looking out of the window at the river. It seemed familiar, that angle, that part of the river. She wanted it to be unfamiliar, brand new and normal. Was she in for another horror-filled Paris night? She phoned Jay and he told her to go out and get some food and plenty to drink.

'If I go out I'll –'

She did sound different. There was a strange note in her voice. She was desperate to get out.

'Shall I go to a hospital?'

'It's just a city, Vicky.'

'Shall I get a cab to the next city?'

'I don't think it will make any difference.' He did not realize it was the city that was becoming a very personal matter. She was very distressed. Even the room was against her. She did not want to look at it.

'I want to get out. And I'm scared. Scared of what I'll do. That's it, Jay.'

Jay wondered how wrong this peccadillo with the music world had gone. She had only been away thirty hours. He said he would phone his friends and get them to visit Vicky with a doctor. He would call her back.

He did not ring back because the hotel switchboard closed at one am, and she spent the night lying on top of the bed, unable to move, drained. It seemed that all the unsettled spirits in the atmosphere came tumbling, one after another, through her mind. And she knew she was cursed. She had done a terrible wrong. With the dawn light she saw that the BBC machine with the tape of Serge Marais, confirming their affair, was gone.

She closed her eyes. 'It's exhaustion. That's all it is. Sleep will make everything normal.'

At seven am she phoned Jay and said, 'You'll have to come here, Jay. Somehow, I'm all wrong.'

She was sitting in the street outside the hotel in the sun when he arrived. He thought it was for pleasure until he saw her face. The hotel had just put her out. They said they needed the room and no, she could not have another one, they were fully booked.

Jay went to the desk and got the manager and abused him in very good French. The manager did not give it a thought: who cared about foreigners, after all?

Jay went back to Vicky. 'Next time I come to this city it'll be at the head of an invading army. It's a beautiful place but the French don't deserve it.'

'And you've only been here two minutes. It doesn't work for me, Jay, and I know why.'

He got her into a café and made her eat and drink. She held onto him all the time and would not look at anything or anyone else. 'Just get me out, Jay.'

'Sure. Let's walk in the Luxembourg Gardens.'

Her stomach rolled with panic, 'I mean out.'

Seeing her face, one word filled his mind: possessed. It just about did justice to the horror he saw there.

· *Twenty* ·

As soon as she was on the plane and away from the breath of Paris, Vicky was herself again: twenty-seven, cool, working, self-sufficient. Before they had got on the plane Jay had made some phone calls trying to locate the Nagra machine. It was very expensive and probably stolen. She did not tell him the most expensive part of it – what was on the cassette.

Jay was supportive and undemanding and he tried to be good company. He did not ask her what had happened. He had tried a question or two outside the hotel and it did not go down well. When she got to London she looked relieved, and breathed deeply. 'It's neutral here. It's alright.'

'What does neutral mean?'

'In Paris, it's all big atmosphere, big moments on every corner, as though –'

'As though?'

'There's something in the air. It doesn't suit me. It really doesn't. I've had my troubles there before. My marriage broke up, right in that city. The place is against me. My film was withdrawn. It's destructive, punishes me and, in addition, I feel really upset, like I'm becoming somebody else. In the past I've had allergies there, couldn't breathe, no room in the hotels, trouble getting money changed, missed trains. It's anti-clockwise, whereas New York, for me, is clockwise.'

Back at the flat, she made some tea and lay back in a bath, washed her hair, then went to bed. Jay's friend phoned to say the Nagra had been found in the second hotel Vicky had been unable to get a room in. 'Are you involved with her, Jay?'

'No.'

'Because there's something on the spool. I didn't know whether or not to send it on.'

'Send it.'

He watched her sleep and thought for a moment that a vampire had been at her throat. He thought she had been chemically changed in Paris, as though linked with something unsuitable. Was it inside or outside or herself?

The next morning, she got ready for work. 'I hope I'm not like my mother.'

'What does that mean?' said Jay.

She did not want to lie so said nothing. 'Could I slip out of myself and become someone else?'

'No,' said Jay.

'Could I go back in time?'

'No. You're in a time-lock. You start and end in the same structure. You're not programmed to include a chunk of another century. I know there are those who would disagree. There have been plenty of accounts of past life experiences and some people believe them. I think it depends on your religion and what you believe. I do not find it acceptable myself. Do you hear voices?'

'No voices. I'm not schizo.'

She was at the studio when the Nagra machine was returned to London. Jay was intrigued by the tape. Serge Marais, invincible, unchallenged by most situations in life, had been made desperate by this quite attractive, pale, English radio producer.

And then he thought about the room in his dream with the stove, unlit. The room seemed freezing. It could be Paris. But when he mentioned it to Vicky, later, it clearly meant nothing.

Her mother's doctor noticed Vicky had a greater authority than before. She looked like someone for whom things were going well. He was surprised she had come to him with a problem.

'I want to know if what my mother has is hereditary.'

'Meaning?'

'Could I have it?'

'No,' he said simply. 'But you could be affected by her illness because she brought you up.'

'Does it have a name?'

'Recurring depression. And this time she's had a traumatic shock of some kind as well and can't come out of it, or even recall it. Or not verbally. She may never be well enough to recall it. Also, I think she's a lady who has found life rather difficult.'

Vicky thought, you can leave out the 'rather'.

'Her problems go back to her childhood. She has difficulty coping with people she doesn't know and she's certainly not had a happy marriage. She's suffered from violent rages and used alcohol to soothe herself but, as you know, it didn't help. I think your mother is a frustrated woman who didn't get what she wanted and feels depressed about it.'

'Has she said all that?'

'It's a conclusion we've made from the notes on her other in-patient admissions.'

'But is she mentally ill?'

'Unstable, can be violent to herself and others. Very depressed. And she's had a traumatic shock. A lot of problems for one person. But she doesn't have excitability or any up-moments so that rules out several illnesses we would otherwise have considered. She has black thoughts but not hallucinations.'

'She thinks I'm dead.'

'She thinks you're alive, Miss Graham. She thinks her daughter's dead. That could be a hostile reaction to you, couldn't it?'

'She never treated me very well. I've always been an unpaid nursemaid.'

'I think you've done very well, considering the parents you have.' He was ready for the next patient. He said again that her mother had nothing transferable. But Vicky stayed in her seat and wanted to talk. She described the feelings that had overwhelmed her in Paris. 'Are you sure those are not her symptoms?'

'What you describe sounds like acute loneliness and fear at being abandoned, even bereaved. Desperate but not insane. And there's a slight loss of reality caused by the sleeplessness, strain, exhaustion. It sounds as though you located a remembered grief. You didn't want to recall the feelings, so you panicked.'

'Remembered grief,' she said thoughtfully.

He walked with her to the ward where her mother sat, a box of jigsaw pieces untouched in front of her. 'As your symptoms occur only in Paris, why not give it a miss?'

'And, doctor, are you sure – you know –' She looked at her mother.

'You have no signs of insanity.'

Vicky thought that was the biggest compliment of the week.

She sat opposite her mother and looked at her hard. Today, she was without fear. This woman had brought her into the world, but was concerned only with herself and her own actions. She had never given her child love.

'You may hate me, Mum. But I just realized, I hate you too.' And her face flooded with heat. She did not remember each and every bad time but the whole memory of childhood was black, with no redeeming moments of closeness. 'I can't tell you what I think. I never could. Because you're sick. So I have to keep it inside myself, all of it.' She got up and left.

On the train back to London she felt worse, not better. And you were supposed to feel easier once you had got something off your chest. Now she felt guilty as well as sad.

Serge called her from a public box in Italy. His voice was harsh and expressive. 'I'm trying very hard but I can't stop thinking about you, wanting you. I smell your skin. It has a very special, lovely smell. Is it perfume?'

She did not think so. Nor did he.

'Life is terrible. You plan it so you do everything right. You are committed to your partner. You stay loyal. Then you fall in love. It's like tripping over the mat. God always has a joke up his sleeve.' There was a beeping sound and he put in more money. 'We're on the way to Greece. Driving.'

'Are you happy?' she asked.

'What do you think?'

'But you seem to have made a decision.'

'The only decisions I make are in the world of Beethoven, these days. Thank God I was not destined to be a bank manager. I would have ruined the economy. I must see you. Come and meet me.' His voice was full of contrasts, like the life he was offering her. 'I will go straight to Greece and spend one day there, because my wife's parents are invited. And her brother. So you see, she surrounds me with family. They are very nice but I don't want to see them this year. So let's meet in Florence. Take a flight, Friday night, and I will invent a reason to be in Italy.'

'Serge, I said to you, I can't take the married –'

He was cut off. She waited by the phone. When it rang, Lorraine said, 'Vicky, I must see you. Can you –'

Vicky slammed it down. It rang immediately.

Serge said, 'I know I am not free. I don't know if I can be free. But I need very much to see you. I want to talk to you. That's what I'm asking.'

'I cannot be involved with a married man.'

'What kind of woman are you?'

'A wise one.'

'You speak as though I'm contaminated. I happen to be married, yes. But I love you. I think you love me. Perhaps a new phase is beginning for both of us. We should at least talk about it. I can't just take eighteen years of marriage off like an old coat. You wouldn't like me if I could. But come to Florence. I will make the arrangements. Satisfactory ones, this time. You have to be patient with me because I have had no practice in this kind of thing. And I –' He was cut off. This time she thought it was not a coinbox problem, but his wife. She felt extraordinarily light. Was it happiness? Could she trust love?

Lorraine rang back and Vicky felt good enough to be polite.

'Why don't you get your anger out and say you hate me, Vicky, because I went off with your lover? I want to tell you; he's not mine, but I am sick and tired of your hysterical phone calls dragging him all over Europe.' Lorraine sounded tough and nasty.

But Vicky had only called once. What else was Jay up to that had to be labelled as a mercy flight to save Vicky Graham?

'He's chosen to be with me, so get that straight.'

Vicky laughed.' I can't account for much of his time. And I don't hate you. Your taking him away changed my life.'

Lorraine paused. 'D'you want to come to a screening with me and a party afterwards at the River Room? There's a producer interested in your short. He loves the idea of the horse angle.' Then she remembered Vicky hated agent-talk, so changed the subject. 'Or come to the healer with me. He asked about you again. You're bound to get something out of it.'

'What did he say about me?'

Lorraine paused, then told the truth. 'That you're in blackness.'

· Twenty-one ·

When Jay came in, Vicky was pushing a Hoover around. That did for housework.

He picked up a discoloured duster and threw it away. 'You always live so down. You don't have to.' He picked up some rush matting and threw that outside. 'I don't understand you. You could live so well.'

'Well?'

'You were married to a Tyrell. Jason Tyrell Corporation. You could be high in a Manhattan penthouse and own all the floors beneath it. You could have cleaned him out. His father, let me tell you, did not go for the gay angle.' Lots of people he knew lived worse than Vicky. It was just that down reminded him of the icy room with the bare floorboards. He did not want her anywhere near that kind of association.

Vicky did not want to live luxuriously. She had never actually thought of it. She had lived, more or less sparingly, in rooms that were unfinished, unresolved. They were more work rooms than homes. She had no homemaking instinct. When she needed comfort, a smart setting, she would call on Lorraine. She did not particularly like living frugally, but it felt right.

'That could be why you're so unlucky,' Jay said.

She flung down the dustpan. How many people had yet to tell her she was down, black, unlucky? She was, in fact, very up. She was one of the minority that had a reciprocal love affair going. 'Jay, sod off back to where you come from. Then you don't have to see it.'

'A down expectation does not attract success. A guy came into Lorraine's agency, actually looking for a woman director, so they put out a ton of names. All those feminist chicks that, in a sane world, would be locked away. So I suggested you'd be good for what he wanted. I ran the horse movie. He said, "She's good. But I have to commit now. I only have one day in London." So where are you? Paris. So he settled for someone half as good who actually got her butt in the right place at the right time. She had high expectations.'

'Why don't you actually move into Lorraine's, if it's a bit of luxury you're after?'

'Because you're all down and covered in cobwebs you think you need a superstar to make up the balance, but I'd be careful there. All that charm and charisma's candyfloss. A little sugar makes a big show of pink nothing.'

She laughed. 'You're jealous. Of him, I mean.'

'You can do a lot better. You're something he needs. He'll get it, use it and then he'll be finished with it. He'll never leave that wife. She's part of the music. Whatever he does, he'll justify as necessary to his performance. Morally, it doesn't stand up of course. Just because he conducts Beethoven and there's a cool million in it doesn't mean he's exempt from moral law.'

'My, Jay! I've never heard you concerned with sin! There are such things as double standards, don't forget.'

'What you're doing is wrong for you. Go to filmschool for three years. Be the best you can. Not a solution for him because he's screwed up.'

'Why don't you let me make my own decisions.'

'I wish I could, Vicky, I wish I could. But I have to know you're alright.' He felt he was fighting for her survival.

'Does it matter that much?'

'Obviously it does. You must mean quite a lot to me.'

And she did. There she was, a victim, half-revealed, her true tragedy only sensed, its shape and devastation not known. He would help her to avoid it. If she did not, he would write about it.

He helped her set the rooms in order, his kind of clean, then took her for a Chinese meal in Hampstead.

*

She filled every vase and jug and milk bottle she had and there were still red roses to spare. They had arrived without message. Then he phoned with details of their planned meeting in Florence. She decided to take happiness where she found it. She had had little enough. So it came from a man who was married. Since when was life perfect? Jay had not missed much. He was standing in the kitchen surrounded by roses, disapproving.

'No sermons, Jay.'

'Just make sure he takes you somewhere easy to reach. Shall I pack my rescue bag?'

'It's alright, sweet. I'm not going to Paris.'

The phone rang.

'That'll be the wife,' said Jay. 'She's not going to let thirty million dollars just walk away.'

Kirsty Cobb said, 'Get in here, Miss Graham.'

'For what reason?' Vicky's voice shook.

'Since when was impersonation part of your job? You're not very good at it.'

Vicky slowly gathered up the remaining roses and gave them to the old man next door.

Kirsty was doing some serious drinking in the pub around the corner from Broadcasting House. Her day had started well. She wore a beautifully-cut red suit that highlighted the voluptuousness of her body. Her hair had been cut and all the silly blonde curls were gone. The fairy story illustration rosy cheeks had also disappeared, along with the Cupid's bow lips. Her make-up was flawless. It had been put on for a good day.

'I hate being used,' she began. That was not forceful enough. She added an expletive. 'The controllers had found some serious actors. And I think, great, something big in the air for me. Shakespeare's good but this looks like classy, international, visual stuff. Then one of them, a lawyer, says, "Stay away from Serge Marais." Well, you can imagine, with the drinking I do, I did wonder if I'd had him or whether this was the DTs. The lawyer said that if I see him again I'll go down for trying to sell the latest high tech stuff my graduate friend is about ready to put on the market. And one of the companies has already made him an offer, telephone number figures. So I decide it's time to give up the sauce. Alcoholics Anonymous for me. Then I start thinking about you. It's always the quiet ones you have to watch. Where were we when I started to become Vicky Graham?'

Vicky, stunned, had to sit down quickly. This story did not go with the red roses unless Serge was so ambivalent and in such confusion he was going mad. There was enough of it around.

'I could have handled a friendly request, Vicky. I'm not ungenerous. But I hate being used. I've had quite enough of that.'

'I'd better go and give in my resignation. I'll explain what I did.' How could she explain it? 'Was he there?'

'Not he. The wife. It was her lawyers. She's very married and she means to stay that way.'

'If you like, I'll tell you how it happened. I haven't told anyone else. It's the least I can do. I'm sorry I used you. It was a rotten thing to do.'

Kirsty tapped the counter. 'You'd better get me a refill.' She could think better while drinking. 'You know, you could have picked a better person. My name stinks. It's hardly "open sesame", not in the media. Did he buy the funny sales talk or was it bedtime straight off?'

Vicky did not want to talk about it after all and started for the door. 'I'll go and tell them and get it settled. It's not actually like me –'

'Oh, I don't know. You're ruthless.'

Drunks were supposed to tell the truth. Vicky accepted she was many things, but never ruthless. She opened the door.

'Don't be in such a hurry to hang yourself. Before you go, the BBC have not got anything against you. I have. The conversation with the lawyers was in private. The controller doesn't know one word about it. So keep your job. You'll need it. He won't leave that wife. Finish your drink.'

'You sound very sane, Kirsty.'

She gave a laugh. 'The wife is part of his world, his career. From what I hear, she does everything for him. She's trained to keep him on top form. Are you going to run around carrying his music scores, holding his silk scarves, standing still while he screams at you? Always on planes? They travel, those music people. He used to do thirty-four concerts in thirty-five days. You won't get over your jet-lag before you're off again. And I know you're certainly not robust.'

Vicky thought there was a lot of sense in what she said.

'Don't let it get public. That's what happened to me. All that shit I pulled might never have happened and no one would have been any the wiser. But I told my best friend and it went round like a bush fire. And I thought, what have I got to lose? So I broke into his house. I just took the next step and the next one – all disastrous. So she comes flying at me with a tin opener. I was desperate, but I still didn't get any relief. Nothing was resolved, except my career. I came out of it looking a damn fool. When desperation sets in you don't have a choice.'

'Shall I demand that either he leaves his wife or I don't see him?'

'You can't demand that anyone do anything. They do what they want.' Kirsty finished all the drinks and reconsidered ordering another round. 'Get that wife off my back. Tell him to straighten it out.'

'Is there anything else I can do for you, Kirsty?'

She laughed. 'Get me his autograph.'

Later, Vicky remembered only one thing from the conversation. The half-drunk woman saying so vehemently, 'You're ruthless. Oh, but you are.'

· *Twenty-two* ·

Vicky took her mother home to her father because he said he could not go on much longer. 'I don't think I can live without her.' Vicky thought it odd, because they had such a terrible marriage. Yet love hung around in the meanest exchanges. As a child, she had been ashamed her parents were not like other parents. They did not seem like a couple. He was more like a grandfather to both of them. And Ruby used to shout and people would stare. The rumour went around that Mr Graham had married his maid. Vicky could not wait to escape, and got a job in London before going to university.

Ruby seemed to be little changed. Hospitalization had done nothing except make her safe. She arrived back with six different kinds of pill, which Vicky saw her father could not administer. She wrote a list telling him exactly which pill to give and when. 'D'you want a nurse to come in? You might muddle them up.'

'No, no, no!' He was angry. 'I can take care of her. I want to keep her out of those places.'

'I really think you should have someone to go shopping.'

He told her to mind her own business.

'It's my business, though, when it all gets too much. Then I have to come running down here. I want you to have a home-help.' She started to ring the GP. He snatched the phone. Her mother sat in the corner chair as though she did not belong to any of it. Somehow, Vicky did not feel it was a situation with any future.

Then her mother said, 'Help me.'

'That's it,' said Vicky. 'Either you allow some help in here or I walk away.'

Her father was very old and too proud. She grabbed her bag and jacket but then her mother said something different. 'What was that?' asked Vicky.

'Don't leave me, Vicky.'

Vicky knelt beside her and took her hand. Italy was slipping further and further away. 'Shall I make you some tea?'

There was no answer.

'D'you want to be here, Mum, or shall I take you back to the hospital?'

'She's not going back, Victoria,' said her father.

Vicky had to return to London for an afternoon rehearsal. Her plane left that evening. It was now mid-morning. If she spent any more time absent, the BBC would ask her if she had a problem. She had so many, she did not know where to begin. Then they would replace her. From past experience she knew that mental illness was untidy, involving a lot of trials and false hopes and new starts. The end result was invariably another ambulance. When she came back from getting fresh milk and fruit, the place was in disarray. Her parents had had some kind of a fight. Vicky ran to the surgery. The doctor, a young woman, went back to the flat with Vicky immediately.

'I can't give up my work to look after them. I need money. And I can't go on paying for her privately. She won't stay in the public hospital and I don't blame her. He doesn't want her to be in any hospital but he can't look after her. And they fight. I can't take it.'

The doctor responded to the realization that the sane one was crumbling. When she got into the flat she was forceful and insisted on a home-help, a nurse, meals-on-wheels. Vicky's father started crying.

'You're upsetting your daughter, Mr Graham,' the doctor said coolly.

Hadn't he always? Vicky was sick and tired of being in the middle, the victim.

The doctor offered her father some medication. She tried having a normal conversation with Ruby, who, now her husband was crying, seemed to take – was it an interest? Her eyes were no longer staring straight ahead.

'Do you want a home-help, Mrs Graham?'

Ruby started to breathe violently, erratically, and then she screamed. She screamed out all the screams of the world. Vicky covered her ears and thought of Serge Marais. Oh yes, I'll go to him. Nothing can be so bad after this.

· *Twenty-three* ·

The plane was delayed and Vicky arrived in Florence over an hour late. A chauffeur holding a card with her name on it waited at the arrivals gate. She supposed Serge was outside, not wanting to be seen. Swiftly, the chauffeur took her luggage. There was more of it this time because she anticipated a longer stay. She was surprised to see the Mercedes empty. The chauffeur put the cases in the boot and opened the car door.

'Where is Serge Marais?'

The chauffeur did not speak English. He gave her a letter and indicated she sit in the car. She stayed standing and read it. She was not altogether sure the wife was not paying the chauffeur's wages. But the letter was in Serge's writing and explained that the plans had been changed. She was to fly to Paris.

'Paris!' she said, shocked.

The chauffeur nodded, smiling. 'Everyone like Paris. Yes?' He indicated that he would drive.

She made the gesture for a telephone. 'I have to speak to Serge.'

The chauffeur locked the car and took her back into the airport building. Using a phone card, he connected her directly with the Maestro who was waiting in the rehearsal suite.

'Darling, at last I have the way out. I have been offered a series of concerts here in Paris and my company will put them onto video. This is fantastic because my wife and family stay in Greece. So come here. Your plane was late so now you've missed the last connection. But Remi will drive you. He's Romanian like me. Very safe. He is my personal driver. He will bring you straight to me in Paris.'

'Serge, why don't you come here?'

'Vicky!' He exaggerated the word. 'I've just told you. It's all beautifully arranged. Fixed. You like Paris, don't you? For me, it is fantastic. It really lifts me, my work.'

She got into the car and thought, I like Paris, don't I? It certainly crops up often enough in this affair.

Perhaps she had been dwelling in blackness because the moment she started living with Serge, she knew she had entered bright light. It was better than that: her life divided into the agony and the ecstasy, with nothing in between. Black, golden, very high, very low. She reckoned she had experienced the low. The future was brilliant. The moment he touched her hand, held her, the decision was made. They would never part.

He wore a rust-coloured corduroy suit, an open-necked grey shirt, leather moccasins.

'Let us go and see eternal Paris, and let it see us.'

Serge himself arranged with the BBC for Vicky to continue working for them on a freelance basis. He could see she would feel better if she had some independence. He made the offer more attractive by promising her first assignment would be an hour-long documentary on himself. Because he was mad about her, he wanted to see the short film she had made. 'POV Horse. Shall we call it that? Of course, I'll get it released, and you'll make others. Whatever you want.' How he loved her body. How glad she was she had kept it firm with exercise and yoga. Her breasts fascinated him. He longed to touch them.

He took an apartment overlooking the Bois de Boulogne and she thought, now my life begins. And with him, the city sank back to normal. She was now part of his life, his rhythm, and his vibrance and love protected her. In the first week he bought her clothes because he liked to adorn her body, and jewels which she did not want. He took her around openly and said she was his biographer from London. He gave her a limitless bank account.

'Spend money. Whatever you want. You don't have to account to me.'

The first thing she did was draft a banker's order to pay for her mother's clinic and arrange for a car to take her father to visit daily. She also asked for him to be given a meal at the clinic and anything else he seemed to need.

Serge bought her a movie camera and installed a home movie room. Without really knowing it, he was trying to make up for what she had never had. He needed to give her constant love and gifts. He put off the first series of concerts, called it being ill, and spent every living, breathing moment with the quiet, Pre-Raphaelite girl, who did not seem in the least English, who gave him a rebirth and a new lease of life. She re-awakened the sensuality and joy in living he had not felt for years. His need for her was absolute because with her, he felt free and without her, nothing.

Her submissiveness aroused him and also allowed him to be in charge. He gave, she took everything. He moved towards ecstasy with the sexual practices she allowed him. No woman in his life had ever given him that experience.

On the first night she said, 'What will you do about your wife?'

'Now I know, she will know.'

'Know?'

'I have to be with you. I am now sure.'

'But what will she do?'

'What I would do. So I'm prepared.' He did not say any more and did not want to spoil a golden time, which he believed was a gift from the gods in return for all his hard work.

On a spectacular August night they dined in the garden and he told her about his life. It was all music, and success had come so easily. He did not seem to have encountered any obstacles. 'They tell me it's because I have a lucky Karma. You know about that?'

She had heard about it.

'Do you believe it? That we return here until we are evolved enough to go somewhere decent?'

'Do you believe it?'

'Yes, I do. It's the only solution that makes any sense. I can't believe I'm going through all this complicated struggle to develop just to end up under the earth, a dinner for worms. And I am impressed by the accounts of people who have been declared clinically dead and then brought back. They have different values after that experience. In any case, it makes life a better place because they know there's something marvellous at the end of it.' Then he spoke with great warmth about his mother. 'She made it possible for me to study the violin. And then I joined the Berlin Philharmonic. My father was a surgeon and wanted me to study medicine.'

She asked if he had had a happy childhood.

'It couldn't have been better. It was a very lovely time. And then, when I was seventeen, my father ran off with someone and my mother was shattered. I saw her go through all that suffering and I vowed it would never happen to my wife.' He stopped, appalled by what he was saying. 'Maybe I'd better reconsider my attitude to my father now.'

'What was your mother like?'

'I never knew it, but she had an inferiority complex. He was very attractive, brilliant. She was just a woman who ran his home. She put all her dreams into me. I can never repay her.'

'Where is she?'

He pointed upwards. 'She'd better be.' He laughed. 'And your mother?'

'She likes animals,' Vicky said promptly.

'Lives in the country?'

'In Hampshire.' She sounded as though she was trying to pass an oral exam. 'With my father.'

'Doing?'

Once again she gave them the lives they should have had.

'So they are English country people. All those grand country weekends?'

'Not exactly.' She almost told him the truth. But it might ruin everything for her. How could he be sure a violent mother did not pass it down to her children, that she would not end up the same? She would say nothing, ever, to anyone.

'They don't socialize.'

He watched her without seeming to. Every time he mentioned

her mother she became blank and very careful, a little like he imagined someone would behave who had been in prison and did not want it known.

He changed to the subject of his obsession with home videos. 'I will film all of my performances. Then, when I die, I won't be just a memory. There will be a volume of work exactly as though I was still there.'

'So you *do* want to be immortal!'

'Of course. I have everything else.'

'So people will see you conducting?'

'Of course.'

'But isn't the music, the sound itself, more important? That can be captured on cassette or LP.'

'I want to be seen, recalled on film. I video many things, actually. Because I don't like to lose one moment.'

Her eyes slid sideways. 'Oh no.'

'Oh yes. It's wonderful. D'you want to see? It will make you self-conscious perhaps, so you won't give yourself so marvellously. What do you think?'

'I don't want to see.' She could not bear to see herself out of control. She did not want to know how she looked.

'But I do need you to help me. Because I am sure you are more proficient than I am and we can get a better focus and more angles. So why don't we just see a few minutes together, then we can – well, whatever comes to mind. And afterwards you will be critical – of the camera, naturally.'

How she loved his voice. It was so seductive and charming, although sometimes loud, angry, cold. It was a voice that helped him get his own way. It was always alive.

'Have you ever seen people making love?' he asked as he set up the screen. 'No, I thought you hadn't.'

'Have you?'

'No. But I've thought about it.'

Then he sat next to her and the film flicked on. He pulled her onto his lap and caressed her and she watched herself on the screen. They watched for longer than a few minutes.

Someone else was watching them on the bed.

'Run it back,' she said.

He was in a high state of excitement. She reached across and spun the film back a few seconds, then sat forward, to concentrate.

As the bed swung with the action she was drawn to the window. That was where the person watched. The whole scene was from the point-of-view of the watcher near the window. It was not from the angle of the camera. 'That blackness there. Look!'

Serge said it was a shadow, obviously. Was it? Why would it have such a distressed feeling.

Before she went to bed she checked the window, its angle from the bed. The curtains were white and they would not leave a shadow.

Jay was still in her flat and admitted he had company. Did she mind? She did not know if she minded.

'Don't let her use my clothes.'

'Honey, this one's a smart dresser. You're far too arty for her.'

'I was joking,' said Vicky. 'But you can wear them, Jay.'

'When are you coming back?'

'Never.' She hoped the phone was not bugged. Serge had a mania for electrical devices.

'Jay, I picked up a dark area on a video film we made. It was over near a window. It seemed to me someone was watching. Could the darkness be a flaw or –'

'Take it to a lab and get it checked.'

That was one film she could not take.

'I could see the person, almost. I just know they were there. I wanted to ask if you knew the word Lunia.'

'Moon?'

'I had a dream about a highly-painted woman in very colourful make-up. And the word was coming out of the side of her head like a decoration.'

She went back to the experience of the video. 'I had the definite feeling that someone was watching. In the end, that's all I watched: the presence of the person watching me. I felt it.'

By now, Jay had got an idea what kind of video they were talking about.

'It could be guilt about the wife, or perhaps you turn on when you think someone's watching you.'

'I think it was a man watching. To do with me.'

'Behind the curtain, you mean?'

'I kept looking up, expecting to see a face. I felt the eyes. I kept looking for him, wanting to see him.'

Jay could not find an explanation for that. It was customary to feel emotion while watching something on screen, but not to feel emotion coming from some person on the screen, in this case, hidden in shadow, unless you took a lot of dope, which he felt was not her fix.

'Then I went to sleep and saw the painted woman in my dream. She carried a parasol or a fan, very elegant –'

He remembered the word Lunia. 'It's a name. Russian or Polish. Vicky, I think you're looking for reasons not to be happy.'

'No, Jay. It's the best time I've ever had.'

In the third week they explored Paris, all the parts he had not seen. He loved walking in the summer nights along little-known streets. 'They are right, who say it is the city for lovers,' he said.

And, briefly, she remembered the bad nights in the hotels. The distress seemed to come out of the furnishings. Was it loneliness or rejection, as the doctor had suggested?

Serge felt freed of his vocation for the first time ever. He was in love and enjoying everyday things. He liked going to jazz clubs. The music, so different to his own, excited him. It was in his blood if not in his repertoire. It was the one enjoyment he had not shared with Anna. He had gone to clubs in New York, New Orleans, Europe, but always alone.

One night, towards the end of August, they stopped at a brasserie called the Rotonde. The terrace was crowded so they sat inside. She wanted a coke but ordered Pernod. They were sitting at quite a large table and he was telling her an anecdote about the music world and, as she laughed, she was aware of an absence at the table. The hair on the back of her head stood up and she was freezing. Not a presence, an absence. And she looked at the space around the table and then at the people by the bar, disappointed because they were modern and not what she wanted. And the lights were too bright. She put it down to tiredness. She said, 'Serge, do you find a – well, something wrong at this table?'

He did not.

'Like a feeling of loss. It's a terrible feeling. It's –' And she stood up. The longed-for one was not beside her, even in the country, even in reality. He was so far off she did not know if they would ever meet again. She ran out, blindly, and could hear wheels, noisy engines. Her mind said, 'It's only the trams.' And a man called to her and others joined in.

'She comes with us.'

The men all wore hats. And then the crossroads in front of her eyes was full of modern people and arms were around her, comforting her. She was not quite sure where she was, who the man was.

Serge said, 'Do you feel ill?'

And she realized he was not the person she wanted at all.

Automatically, she started walking around the corner of the Rotonde, across a street, along a narrow street. It was the instinct of a dog making for home. The street, the Rue Grande Chaumière, was full of art shops and studios of painters, long dead, now famous. Then, realizing what she was doing, she stopped.

'Who do you know in this street?' Serge said. 'You are walking as though you are going somewhere familiar.'

'Jesus, I've got to get out of Paris.' And she spun around and started towards the crossroads.

He caught up with her. 'What do you feel, Vicky? Tell me!'

'Doomed.'

When they got home he made her a peppermint tisane with honey because he believed she was in shock. He wanted to think she was pregnant but she had already told him about the coil. She tried to say it was something she'd eaten but he would not accept it. She became angry because, being used to fending for herself, she was not often challenged. Did she feel in trouble? he asked. She was almost ashamed of the extent and number of her misfortunes. To put a stop to the discussion she said she occasionally had a blood-sugar level crisis. Then she changed the subject. Nothing would be allowed to intrude onto her happiness.

'I don't accept this. Do you think if you tell me the truth I'll be put off you? Why are you so defensive? You looked to me as though you'd seen a ghost.'

So she trusted him enough to say Paris did not suit her. 'It's like a magnetic field. When I get away from it, I'm alright. It's as though I'm pulled back into –' She could not go on.

He wanted to know what came into her mind, however ridiculous. He wanted to help her.

'I'm becoming aware of another state of being that has to do with me, yet it's not to do with my life. I think, when I come here, my normal life links into another life. And because the sensations are so powerful, I'm going to assume it's mine. A life from the past. So then I ask myself, why does it happen? Because something is unfinished, or I'm not properly protected mentally, or something so terrible happened here I'll remember it for eternity? The town says, don't come here, mademoiselle, thinking all is forgotten and forgiven. Miss 1988 Radio Producer, all neat, going for happiness with a man –' And then she wished she had not told him. She had learned with Dean, do not reveal your weaknesses.

He said, 'I think past lives can overtake you for a reason. A chink occurs and parts are re-experienced.'

'So you believe in it?'

'Yes, I do, but I don't make a point of becoming involved with it. I try to do the best I can with this life. My mother told me that, when I was very young, we went to stay with some relatives in the country. This was in Romania. And as soon as we got there, the other boys started to throw stones at me. I went running away from the house, along a lane to the nearest village. And a man stopped me and said, young boy, where are you going? I said, to the nuns' house. Satisfied, he let me go.

And I carried on running and arrived in a square and went straight to the last house on the right. I knocked on the door and asked for the abbess. And they said, what is this? We are a printing house. Meanwhile, my mother, seeing I'd disappeared, went to look for me and met the man I'd passed on the lane. He said, the boy went to the nuns' house. My mother said, but how would he know about a nuns' house? He's never been here in his life. The man said, it's no longer the nuns' house; a printing business is there now. But for hundreds of years nuns lived there and it's still called the nuns' house. And she came and got me and said, quite obviously, in another life, I'd known this was a safe place. And in this life I went there for refuge.'

She felt comforted by him. His story, although fascinating, had no connection with her experiences, which were far from pleasing. 'What should I do?' she asked.

'Let's get your film released. Let's start making Paris know that you are a winner.'

He put a good face on it but, in the night, he thought again of the scene at the Rotonde. How cold she had gone, her skin up in gooseflesh and so pale. And her expression had been different. It was one that belonged on a younger face, as she sensed whatever it was, the thing that had disturbed her. She looked captivated, completely in love, almost in a state of worship. She'd never looked at him in that way.

· *Twenty-four* ·

First, Serge's lawyers asked if Madame de Fleury had had a reason for injuncting Vicky's horse film. Had Vicky knowingly been vindictive?

'I'd never seen her in my life.'

And the door opened and in walked the woman who had spent thousands of francs because she thought a low-budget piece of celluloid mocked her.

She was dressed, over-dressed, in green silk with a short veil over her forehead and some serious jewellery on her ears, around her neck. She was impressed by the presence of Serge Marais which was the reason she had agreed to come to the meeting. She repeated her original statement: she had been unfairly characterized on film and the French courts had agreed. She made it clear, however, that if the Maestro saw a point to the film, she would allow herself to be persuaded to lift the injunction immediately. She adored his performances. He could do no wrong. She barely glanced at Vicky. The lawyer showed the film and Serge asked with great charm which parts offended her. She had a string of reasons. The owner's walk was the same as hers, the shape of the buttocks, her style. She did not like the implications of doping. The ill-treatment of the animals was damaging. Serge thought her reasons sounded over-rehearsed. He took her into another room and shut the door.

'May I call you Ginette?' She loved that and accepted a cigarette.

'Why does Vicky Graham upset you?'

'Me!' She stopped being playful and gave a sharp laugh.

'You saw her on television, didn't you, and you saw clips of the film. I am sure, Ginette, you are a woman of strong intuition.'

'I know what I'm looking at, yes.'

'Did she remind you of someone who'd perhaps behaved unfairly towards you, or –'

'No, darling. You are on the wrong track. My husband did not fancy her. She was there on the set, but I hardly noticed. I had some guests. And then I looked at her and immediately turned against her. I couldn't say why. And I still can't, now.'

He stayed quiet, waiting for what else had occurred to her.

'I don't know why I don't like her. But she disturbs me. I can't give an explanation. I'm sorry. Shall I think about it and let you know?'

'D'you want to talk to her?'

Ginette said quite candidly, 'No, I don't want to talk to her because I've done her a wrong. She reminds me of something, and, more, I think she shouldn't succeed.'

'Why shouldn't she?' Serge was amazed.

'Why should she? When I saw her on the television I thought she should not have too much exposure. In a worldly way. She will find it very hard; I know these things. Yes, I did take against her.'

Serge said softly, 'Madame, you are a jealous bitch.'

'Perhaps you should ask what *she* is!' she snapped.

This reaction seemed too extreme for someone Ginette had never even met before. She agreed, finally, to lift the injunction. As a farewell she said, 'Sometimes you see someone and fall in love immediately. You don't ask the reason. And other times you don't like the person. Then you do ask the reason. And there isn't one. Just instinct.'

He stood silent and thoughtful when she had gone. She had seen something in Vicky that disturbed her, that outraged her deepest beliefs to the point where she made a ludicrous legal move which cost thousands. He was quite sure that, although her dress sense was eccentric, she did not go around squashing careers because she felt hate at first sight. 'She saw you on television and turned against you. And she can't say why.'

Vicky thought, people do in Paris. That's exactly what they do. Even waiters, who in another city would be pleased to serve me, treat me in a surly manner. People shut the door in my face. Always have.

'Perhaps her husband was watching the television too,' said a lawyer. 'Perhaps he liked Miss Graham.'

'No. Madame de Fleury has her own antagonism. Something about Vicky set it off. What's her background?'

The junior lawyer said, 'Not much is known about her early life. She was a Bohemian in the artists' quarter. She modelled in the thirties. I think she's older than she appears. Then she married de Fleury and became a business woman.'

'Any convictions? Notorious affairs? Scandals?' asked Serge. 'Any children?'

The lawyers shook their heads.

'Get the film on a general release and get it on television. I want it to be very successful.' As they went out he said quietly, 'And I don't care what it costs.'

He took his darling Vicky for a celebration lunch at the Brasserie Lipp.

After a rehearsal he met Vicky at the Café de la Paix near the Opéra and, as their eyes met, all the pleasures of the night were remembered. What a setting – free of every inhibition. Sex with her was the most important thing in his life. The visual images of what they did remained with him throughout the day. Their hands met under the table, his eyes burned into hers and he wished he had some sexual energy left to have her again. He would take her into the lavatory and do it against the wall, the sink. He looked at the menu and tried to think about something else.

'I found out something about Ginette de Fleury,' he said. 'She was the illegitimate daughter of one of the painters. Soutine? Was it Braque? Not Picasso. She was born in the early twenties. Maybe a little earlier. Maybe she was Utrillo's daughter? Did he have one? She was brought up in La Ruche. Have you heard of that? It's a circular building with staircases full of artists' studios. They all lived there. Chagall, Soutine, Kremegne, Modigliani – an endless list. Ginette was very poor and only just got by. I wish I could remember who her father was. Anna would know.' He stopped, 'Well, I'm going to say it sooner or later: Anna. I've said it. Alright? Are we both alive?' He took out a small street map to show her La Ruche. Her eyes moved away, east, to the words Père Lachaise, and it was as though a cold wind blew through her. Père Lachaise. The words terrified her. She forced herself to say them.

'The cemetery. Let's stay with the living.' The names that she saw were the hospitals, the hospices, the graveyards. He saw only the places of beauty and the smart hotels. The hospital names worried her, caused an immediate stab of fear. It subsided. But not Père Lachaise. It all had a blackness over it, the streets, the squares, the gardens. Restlessly, she stirred, wanting to leave. 'I won't win in this place.' Black with a gold cross. Hell and God's protection. That was Paris for her.

Serge was wonderful to Vicky at all times. She was effortlessly happy and the relationship worked because there was such harmony between them, which went on whether they did something together or not. Wherever he was, she was in his thoughts. In her case, it was slightly different. He was in her mind but so was something else. There was a darkness in the sunlight. It happened as it had at the Rotonde when she was not thinking about anything in particular. Carefree, she would sit at a café table in the sun and she would suddenly notice the empty chair opposite and her mind would leap in expectation; more, elation. And then only Serge would sit down. Montmartre was worse. Up there, on the Butte, she expected to see – the figure was a mere eye-blink away. After the moment of expectation there followed a lowering sadness, a sense of loss and then the unbearable, the panicky blackness, a bitter, choking, unsobbed-out grief. For no reason, a beautiful doorway, a street corner, would depress her unutterably. And in the end she gave it the name the doctor had chosen, 'Mourning'. She was aware that her skin was very thin and it kept her in, with its modern silky covering, and the rest out; the buildings, the streets, the people. But the skin could do nothing about the past. She had to say again, 'Paris does not suit me and I don't think it likes me. The happier I get with Serge, the worse the reaction from the city.'

They had few secrets. She knew he was over forty-eight, and

had always been faithful to Anna. He found out that Vicky had never had an abortion or a miscarriage. Children had not exactly entered her mind. They said what was in their thoughts and lived for the present. Both agreed it had been an ideal summer. Still he did not perform. 'You came into my life when I was desperately looking for a way to climb down from the podium and take the subway. I am so grateful.'

And he believed his love would protect her from the hostility of the city. He had seen it in small ways. A waiter would not be friendly, women spoke politely but their eyes were cold. 'But the French are insular and impolite,' he said. He always had to find rational reasons for what happened to her and how she was received. Yet it was as though her past acts were a stain across her face, inviting a swift and unpleasant reaction. In other cities she was quite different. He decided if they did continue together it would be elsewhere.

· *Twenty-five* ·

One secret Serge did not share was his meeting with Anna. He called that a six-hour business trip to Switzerland.

Anna waited in their mountain home and he dreaded seeing her. The children were not there but Anna's mother and father waited in the garden, in case they were needed. It was one of the worst times of his life. She said everything to keep him and, when that did not work, fell at his feet, sobbing. Her life was at an end. He felt like a murderer as he crouched down beside her.

'Anna, I think I am with her for the music. To make it different in some way. It's an artistic thing.'

'But you don't work. You cancel every concert. You say you were sick and the insurance pay, yet you are seen all over Paris with this so-called biographer.'

'Anna, I am sure it will –' He made a gesture for disappear. 'You may or may not want me back, but I will come back, I promise you.' And in that moment he hated himself for leaving her.

She said she would Hoover him out at the bank and the English bitch would get nothing. He would not see his children. Let him go to court. She wanted all the property. 'I put my life into it. I gave up my vocation for you. I was at university studying to be a chemist when you swanned into my life.'

He recalled a dalliance with physics. He would hardly have called it a vocation.

'I will ruin her. Believe me, people will not accept her. I'll see to that. Miss Cobb will be detested.'

He saw this was no moment to tell her he was not with a Miss Cobb.

'Will it help, Anna, if we go on seeing each other? I'll willingly see you every week and –'

'Absolutely not. What are you hoping for? A threesome? Next, she'll be in the house. You're at a funny age.'

He leapt at that explanation with relief. 'I think you are right.' In Anna's company he always felt slightly defensive. He dominated her in the obvious ways and shouted a lot, but, in truth, she dominated him. She was strong and silent, sometimes accusing and always absolutely right. He did not have fun with Anna. Life was serious. She hated the second rate, the lightweight, the fashionable. She had foolproof taste, exemplary standards. She was a perfectionist. In bed she was satisfactory. She did the right things. But for a long time it had not pleased him. Years before the submissive, auburn-haired, so-called Miss Cobb came into his life he had been longing for sensual acts that would take him way beyond the marital bedroom. He wanted to return immediately to Vicky.

'I still love you, Anna. I feel no differently towards you. But I need this girl for the stimulus she brings me, so that the music is –'

She threw a lamp at his head. Bloodied, he tried to leave.

'You stay, you bastard, while I read you a list of rules concerning our family.'

As the visit had gone so badly, he did not see why he should not ask a rather flippant question: 'Who was Ginette de Fleury's father?'

'Why? Do you want her too? Will a seventy-six-year-old stimulate your music? She's at least that.'

'Who was the father?'

'How do I know? It could have been any one of the artists in Montparnasse at that time. Whenever a child was born they'd all look over the crib to see whose it was. Everybody had everybody else in those days. You'd have liked it, Serge.'

He let that one pass. 'Who was the mother?'

'She modelled for –' She paused. 'Modigliani. I think she was in love with him. All the women were. But she certainly didn't get him. The father was possibly Modigliani's dealer, a Pole named Zborowski. You should ask her. She'll lie to you and say it's someone like Picasso.'

And then she remembered she hated this man to whom she was casually gossiping about a past that had nothing to do with either of them. She grabbed a paperweight and threw that. As he made a hasty exit from his house, Anna's father said, 'You'll be dealing with lawyers, then.'

Anna moved fast and claimed all Serge's property, except the château south of Paris, which was in his mother's name. She left him one car and his boat. She took all the real estate. He would have agreed to everything because he felt so guilty, but his lawyers did not, and they fought, even if he would not. They also checked Anna's private life; how they would have loved to sniff out a secret sin! But her past, like her appearance, was impeccable. She would not allow herself even one small orgasm with a stranger until she had secured every brick, every blade of grass, tree and bank account.

Before he took Vicky to the château south of Paris, Serge tried to prepare her. 'It's quite a big house. With grounds.'

'Did you live there?'

'Sometimes. We used it for entertaining.'

'How big?'

'Well, it's not small, you understand.'

'Ten rooms?'

'A few more.'

'You seem rather ashamed of it.'

'I think you see me as an artist. I am, in fact, a very rich man.' He looked at her eyes. When displeased, they were immobile, but Vicky was not upset about her lover having a big house with a couple of lawns.

The Romanian chauffeur drove them to the château because Serge needed to sit in the back and go through the lists of his possessions. As they approached Versailles he said, 'It's got thirty rooms, Vicky. It's not exactly a house, more a château.'

'Who lives there?'

'The staff and guests.' For the first time in his life, he was uneasy about his wealth which, in turn, made him angry, even resentful. 'I'm sure you can handle a château or two, can't you? We don't all have Bohemian lives.'

'I don't, Serge.'

'No, but you look as though you might,' he said quickly. 'I think that time would have suited you. Paris in the twenties. Or even before. But then, the artists were mostly foreign, not French. You don't look as though the nineteen-eighties are your time. Paris 1917. That's when I see you.'

The eighteenth-century château with a lake, forest, river and mill, silenced her. Once inside, she followed him through salon after salon full of art treasures. She had never been anywhere like it and said so.

'It's yours.' He said it simply. He showed her the Chinese collection of T'ang bowls and Buddhas, and pieces of pottery from the Chou dynasty. And jewellery and soldiers which had been unearthed from an emperor's grave. There was primitive art from many countries, Italian church paintings, sculptures by Brancusi, several Picassos, two Bonnards, several Modiglianis, a Soutine.

He held her hand tightly. 'I thought you might be put off. But you had to see it. I am, you see, a very rich man. I know it may offend you.'

She was still too taken aback to know how she felt.

'You've seen me without the trimmings. But they are very important. Mostly, they are on loan to exhibitions. I am always willing to have anything here shown publicly, as long as my name isn't associated. There are more paintings in our house in Montreux. I also have an American collection in the Manhattan apartment. I love, adore collecting paintings. I could have put my money into stocks or land. I chose to buy what I loved.'

'So you made it all from music?'

'Of course not. I get good fees but I invest well. Then I use the interest from the investments. I am trying to build up a Persian collection but I've had trouble buying into that area. The bedrooms are upstairs.'

Vicky could not imagine living there. She would be crushed to death by the works of genius on every side. She kept saying what she thought he wanted to hear.

'So you collected it all over the years?'

'Together. We always did it together. Anna has an incredible nose for what's going to . . .' He realized he was putting far too much financial emphasis on these objects of love.

Vicky was sitting cautiously on a spindly piece of furniture. It was a queen's chair and probably had not actually been sat on since its owner died. Serge squatted beside her. 'Choose your favourite painting, sculpture, bowl, necklace. Because it's yours.'

She looked at the Bonnard woman bathing, then she looked at Munch's girls on a bridge. Back to the Bonnard.

'Go right up to it. Come.' He took her hand. 'You can even touch it. You're not in a musuem.'

He walked with her, slowly, along the display wall. She looked at the Modigliani of a woman in a hat, then a Soutine piece of meat, two Modigliani nudes. Back to the Bonnard. Then she saw a Matisse. A window opening onto a harbour in the south of France.

'I love that.'

'Why?' Now he was enjoying himself. He had won her over. The puritanical doubts of a poor person, which he had dreaded, were quashed. He had made her greedy.

'Because it's so life-affirming and it cheers me up.'

'It's yours.'

During the drive back to Paris she thought of the starkness of her youth, how her father would never spend money. Insecurity made him save. So they ate sparingly and he said it was good for their health. They did not entertain and they did not take holidays. Ruby's illness at least made life cheap. Vicky thought of the almost deliberate sparseness of her life in London. Whatever she owned she had worked for. And she was glad she had had that experience. Not having quite enough felt right to her. Abundance was indigestible. But she had wanted the painting. It was one of the greatest in the world. She now owned a Matisse. She had accepted it because she did not know how long Serge would go on wanting her. She suspected the limitless bank account would fade with his passion. She accepted the painting for her mother's sake. Courtesy of Matisse, both her parents were now taken care of, at least in the material sense.

· *Twenty-six* ·

Jay gathered his things together to go back to America and realized Vicky had fewer possessions in the flat than he did. She was not an acquisitive person. There were books, shoes, records, special letters and a few clothes, but no photographs. He thought she had had a little life, unmarked, unadorned. There was not even any jewellery.

He had spent a month doing research into victims and felt, one of these days, a piece of writing would come out of it. For now, he would get on the Artificial Intelligence programme and try and get 'Scam' sold without actually having to stay in Hollywood himself. He had tried to cut down his visits to Lorraine, who seemed to think their relationship was deepening. For him, it was over. When she threw off her clothes and bared her breasts he still had a mechanical response and he would take her, against a table or hanging over the bed, because he loved sex, but not necessarily the recipient. Afterwards, he would watch television or a video because he hated conversations which always went one way. If he was dumb enough to marry her, he knew, as sure as hell, he was bright enough not to stay with her. Also, he had been seeing a very young music student who often called at Vicky's flat for coffee in the mornings.

He decided to spend some time in the country outside New York and cleanse himself of people, their needs, his needs. He had no fear of being alone. In fact, it suited him. He could go for days without speaking to anyone. Because he could always find sex, he did not need to look for it. He did not have to keep a partner always on call. So many men he knew did not want to keep making love to their partner, yet felt if they did not, she would go off with someone else. Then, when they wanted it again, there would be no one. That, to Jay, summed up relationships. Keep the larder full or you will starve.

As he did not know where to call Vicky he left a long note, saying he would always be her friend, and he did not mean to be critical of her affair with the conductor. Something about her brought out a puritanical streak in him, for which he apologized. And he wished Lorraine could be more like her. From Lorraine, all he ever heard was, I love you, no matter what he was doing to her.

He Hoovered the flat and swept the patio and gathered a few September flowers to put in a vase. Then he decided to wash the curtains and while they were churning around in the machine, he cleaned the windows. Then he stopped. Christ, he was nervous. He leaned against the patio wall. He did not want to leave Vicky. Was he perhaps in love with her? He did love her. He supposed he did. As he had never had a platonic relationship with a woman before, he was not sure.

He hung the curtains back although they were slightly damp. If he said so himself, the place looked great. He polished the brass fireplace and by the side of the false coals he found a postcard. On the front, the Eiffel Tower. On the back, a message from Dean.

> 'Sitting in the Coupole with new friends, I thought of you. Paris beautiful, as expected. They've knocked down that old place near Les Halles where we had onion soup with the working girls, but they can't destroy memories. Whatever they build there, I'll still see the zinc counter and you, my sweet.'

Jay sat down very slowly on the floor. There, in the message on the rather gaudy postcard, was the key to what was wrong. Thoughts were not just steam in the air, but things, solid, unchanging. Memories did not disappear. They were actualities which could be recalled at any time. And the clock ticked loudly as he recalled the room with the red walls, the stove, the uneven floor. Dust everywhere, coal scattered. He thought he wanted to add a lot of cigarette ends to the image but was not sure. He had almost got it, then it was gone. The clue. He looked out at the modern street. A popstar lived opposite and was throwing out a groupie. I'll always see you, my sweet.

It was as though Vicky moved to and from her place of work, her lovers, the shops, her parents; she slept, dreamed, laughed, while eyes like a gun barrel were pointed her way, watching her. They were the eyes of a creature of prey.

The sound of coughing woke her. It was an irritating, dry cough. Silence. Then it started again. It began to get on her nerves. 'Oh, do stop,' she said. On and on went the cough. She covered her ears. Then a sickly attack built up and the coughing man spat phlegm onto the floor. She heard a wet splash. She kicked him. 'For heavens' sake!'

Serge sat up.

'Stop coughing,' she said.

'Coughing?' He cleared his throat. 'I wasn't coughing.'

'It woke me up. You spat on the floor.'

'You were dreaming.' He looked over at the marble floor. She got up and walked around the bed and looked for the phlegm.

'There's nothing there.' She moved her hand angrily over the floor.

'Stop having nightmares and go back to sleep.'

'But it wasn't a nightmare.'

She lay, her back against his, and she could smell cigarette smoke, dust and a very particular eau de cologne.

Jay was about to leave when the phone rang and Vicky said, 'I'm coming back.'

'But I'm off to New York.'

'Jay, I need to talk to you. I'll only be a day or two. I'll have to come back here afterwards. But it's OK if you have to go.'

He dreaded the day when she found out superstars were not special.

A chauffeur-driven pale Mercedes brought her to the door and the Romanian carried in her luggage, one slim Gucci case. She was dressed in a long, elegant Chinese dress with very high-heeled shoes. Jay could see that the Maestro had very definite tastes. The slit up the side of the skirt said he was playing out some fantasies. Her hair was silky and piled up and her face caressed and smooth. She was beginning to play the part. Jay thought the Maestro would only be really happy when she ended up looking pampered and owned. He tried to get the picture of a deluxe poodle out of his mind. The chauffeur did a lot of smiling and left. Jay was not fooled by the goodwill. He had seen the way the guy walked and the size of his arm muscles.

Vicky was hardly inside the flat before the phone rang and the Maestro wanted to check she was safe and where she should be. Jay thought he was already making a little mistake. Vicky was not used to love. She was not someone who liked everything to come to her. She wanted a space so she could do some chasing. And then the embrace, when it came, was the more exquisite. Vicky definitely needed space in which to feel tantalized, even unsure, if she was to be at her best. But Jay thought the Maestro would not appreciate the advice. During the love talk, Jay left the room and made some coffee.

'I see your horse film is coming out in France. That's great!'

Vicky kicked off her shoes and let down her hair. 'I'm going to make another. A feature.'

'What, you've got pre-production money?'

'Serge has pre-production money. And he's got Gaumont in for the rest.'

Jay thought, that was great as long as everything continued hunky-dory with the love affair. As though guessing his thoughts, she said, 'I never thought I'd be so happy.' She bit her lip. 'And if it doesn't work out, he's given me a Matisse.'

Jay was speechless.

'The only trouble is, it's in his house near Versailles with the other paintings. I mean the French stuff like Renoir and Modigliani –'

'Modigliani wasn't French.'

'Wasn't he? Oh, I thought he was. And I'm worried about her, the wife, that she'll come in and claim the lot, including my present. So how do I get it out of there?'

'Has he given you an allowance?'

She opened her bag and flipped out a string of credit cards.

Jay pretended to be impressed. 'It just shows you, kid. If it's supposed to land in your lap, it does, You didn't get it with Dean. But this is real.'

'And I've got a car and I'm having driving lessons and another allowance for clothes. He wants me to have plenty of those. I absolutely refuse to wear jewels, except in bed. But don't go thinking I'm loaded because I have to pay for my mother, naturally, and he doesn't know about that. And I'm putting something away for a rainy day. A flight fund. I can't believe I'm so happy.'

Happy! He had never seen anyone less so. Keeping her mother: that was a new one. Wasn't she residing on a country estate? 'Are you hungry?'

She said she would have to get a takeaway because she could not go out in case Serge rang. 'How is it with you, Jay?'

He told her one or two of his plans.

'Serge has fixed my job, so there's no hard feelings. I can go back, and do some freelance productions. Well, I've earned it. I certainly worked hard enough.'

Her thoughts were all over the place and this was not even Paris.

'I've put your letters and phone messages by the bed. Micky Duke came round to see you. He obviously misses you. I didn't say anything, even to Lorraine. Especially to Lorraine. Vicky, I don't think I can help you get that painting out. I can see it's tough, with the wife grabbing everything and I can see you can't ask for it because it looks pushy. I don't know what you can do.'

'Oh, that's not the problem,' she said, almost airily. And then she told him about Paris.

He showed her the postcard from Dean. 'You can't dismiss memories, or shrinks would be out of work,. Memories are solid things. They don't evaporate. They can be activated by the person coming into contact with something from the past. You see a photograph, you feel sadness. That time has gone. In London, you can go anywhere because nothing big has happened here, so you just go on with your everyday thoughts.

In Paris, you step into a street and all the memories of what you've experienced are activated. The good, the bad. You're overwhelmed.'

'But, Jay, nothing has happened much in Paris. My visits were entirely low-key until now. I really did not suffer over Dean. You're right about the memories. But they are from another time.'

First thing in the morning, she took the train to see her mother. The clinic had spent some of the extra money she had sent in buying Ruby new clothes. The hired car brought her father to and fro for daily visits. Occasionally they persuaded him to eat. Vicky could see that money did solve some problems.

Her mother was sitting in Occupational Therapy, holding what looked like the same piece of jigsaw. Six weeks had passed, but the jigsaw was still as chaotic as her mind.

'I can't do these, Vicky. All the pieces look the same.' At least she was coming nearer to reality. Vicky was pleased.

'No, I can't do jigsaws,' she said. 'They drive me mad.' Vicky realized that was an inappropriate statement to make in such a place.

The OT girl said, 'Mrs Graham, keep the sky together. That's the blue and then let's have the green at the bottom. Grass.'

'I know that,' said Ruby. 'I'm not stupid.'

'It's like a painting, isn't it – a jigsaw?' The girl spoke enthusiastically and Vicky nodded.

Her mother said, 'My daughter used to paint and draw beautifully.'

'Me?' Vicky asked cautiously.

'When you were young, you did some very good likenesses.'

Vicky looked at the girl and shook her head.

'Well, tell her,' said the girl, quite openly.

'I didn't, Mum.'

'Not you,' said her mother. 'My daughter, I'm talking about.'

Vicky sighed and realized not too much had changed.

'What did she look like, your daughter?' asked the OT girl.

'Too thin. She had plaits.' And her mother stopped and thought about it. And they both watched her as she tried to come back from a state of darkness where the main language was 'help me'. 'I see the girl with the plaits as clear as I see you. And I know she was my daughter. Then I see you, Vicky, and – how can you be two people?'

She thought about an answer to that. There was not one. 'I just feel I've come back from a very bad place.' And she got up. So did the OT girl, unsure of what the patient would do next.

'How can I remember all that? Her drawing and all, if Vicky didn't do it?' She looked at Vicky. 'It's like you were before you were you.' She sat down, placid, too calm. 'It's all these damn drugs. They give me really bad thoughts and then I worry about something else.' She looked at Vicky, as though remembering something, and she ran her fingers along her mouth nervously. 'My daughter is dead.' She stayed silent and did not speak again.

The doctor was watching some patients playing croquet. He had a broad smile and was the sort of man Vicky felt she could trust. They talked briefly about her mother. 'She slips into depressed thoughts and feels anxious. We try to get her interested in a hobby. Do you know what she likes?'

'Animals.'

He nodded. 'Miss Graham, she's a difficult person and I don't think that will change. But I think, in time, she'll be able to cope enough to live in a sheltered housing arrangement. With medication for the depression.'

'Did you find out what so shocked her?'

'That's buried. She can't face it yet. She has a lot of kindness in her.'

'Not for me!' answered Vicky, ashamed of her anger.

When she got home there were half-a-dozen calls on the answering machine, all from Kirsty Cobb. In each one she sounded more sober. They were all pleas for help. In the last, she said, 'Just get here.'

Vicky took a taxi to the flat in Little Venice. Kirsty just about opened the door. Her eyes were black-circled, her face white and puffy. She still looked a lot better than Vicky's mother. She was crouched over, a bow of misery. Vicky saw the pills immediately, dozens of them, loose on the carpet, the sofa, in the cushions; little white, blue and yellow shapes like confetti.

Vicky put her arms around the woman and tried to soothe her. 'How many have you taken, Kirsty? I've got to know.'

'Too many, because I threw them up.'

Vicky scooped up all the pills and put them in her pocket. She made Kirsty drink a lot of water. Did she call a psychiatrist, a priest?

'I wanted to do it. Be out of it.'

Vicky said quietly, 'It's no answer, believe me. You can't do that.'

'What do you mean, no answer? It's oblivion and that's what I need.'

Vicky said she was wrong.

'Why?'

She didn't know. She just felt it was a bad mistake. It was against life. You did not do it, and you stopped others from doing it. It was an absolute duty. 'You've seen him again, I suppose. And it's upset you.'

'I haven't seen him at all and it's upset me. I can't go on any longer. I'm sorry.'

Vicky went into the kitchen and put on a kettle. She planned to make Kirsty a hot tea with honey and lemon. It had soothed her, when Serge ordered it in Paris. She made sure she could still see what Kirsty was doing. 'You'll get over this,' she promised. 'You'll be glad you didn't do it.'

'Oh, don't give me sweet life talk. You're not responsible for what I do. I called you because I want him to get this.' She fumbled out a crumpled envelope from her dress. 'Make sure he reads it. Most of my letters he throws away unread. And this one's for my family.' This, a more formal letter, lay on the table. 'Just tell them I couldn't go on with it all. I'm sorry. Do make sure they get the letter. You owe me something, after all.'

Vicky realized there were other pills in the flat, stronger ones. 'Can't you see, your feelings will change. In another month you'll look back at this moment and say, I must have been mad.'

'Oh, Vicky, please stop. I thought you would be the last one to come out with the stay-alive sales talk.'

The kettle was boiling. 'I'm going to make you a drink,' Vicky said, 'and we'll decide what to do.' She went into the kitchen and speedily poured water over a teabag. She brought the honey back with her and did not bother with the lemon. She did not trust Kirsty.

'Why stop me?'

'Because I have to,' said Vicky.

'Are you religious?'

'I just know it's not the right thing to do.'

'That's your problem,' said Kirsty.

'It's against life. It's wrong. So people have to be stopped. You must not do it!'

'You're very adamant. Have you tried?'

'Never!' A psychiatrist's influence would not work quickly enough. For a wild moment she considered taking Kirsty to meet Jay. Then she remembered Lorraine's healer who seemed to be in touch with two worlds. He might have an immediate effect. She phoned Lorraine and took down the number.

Although it was late, the man recognized an emergency and agreed to see Kirsty. First he spoke to her on the phone, and what he said insured she would stay unharmed at least for the minicab journey.

He was well-spoken, soft, intelligent, thin, balding and about forty. All Vicky really saw were his eyes. They were quietly alive, observant, and optimistic. The house, ordinary in itself, had a calm you could lie against, a calm like thick cream or blue light, beautiful beyond words. She waited whilst he dealt with Kirsty and her needs. She was hungry, had not eaten since breakfast, and anxious because she had not phoned Serge, but all of it was swallowed up in the thick calm. Twenty minutes went by and she was at peace.

When the healer brought Kirsty out he led her to a leather couch. 'She'll have to rest for ten minutes.'

'Will she – will –'

'She'll be alright. She knows her solution now. She's calm.' Kirsty's eyes closed and she was asleep, 'I think you need to see me too,' he said.

'Oh, no. Not me,' said Vicky.

'I think that's why you're here.'

'I brought her.'

'You were brought here. The spirit works in a marvellous way. You wouldn't come yourself so you brought someone else in need. All the time, Mademoiselle, you stay in blackness, you won't progress – everything you do will be thwarted.'

'Why did you call me Mademoiselle?'

'I feel you've been very unlucky and you wonder why.'

'I'm sure Lorraine told you that.'

'You live in ignorance. You cling always to the past. You won't let go. So you can't go forward.' His voice was slightly hypnotic. She could not avoid hearing it.

'Believe me, there's nothing in my past to cling to. I'm sorry, I don't believe you. But thank you for helping Kirsty.' She started to shake her awake. 'Could you call a minicab, please. How much do I owe you?'

'Whatever you can afford.' He pointed to a box with a slit in the top. She stuck in a five pound note with difficulty.

'You always pay, don't you?' He sounded quite sharp. 'You pay and pay. You could have taken her money. You pay because you think that way I will pay back what I did.'

'Did?'

They looked at each other, and he saw she did not want his help. He rang for a cab, and said it would be a few minutes.

'Are there really spirits around?' she asked.

'Of course. They visit us all the time.'

'Why?'

'To protect us. To advise us. They help us when we're ill. Sometimes they just come to say hello. And sometimes it's for more selfish reasons. The man you're attracted to wants you to make some changes.'

She nodded.

'He drinks and I see colour all around him.'

Was music colourful? She supposed it was. 'He's a musical conductor. He doesn't drink.'

'He's a painter.'

'Absolutely not.'

'He's a moody person. I expect you know that. But he loves you. He's quite extraordinary and he's psychic himself. Perhaps he doesn't know it, but his paintings show he is.'

'But he's not a painter.'

'But he is. You do need help.'

Vicky got her friend into the minicab. When these people got it wrong, they did so with no half-measure.

· *Twenty-seven* ·

The next morning, Kirsty looked different. She was calm and her eyes were quite innocent. They had lost their stricken look. Vicky had slept on a pile of cushions beside her bed, just to make sure. She had dreamed in colour about the woman, heavily-painted, striking a pose with a fan. And, slanting out of the side of her head, the name Lunia.

'I really must thank you for taking me to him, He's – well, I suppose it's healing. After a while, he asked me what questions I had, but it was all so perfectly peaceful when he put his hands on my head that I had none. Normally, I'd have had dozens about "him". The questions seemed unimportant in that wonderful peace. I'm going to see him again.'

As Vicky drank her coffee, the image of the over-painted woman was still fresh in her mind.

When she got back to Hampstead the phone was ringing. Serge was charming but definite. 'On the next plane, please, Vicky. The driver is on his way.'

Jay said he would come with her to the airport.

She said, 'When I'm in London, I'm neutral. It's all down to me. Good. Bad. When I'm here the thought of Paris doesn't bother me. I'm not insane, am I? Why would I save the cursed performance just for Paris?'

'Have you spoken to him about it?' asked Jay. He could see she was nervous about going back.

'Not entirely. It wouldn't be fair. If he knew –' She stopped. She was going to say if he knew about my mother he would go back to his wife. Run back.

'You don't think it's OK to talk about what might be termed

failing?' It sounded harmless but his eyes slid sideways, watching her. She was definitely defensive. 'You think there's something wrong with you?'

'No, I don't. That's not right at all. But I've got the feeling, in Paris, that people respond to me as though I've done something or am something – And I don't like it.' She thought of the healer saying, pay. For what you have done.

'What about when you're with him?'

'Oh, with him it's all bow and scrape. Yes, sir, no, sir, three-bags-full.'

Jay thought it could be a simple story of a girl with an inferiority complex hiding it for a while in a superstar's aura, until she said, 'And I woke up and smelt dust and cigarette smoke.'

'What sort of dust?'

'Well, the sort you smell. Coal dust perhaps?'

'Coal?' He sounded as though it did not exist.

'I heard coughing and a spitting and I woke Serge. But it was not him. He hasn't got a cough. I really love him, yet every move nearer to him brings more of those frightened thoughts.'

'You don't have a room with a sloping kind of floor?' And he described the dusty room.

'Not quite,' and she laughed. But as she went to catch the plane she thought the room he had described seemed familiar. She did not remember, though, that she had put it down on paper as a casual doodle, while sitting at her desk in the BBC.

Jay waved goodbye and remembered Lunia, who she was. He went cold.

Serge stood at the kitchen stove in his shirt-sleeves, forking around a ratatouille. The rice was ready, perfectly cooked basmati with a small knob of soya margarine on the top. All his movements were graceful. He had such dignity. She waited at the kitchen table, watching him.

'I haven't cooked before, so it's another first for me. Well, I did as a student occasionally.'

'You do it very well.'

'My mother taught me.'

'You mention her a lot. You must miss her.'

'Of course I miss her because, although I know she is around me, sometimes very close, I can't talk to her. Sometimes when I'm confused she draws very close and I feel her soothing my forehead and even imagine I smell her perfume. Perhaps I do. And, within a short while, the confusion is quite gone. But now I am with you, I feel peaceful.'

He had seeing eyes. She had heard them described that way. He studied Eastern religion and did yoga and meditation every day. He had been described as a profound person. She could not equate that with all the collecting of objets d'art and wealth.

He put the food on the table. 'How is your mother?'

Had she said she was ill? She could not remember. 'Like she always is.'

'What does she think of me? You and me?'

'She's in her own world.'

'I want to spend the rest of my life with you. Do you agree?'

Vicky felt a rush of pleasure, of delight. 'Are you sure? What about your wife?'

'Oh, she'll take me to the cleaners, predictably. But I feel so free with you. We bring the best out of each other. We interact in a way that is fruitful. We bring out of each other things that, on our own, would not be discovered. We are very, very lucky. What do you think?'

'That you're a great man and I'm not on the same level.'

'Why?'

'What you do is superlative. You're world-famous –'

'I present music, you receive. We are both involved in the process. The music is the thing that is great. So what do you say?'

'If you want me, I'll come to you.' What an uncharacteristic thing to say, she thought. The kitchen was now cold, all cosiness gone. Her breathing was faint and light and she could see him now quite clearly in her mind's eye. Dark, curly hair, black eyes, white skin, dark beard coming through where he had not shaved. He was tired and shaky and coughing and he turned the street corner and came face-to-face with her. And her heart leapt with joy. He was in the world. He laughed, a hard, racking sound and she wondered how the malevolent could be so fascinating. He read a printed page, one of many, stuffed into his corduroy jacket. It was called Les Chants de Maldoror.

> 'If men were happy on this earth, one ought, then, to be astonished. The madwoman makes no reproaches, she is too proud to complain and will die without having revealed her secret to those interested in her, but whom she has forbidden to address her.'

As he read, she looked at his hands. They were beautiful, never to be forgotten.

'If you want me, I'll come to you,' she said.

And he looked up from the page and laughed, a small, dry, sarcastic laugh. He could have anyone. But his eyes were gentle and showed he was still capable of love. He put the page back in his pocket, and shivered. The day was warm but he was ill.

Vicky was staring at the lamp.

'So it's yes,' said Serge.

'Oh yes,' she said. 'I want to make you happy.' Her voice was more sensual than he had ever heard it.

'You can't make me. I am.'

'Serge, one thing. I want to get out of this city.'

He reached across and tried to take her hand, but she seemed to avoid him. She decided the next day she should get an exorcism.

Serge sung to her, lovely songs by Schubert, and slowly the warmth of the kitchen came back. But everywhere she looked she saw his eyes, the eyes from her childhood, when he had taught her to make lily ponds and daisy-chains. She thought, he was my only friend.

· *Twenty-eight* ·

Anna phoned the next day. She, too, was in Paris and was prepared to forgive what she called a menopausal peccadillo. Serge said that was nice of her but that was not what he wanted. He would never go back to her. She said she would never allow him a divorce.

'Why don't you see how much you love the girl when you start trying to work? You're scared to work, Serge, because you'll have to face the fact she does not fit in.'

'Not at all. I just want to be alive in a different way.'

There was a nasty pause. Then he said, 'But I'll look after you, Anna.'

'You certainly will,' she agreed, and hung up.

He did two things immediately. He rang his impresario and said, 'I'm going back to work.' And he told Vicky he was going to make her a rich woman. She had not seen him in such an impulsive mood since the days when he had been trying to choose which woman to be with.

'With you, I feel alive. You are the unique partner for me. So I am going to ask Anna for a divorce. She'll take me for all I've got –'

And Vicky thought immediately of the Matisse. Would that be part of the 'all'?

'So what I'm going to do is quickly make you very rich. I'll give you a lot of presents. It's not very nice, perhaps, but she won't be either. She'll have her share. My children are all provided for. When we marry the presents revert again to me. Is that alright?'

She had no response.

'And you should now start working. You want to make a film, don't you?'

In the days when she had made the horse short she was hungry and passionate to make something. She had spent years trying to get financial backing, to get a break, showing the script around, getting near it, but never there. Then she had mortgaged her flat and made the film herself. And she thought while making it, now I know why I was born. It was an exhilarating, marvellous experience. Since it had been snatched from the public gaze by the eccentric horse owner's wife she had not put herself wholeheartedly behind anything. Her attitude had been, let it come to me. And now, finally, a huge chance had been offered to her. And she had no idea what to make.

'It sort of takes you over, making a film, Serge. I'd rather be with you and just spend time being happy.'

He sat on the bed again, very pleased, stroked her hand, always tactile, loving. 'But I have to work. I have to rehearse. I, too, would like to go off to a desert island but –' He thought he should do what he was put into the world to do. He had understood music before he had learned his first word. He had always known how to do it.

'Do you want me to come to your rehearsals?' she suggested.

'I think that would be difficult. You see, Anna was always there. I think I should leave that to her.'

'What, you mean she'll be there now?' Vicky was alarmed.

'No. But, out of respect, there should be that space. That's all. She put a lot of her life into me.' For a moment he was angry. Why couldn't she understand? Did everything have to be put into words? He lit a cigar and waved the smoke away from the bed. 'Once you've found something to do you'll feel secure. The impetus will come back. I think you have a particular way of looking at things. Otherwise I wouldn't encourage you to do this. If you like, Gaumont can send you some scripts to consider.'

'No no!' At least she was still able to find her own material. She thought she should do something of Jay's, but was not sure she was competent enough yet. What she really wanted was to make a film about her mother. Life's failures interested her far more than the ones who succeeded. The outsiders, the losers.

She thought how ironic that was. You could not imagine a bigger winner than Marais, and she was living with him.

The lawyers and people who looked after the Maestro's empire gathered in the château near Versailles. Serge was still wearing his rehearsal clothes, the famous long black cardigan and white scarf. He was pointing out the art treasures that would now be put in Vicky's name as the men made lists. She was dreading the moment when they reached the Matisse. Was it hers? Had he forgotten? Should she speak now?

'Who was this woman?' A dealer pointed to a Modigliani portrait.

'Jeanne Hebuterne,' said Serge.

'But she has brown eyes in this one.'

Serge moved up to the picture. 'She looks as though she's just made love. She's still got damp skin. Maybe passion made her eyes change colour.'

'I hope so,' said the dealer looking at the dishevelled, still-aroused woman. 'There are a lot of good fakes around. Maybe we should ask Lanthenam.'

'It's always been disputed,' said a lawyer. 'It may not be Jeanne but one of her friends.'

Serge waved a hand at the Matisse. 'Don't list this one. It's Vicky's. I've made her a gift.'

Vicky was relieved she had not said anything.

'Miss Graham, are you interested in art?' asked a lawyer.

'I like looking at it.'

'The Maestro adores art, as you see. It's his main investment. Do you like Picasso?'

'No, I've never liked Picasso.' She said it absentmindedly. She was watching Serge for the moment he would leave. Then, realizing what she had said, added, 'I don't know why.' Why had she said she did not like Picasso? She stood in front of the Matisse. It represented a great deal of security: her mother, father, even a film, taken care of. It seemed a brutal way to look at art and she moved into the other salon where assistants from the Louvre were wrapping the Chinese treasures.

Before going to lunch she signed her name on the documents. She was now a billionairess.

Serge said his first concerts would have to be in Paris because he owed the French a great deal. He had continually let them down in the past months. 'Then we go to America. Be fit, Vicky, because the tour will be arduous. We'll be moving non-stop for three weeks.' And with that advice he disappeared into his rehearsal suite and she did not see him again for hours. He now liked going to bed at ten o'clock in the evening and getting up at dawn to meditate and practise his yoga. During breakfast he was smiling and talkative but she felt he would have preferred to be silent. He had experienced what he had most wanted, the rebirth. How would that affect his music, sensitive to any slight change in habit or mood?

Instinctively, she felt it best to leave him alone. She returned to England to make a necessary visit to her mother and father.

Back in London, she waited in the gynaecological clinic for nearly an hour because she needed a new coil fitted. It was a hot afternoon in late September and all around her pregnant mothers fanned their faces with magazines. A particularly pregnant woman got up and waddled into the doctor's room and Vicky took the magazine she had been holding. It was still damp from her hands. Idly, Vicky turned the well-fingered pages, trying to find something to interest her. On the diary page she saw a photograph of a painting of a woman. Underneath, a paragraph described its sale at Sotheby's, where it had fetched a record price of one million, eight hundred thousand pounds. It was a portrait by Amedeo Modigliani of his last mistress, Jeanne Hebuterne. A couple of paragraphs outlined his life: he had come from Italy to Paris in 1906 and, as he predicted, he had had a short but intense life. Known as a painter maudit, or cursed, he had destroyed himself with drink and drugs. His life was mostly spent in wretchedness and poverty and he had never received the acclaim he desired. He was said to be psychic. Women found him very attractive but he never brought them any happiness. A day after his death, his devoted mistress,

Jeanne Hebuterne, aged twenty-two, unable to face a life without him, climbed to the top of their house and, although nine months pregnant, threw herself from the window to her death. Their first child, a girl, was brought up by his family in Italy.

Vicky sat completely still, hardly breathing, her mind stunned, her hands damp on the page. The story was familiar. It was something she had always known. She did not refer to it directly, but her everyday actions and responses were in some way a result of its happening. The magazine was several months out of date. She furtively tore out the page and left, without seeing the doctor.

She walked the streets of Hampstead, seeing nothing. The effect of the magazine article was like hearing very bad news. Nothing could be the same again.

The first concert she attended as Serge's new friend was the most exciting night she had ever known. To be in the company of a celebrated man gave her a fantastic lift. To be the receiver of his love dazed her with joy. He had greatness. Everywhere they went, the response to him made it obvious. This was a brilliant, unique person. She sat in the house seat between the minister of arts and the impresario. All around, people watched her behind their programmes. She wore a simple black dress with gold bangles clamped the length of one arm and gold shoes. The black dress had one thin gold strap. Her make-up was flawless and she looked as good as it was possible to.

Quite calmly, Serge Marais walked onto the platform and conducted 'Il Trovatore'. Long before the end, she was dreading the backstage line-up. This time, she would be beside him as the famous bowed over his hand and offered him their continuing worship, gratitude and, in some cases, love. Many of his followers idolized him, others wanted to sleep with him, others just liked seeing a legend close to. When his divorce was final he would marry her the same day. She knew, as did all his staff, that Serge was having appalling rows with Anna. It was as though a zoo door had been left open and ill-assorted animals were assembling for a fight to the death. Her parents were involved, her brother, lawyers. Vicky noticed the impresario had a long scarlet scratch down his cheek. No amount of camouflage could hide the work of those sophisticated nails.

In the last act her mind wandered off to the gynaecological clinic at her local hospital. The feel of the glossy magazine, out-of-date, much handled, slightly torn, was still on her fingertips. And that one paragraph under the reproduction of the Modigliani painting had given her much cause for thought. It was a confirmation, a proof, without the evidence. She thought of the painter's suffering and escape into the false paradise of drink and drugs. Why did he decide not to live? She preferred to think that, than that he had decided to die. The story of Jeanne and Modigliani seemed so familiar. It could almost have been told to her as a child. Her first action the following day would be to assemble all the facts about his life. The biographies were out of print. She would have to try libraries and second-hand shops.

The applause drove her to her feet. The impresario said, 'He chose his favourite opera for you,' and propelled her through the crowds to a secret door that put them immediately at the head of the queue.

Serge came off the stage, wiping his head and face with a towel. Still involved in the music he looked at Vicky as though she was a stranger. Then he laughed and kissed her. The impresario draped a long black coat around Serge's shoulders.

Vicky realized how energized, how alive Serge was. Even his skin seemed to vibrate. Did the music make him like that? He received only the first part of the queue and then lifted his hand and made a short speech to the unlucky. On a cloud of charm he turned and took Vicky by the arm to leave the building by a private exit.

'Let's go and celebrate!'

'You deserve it,' she said.

'Not for tonight. For being happy. What else?'

Anna was outraged by her husband's cavalier treatment. How could he give that girl all those paintings as gifts? 'It's my life he's giving away and I won't accept it. Bring an order against him.'

'He claims that he made the money to purchase the art acquisitions.' The lawyer repeated the phrase, putting an emphasis on the 'he'. 'That he also purchased houses and real estate and –'

'I know what the hell he's got,' sneered Anna. 'I helped him get it.'

'And he's decided to make them over as a gift to his lady.' The lawyer monotonously listed the property that remained, which would be divided up by the courts.

'I want those paintings,' said Anna.

'The Maestro claims the property comprises your family estate. The paintings are lawfully his.'

'Will he win?' asked Anna's mother.

'I'm sure he won't lose,' said the lawyer.

'So my daughter is just to be shed, like an old skin,' said the mother.

The second lawyer said, 'We can put in a counter petition. Madame Marais has objected to the divorce, but I think, financially, that is unwise. He won't return to his marital home – he'll go on living with this girl, and she'll keep the art collection and the properties he's given her. And I think Madame Marais will feel the squeeze. Apparently, he will not make an allowance, except for the youngest child, unless his wish for a divorce is granted.'

'But who knows how many other presents he'll make along the way,' said Anna's father. 'And what if she has children?'

'Are they happy?' Anna hardly dared ask.

Neither lawyer wanted to answer that.

'So he is,' said Anna's father.

'And the children?' asked her mother. 'Does he just give those away too?'

'He's already set up their trust funds. They're very well provided for, Madame. After they reach twenty-five, that is.'

Anna said, 'I never thought it would go this far.' She thought about the girl, the photographs she had seen, what she remembered. 'In my bones, I know it won't last. She's covered in clouds, mysterious, undisclosed. It'll draw him to begin with, then it will worry him. Then it'll get in the way of what he's doing and he'll run back to me, to what he knows. Because he hates the obscure. He won't challenge her because he always takes the easy option with people.'

Anna would get even. Music was his life. The prison door had clanged shut a long time ago and she was inside too – the prison of perfection, and you did not just stand up and walk away. Serge had tried this pitiful escape, to be an ordinary man, in love with a quiet, ordinary girl. But he would never escape the quest for perfection. Life, or whatever he now called it, would pale and he would be drawn back to his true self and she, his partner, would not be there. That was her revenge.

The Romanian chauffeur took Vicky to the château because she wanted to look at the Modigliani pictures. All she had retained of his work was that he distorted faces and gave his subjects long necks. Yet, as she looked at them, they did not seem distorted at all.

One of the Louvre assistants accompanied her and advised she keep the Matisse in the château. 'For one thing, there is proper surveillance: we look after the paintings.' And he described briefly the work of a picture restorer.

Vicky stopped in front of the first Jeanne Hebuterne painting. The assistant said, 'Every time he painted her he made her look different. Was she changeable or did he see her differently?'

He took Vicky to a sideroom where some recently acquired drawings were being hung. On a stand was a picture she thought she recognized. 'That's a Modigliani, too, isn't it?' And she approached and then stopped sharply. Here was the elegant woman with narrow eyes, holding a fan. So her dream had been wrong. The woman was not over-painted. The dream was, in reality, a painting. And there on the canvas was the name, Lunia.

Because it would be his last night in Paris for some time, Serge chose to eat in Montmartre. Silently she walked beside him up the famous Rue Lepic, past the Bateau-Lavoir, where Picasso's crowd had lived, up to the Place du Tertre which Utrillo had immortalized. And she could hear a voice above her heartbeat saying, well, how does it feel to have everything? Fame? Celebrity? Wealth? Health? Even love?' She was relieved when she realized it was the impresario talking, chiding Serge for being so lucky. And she thought of Modigliani, the unacknowledged artist, in a frenzy of self-destruction, and the girl who died for him. She imagined how he had walked these same streets without choice, all the usual benefits of living taken away from him.

They ate excellent couscous in a simple place, away from the tourist restaurants. Serge said, 'After America, we take a holiday. Where would you like to go?'

'Nice,' she said.

'Do you like it there?'

'I've never been. It just occurred to me as a place to visit. A new place.'

'It's so built up,' said the impresario.

'No, we'll go,' said Serge.' It will still be warm in October. Nice itself is not so charming now, of course. A lot of that coast is ruined. Cagnes is pleasant. And there are places towards Italy.'

As she ate the couscous and looked at her lover she thought, Nice takes me out of Paris. It's the way out.

· *Twenty-nine* ·

'On September the twenty-second, my life changed,' Vicky told Jay in America, as they sat in a hotel in Cleveland. Serge was doing his tour of North America and Vicky was trying to keep up with it. She had called Jay in his rented haven in Connecticut and asked him to join her. 'Serge says I'm to have some friends. I can hardly let Lorraine loose on him.'

Jay looked uncomfortable in the hotel suite.

'You don't approve of him, do you?' she said. 'Is it because he's so successful?'

'I hope so,' said Jay. 'No, I don't like him.' He sounded curt, hostile. 'All that dazzling crowd-appeal makes me cautious. Is it an act? He gives himself to the music in front of thousands of people. But does he truly? He looks overcome and exposes his soul? But is he really? And the only reason he's making those CD videos is because he's good-looking.'

'Music is his life.'

'And you? Where do you fit in?'

'I'm the reality.' She blew her nose. She had a cold which she was trying to hide from Serge. Early mornings at the airports were the worst part. She would take homeopathic remedies and smile a lot and say she was thrilled to be along when she was just dying to be back in bed, the covers over her head.

She poured Jay more tea and assured him the Maestro was busy rehearsing.

'So he proposed to you in September? That changed your life?'

'On September the twenty-second, I was sitting in a hospital waiting room in London and I picked up a magazine and read about Modigliani and his mistress, Jeanne Hebuterne. And it was as though I was reading something I already knew. Was it a story from my grandmother? I've just read a biography but I long to know more about him. It's like rediscovering a friend. I suppose it must have something to do with me. That's what I wanted to tell you. There's a lot more to life than I realized. The painted woman I dreamed about was really a painting by Modigliani of Lunia Czechowska. What you said about memory remaining and being activated could be right. Thoughts are solid things, you said. All those memories I feel in Paris, yet nothing much happened there in my past. So it's another past, isn't it? From another life.'

'How do you prove it, Vick? There's no scientific research that I know of that would reassure you. You'd have to go to a psychic or be hypnotized.'

'The Lunia picture convinced me. I'm experiencing it again, that life. Re-living its dreams or – I'm not over that life. I really could see him, Modigliani. Yet he didn't really look like the photographs I've now seen in the biography.'

'So what are you going to do about it?' he asked.

'I'll have to read all the existing material on his life, but it's mostly out of print. I can't get hold of anything until I'm in one major English-speaking city for more than a night. I wondered if there was anyone still alive who knew him. He died in 1920, January the twenty-fourth.'

'They'd be in their eighties or nineties. Not in the best shape to remember things. Do you want me to try to find out for you?'

'All I know about him is he was desperately poor, ill, ignored, unsuccessful, an addict, didn't fit in with his own kind. Picasso thought he was a drunken show-off. He became increasingly bitter, had a terrible temper. He believed fate conspired against him.'

'All I've got to do to remember all that is think about Serge Marais. Because he's the opposite.'

'I had to think of a place to go for a holiday. I said immediately, Nice. Why Nice? Then I read in the book that he'd left Paris and gone there for a year.' She sat still and thoughtful. Then she said, 'He was ruined, and so utterly beautiful.'

Jay was taken aback. 'Why do you say that?'
'I'm on his side, Jay.'

Serge asked to meet Jay Landis. He had heard about his plays, his prizes and read his reviews. She said, 'He was my lover. I want to get things straight.'
'Yes, I know that, but you didn't love him.'
'How can you tell?'
'Because I am the first you've loved, I can tell that.' And that made her more special. He would never let her go. 'Bring him to lunch. Why not?' Quickly, he looked at his diary. 'Sunday, New York. I want to meet him because he studied physics. That always interests me. Isn't science how we met?'
Serge chose a restaurant on the East side, frequented by European refugees who had known his father. He had an hour to spare, after which there were domestic matters that needed attention a few streets north. He started talking immediately to Jay about what interested him, because he rarely had free time and hated to waste it. CD videos, recording systems, what was new.
Jay's answer made him drop his potato dumpling. 'I think the newest information is that cassettes self-destruct after eight years.'
The shock induced Serge to order a drink. Vicky could see Jay was enjoying himself.
Jay said, 'The big companies will deny it, but the tapes are unstable. And the tape you're using for your home visual productions could wipe out in five.' Jay's mouth was small and hid untimely smiles, but today it broke open in an emormous, radiant filmstar grin. Who was big enough to tell the Maestro that news? It was a moment he would always relish.
Vicky said quickly, 'It's not a joke, is it?'
The men ignored her. Serge was thinking of the thousands of reels of celluloid and tape bought up by his company, all dying. 'Can you substantiate what you've just said?'
'Why don't you just go ahead and put what you've got on the market. Then you don't take a loss.'

'And have all my work erased after a few years?' Serge was appalled.

Jay gave Serge the names of the companies who would be honest about the news and the ones who would deny it. 'I don't think anyone anticipated this happening. Think of it like a virus in the celluloid world. One reel has got it, they all get it. Like flu. Still, you're lucky. You've got plenty of art works on canvas and they don't go off so easily, even if their creators were sick.'

Serge said he had to go uptown to his penthouse on 72nd Street. It was one of the marital properties, so Vicky was not invited. 'I have to see my eldest son. He's off to university.'

Jay said, 'Why don't we all travel up and I'll take Vicky around the art museum.'

Before they left, Serge said, 'I'd still like you to give me some confirmation of the self-destructing tapes.'

'Sure,' said Jay, as though it was the easiest thing in the world. 'I knew you'd ask for that. After all, who wants to hear poisonous rumours over lunch if they've got no foundation?' And he gave his enemy a slim envelope.

'And don't let Vicky get too tired. She's frail.'

Jay hoped 'frail' was not a euphemism for pregnant.

When he had gone Jay said, 'You're going to have plenty of time on your hands to read about Modigliani now. He's going to be busy re-recording every piece of music he's ever touched.'

· *Thirty* ·

Vicky crossed one of the busiest streets in the world in the noonday crush and sped along the side of St Patrick's Cathedral. There was no chance of slowing down – the crowd set the pace. She took a sharp left, up to the side door of the cathedral, which was packed with tourists and the religious. It was a very sultry day, the humidity phenomenal. It was like trying to breathe through a wet blanket. She was going to arrange the tickets for the Nice holiday, and thinking little material thoughts, when suddenly, like a figure on a screen, he filled her head. She could see brilliant Mediterranean blue sky and him against it, with his black curly hair and pale, classically-shaped face and dark joyful eyes. He was smiling at her and a front tooth was broken. Around his neck was knotted a red scarf and his suit was dark, of a ribbed material like corduroy. He came towards her as though he had travelled a long way by foot, like a wanderer, not a beggar. He was full of good things, of qualities, knowledge, poetry, love, wit. And he came down the hill against the sky towards her, smiling. She closed her eyes. He remained in her mind, and how she wanted him to stay there. His eyes were flecked with gold light. Oh, God, I've known such happiness. And the memory of it, still there, made her higher than any drug. Tears of exultation flooded her face.

The healer opened the door himself and made it clear he was finished for the night and was very tired. Her impetuous call from the airport had kept him up so it had better be important, he said. Because he was in touch with the spirit world did not mean he was a saint in his own life. Bad-tempered, he put on a white coat and led her into a healing room. It was not as she expected. There was no incense, music or candles, no suggestion of mystery. Except for the thick air of peace, it could have been an examination room anywhere in the world. He asked her to lie on a narrow leather bed. 'You've been offered the chance of help many times. You never took it.' He was irritable until he put his hands on her head.

'I have no one else to go to,' she said truthfully.

'You have had a hard time of it, haven't you, Victoria? A lot of it has been caused by your actions in the past. We have to pay for what we do.'

'Do we?' She sounded suspicious. 'Who cares what we do?'

'We have to answer for our actions when we go to the other side of life. And then we come back here and put it right. It can take many lives.'

'So they do really exist, spirits?'

He did not answer but moved one hand to her solar plexus. She felt a slight change of temperature but otherwise no difference.

'Why am I so unlucky? You said to Lorraine that there was a reason for it.'

'Until you change, Victoria, the condition around you can't lift.'

'But I have changed. I'm marrying a fantastic man and I've got a new life.'

'And you're the same.' He said it swiftly.

'I'm not!' She sounded wilful.

'All the time you cling to the past condition, you won't progress. You have to let it go. That was your spiritual lesson. You can't cling to that sensual life which has put you in bondage.'

Was he telling her sex was wrong?

'You chose, as he did, to take certain actions which you cannot fulfil. You must turn your back on him.' He sounded very firm, angry. 'Let it go. Life offers a great deal for you. You've got a talent which you've hardly touched. Do you understand about paying for what you've done?'

She said she did, but she did not.

'Do you understand wrong-doing?'

In a general sense, she did.

'Wrong-doing is that which goes against progress. Stopping the progress of yourself or others to evolve, to evolve spiritually and to be free, is wrong. You must untie the bonds that keep you returning to this earth-world. You cannot take away another person's freedom of action and choice. You are not controlling their lives. You are master only of yourself.'

She did not know what he was talking about. 'I have never taken away someone's freewill.'

'I say you have.'

'You think I've done something wrong. You said that before.'

'And you came into this life with a great deal to put right. To do this, you must let go of the longing. It never did you any good. Nor does he. He can't help you, nor you him. The passion, the ecstasy you experience, is not the point of life. You come here to learn and to evolve to a higher state.'

'What did I do? The wrong thing?'

'If I told you it would not mean anything to you. It's very rare to come into this life trailing memories of other existences.'

'So God in His mercy gives us a clean sheet each time? Our remembering nothing is really merciful?' And she could see it would be unbearable to remember, not just childhood, but crimes down the ages.

'Once you've paid your debts you'll be free. And life will be sunny for you.'

She thought nothing much had happened to her body until she tried to sit up. She could not move. She felt heavy, immobile, as though filled with wet sand. His hands persuaded her to stay still.

'During the bad moments, remember you chose to come into this body in this life so use adversity to advantage.'

'But I've found happiness. Why don't you mention that?' Had she come all this way for bad news?

'There is a man for you. Believe me.'

'Are you saying I shouldn't get married?' She felt frightened, the calm feeling quite gone.

'I don't think he's in a state to marry you. Not as I see him.'

She sat up swiftly, did not want to hear any more. Was Serge ill? Had the news of the disintegrating tapes hurt him? Was his wife back? 'You did say something last time about a painter.'

'That's the one I see.'

'You've got it wrong, so wrong!' And she wished she had not come to see him. 'My fiancé collects paintings. He is not a painter.' She waited for him to apologize.

He said quietly, 'I have not got it wrong.'

When she left the waiting room she could see why some people loathed clairvoyants. She was one of them.

She fumbled for a five pound note, but he took her hand and sat her in an armchair. 'You don't have to pay me. And you have to rest a few minutes before you leave.'

She sat back unwillingly.

'You haven't told me what it is that is so urgent. What made you rush here from New York?'

'Could I be possessed?' she whispered.

The man smiled warmly. 'One in a thousand cases is about possession. Usually when strange states occur it's caused by taking drugs or it's a reversion to a former life.'

'Can people be aware of their former lives?'

'Only in glimpses. You wouldn't see the whole thing. And there would have to be a reason. It's usually to help you evolve faster in this life to give you a clue as to what you should do next, the right path, what to embrace and what to avoid.'

She described her experiences in Paris and the man who now came into her mind. And the sound of coughing, the painting of Lunia, the finding by accident of the article about Modigliani's life with Jeanne.

'It was no accident,' said the healer. 'You're being made aware for a reason.'

'Could I have been alive at that time? One of those people? Is that what it is?'

'Unfinished business,' he said quietly. 'Our past lives are all stored in our subconscious. And one of yours has been activated. In your case, when you go to Paris there's a considerable overlap between this life and the previous one. This life links into the past one and you have uncomfortable feelings and thoughts. But it's only memories. You can only experience what has already happened.'

'So I can't become that person?'

'You can take on some of the aspects and ways of behaving. But what's the point? You've already lived that life. You won't learn anything or progress. And people would find you rather odd.'

'So what should I do?'

'As I said earlier, turn your back. A soulmate is not necessarily a good thing.'

'But I want so much to see him. It's the most important thing in my life. It is Modigliani I see, isn't it?'

'I told you your soulmate was a painter.'

'Seeing him is even more important than Serge.'

The healer put his arm around her. She felt a sweet calmness pass into her body and everything seemed tranquil. And then the next thought came and with it the longed-for one, sodden with rain, standing in the dark, stormy night. She knew she was inside a church, fortified, protected and yet she could feel him outside, was aware of his desperation, fury, that she would not come out to him. The mental experience was more powerful than other, everyday thoughts. It was etched already onto the skin of her mind. She could not hear anything but the priest was in front of her and what he was saying, its meaning, passed directly by thought to her mind. He wanted to save her soul. But her soul was outside with the madman in the gutter, shouting and raving in his drunkenness. She sat, scarcely breathing, her physical body in the healer's house of the present world and her consciousness back in the past where it was all much clearer, the colours so vivid. In the church a familiar woman sat close beside her. Further along the row was a disapproving man with a white beard. She tried to see more but the other-life glimpses had their rules. You saw only what you were shown, only what had already been experienced.

When she left the healer's house she was still back in – she was sure it was Paris. Serge no longer existed. The North

London streets were a flimsy grey structure that would dissolve so easily, if she was not careful, into the rich colours of the past. As she left she said, 'Pray for me, please.'

To whom was she speaking? The healer or the French priest? It seemed to Vicky a very serious thing to ask.

Lorraine was wearing a towelling exercise suit which did not suit her. She had grown larger and her curves were more obvious.

'The healer screwed me up, Lorraine. They're dangerous, those people. He's got Serge all muddled up with what's been in my mind lately. I've been quite fascinated by the painter, Modigliani. And the healer must have read my mind and thought Serge was a painter. So you see, he just reads minds. He knows nothing, so be careful.' Vicky thought, Lorraine sinned a lot more than she did. What was she paying back, exactly?

'Can you read my mind?' asked Lorraine.

'Up to a point.'

'What am I thinking?'

'What should you think? That you're up the swannee because a mind-reader pretends to be a spiritual healer?'

'You can't read my mind, nor I yours. He's not wrong and you know it. That's what I was thinking. Why don't you go and see a clairvoyant who specializes in past lives? If that's what's worrying you. I'm sure Jay would help you. He thinks about nothing else.' She sounded bitchy and regretted it. 'I suppose you think I've put on weight?'

Vicky made a minimal gesture for Lorraine to interpret as she chose.

'Of course I have. I'm having a baby.'

'Oh, no,' said Vicky. Then she saw this was supposed to be good news. 'No, really?' Her voice lifted.

'I know what I should go and have done but I'm not going to. I really love Jay. At least I'll have his child, I'm thirty-seven. It's now or never.'

'Have you told him?'

'He said it wasn't his.'

'But that's ridiculous.'

'He said his best friend slept with me in Los Angeles. He can't bear to think his current mistress sleeps with someone else. He's very proud, you know. Cock of the North. Yet he sleeps around all over the place.'

'Did you? With the best friend.'

'No, but I wish I had. I went to him for comfort when Jay was being vile. It's Jay's child.'

Vicky thought, he has so many, what difference does one more make? She saw there was no space for her kind of problems. Everything in that room was present-day and only too predictable.

Lorraine suggested she go next day to a clairvoyant for a past life reading.

The next day, Vicky went to Munich to meet Serge. She thought if she was being drawn back into the past she would deal with it as she had everything else in her life.

And during the next few days, whenever the beautiful man with the broken tooth, or some aspect of Paris, came into her thoughts, she concentrated on Serge and the present time.

· *Thirty-one* ·

They did not seem able to get to Nice. First, there was an air traffic control strike. She had heard about that in New York and had been on her way to the TWA office to try and arrange another route when she had decided her destination should be the healing sanctuary in London. When she arrived in Munich, she discovered the French hotel suite Serge preferred had now been re-booked. Serge said he would rather wait for that to become vacant than take his chances on the Côte d'Azur. Then they decided to go by car and stay in the hills above the resort, but she caught another chill. When they did set off, the car broke down. Serge tried to book a flight. Impossible. The whole of Air France was now on strike and he couldn't be sure of getting a flight from Nice to his next concert destination.

'It doesn't look well, this trip to Nice. For some reason we can't get there. I've never known a destination be so difficult. Shall we disobey fate and take a train?'

'It really isn't important,' she said, 'just a whim. It's not as though I've been there.' She was scared of finding out that she had been. She thought of the vivid image of the dark, curly-haired man coming down the hill against the brilliant sky. She would swear that was Nice.

So they went to Greece. And those were lovely days, full of music and pleasure. Serge felt that he had now got her on his own ground, and she was starting to look well and brown. 'With me, you'll flourish, you see,' he said.

And she was glad the first part of her life had been as it was. It made happiness with Serge Marais all the more exceptional. She loved the way the light passed through the temple at

Corinth, pink, mauve, with gilded outer rays, She wanted to capture it, take dozens of photographs. It still did not do what she had seen justice. She thought that here, being in a new place, there would be none of the haunted, overlapping quality of Paris. Yet as they stood by the temple – he was kissing her at the time and saying he had never been as happy – she heard that cough from an irritated throat, from undernourished lungs, like a miner's cough. And then a merciless laugh, short, cruel. And she pulled away from her lover. He did not look as though he had heard it. Perhaps there was another visitor in the temple. But the laugh seemed to be directed at her. She stayed on after Serge had gone back to the hotel, waiting, but nothing happened.

She decided she would have to fight back. It was the past interfering with her present, putting blinkers on her life. She would have to know as much as she could, read the books, settle in a city and do some research. She would call it making a movie so Serge would not be intrusive. And when she knew all there was, she would have something to fight back with. As it was, the past claimed her when it chose and she was a victim. She was looking at one of the most impressive sites in the world and yet she saw a wall painted orange. And there was a painting on an easel to the left side. She could see the scarlet paint was still wet, and the corner of a thick, old, wooden table, scarred and cut. To her right, there was a window. She felt hot, unable to breathe, and she opened the window which looked onto a courtyard. Opposite, all the windows were open. And the air outside was the same as the air inside. There was no difference. In the air was a heaviness, a darkness, a certain perfume that was undeniably Paris, and she was not Vicky but someone who so appreciated the difference between colour and texture, that the scarlet of the paint in contrast to the roughness of the bread crust on the table gave her an exultant sensation. She felt so alive and so hungry for colour and textures, they fed her, as food did Vicky. The luscious yellow petals of the summer plant gave her joy. And the table, she saw, was scattered with painting tools and bottles and the floor was wooden with painted, uneven boards. She felt heavy, as though her abdomen was pressing her stomach upwards – she knew it would be a case of having to squeeze past the table-corner to leave the room.

Now she was full of apprehension. Should she go out into the street and look for something to make her apprehension lift, or stay where she was? The cause of the unease, she was sure, was a man. And then came fast footsteps, quite heavy, up flights of stairs, undeniably his, and she heard him singing and whistling, heard it in her mind – there was no sound. Her heart soared because the door would open and he would give her the unimaginable. He so changed her, he filled her with light, like a carousel, when he was there, when he was absent. The light, the dark, the absence was unendurable. Now she saw the portrait of Lunia, yet another one. They must have spent a lot of time together.

Tears splashed through her fingers, and an American voice said, 'These temples are moving, aren't they?' Vicky moved off, dizzily, down the broken stone steps, off across the dry earth. She was pulling the past with her, one boat, rescuing a capsized boat. There was no choice about it. One thing was certain, she was not free.

'What do you want?' It was said silently, in her mind. The rules of the past answered. Silence. Patience.

She spent her time searching out books about Modigliani. She read them, devoured them, as she sat in the Tate Gallery, the Victoria and Albert Museum, reading the few remaining works. Serge could see she was preparing a movie, and that satisfied him, because he could now pour himself into his music. They made love every day. The intensity, the hunger, had not changed. They played backgammon before going to bed, and at dawn she joined in his yoga sessions.

Then, one day, he was tired of her. How exhausted he was by her submissiveness. He longed for Anna, even if she was, by now, stored in ice. Her heart, anyway, and his bank balance. And he went to the rehearsal thinking, it's not Vicky I'm tired of but habit. Everything, however wonderful, becomes habitual and, from then on, it's downhill. She was so predictable in her pastel dress, always wanting to please him, to remind him of her body, its pleasures. He wondered if it could be a liver attack he was suffering from. By lunchtime he still felt dull and flat about Miss Graham, and tried turning his mind to some of their more spectacular sexuality when her enjoyment turned from submissiveness to violence, to dominance. Afterwards there were tears, always silent, not from grief but from release. He thought about it and could do without it. 'My God, I nearly married her.' He telephoned Anna and arranged to meet her in New York during his next concert tour. He dreaded going back to his house in Chester Square. Of course, Vicky might be in her Hampstead flat, seeing her friends or whatever she did. But when he got home she was there, yet absent, and his very soul seemed to leap out and reclaim her. It was as though she belonged to another man. He wanted to say, are you unfaithful? Have you been sleeping with someone? Tell me. And he knew he would never be free of her or tired again.

'Do you love me, Vicky?' He had to ask twice because she was so far away.

· *Thirty-two* ·

When Vicky told Jay she was going to marry the Maestro he knew why he had seen her as a victim. His presentiments were correct – he was satisfied. He had become a little overwrought with his original prognosis, but then her Parisian performance had been out of the ordinary. He concluded that all the so-called psychic activity was symbolic of her downfall with Serge. She had been on the wrong path and she would end up in a hellish room with coal dust on the floor. He did have a problem with the Lunia picture: how could she have dreamed it? So he called that coincidence. He saw any woman married to Serge Marais as either a speculator or a victim. You could be as out of place in a palace as a gutter. Vicky would be sacrificed for the great man's needs. Marrying Marais was not an ordinary mistake. It would lead to spiritual suffering. Of course, the lavish wedding he would give her did not quite fit in with the bare room with the creaking floor and dust. What Jay had seen was a presentiment of spiritual mutilation. He kept his thoughts to himself, but he did take Vicky into Central Park and try, with the wisest part of himself, to give her the best advice.

'I don't think it's right for me to shout my mouth off if I can't offer you better myself, and I don't approve of him but I can't marry you. If ever someone tries to stop you doing something, make sure they've got something to offer you that's better. If they've just got advice, tell them to piss off.'

'Piss off, Jay.'

'He's had to cut a lot of corners and make a lot of selfish moves to get where he is. Do me one favour: ask yourself if you would rather go to filmschool for three years? And I'd help you and give you stuff to direct and when –'

'He likes you. He said he'd like to get some professional advice on handling past wives.'

'Well, as he's not a resident of the United States of America he doesn't have alimony at the door every month, so he hasn't got too much hanging over his head. Except maintaining a high standard. For all he knows, he could go off in his prime, like a ripe apple. You'll hold his hand. You're young enough. If you're serious about making films go to filmschool.'

Vicky thought Jay in a bitter mood was someone to be avoided. 'At least I'll have a cleaner to sweep around a bit.' She laughed.

Jay was confused by his feelings for her. He wanted to protect her, yet it was not a parental feeling. More that of an advisor, even a priest.

'Anyway, I'm not going to do a film because I've started writing something.'

'Yeah? What's that? Your journal?' he said.

'I think it is. Yes.'

'By the way, I did try and check out if anyone's still around who knew Modigliani. You asked me to, remember? But they're all deceased.'

'I don't need that now.'

On the way back to Serge she thought about choice. 'That is a luxury. I don't think I've had a lot of it. I've been able to choose how I view what happens but not what happens. Now I can.'

Jay put his notes on victim research away in the dead ideas file. There was not anything to write about after all. Vicky being reduced to a marital slave for Marais was too depressing to think about and he was glad he would be in Artificial Intelligence and would not have to witness it. He certainly would not attend the wedding. There were so many women around playing the victim. Lorraine was one, always loudly crying wolf, ruined by men, always hurt, constantly devastated. He got a cry wolf howl daily from her London office. The real victim was not aware of it, her state or need.

They met Dean Tyrell in the VIP lounge. He was taking a flight to Amsterdam, accompanied by the director of a symphony orchestra. Dean was dressed in David Hockney style, with a colourful plastic watch, a bright paper tie and his cap peaked low over his forehead. He was well-muscled and full of a rough street energy that could be put down to drugs.

He did not recognize Vicky, nor she him. He did recognize Serge Marais, and so made the assumption that the elegant girl with him was his one-time wife. Vicky noticed immediately the physical changes wrought by his new life-style and covered shocked surprise with polite greetings. His mouth looked hard and his eyes provocative. He was someone to watch out for. The cap hid some slight balding.

Dean thought she looked sleek, like a pampered cat. She would be wearing fur next. Dean did not think she was quite pretty enough for the role she was playing. He thought the Maestro was divine, and always had, but there was not a gay bone in Serge's body.

When Serge was called to a phone, Dean spoke openly to his ex-wife. The symphony director discreetly left the table.

'So, how's tricks?'

'Just as you see, Dean.'

'She's playing it quiet, the wife. I'd watch that angle. Because she's never quiet.'

'Well, as long as we're both happy.' She could see he was not and no longer expected to be.

'He's not the right one, either,' he said softly.

'I'm sorry,' she said. 'He looks nice.' She thought he was talking about his lover.

'No. Serge Marais. He's not the right one.'

'What does that mean?'

'You haven't found who you're looking for. You're still seeking, I can tell.'

'I'm happy, Dean.'

'I can tell you're not.'

She said urgently, 'Please don't tell him about my mother.'

Dean made a gesture promising silence.

'And don't talk about me. I just don't want to sound like a failure.'

'Dear child. He loves you. It's you he's marrying. So you went through a bad time for a while. He won't ever go through one, so it won't worry him. People are only put off by your weakness if they suspect they might have it too.'

Vicky thought he was right. But her life was better with its omissions. If she put in the months of loneliness, the inability to get a film career even started, the failed marriage, even the Maestro might feel threatened. Was failure catching? She censored her past ruthlessly.

'How is your mother? I'll never forget Ruby.'

'The way you remember her. How's yours?'

'Mean. Marais is staying away from us. He doesn't like me.' Dean shrugged.

'He's hardly jealous.'

'I'm just a rich fag who writes poetry and should have died with Kerouac. I liked your film about a horse's life. I caught it in Rome. It's getting noticed, so follow it up. I like your way of seeing things. Make one about Ruby.'

Serge was coming towards them.

Dean said quickly, 'You're still seeking. I can see it in your eyes. You deserve the one your soul loves.'

When she spoke her voice was almost wistful. 'I've never found him.' But she knew she had.

· *Thirty-three* ·

Amedeo Modigliani was born in Livorno in July 1884, the fourth child of his parents, who were Sephardic Jews. They had been comfortably off, but during Amedeo's childhood the family went through financial reverses and were only saved by his mother opening a school. 'Dedo' was the youngest and his mother's favourite. The father, a failed businessman, faded into the background. Dedo had frail health and nearly died from an attack of typhoid fever at fourteen. His family was an educated one and keen on literature and art, so he acquired a cultural background. He gave up academic studies and took art instruction from a well-known painter, Micheli, in Livorno. He became very ill again in 1900 with pleurisy, which was to lead to tuberculosis, and his mother took him on a recuperative holiday through Italy. For the next years, until his journey to Paris in 1906, he studied art in Florence and Venice and was financed by his mother's brother, a businessman in Marseilles. In 1902 he tried to work seriously in stone and make sculpture his future, but the dust and heaviness of the material were not good for his lungs.

Arriving in Paris in January 1906, he at first lived well in a hotel near Rue Madeleine. He began life-drawing at the Colarossi school in the Rue Grande Chaumière and, when his money ran out, moved to a shack in the Maquis area of Montmartre. This was the slum frequented by crooks, drug dealers and artists. His good looks and sexual charm attracted women and he had many shortlived affairs, often using the women as models. He mostly starved, as did many of the artists of the time, but was always clean and dressed with style, often wearing a scarlet sash around his waist and a red scarf. He relied heavily on alcohol and hashish, and the regular monthly allowance sent by his mother was spent immediately on these artificial paradises. His work was not acknowledged and he became more and more depressed. He made many ever-deteriorating moves around Montmartre in the next few years until he moved to Montparnasse in 1909. In 1906, three of his paintings were exhibited in the window of Laura Wylder's gallery, and in 1907 two oils and five watercolours at the Salon d'Automne. He did not make a sale and his one and only patron was Doctor Paul Alexandre. Modigliani was fascinated by Cézanne, and primitive art. He refused to become part of Picasso's group, the Cubists, at the Bateau-Lavoir. Neither would he sign the Futurist Manifesto. Throughout his life there was a tension between the two men. Picasso spoke slightingly of Modigliani's showy drunkenness but was jealous of his eloquence, style and luck with women. Modigliani resented the Spaniard's sarcasm and move towards the bourgeoisie. In 1908 he lived briefly at an artists' colony in the Rue du Delta, run by Dr Alexandre, but in a drunken rage he destroyed other artists' work and did not return. He had a flamboyant affair with La Quique, a beautiful, tempestuous Montmartre circus performer. In 1909 he moved around Montparnasse – fleetingly at La Ruche, Cité Falguière and the Convent des Oiseaux. The sculptor Brancusi revived his interest in sculpture and, for a while, Modigliani worked with him. He returned to Livorno in the summer of 1909 and sculpted in Carrara but his real home was now Paris, the place in which he had to succeed, the art centre of the world.

He returned to France in September and lived in temporary dwellings. In 1910, six of his paintings were hung in the Salon des Indépendants. He was increasingly bitter because he was not selling any work and had had no critical acclaim or acceptance, whereas other, lesser artists were thriving. His aunt, Lo Garsin, appalled at the state of his health, insisted he join her on the Normandy coast for a holiday but each time she sent him the fare he spent it in the Rotonde or the Dôme. Finally he arrived in a storm in a horsedrawn carriage, wearing only a shirt. He had been first to see the seaview at Fécamp. Aunt Lo decided he was too much of a responsibility and returned him to Paris. In 1912 he decided to concentrate on sculpture and exhibited seven heads en bloc at the Salon d'Automne. In the terrible winter of 1913, poor and starving, he had a physical breakdown and returned to Livorno. The sculpture he produced was not appreciated by his Italian artist friends and in a rage he tipped it all into a Livorno canal. On his return to Paris he was taken up briefly by the famous dealer Cheron, and then by Paul Guillaume.

In 1914 he met Beatrice Hastings, the South African writer, and lived with her, on and off, for two years. Beatrice was intellectually his equal, she was his model, lover and he painted her. She kept him. His work was now handled exclusively by Guillaume but did not sell. After leaving Beatrice, he had a short affair with Simone Thiroux, a warm-hearted Canadian girl with some money of her own. In 1917 he left Simone, who was now pregnant, denying he was the father. She gave birth to a boy who was later adopted. In 1916 he met the Polish poet Zborowski who, very taken with Modigliani, became his dealer.

He spent his life on the streets or in bars and never lost his wit, sarcasm, intelligence or love of poetry. When Zbo took him on, his health was deteriorating and his allowance had stopped because of the war. His brother, Emanuelle, now elected to the Chamber of Deputies, had tried to persuade him to return to Italy at the outbreak of war. Whatever Modigliani's situation, he was always in contact with his mother and desperately wanted to prove that her belief in him had been justified. Although ill, he still had great charm, and captivated women, but could not sustain a long-term relationship. He was quarrelsome and violent, yet generous and kind. His friends were the outsiders, the poor ones, misunderstood like himself, the painters maudit – Utrillo and Soutine.

He painted with great bursts of energy, aided by alcohol, but his hand, when he sketched, was always steady. He drew tourists in the Rotonde and the Dôme for the price of a drink. He was better than his situation, which gave him a kind of arrogance: he would not accept pity and he set the street price for his work of five francs. If an American tried to give him twenty, he was offended. He liked to complete a painting in one or two sittings and could not bear work to drag on over a period of time. It is said that Lunia guarded the door while he painted nudes. To protect his privacy or her heart?

In 1917, sometime around the Easter carnival, he met Jeanne Hebuterne, an art student, and they fell in love. She came from a bourgeois Catholic family who disapproved of her liaison with the drunken, penniless, Jewish painter. Jeanne modelled for him, and when she was obliged to leave home, they lived together in small hotels and later at the top studio in the Rue de la Grande Chaumière. He had his first one-man show at Berthe Weill's Gallery in December 1917. Because his nudes were shown with pubic hair the police closed it down the same day.

In 1918 Zborowski took Modi and Jeanne to Nice. Included in the group were the painter Foujita and his wife, Soutine and Jeanne's mother. Jeanne was pregnant and the rows between her mother and Modi were dramatic. For a time he moved out and lived with the Osterlinds near Renoir in Cagnes. Jeanne gave birth to a girl in Nice in November and Modi got drunk and forgot to register the birth. Then he had his papers stolen so could not return to Paris as he wanted. He lived from hand to mouth and often could not find models, so painted two landscapes. He became ill with the Spanish flu and during this time the Osterlinds helped him give up drink and drugs. He saw Jeanne from time to time – she could not cope with the baby and a wet-nurse was employed. Her mother, unable to tolerate the situation, returned to Paris, and Zborowski, unable to sell any work in Nice and so support his painters, also returned. Modi got drunk again with his companions, Blaise Cendrars and Léopold Survage. Some of his friends did not even know he had Jeanne and a child living nearby. He was determined to get back to Paris to his old haunts and, as soon as his new papers arrived, travelled back alone on May 31st leaving Jeanne behind, pregnant again.

In Paris he painted Lunia and they resumed a close relationship. She said she would not give in and let him sleep with her because of his association with Jeanne. Under Lunia's influence he gave up drinking and tried to regain some semblance of health, even talked of going back to Italy. He was dying of tuberculosis but still had great life force. Lunia and Hanka Zborowska decorated Modi's new studio in the Rue de la Grande Chaumière. Jeanne sent a telegram from Nice asking for the train fare to Paris for herself and the wet-nurse. She arrived at the end of June to live with Modi in the new apartment. Modi started drinking again, she could not manage the baby, and Lunia and the Zborowskis looked after the little girl until she was put in the care of a nurse near Versailles. Jeanne, pregnant, had to deal with Modi, who was often too drunk to get home. Frequently she had to search for him in the police stations.

From the time of his return to Paris to his death in January 1920, he painted some of his greatest portraits of Jeanne, Lunia and Hanka. He wrote a declaration, stating he would marry Jeanne Hebuterne as soon as his papers arrived. But he spelt her name wrong, called her Jane, and his papers had already arrived. It was signed by Lunia, Zborowski, Jeanne and himself.

In the summer of 1919 his work finally started to gain some recognition: a painting of Lunia was bought for a good price in London by Arnold Bennett; Osbert and Sacheverell Sitwell sponsored his work; Francis Carco praised it in a Swiss magazine. His first good review came from a London Jewish paper. When Modi received it he kissed it. 'Now Mama will be pleased.'

He painted up until his last days – he knew he was dying but refused medical help. He almost sought death out on the streets in the icy winds of winter nights, walking drunkenly without a coat. Earlier, Lunia had tried to make him return with her to Nice but he decided to stay with Jeanne. In his last week he lay dying in the studio and Jeanne stayed beside him but did not get help. She was due to give birth to their second child at any time. They had only alcohol and tins of sardines to live on. She made several drawings of ways to kill herself. Nobody came near them and there was no coal. Finally, Ortiz de Zarate, a Chilean painter who lived downstairs and frequently carried Modi up to his studio drunk, found them both lying on the bed, almost dead. He rushed Modi to the Charity Hospital where he died on January 24th. On January 25th, at four o'clock in the morning, Jeanne jumped to her death from her family's apartment in the Rue Amyot. Modi was given the funeral of a prince. All the painters, models and characters of Montmartre and Montparnasse followed the cortège to Père Lachaise cemetery. As the procession made its way to Modi's burial place, his work doubled, trebled in value. It continued to rise to colossal prices from the moment of his dying. Jeanne was buried almost secretly in Bagneux cemetery, outside Paris. Several years later, the Hebuterne family finally agreed she should be reinterred in Modi's grave at Père Lachaise cemetery.

Throughout his life Modi quoted from memory Dante and Lautréamont. He was described as a child of the stars. He was the love of Jeanne's life and she loved him more than life itself. Modi loved life more than he ever could a woman.

Vicky added the last two sentences and knew them to be true.

· *Thirty-four* ·

It was while walking along Pacific Palisades in Los Angeles that Vicky saw Paris so clearly – Paris in the sun, a bright, optimistic light everywhere, and she felt herself walking down a main thoroughfare in a blaze of light. She was ecstatic. She was in love. She was going to meet the man she loved. There was no joy like it. Life was marvellous, more, divine, and she could see colours so much more clearly then she did now. She passed along the cafés, her body weightless and free, and, amongst the crowd on the corner terrace, he stood, his back to her, a glass in one hand, a cigarette half-smoked in the other. All his simplest movements were something people watched. He had wonderful reflexes and balance, even drunk. And then he turned and she could see in his glance that her love was reciprocated.

Vicky sat absently on the Los Angeles grass, trying to keep hold of the picture. She wanted her consciousness to move in closely, like a camera, but her mind would not. It would not do what she wanted. She was shown these vivid moments of life and she must learn to accept them as visions that could not be improved upon or altered. The past could not be changed, nor called up at will.

So she saw Modi from the angle she had seen him before. His eyes lit up and she felt a swoop of wild joy such as she had never known – up she went to a high place. She could smell flowers, could see from the Montparnasse trees it was spring.

'Who am I?' she said.

The recollections of Paris were accompanied by feelings she, herself, Vicky, did not experience. She was aware of a difference in her emotional state. She was limited in what she saw by the angle at which she was placed. She could not see herself and had no idea what she looked like, only how she felt. There were no sounds and speech was given to her by thought. A sentence was there in her mind. An atmosphere was always present. She was very aware of textures but could touch nothing. Being part of that life, even for a short time, made her feel extraordinary afterwards, as though she had been in a time warp, as though she had been to Mars.

But it was a world of memories. They were stronger, clearer, more enduring than anything from her childhood or present life. As she went further back the recalled images grew stronger. Nothing else she recollected had this intensity, not even her meeting with Marais. Yes, she could not choose her recollections, nor could she see them from another point of view. She tried, as he stood on the terrace with a bearded, svelte man, to go up behind him and touch his back. She knew the café, yet its name she would only be able to see from the street. All she was doing was reliving what she had already experienced.

'Who am I? I was in love with him. I am supposing he is Modigliani, partly because of what I felt when reading about his life, which seemed familiar. His face is not exactly as it looks in the photographs in the books. In none of them is he smiling, but with me, he smiles. Only the last known photograph, when he wears a beard, his eyes serious and intense as he saw death, that photograph I recognize.

So I was someone who loved him. Beatrice Hastings? Simone Thiroux? Jeanne? Someone not even recorded? Or Lunia? She saw the last was impossible because that woman had still been alive when she, Vicky, was born.

On the plane to Toronto she asked for more iced tea. She had a passion for it, very cold, with lemon, herbs, sugar and spice. Serge was talking to her about the video marketing company. She always found what he said interesting because of the tone of his voice. This time he said, 'We get on well, don't we?'

She nodded in agreement. What had he said?

'Cool?' he asked.

'I like it that way.' She thought he meant the tea. He was talking about her response to him.

She could still see the shanty town shack and a door, half-opened, showing a piano draped with a colourful scarf. It looked incongruous in that squalid area. And the painter was well-dressed in his velvet suit, leaning in the doorway, waiting. His hair was curly and wet from bathing. And he looked expectantly in the direction of Paris. He went back into the hut and reappeared with a zinc bath, which he emptied onto the litter-strewn track. He leant the bath against the wall. Along came a dark-eyed beauty with a voluptuous figure and a small waist. He smiled at her, she smiled back – there was intimacy in their look, and desire for gratification. He touched her as she passed him and, before the door was shut, she started taking off her blouse and threw it over the piano. Vicky, the one outside, winced with pain, a searing pain like teeth in her heart.

'Perhaps you're not sure, Vicky?'

'I'm sorry. I didn't hear you. My ears. We must be going to land.'

'I told you not to take so much iced tea. It's bad for your system. We are not going to land.' And he smacked her hand playfully.

It was a lapse from reality, this sudden conversation in a plane. She saw again the shack. He looks so young, and I must have been very young. The pain did not feel young. And she went back, slipped back, to where she felt most alive – the heat of Paris in a summer that felt safe again. She guessed it as being just after the First World War. There she was, in the narrow room, standing by the table which was marked and scarred. It was functional. She could see only its corner. She would have trouble manoeuvring herself past it, so there was little space. To the left stood the easel. On it was a canvas covered with the colour crimson, still wet. She was so aware of the difference between one colour and another, between shape and texture. She felt this difference in her stomach, all over her body.

It was too hot, there was no air, so she opened one of many glass windows. One side of the room was entirely glass. The air in the courtyard was no different to that in the room. Opposite and all around, other windows were open. She felt a stab of suspicion. He was not in the room, nor in the next, nor the one at right angles by the main door where she kept her clothes. She felt nervous. Should she go and look for him, or stay? She was panicky because he might be with someone else. The thought of him on top of a naked woman, thrashing about in a hotel bed, was unbearable. She might miss him if she went out. If he was with Lunia then she would find him at the Zborowskis' at 3, Rue Joseph Bara.

So who am I? One of the women mentioned or the countless others who loved him? She could return to the narrow room if she chose. It was still there, the doorway of her mind was open. And beyond the easel was a bulge and a little piece of corridor and another room. Then came an orange wall, a red wall. At the end was a door and the floorboards were noisy and uneven, and full of dust and bits of coal and cigarette ends. She thought she should sweep up, but she hated sweeping, any kind of housework. She took a piece of pencil and sketched the tree in the courtyard. Drawing took away the pain, some of it.

· *Thirty-five* ·

When Serge returned to the hotel she was still reading books about the painter Modigliani. She was so engrossed in what she was doing, she did not even hear him come in.

'Which city are you in, Vicky?'

She looked up, pleased to see him but distracted. No, it was worse. She was a long way away. Immediately, she covered some handwritten pages. By now she had remembered which city this was. For a moment she had nearly said Munich. But this was Toronto. Tomorrow, Munich. She made him some tea as though it was an obligation, as though he was imposing himself on her life.

'I didn't know you were so interested in art.'

'I'm not. I'm interested in the people who make the art.'

'Why him?' He counted the books – five.

She did not know what to say.

'Are you going to make a film about him?'

A lie would have taken care of it, but she said, 'There was a film, but very romanticized. Gérard Philipe played Modigliani. I'm getting it shown for me. It's in French.'

Serge had turned to an illustration of a nude and saw the model was at the height of sexual pleasure. 'The way her body is twisting, hands clenched. I think he had a very definite physical effect on women. Some potent power that mesmerized them. They dropped like flies around him.'

'How do you know?' she said.

'It's something that's known. He had quite a reputation for sexual prowess, though how he did it on all the drink and the drugs, I don't know.' He went on looking at the picture. 'He could immortalize that state of being, that sexual heat. Oil paint didn't get under their skin. He did.' Then he looked at the other books. He actually wanted to see what she was writing.

'I've read all these books.' He tossed them aside but she had moved the writing. 'He certainly understood a woman's sexuality, but he must have been satiated, exhausted.'

'Why?'

'Because they came to him. He didn't have to choose them, go after it. It was always there, in front of his face.'

'Well, you should know. Enough women throw themselves at you.'

'And you're one of them.' He grabbed her. 'So what are you writing that is so secret?'

'Notes.'

'I love notes,' he said.

'The simple facts of his life. It's hard to know what he was like from the books because they're all, to some degree, coloured by the legend, and the reaction of his friends to his lonely death, her suicide, and the reputation of genius that followed.'

'How will you know,' he said sharply, 'if not by the books?'

'From people who may have known him,' she answered promptly.

'Oh, I see.' She still had not shown him the notes.

She told him how difficult it was to track down books because they were now out of print. 'If one book printed in, say, 1930 exaggerates a detail about his women or drinking, it's taken up as a fact in the next and enlarged further in others. So by 1963 he's drunk, drugged, sick, never eating but always able to have women. He's a clinical phenomenon. His daughter, Jeanne, tried to balance the story by writing her account, "Modigliani without Legend", but succeeded in writing another type of legend. That's my view. I'm sure she understood less than anyone because she never knew him. She was fourteen months old when he died and what were his friends in Paris going to tell her? Would they tell the truth about her dead father? To the orphaned child of a self-destructive man and suicidal mother? Modigliani belonged to his Bohemian friends in Paris, not the family in Italy. What did they know? As she said herself, the artists felt he was theirs and considered her an outsider.'

The truth, it seemed to Vicky, would only have emerged when it was safe. In other words, when it could no longer hurt the daughter.

'Why don't you talk to her?' Serge said.

'She died in 1984 in Paris. Jay found that out. And now they're all dead too.'

'Try Ginette de Fleury. She's very much alive. She was part of that Bohemian world and she owes you something.'

'But she's in Paris.'

'So will we be. I have to be there in January.'

Vicky kept her fearful reaction from him. 'How long for?' Her voice sounded ordinary, to her.

Furious, he said, 'You snivel about that city, yet spend hours reading about it. You don't even hear what I say! Half the time you're just not here. I suggest Ginette de Fleury, you don't respond. Get your knowledge from the books, then.'

'The books!' She was scornful. 'They're so subjective and, from what I read, if they don't know, they fabricate. It's all surmise. He probably said this. Imagine he felt that. They were left alone for a week in an icy studio. He was dying, and then she killed herself. Every one of his friends is going to cover that up. They'll all have a story to deal with their sorrow and guilt. The minute he died he was proclaimed a genius. So he was no longer a quarrelsome drunk but someone of immense value. They would all have to change their views, rewrite their anecdotes. And because he's now a genius, every woman in Paris will have been to bed with him. Do you see?' She had completely dismissed his anger.

'So you're making a film about un-making a legend? I like your work, what I've seen of it. You see things always from such a definite angle. That is what you're going to do, make a film about it, isn't it?'

She said yes.

'You could have told me.' He was beginning to feel left out and did not like it.

When he had gone she took the notes from under the bed and wrote on the front, 'These go to Jay Landis, who might find them of interest, if anything should happen to me.' They were not just statements about the painter's life but a record of what she had seen and experienced.

She kept looking at the reproduction of the portraits of Lunia but they did not revive the dream or any associations. She was just a woman with a fan. Vicky thought again about the snake she had drawn from her subconscious and put on BBC paper and, above it, the name Lunia. The snake, for her, depicted jealousy and female betrayal. While the Maestro rehearsed, she read and re-read the books, avidly. And when she had to go out she longed to go back into Modigliani's world. How she identified with his bitterness. She could feel his descent towards death, unable to stop the chemistry of drink and drugs which perhaps supported his mind sufficiently to allow him to achieve his last paintings; compulsive, articulate works, all finished in one session. Like a martial arts specialist lunging, he did not hesitate. And they said, some of his friends, that he was psychic and could enter into the person he was painting and she, the model, could feel him, his spirit, against hers. Vicky thought he painted what was there and not what they hoped was there.

She knew it was not a coincidence that she had chosen Nice as the escape from Paris. Jeanne had gone there to escape the bombing of Paris and Modi's decline. It would have offered them a new start. Vicky suspected the months spent in Nice were horrendous for Jeanne. No book had captured that. This feeling also gave Vicky a definite sense of her previous identity.

Vicky wrote in her notepad, 'Can I really have something to do with this man? I've never even properly noticed his work. I've seen it before because I could recognize the style. But no more than that. Yet he's become so necessary to me. More important than Serge!'

She kept the notes locked in a metal case supposedly containing film. It was the one way she knew of keeping a record of what was happening to her. And she knew Jay Landis was the one to take care of it.

*

She was awake. She could see his naked back and his black hair, grey-streaked and long, like a glossy weed on the pillow. Around his neck a charm of gold and a small cross and chain, a present from his mother.

Again she heard the chipping noise, a hammering of metal against stone. Who in hell could be starting manual work near the Maestro at this early hour? There it was again, a chipping of stone and a voice she knew, reciting poetry, a voice full of irony and melody, acid, tantalizing, thrilling. The words were foreign but she knew them. She heard the meaning of the words. She knew the man was reciting Dante and the chip, chip, chip, was the cutting of stone. And there he was, amongst the weeds of the garden. Behind him, a watch was pinned to a tree. He wore a blue and white checked shirt and rust corduroy trousers, and he stood back to look at the sculpture of the head, elongated, African-influenced, primitive and all-knowing with its strange stare. He took a large drink from the wine bottle and saw her. Around his neck hung a red scarf, his hair was blue-black, thick and very clean, his profile beautiful, eyes intense and luminous. He went back to the stone with a flat knife and he worked with such absorption that, as she watched, the stone became part of him and he the stone. She, absorbed by the activity, did not move. He wiped his face with the red scarf and drank from the bottle.

'You still there? You should be in school.'

She wished she did not have long plaits, an ordinary school tunic. She wished she was dressed by Poiret.

His eyes had a tenderness she had only dreamed about, his hair hung over his forehead. And there was no one else in the whole world.

He pointed to her violin case. 'So you play, do you? Play me something.'

She took the violin from its case and played a piece by Bach that she had practised. And he nodded as though taking it seriously.

'It's my birthday today. That's the best present you could have given me. Do you know any Italian music?'

She shook her head.

'Well, come and play on my next birthday. July the 12th. Don't forget.' And he turned back to the stone head and ran his hand over it. She shivered. 'Stones have special powers,' he said. 'Some stones have great energy. I've seen you before.'

She had seen him before too. She used to watch him up at the top of Montmartre, in the bad area overrun by vagrants, crooks and artists. He had stood in his doorway one day, so beautiful, and a dark woman had come up the gravel slope and he had taken her inside and caressed her. She had seen through the window. And after he had moved wildly on top of the dark woman, he had had a drink and started painting her. She had gone up there the next week but he had moved away, some said to the hotel in the Place du Tertre. Others said a middle-class child like her should not be hanging around the Maquis.

'How old are you?' he asked.

'Over thirteen.'

'What's your name?' He held out a piece of stone for her to feel.

She backed away, suddenly shy. He was poor, yet he smelt clean and it was a hot July day. She ran out of the Cité Falguière and into the boulevard, breathless with sudden excitement, and the effect of running made her braids flap against her head.

Vicky touched his back in fear. He turned and it was not the face of the man chipping the stone.

'D'you want it again?' Serge was amused. 'Shall we?' And he got on top of her.

His face had been so clear and well. And she had gone there again and watched him through the fence, banging on the stone, and all around him were heads with long noses. Her brother said the Italian got the stone and wood from the métro station being built in Montparnasse. He collected it in a wheelbarrow. One night she was watching and he lit candles and put one on top of each head as though they were his children.

Vicky held onto Serge as he rocked to and fro against her and thought, what should I do?

Serge Marais knew all about the girl he was going to marry.

When the accountant said, she spends a lot but she's not wearing it, Serge had her checked out.

She had said that her father had worked in military intelligence at the Ministry of Defence and her mother – the way she described her was 'county'. Now he knew that her father had had a quiet position in the Ministry of Defence and he had turned down promotion and kept his home life private. Her mother was frequently hospitalized, nervous breakdown material. Serge was impressed with the way Vicky had helped her father by arranging a car to make his visits to the clinic easier. Serge knew she had visited her mother regularly and paid the bills at the clinic. She made twice-weekly phone calls to her father and the clinic. What was more, she had kept it to herself. She had stayed in a low promotion job in radio instead of going to filmschool, to help her family. Her marriage to Dean had been a disaster but she had left him his money. Her life had not been easy. Dean Tyrell described her as 'a generous girl. Lovely and generous.' Nor had she clung on to Jay Landis. When it was time to go, she had let him go. Her life almost made him cry, the sadness of it, the humility. It made him love her more.

Serge was sitting at the kitchen table in his house in Munich, changing a plug on the clothes iron. His hair flopped forward, his feet were bare, he felt quite ordinary and stable, as though his life would go on indefinitely, calmly. Then his eyes met Vicky's and he remembered their night of sexuality, climax after climax, that went on till dawn and he looked away – all that heat aroused him.

'Come here.'

She got up from what she was doing and sat beside him and he put his arm over her arm on the table as he continued changing the plug. The second they touched there was a flare of excitement and their arms pressed together, throbbing. He looked into her face. 'Five o'clock, OK? Be there.'

'In the bedroom?'

'Just be around the house. I'll find you.'

And she got up, breathless, knowing they would repeat the experience of the night before with the fresh energy of late afternoon.

Serge decided that, after the siesta, he would challenge her about the sick mother. Why couldn't she trust him enough to share the pain? But when it came to it, he could not say a word. She lay beside him, miles away. There was something otherworldly about her eyes. He immediately noticed she was distant in her replies, two beats, maybe three, before she responded. He tried to get her to talk about that.

Vicky could hardly say, 'I'm obsessed by a dead painter.'

· *Thirty-six* ·

She tried to lose herself in the beauty of the music. Serge's world was an oasis of the harmonious and uplifting, in which people gathered as they once had in churches. Perhaps God was there, in the harmonies of Beethoven and Bach. The audience sat in their nice clothes, wanting to be rescued.

It was his last concert in Munich, packed to capacity. The concert hall was too hot. Had they turned up the heating because it was November? Vicky nudged the impresario and signalled that she was hot. He was surprised as for him, the air-conditioning was too efficient, the draught steely. It was as though the air was tinned. She insisted it was too hot and threw off her jacket.

'It is the beginning of November. There should not be air-conditioning,' he said.

Against the music Vicky could hear the sound of an insect. It whirred and bumped against a window. Yet the music still played. She watched Serge. What passion he evoked as the music reached a crescendo. She thought of him, how he moved in bed, and the pleasure of that should have cut out all fear. But the insect buzzed against her ear, her hair, back to the window, jumping against the glass in the hot room. She could see the top of a tree and windows opposite, and he was beside her. When he spoke he reeked of drink and ether. And now that he was so real, there was no other reality.

'Just open the window. Now, be free.' The window opened a small way and the insect zoomed out into the courtyard towards the tree.

She could feel his hand on hers, one touch, more provoking

and powerful than anything she had known since. Her mind hovered, half in the concert hall, half in the narrow room. His hand on her hand gave her expectation of joy. And she thought, only the music I'm listening to is that good. She returned to the hot room and felt his breath against her face. He had sketched since nine at the café and an American tourist had tried to buy, not the drawing, but him – he had written in big letters across a quick self-portrait, 'Not for sale'. He had torn up the one of the tourist. There was no money. Nothing. And he had had three more teeth pulled. She listened to his melancholy. Just being near him was enough. She was – complete.

And she tried to see him, but these memories from long ago presented themselves always as they chose. You saw only what was there, from the angle shown. She could feel the texture of his shirt and something silk wound around his waist. And there was passion, delicious, coming and going towards ecstasy like the music.

His body was so white and perfect. She knew that he believed he was dying and she would not have it: he had to live.

Vicky closed her eyes. 'I couldn't let him die.'

The Bach ended. Vicky said, 'I am possessed.'

Modi said, 'I gave my other shirt to Soutine. He wanted it.'

And she knew Soutine wanted all Modi's clothes. Wearing them made him feel more attractive, as though some of the Italian's charisma wiped off on him. She had heard that Soutine had seen a man in the street wearing Modi's type of blue and white check shirt and, thinking it was his adored friend, followed the man for two days.

'Will the possession just go away as it came? And by who am I possessed? Not by him because I can see him. By Jeanne, the person I was?'

She left before the applause was over, ran to the administration room and phoned Jay. She told him, 'I'm haunted, taken over. Please help me. It can't be right.'

'Is it him? Serge? Is he getting you down?'

'Jay, I'm sitting in Munich in 1988 and my eyes see Paris 1918.'

*

The house was old and Victorian and the rooms were empty with just a few possessions in the corners. She believed it was the house she had lived in during her teens, after leaving Hampshire. The man she was expecting came up the stairs and she was so relieved. How she loved him! He was small and dark with curly, wavy hair and a stocky build. She was not pleased to see a woman walking behind him, a tall blonde who looked like a policewoman from her favourite TV series. The man said quite curtly, 'I'm going.' And he took his woollen sweater and his book and she knew he was going with this woman. She knew he was having an affair with her. He was perhaps even in love. This was no time to find things incongruous. Her heart was in danger. Vicky took hold of the blonde and pushed her into the front room of the empty Victorian house. In a fury, she pushed her head through the sash window, smashing it. The woman's face was gashed and streaming with blood. Vicky waited, expecting her to die. But the woman, in spite of her injuries, pulled herself back from the glass and straightened up and went to the man waiting in the hallway, and they went swiftly down flights of stairs to the front door. Vicky ran after them. They had disappeared around the hedge. Vicky ran into the street and screamed, 'You can't leave me. I'm pregnant!'

Serge woke her up and put on the light. He held her, soothed her. 'You were having a bad dream. What was this about a baby?'

And she told him the dream, as much for her sake as his, so she could remember it in the morning. 'And the woman was so tall and strong. Yet I pushed her into the front room –'

'The old house means the past,' he said.

She agreed with that, but with nothing else he had to say.

It was dawn when he at last lay down to sleep. 'Perhaps you want a baby,' he said.

Oh God, no, she thought.

And then he told her the good news. 'I've found a way out for us. I'm going to cut the number of my performances. After our wedding I'll do only twenty a year.'

*

She saw him on the terrace of the Dôme, dirty, sleepless, wearing a sash around his waist. She was standing diagonally opposite and in front was a barrow of spring flowers. She was aware of the big bunches of yellow dew-moist primroses. And she watched him, her heart lifted and she knew joy. The prison walls of her childhood dissolved like soggy cardboard and she was free. And forever afterwards she would associate primroses with happiness. He did not see her. She knew his name and his reputation because she had watched him on and off for years. And her friend, Julie, used to call him 'idol'. He was everything her parents would hate. Yet he was the man she was born to love. It was just bad luck that he was sick, dissipated, ruined. She had no choice. She was just nineteen.

Vicky kept to a routine so that her days were ordered and calm, with time left over for any sudden demand from Serge. Although his schedule was planned weeks ahead he could not predict the crises caused by his children, the sudden meeting with a friend who happened to be in the same city. And as she washed her hair or did some exercises, she would be taken there. Between one thought and another she would be back in the Rue Lepic, walking with her friend Julie, looking for the fantastic, wicked places; the Moulin Galette, the Lapin Agile. A boy accompanied her. Was it her brother? And in a café in the Rue Lepic she saw him. The boy said, 'That's the Italian painter, Modi. He's a Bohemian.' And a thin, pale man sat with him, dressed in a tall hat and gloves. 'I think he's a poet,' whispered the boy. 'He does astrology.' And Julie pushed them, giggling, into the café. Modi was reading a sheet of paper. He burst into tears, and she knew the letter was not from a mistress. What woman would leave him? She knew it was from someone very special, his mother.

Now she was in the Boulevard Raspail. He stood in front of a statue, reciting Dante. And then he started to take off his clothes. How beautiful his body was! She saw the crowd watching him. 'He's like a god. A Greek god,' said a man. An English woman pulled at his sash and he went twirling into the darkness, whirling, laughing, and just disappeared.

She was in the wet, smelly, steaming, smoky room and they were all pushed together, drawing from the nude. She was watching him, how he drew very fast with one unbroken line, utterly sure. He looked up and saw her watching him, and smiled slightly as though he recognized her.

Then the Panthéon rose up like a monster. The landscape was bare, then that building, huge and fat, blocking her way. Her heart was actually in pain, her chest stretched. Could a heart break? The boy said, 'He's not Catholic, he's a Jew.'

And the woman said, 'Don't make me shiver.' She wanted to go with him. 'Listen to your brother. You're to go to Brittany. That's it.'

She ran round the full extent of the monument but she could not escape. Tears spilling down her face, she prayed to God. Her prayers were not answered. 'Without him, I can't sleep, eat, live.' And the oriental turban fell off and her plaits came loose and her heart broke with love.

'Although I walk through the valley of the shadow of death, I will fear no evil.' It was Jay's voice.

'At least listen to your priest!' the woman shouted.

'Oh, Maman!' She had to go to him. He was waiting the other side of the Panthéon.

As she whirled round the Panthéon her friend, Julie, was waiting, and she listed the women Modi had slept with. She pressed her face into the gritty wall of the monument and sobbed. How deceived she had been.

She whirled around to the other side and approached it slowly, her father's arm in hers, in case she slipped on the ice. Her stomach was huge, the baby low, pressing. Her heart, as though broken, had spread out across her chest like a slaughtered animal. Pain still crept through her, worse, desperation. Ahead was the Panthéon. 'I hate that building.' It still stood, yet he was dead.

Her father replied, 'Come now. You've seen it every day of your life.'

'But he's gone.' And she did not speak again.

*

Serge came in as she was packing a case. 'We don't go until tomorrow. Why pack now?' Then he noticed it was a small, slim suitcase. 'Where are you going?'

'London.'

'But I'm in Rome tomorrow.'

And she looked at the face of the man opposite, at the room, the bed, and it was all unreal. Flat, grey, like a skin she could shed.

Jay said, 'Lo has found two women who sound right. They can tell your past lives. They live miles out, in suburbia, and we have to be there at seven this evening. These people always live in the most difficult places. It costs plenty too. But let's give it a shot.'

He hugged her to him, kept holding her, so pleased she was back in his life.

After lunch Vicky walked across Hampstead Heath where they flew kites. Around the hill she could see London.

Yet, all of a sudden, she saw her body whirling down from a window. It landed in the narrow street. It fell like a sack of potatoes and an object was flung out from between her legs. She believed it was the baby. She could see passers-by, the position in which she lay, the darkness of a winter dawn. The road was narrow and situated east to west, somewhere between the Panthéon and the Luxembourg Gardens.

As she walked on Hampstead Heath she could see the body from above. Her mind hovered, taking in every detail. The corpse was trundled across Paris in a workman's cart, to and from the studio in the Grande Chaumière and the police station. The concierge did not want to take it. 'Monsieur Modigliani does not live here now.'

'Where is he?'

'Dead.'

'But the police insisted it lie here,' said the workman. 'The parents won't take it.'

And dizzily the body curved round the flights of steep stairs, back up to the studio, its door hanging open.

Vicky cried silently, tears flooding her face, because her body had not been wanted. Nobody wanted her.

And she saw that killing herself with the child inside her was a terrible act. That was why, in this life, she was the only child of a disturbed, often terrifying, woman and a weak, unloving father. She could now rewrite the story of her life. Instead of being the victim, unlucky, she was a person who wished to repair an earlier wrong. Vicky's life was payment of a former spiritual debt. How terrified she had been, seeing her mother try and kill herself. She had experienced the horror of the manner of death and also the terror of being left at the mercy of a not-particularly kind world. She had had to endure such a childhood to repay the Lords of Karma and her own spirit. She no longer resented her mother, or expected anything to come of her own suffering except repayment. Seeing the futility of suicide was part of the price.

She now knew who she was. And she heard the Frenchwoman scream as she had wanted to so often at Ruby, 'You think only of yourself! There are other people in the world, too. What about us? You're ruining your family. You don't care that you break our hearts.'

· *Thirty-seven* ·

Because of the rain the taxi took two hours to reach Croydon and then it was impossible to find where the two women lived. Jay said, 'Don't tell them anything. Have you got the photographs of Modigliani and his women?'

'You haven't told Lorraine about me?'

'How can I tell someone you were Modigliani's mistress? I don't even tell them you're marrying a superstar. Don't, Vicky.'

'What?'

'Keep slipping back. You keep going back there. I feel I'm going to lose you.'

When they finally found the right flat they were over an hour late.

At first the women would not open the door because they were not expecting two people. The number of bolts that were drawn and chains and locks undone before the door actually opened, suggested they were either frightened of burglars or on the run from dissatisfied customers.

The women sat close together on a small sofa. Jay chose a high, straight-backed chair. Vicky was given the comfortable armchair. The women, like Tweedledum and Tweedledee, had the same shade of dyed gold hair. One wore glasses and her eyes were round and magnified so that they looked kind. The other looked distinctly worldly and had seen enough to distrust. They were not happy about Jay. Was he a reporter? A policeman? What was he? They told Vicky they would prefer him not to be there because the vibrations would get mixed up. Vicky replied she wanted him beside her and would take that chance.

They spread the photographs of Modigliani and his mistresses across their knees, including a reproduction of the painting of Lunia. There was no photograph of Simone Thiroux so Vicky had included a copy of the letter the woman had written after the birth of her son, a touching, beautifully written letter asking the painter to see her one last time.

The woman with worldly eyes was watching Vicky. 'You were never bonded. Do you know that? Your mother never bonded with you.'

'Bonded?' said Jay.

'A mother has to bond with her baby during pregnancy.' She peered at Vicky. 'Your father wanted you. So there was bonding with him. That's why you have such low self-esteem.'

Vicky made the face of someone with low self-esteem. She did not believe it. She just felt she had had a hard time.

'You had low self-esteem then, and you have now.'

'Then. So I am one of these people?' She pointed to the collection of photographs.

'You know you are.'

'It's quite incredible,' said the kinder woman with the glasses. 'The likeness. Look at the neck.'

'So I'm him? The painter?' said Vicky.

'You know you're not,' said the harder one.

'Is he around?' asked Vicky.

'Most definitely.' And the woman with glasses held his picture straight out and looked at him as though he was standing in front of her. 'Here, he was in his chaos.'

'And now?'

'He didn't do you any good then. Or now. What you felt for him was a longing, a oneness, a clinging, a belonging, a wild happiness, a hunger –'

Vicky agreed to all of it.

'It's wrong! Infantile. That's the feeling of a child for a parent. That's not love. Love is free. Respectful.'

They all sat in silence, in respect of what had just been said.

'Love lets you be free. Lets you be yourself. Love is harmony. You searched for that clinging, bonding tie and you still do. And he fits into you like a hand into a glove. But it's wrong. Turn your back on him. Only new things, new states of being will take you forward. Do you want to grow and learn and make progress?'

Vicky said she did.

Jay was now worried. Did they think he was Modigliani? Did they imagine he was doing her harm? He tried to say they were not together.

Vicky said wilfully, 'But he's my destiny!'

'Destiny!' The tougher woman shouted. 'All destiny brings you is lessons. Happiness comes from the unexpected.'

'Is he alive?'

Both women looked at Vicky and took it in turns to speak. 'If we say he is here you will go straight to him. If we say he's in the spirit realm you will reach out to him. And you'll go on interfering with each other's lives. You with his, he with yours. You did before and you do now. Give him up!'

The women turned in unison to Jay.

'Hey!' he said. 'I'm not him.'

The women smiled and shook their heads. They liked their little joke. 'Of course you didn't paint. But you're still giving her wise advice,' said the kind one.

Jay nudged Vicky. Time was running out. He indicated the photographs.

'So I was with this painter in my past life?' she said.

'Of course. Your last life and one before that. You've known each other through many lives.'

'But which one is she?' asked Jay.

First they lifted the photograph of Beatrice Hastings and Jay was triumphant. Got you, he thought.

'Not her,' said the tough one. 'He didn't fit hand-in-glove with her. She challenged him. They fought, drank too much.'

Then came the reproduction of the painting of Lunia. 'Not her. She couldn't get him away from you.'

Then came Jeanne.

'And now you feel sin. You're guilty for what you did. You're full of sin. He has it, you have it. Both of you. I always see you born in Paris. Why, I can't imagine. You have known terrible deaths there. Before your Parisian lives you were far more evolved. You were somebody. But you fell into sin, into ecstasy. All earthbound. For you, Paris is a purgatorial path. You were in purgatory this last time. You saw him die and you couldn't go on living without him. He was your life. You threw yourself out of a window with a child ready to be born inside you. And then when you'd done it, you saw it was no good.'

'No good?' she whispered.

'You still existed. You were there, attached by the etheric cord to the body. I see you hovering just above as you realized what you had done was for nothing. You were a conscious being in your etheric body and you still felt the same pain. From there, you should have passed to the halls of rest, the spirit realms.'

Jay wanted to know something about the etheric body.

'It contains your consciousness, memories of all your lives, desires, personalities, nervous system.'

'Can it be seen?' asked Jay.

'A psychic can sometimes see an etheric body leave the physical body at the point of death. It usually leaves from the top chakra, above the head, and remains attached to the gross body for some time. This explains people's death experiences. They are clinically dead, yet can see their body and the room around them. Then they are brought back with after-death memories.'

'Is it like a ghost?' asked Vicky.

'It's a spirit. But you remained earthbound. You did not go to rest. You hung around in the ethera, waiting for him.'

'Why did I do it?' Vicky sounded broken.

The woman with glasses said, 'He asked you to join him. You made some promise before he died.'

'It's in the books,' Vicky whispered. 'You could have read it in the books.'

Jay thought she looked in bad shape and that he should get her out of there. He prepared to leave. Vicky shouted furiously at the women, 'Tell me something I don't know! Give me one piece of evidence. I know the books very well.'

Unperturbed, the first woman said, 'I see you by a river. It's a very hot day. You've just made love. He went on wild sprees. He could fit into any woman's fantasy, that was his talent. He was psychic. You weren't over the excitement when he said, "I can make you do anything. You'd die for me if I asked you to."'

'Do you remember that?' asked Jay.

Vicky shook her head.

'And when he was dying he made you vow to go with him, to join him in the afterlife. He said, "You'll always be mine. You always have been." Your pact was beyond religion or God, right or wrong.'

'So, how can I prove that?' said Vicky.

The tough woman looked at her with eyes narrowed. 'You won't have to.'

Jay did not like her tone. 'Is it in the books? This pact? What did it say?' he asked Vicky.

'As he was taken to the hospital he said, "I've arranged things with my wife. We'll be together in eternity." So some biographers suggested there had been a pact or vow.' She sounded exhausted but she turned back to the women and asked, quite desperately, 'Is he with me? Modi?'

'Only if you let him be. You live in this life so get on with it. You have a lot of things going your way. Don't ruin that. The session will cost one hundred and twenty pounds.'

Jay choked. Vicky wrote the cheque, almost embarrassed by their greed. The first woman, making sure Vicky wrote the right sum, said, 'You must have fun. You never have any fun.'

Before she let herself be shown to the front door Vicky asked, 'Is he one of the men around me?'

'Yes.'

'So he's alive?' She was surprised. How could she see him so clearly in her mind?

'In one place or the other. Ask him.'

'How can I reach him?'

'My dear, he reaches you.'

Jay said, 'So you do believe we go on afterwards? Really?'

The women kept looking at Vicky. 'Our spirit friends don't come unless there's a reason. What is his?'

Vicky had never questioned that. 'Good or bad?' she asked.

'Make sure it's good. You're born here and he's in spirit. So you're not meant to be together. You've been kept apart and given a new chance.' And the women guided Vicky into the hallway.

By the time they got back to Hampstead Vicky felt flat and disappointed. 'How the hell can I prove any of it, Jay?'

'I don't know. Nor do I understand why that life has surfaced. It's like you're a magic painting book. You're in a black and white design. Then Modi wets it with his tears and you come up another design altogether and in bright colour.'

He took her out for a Chinese meal at her favourite restaurant in Hampstead and he felt the original feeling of disquiet he had had when he first sensed she was in danger. He could tell when she was slipping back to Paris. It was more concentrated than day-dreaming. Her breathing changed, became faster and shallow, and her eyes looked down, resting on some object without interruption.

'Stay in this life, Vick. Don't keep going back. How do you know your mind can take it?'

'There has to be a reason why I'm shown that time, that happiness. I can't begin to even – I want to see him, Jay.'

· *Thirty-eight* ·

Vicky's mother was a lot thinner and a lot more trouble. Vicky took her over to her father in a car. When they arrived he was lying on the kitchen floor, mouth stained with food, asking for his wife. The ambulance men waited in the passage. The young efficient doctor bent over him, holding his hand.

'Mum, it may be the hardest thing to do, but please be with him,' said Vicky.

The neighbour had phoned the clinic while Vicky was visiting her mother to say Mr Graham was not feeling too well. He had sent for the doctor. The doctor rang and said it was serious but Mr Graham refused to die in an ambulance. He would die in his own home and he wanted his wife beside him.

The doctor said, 'It's his right.' She had given him a shot for the pain but he was slipping fast. The ambulance men still waited – there was no rush.

Ruby said, 'Get up. It doesn't do any good lying there.' And with gentleness she tried to lift him.

'I'm dying, Ruby. And I'm scared.'

Vicky, kneeling beside him, said, 'Don't be, Dad. We all go on, I promise you that. It's like going from one room to another. It's that easy. And it's not the end of anything.'

'So, if you're right, we all come back?'

'Yes, Dad, I promise.'

'Then why isn't Julius Caesar here?' And he started to gasp.

Vicky could not watch him die. She held his hand and tried to give him all her strength. Of course, she thought, I forgot to tell him Julius Caesar does not come back as Julius Caesar but as the result of his actions as that person.

She kept her father's death quiet. She phoned Serge and said the cremation would be the following day and asked him not to come. After all, he had not known her father.

'But I want to be with you and help you, Vicky.' It hurt him a great deal that she would not share her life with him. Did she think he was a snob because her mother had a depressive illness and, before that, worked on the glove counter in a London department store? It was one of the things he would confront her with when she returned. The other was harder. The nearest word he could find to describe it was secrecy. What was behind it? What was she keeping from him? She could not have captivated him more by her actions if she had tried. A woman, too available, all over him, bored him sooner or later. This girl prolonged sensation perfectly and did not even know it.

Vicky was the only one who did not cry at the funeral service. Why waste a tear? Her father had not gone. The healer had told her, at the time of death, you were taken over by those already in spirit who loved you. They helped you to adapt to your new condition and then you were taken to the halls of rest. In some cases, the healer said, you refused to pass across into the further realm, preferring to stay near the earth, your etheric body invisible to fully fleshed human beings. You sometimes wished to stay near those you had left in sorrow. Vicky prayed her father had gone to rest. And although she now believed in other lives and the continuation of memory, she still missed him.

Afterwards, she took the messages of condolence and some of the flowers to her mother. How strange it was that, now her husband was dead, she seemed truly alive. She was alert and ready for the outside world. Was it some irrational reaction? Or was the one cure for her condition death? Had she been so disadvantaged by her marriage? Had he driven her mad? As always, Vicky said, 'Is there anything you want?'

'Yes. I want to get out of here.'

'Give it a few more days.'

'I'd like the flat repainted – white. Get a good painter in. And I want a new bed. Give his suits to the old man above the pub.'

Vicky wrote a list. Her mother deserved a new start, yet she felt the return to sanity was so fast it was almost indecent. Her mother showed few signs of mourning.

'Get rid of his possessions and ask the neighbour to defrost the fridge. Don't you try doing it. Sort it out, Vicky.'

Had she loved him? Was she in shock? Did a husband have to die to turn a mad wife sane?

Vicky was exhausted by the emotional strain, the quick preparation for the funeral and her mother's demands.

'Mum.' She tried to hold the woman's hand. The hand stayed away, out of reach. 'You know when I was very young I used to have imaginary friends – and I remember they had French names: one was Antoinette and the other – do you remember?'

'Oh, don't bother me with that now, Vicky. How can I remember that?'

'But it's strange I should give them French names. What could I have known about France? I was two, maybe less.'

Her mother gave it a second of thought. 'I don't know, Vicky. You were a lonely child. But then, we lived right out in the sticks. You didn't get it from me, the French names. I never went there.'

Vicky realized her mother had been lonely too. 'Wasn't there anything good about that time in the country when I was small?'

'Yes, the animals. And there were no people. At least animals are loyal and don't lie to you or let you down or cheat you. They're not people. All they want is love and they love you back. Give me animals any day.'

Vicky realized she did not belong to this woman. She had only passed through her to reach into the world, taking some physical traits and some aspects of genetic heritage along the way. 'You've been ill a long time. Since last June. We're at the end of November now. D'you remember going to St James's? You said, my daughter is dead. Do you remember?'

For a moment her mother's eyes gleamed with panic and Vicky was scared she had gone too far.

'No, I do remember. It was in June, on your birthday. That's when it happened.' Her mother bit her nails and looked at Vicky as though sizing her up. 'I saw my daughter fall out of a window and it gave me a terrible turn. It was – I know it was my daughter, but she didn't look like you.'

'She didn't?' said Vicky quietly.

Her mother blinked over and over again. A nervous reaction to the pills? Another crisis beginning? 'I saw her hit the ground. I couldn't get it out of my mind.'

'Was she pregnant?'

'No.'

'No? Are you sure?'

'You know I had a lot of trouble with your father. I won't go into it, but he wasn't an easy man.'

Vicky's eyes filled with tears.

Ruby carried on speaking, uncaring. 'He was a lot older than me and I should never have married him and that's the truth. He came from a better background than me and they never let me forget it. They treated me like dirt. His mother and those sisters.'

'Oh, Mum, come on. I've just buried him for you.' After a hostile pause Vicky said, 'Just tell me what happened. The girl falling out of the window.'

'I've told you. She hit the ground and I knew she was my daughter. I was – well, I was beyond it, I can tell you.'

'What were you doing at the time?'

'Cleaning the lavatory where he'd messed it up. I was about to get his tea. And then I saw that and it put me in a terrible state so I had a drink, then another, but I couldn't get it out of my mind.'

'You said she used to draw and paint, your daughter. You said she was talented.'

'Well you should know that. I've only got one daughter. Sometimes I see a little girl and she's dressed, like odd in a tunic and she's playing a violin or painting, and I know she's you. Then I see you in the garden when we had the big house, talking to your imaginary friends and that's you too. At other times it's unthinkable. I felt upset that my daughter had killed herself because it could have been my fault. And I remembered, when she was small, I could see her lovely hair in plaits and everyone said she was so talented. Then she went into a grey place, like a marsh. Nothing. And she kept calling.'

'What?'

'She kept calling out.'

'For you?'

'No. A word.'

'A name?'

'No, a meaningless word.' Her mother sighed and lay back on the bed. 'It's terrible, Vicky, when the depression comes on because I don't know where I am and that's the truth. I thought it might be my fault. That's what I thought. Because I didn't love her enough. I know she wore a veil when she jumped.'

'A nun? Was she a nun?'

'A wedding veil. She was going to get married. People came up, really smart people –'

'In old-fashioned clothes?'

'No. Why? Smart, real classy types. You know, Ascot. Definitely not old-fashioned.'

'Can you remember anything else? Please try?'

'I don't see what my illness has got to do with you, Vicky.'

'Was Dad in the room?'

'I told you, I was cleaning the lavatory. He had some music on very loud. And I shouted, turn that off. The neighbours.'

'Classical music?' And Vicky remembered, it was on her birthday that she had seen Serge Marais on television. She felt shaken.

'Yes, classical music. Someone famous was conducting.'

'Serge Marais?'

'Oh, how do I know their names? Your father didn't like it. But he turned it right up and they'd have been knocking. You know, those snooty ones next-door. You haven't said anything to them about me?'

'Of course not.

'He did it to show them he'd got some culture too. He was proud of you being at the BBC. That's why he kept the music on.' She laughed. 'He didn't want them to think we were watching the American soap.'

So when Vicky was alone on her birthday and she had seen Serge Marais by accident, because the television control button had not tuned to Dynasty, her mother had been throwing bleach down the lavatory and hearing the same concert. And during it she had seen her daughter kill herself.

'God, have I got to live near that lot again? All done up, mutton dressed as lamb. Is it worth getting sane for that?'

Vicky half-laughed and prepared to leave.

Her mother said, 'I know the word. The one she kept calling out. Mody. Mody.' And she started calling it as she had heard it in that grey place, endless, with nothing around it. The nurses came running.

· *Thirty-nine* ·

Lorraine drove her to the airport. 'To a degree, I'm clairvoyant but it's not very developed. It helps me a lot in my work. I can tell what to avoid, what will come up roses.'

Vicky did not think it had helped with her choice of men. 'So, what is it like to be psychic?'

'You tune in to people and know things about them by something other than your usual five senses. You see things. It's not like thinking, or making an effort. It's like a vivid imprint on your mind, that you can recall instantly and exactly at any time. A psychic impression is quite different from the usual thinking process and has different colour, a clearer shape and doesn't fade, whereas a thought is lost or, if recalled, vague. And, up to a point, you know what's going to happen to people. But they do have free will and can change the future, you see, except for the chosen experiences which they have to pass through: the events selected by the Lords of Karma, or by yourself before birth. You learn from these events or repay previous mistakes and crimes.'

'What do you feel about me, Lo?'

'What I'm saying. You've got to put right previous wrongs.'

'So I have to pay for my past actions. Alright, I had a terrible childhood. My mother was ill and my father unloving and I was alone. I went through that, didn't I?'

'Vicky, you pay but you don't choose the manner of paying. Only God decides that.' Lorraine was outraged. 'So you were unhappy and didn't complain too much. Put that on the asset list. But you're not the judge of your actions. When that man comes into your mind, kick him out! D'you understand?'

Had Vicky mentioned seeing the painter? 'So Jay's been talking.'

'It's too big a deal to worry about who said what. Save yourself! Tell him to go back to his place of rest. Otherwise he's going to ruin your life.'

'But he's the one I most want to see.'

'Vicky, he's a spirit not at rest!'

'Could he be in that place called the ethera?'

'We could all be there,' snapped Lorraine. 'It's a state of consciousness between here and the spirit realms. I'm not an afterlife estate agent but don't go there. It's limbo. Put him out of your mind now and concentrate on what you've actually got, while you've got it. Don't let Serge Marais feel ignored. They're queueing up to take your place.'

· *Forty* ·

She had to wait to see Serge when she arrived at the hotel in Rome. Although it was after midnight he was surrounded by business associates in a private salon and the Canadian was keeping guard. Was he punishing her for staying away for over five days?

When he finally came up to the suite he was in a sharp mood, distracted by the subject of the unstable tapes with an eight-year lifespan. Did he go ahead and sell what had already been filmed, with the chance it would dissolve in a few years? Or did he re-shoot everything again on different tape? Was that, in turn, reliable?

He said, 'Well, Vicky, don't unpack too much. We're off first thing.'

'Off where? This *is* first thing.'

'Paris.'

She closed her eyes in disbelief. 'Shall I bother going to bed?'

'Oh, yes, let's bother with that.' And he pushed her so she fell backwards across the large, luxurious bed. 'I've been holding it back. All for you.'

He made love to her and that took care of the rest of the night.

When breakfast was wheeled in at seven he said, 'So, how's the feature film?'

She was too tired for deception. 'I'm not doing one.'

'I know that. Why don't you do something for radio?'

She could not think of anything to say.

'You originally wanted to do a documentary about me. Well,

do it.' He opened his arms theatrically and laughed. She thought it was a good idea because it would keep her mind very much on the present. He liked it because it would keep her very near him.

'You've seemed a little way off, Vicky.' That was not quite true. She had seemed a very long way off. 'Why not concentrate on what you feel you know, get back your identity? And we can work on the documentary together as we travel.'

She said her distant behaviour was caused by jet-lag and getting used to the new life. There was nothing to worry about. Being distant was all in the past. She hoped he had not been snooping around in the metal box and reading the notes meant for Jay.

How she wanted to make a good life for him, and allow herself happiness. As Lorraine said, 'If the painter comes into your mind, kick him out.'

She did better than that. When Serge left the room she prayed to God to keep all spirits away from her. She needed guidance to lead a good life.

For her engagement present Serge gave Vicky a locket which had belonged to his mother and asked for all the works of art to be returned to him. He was now safe because Anna had signed all his agreements. The first part of the divorce was through and on the day of its completion, April 6th, he would marry Vicky.

'You want all the collection back?'

'Of course. Except the Matisse which I gave to you.'

They were sitting on the terrace of the rented Bel Air house, surrounded by cedar trees. It was cool for December but the sun was bright. He wore a long grey cardigan and silk scarf and gold signet ring on his little finger.

She now believed prayer worked. Every night she asked for the spirit that haunted her to be kept away. She half-expected him to come into her mind during relaxed times, but he did not. It was as though he was aware of her decision and acknowledged her right to make it.

Serge said, 'I've made my will. I want you to know that. I'm forty-nine and conductors usually live till they're ninety. But, just in case I get run over by a bus, you're well taken care of. I want you to know that. So are my children, Anna, her parents and, of course, any children we will have.' He looked at her, waiting. 'Well, we might, mightn't we? People do.' And he reached across and stroked her with the tips of his fingers. She grabbed his hand, his hair, and they made love violently on the terrace, her body now in a furore of excitement. Afterwards, he said, 'Don't be frightened about making noise. Don't stop.'

'But they can hear. The staff.'

'So? It's my house. You do exactly what you want to do. Go on.' He smiled, teasing her. 'I'm sure you want more.'

She felt hungry for violence and slashed her nails down his back, drawing blood. She clawed the inside of his thighs. Then she looked up, subdued, and said, 'I'm sorry.'

He was looking into her face, liking what he saw, interested in her expession. 'No, go on. You do it if you want to.'

'But it hurts you.'

He made a dismissive gesture. 'Hardly. A few scratches won't hurt me. Go on. More.'

'But why do I want to do it?'

'It's a primitive urge. You want to leave your mark on what's yours.' He, too, wanted her to do more, to make it as earthy, dirty, lustful as she knew how. Afterwards, he said, 'Who taught you about sex? Jay?'

'Jay!' She laughed. 'It's just in me. I don't know.'

'Were you aware of your parents' sexuality?'

'Not at all.'

'So you read books about it?'

She shrugged.

'Come on, Vicky. You're not just born with it in your head, are you?'

She thought, in my case, probably. She said, 'You bring it out of me. Incidentally, who brought it out of you?'

'You,' he said.

She got up off the terrace, put her high-heeled shoes on and went naked into the house. He was obsessed with her body, had photographed it from every angle. How he wished he could have recorded that last act on the balcony. He had expected to get tired of her, jaded, yet he could never get enough of her.

In the bedroom she was splayed back across the bed, one arm over her head, her eyes all-knowing, full of sin, watching him. He wished he had some sexual energy left to do justice to what he was feeling.

'What are you thinking about?' he asked.

'I wasn't.' She did not move. Sometimes she stayed so still, always to advantage, as though someone was watching her, as though she was posing. It was especially noticeable in Paris. She would sit in certain positions and then he could say she did not belong to him. She would sit as though hypnotized, looking into space or inwards, at what?

'I want to settle somewhere and have a home, don't you?'

She said yes.

'I've been offered something I really would like to do. A musical director's job for six months. I only do ten concerts, and –'

She waited.

'And I can put together the whole home movie company right there, with new tapes and –'

'Where?'

'Paris.'

She was appalled.

'It really works for me, that place. And I think that now your film has done well, it will change for you.'

'Do you?' she said softly.

The horse film had collected some fairly good reviews. It was a strong, original, uncompromising piece of work. She did not think it would make a sou of difference to Paris. Their last, brief, trip had been . . .

'You know, Serge, I think it's one unlucky town for me.' She was trying to be very honest with him within the limitations of her problem.

'Try and overcome it. It's only a city.'

'Oh, but it isn't.'

'Did something bad happen to you there?'

She thought, my heart broke. She said nothing.

'If I want to go and you love me you would come too. For me.' His voice was coaxing, so seductive. 'It's only six months, after all.'

She could feel that distress in the air, coming up from the drains, the despair coming up off the cobbled sidestreets, the sun, never more beautiful, as it reminded her of a time that was gone. In Paris, she felt obliged to mourn. She said, 'I won't go near anything that doesn't reek of reality.'

Of course, she knew there was more to his desire to work there than he had said. The Russian pianist, the prodigy she had first heard about from Micky Duke, had defected to the West. He was the wonderboy who excelled in Mozart, the one Serge Marais feared. Every country wanted him but the boy had chosen Paris, a city he could trust and love. Serge, in a shrewd move, had grabbed his rival by discreetly letting it be known he was prepared to conduct the boy's first series of concerts. His offer had been seized upon immediately and the Parisians prepared for what would be the musical event of the decade. Serge made one stipulation: the boy would be under contract to his own recording company. Serge would make sure he received full credit for his guidance and later, while listening to the performances, it would be difficult to discern who was the greater, the prodigy or the conductor. Serge would make sure of that.

'Of course I want him in my grasp,' he had admitted to Anna. 'He can embrace the mountain. I have never truly got near it.' He meant Mozart. He said nothing of his manipulations to Vicky. With her, he discussed the wedding.

'So, who shall we invite?'

'But you've done the list.'

'My people. What about yours? Who will be matron of honour?'

She laughed. 'Kirsty Cobb.'

'Oh, Miss Cobb! Who else?'

She could hardly ask her mother.

'Jay should come, if you agree? And what about your mother?'

'She doesn't travel well. She's very busy –'

'With what?' He spoke as though he was playing chess, always a move ahead.

Vicky thought, busy being sane.

'Why don't you make this a first time, too. Telling a man the truth.'

'If you know, why ask!' she snapped. She sounded, to her own ears, as sharp as Ruby.

'You tell me. You would if you trusted me.'

'I didn't want to tell a lover my mother was mad and violent. He might be put off and think I was the same.'

'Are you?' He smiled into her eyes, his own hypnotic and gleaming. 'Let your mother come to our wedding. She is your mother. We must have one mother there. Don't you think I could look after her, make her welcome?'

'Forget it, Serge. You don't know what you're asking.' How well she remembered Dean at the beginning, all humane and eager to embrace her mad mother. And how well she remembered him at the end; insulting, cruel.

'You don't want people to see what she's like. Is that what you're afraid of? If I accept her, Vicky, so will they.'

She could see he was trying to be nice, but to the wrong person about the wrong mother.

'You love her, don't you?'

'Nothing good ever came out of my being with her so let's leave it. I can get married without her help.'

'That's not very nice.' He closed up the backgammon board, and sat beside her on the floor. 'I want you to forgive her. You're happy enough for that, aren't you? Let it be your wedding present to me.'

'Serge, I can forgive myself. I can't forgive another person. Only they can do that.' She got up from the floor, away from him. He would be asking her to go to Paris again next.

He said, 'I need to go to Paris. I need to work with the Russian boy. I have to go immediately after Christmas because I want to get used to working with him and the orchestra. The first concert is scheduled for February 6th.' He used all his charm, all his captivating ways to win her. 'We need to be together, to sleep together. You know that. And I'll look after you.'

She knew he would try. But even all his advantages couldn't keep her safe. Worldly acclaim meant nothing in the spirit world. If she went back she knew she would be damned.

· *Forty-one* ·

To Vicky, travelling was the most obvious feature of her life with Serge. She went to a gym to build up her stamina, took all the minerals and vitamins that he did, let him guide her in meditation and yoga. But he was a harmonious person who could be himself anywhere and she was not. The constant changes in atmosphere, temperature, language and time made her fractious. They had their first quarrel in Milan. He had taken her to the best fish restaurant there, famous throughout Italy, and given her a ring. It was set with all the right jewels and a message of love engraved on the band.

'Yes, it is incredible,' he agreed. 'And it costs more than the painting Anna thinks she's going to sell well at Sotheby's. I measured it for her and every square centimetre has now increased in value from last year by four hundred dollars.' He felt awkward all of a sudden. 'She always used to say to me, don't tell me to buy a painting because I like it. Tell me what it's worth. Or she'd say, Don't talk about liking art; just the money it makes. She'd have made a fabulous dealer. I've made more money by speculating in art than anything else.'

Vicky felt lowered, depressed and, for the first time, wasn't pleased to be with Serge. She did not want to ask which painting it was that Anna was selling. She dreaded hearing it was a Modigliani.

'Do you like paintings, Serge?'

'Of course.'

'In what way?'

'What kind of question is that?'

'Do they excite you? Enrich your experience?'

'Don't tell me you're one of those people who thinks works of art should be on show to anyone in museums for free!'

'Yes, I think I am one of those people.' She was angry.

'I promise you, I look after my paintings better than a public museum because I have more money than they do. Also, they don't get stolen. I show them publicly when asked. In fact, I've made that a stipulation in my will.'

'Do you like them?'

'Of course. They've made me rich.' He laughed. 'Oh, Vicky, of course they're an investment. They're also, in some cases, works of perfection. And, as you know, I like perfection, or the attempt at it.'

'You don't like paintings, Serge. You're jealous of them because they are immortal.'

Stung, he said, 'I have never heard you speak like that before and I don't like it.'

'Exactly. They go on forever.'

He took her outside into the unseasonable rain and they had their first fight. After that, he spent a great deal of time on his films, trying to achieve the best possible reproduction of all his recordings and concerts.

It was ironic that he, at the height of his career, was losing something that a painter, at gutter level, could only gain. In whatever circumstances the painter left the earth, the work remained. Serge was haunted by Vicky's jibe about immortality.

Again he brought up the subject of Paris.

She had been spending a lot of time trying to keep her future separate from her past, but finally she saw she would not have a future with Serge if she did not give in. She would have to go to Paris. He needed to dominate her, needed her acquiescence and her pleasure in submitting to him.

So she said yes to Serge and to Paris. She said to herself, 'Whatever made me think I'd become lucky?'

Kirsty Cobb came to Los Angeles and asked Vicky to lunch. She was a new person, she said. And it was all thanks to Vicky.

'I still go to the healer. He's changed the vibration I put out. You know, we all send out a signal which attracts a corresponding signal. Change it and you change what you attract. Well,

I've just attracted a brand new job here in L.A., producing prime-time movies, two dozen slots a year. And I need an assistant. You have first offer. I've stopped drinking. I don't even think about him. I've even forgiven myself for becoming a public fool.'

Vicky said she looked fabulous.

'Now all I've got to do is find a man and have a baby. Well, Lorraine has taught us all about happy endings.' She sounded sarcastic. She admitted to Vicky that she knew her invitation was unrealistic because it would not leave enough time for Serge Marais. 'I have to say, I'm amazed you netted the Maestro. These wives are no slouches when it comes to a fight. They give a little rope and the guy thinks he's free. Then they tug him back with responsibilities, the kids, the mortgage.'

'Kirsty, every married man is different.'

'Yes, everyone's different, but it's funny how the same thing keeps happening. You know, I really would like you to work for me. I could be pretty flexible about time and you'd get a free hand. After all, I thought that's what you wanted, to make movies. Or are you just going to grace his days sitting around the hotel, château, or penthouse, a visitor in his life?'

'Why do you want me?'

'Because in a quiet way you're ruthless.'

Vicky felt hurt. 'I spend most of my time actually being supportive to other people. And I shut up about it. Is that ruthless?'

'I appreciate that. Point taken. I called and you came. But you also swanned around Paris selling my secrets, or trying to, in my name. That's an example of ruthlessness.'

'You said I could. You were drunk at the time.'

'I'm never that drunk. You'll say anything, do anything, to get what you truly want. I don't even think you have a choice. You'd die for what you want.'

'I don't feel anything like the person you describe.'

'Of course not,' Kirsty said swiftly. 'We never see ourselves as others see us. Are we right or are they? You choose.'

'I've been called some things in my time but never ruthless, except by you. Twice. You seem to think you know me, Kirsty.'

'Just watching you, Miss Graham. That's all it takes.' And Kirsty noticed her eyes changed when challenged. Hurting bright, like diamonds, and just as hard.

They sat in silence. Vicky felt abused, almost violated. 'All you've got against me is that I have had some fun. I've slept with some big names and you're jealous.'

'Endless submission to act out their fantasies. Perhaps I see you so well because you don't see yourself. You do it by numbers – living. Little neat moves, a competent job in the recording studio, a look up to God every night to make sure everything's alright, save a life here, stroke a cat there. Come on, Vicky, just tell me you're a very together, ruthless person.'

Now they were staring at each other. Did Kirsty resent Vicky for having saved her life? Was that the problem? Vicky got up to go. 'I think, if you don't mind, I'll exist in the quarter-inch of top soil I know about, ignore the acres of ruthlessness beneath and not come to work for you, thank you.'

'Perhaps it is better you keep it all in, Vicky. I'd hate to be around the day you let your wolf out.'

Serge had a stop-over in New York and took the opportunity to complete some negotiations with his wife. Jay took Vicky to dinner in Chinatown. He was dressed in a well-cut blue-black suit and blue shirt, his hair was glossy, his face pale and matt, a face you wanted to look at. He looked like a winner and everyone in the place knew it. He was involved again. This time it was an aerobics instructor with a body as pared down and purposeful as a machine.

'Am I ruthless?' said Vicky.

'Depends.'

She told him about Kirsty Cobb.

'Why listen to her? She's obsessed with an unattainable man. That leaves quite a lot of room for bitterness. Plus you go to Paris using her name and – the irony of it – hook a married superstar!'

'Sometimes people talk about me as though I'm not really here. Like I'm a negative not a photograph. I know my mother had a hard time having me and she should never have had a child—'

'Oh, Vicky, come on! Are we in a perfect world all of a sudden?'

'According to a lot of beliefs, before our birth we choose our parents and so take some of the responsibility for our destiny. I'm not sure I even know what ruthless means.'

'To Kirsty it means you'll do anything to get what you want – to the death. She sees that in you. I don't. But I could find you determined if I thought about it. You're very well behaved and centred with me, but I don't give you any stress. I don't know how you'd be if it all got out of hand. Maybe she's upset because you succeeded where she didn't, with a very married man. She accuses you of tricks. She was herself, no tricks, and got the boot.'

'She said I'd never let go, not when it was time to leave. She talked about me as though I was familiar.'

He waited for her to continue but she looked dazed. She was seeing the junction of the two boulevards and the traffic going slowly because of the rain. It was windy and he was coughing, his coat hanging open. The Polish woman, Lunia, was standing there, the central figure, with her hair scraped up. There was a horrible argument in progress and she felt desolate. Everyone was listening to the elegant Lunia and the cough went on rattling, like gunfire. Of course, he was going with her, the stylish clever woman. There was something definable between them, something there in the eyes and the way they looked at each other, or did not look. Whether they had slept together or not, the thought was there. He could so easily leave with that woman. And she, Vicky, felt raw emotion, pain, thoughts churning. It was agreed Modi should go. Lunia leaned across and with familiarity, turned his coat collar up to try and keep him warm.

Go! She could not be left! It was unthinkable. And her stomach heaved and the baby heaved inside her.

So, he is going for his health. That's what they said. Back to Nice with Lunia.

And she looked at the sophisticated Lunia and wanted to scratch her, maim her, stop her. They were saying he needed the sun, to get away from Paris, to stop drinking and smoking, and that she was the one who had brought him down to this level of chemical dependence. That is what they meant. She could not control him, only add to his disastrous list of responsibilities, bringing yet more into the world. And he was looking at her, his eyes gleaming softly in the night. Life when he was not in it was not bearable. She said, 'You can't leave me. I'm having a baby.'

And he gave a big Italian shrug and chose to die with her rather than live a little longer with Lunia. Lunia slipped some money, the money which would have paid his fare, into his hands and ran towards the boulevards, her face wet with rain and tears.

Vicky did not eat any more food and longed to get away. Where to? Jay was still deftly using his chopsticks. 'You're leaving all this?' he said.

'It's come back – Paris.'

'D'you want to leave?'

'It doesn't make any difference. Finish your meal.'

After Lunia had left he went to the Rotonde with the train fare. He wanted to be on his own. He looked solemn and the others looked at her as much as to say, now look what you've done. They were not French, any of them, except Zbrowski's maid, Paulette. Modi's friends were Russian, Polish, Italian, an Arab. Utrillo was French but he was in the mental hospital.

'Maybe I have to learn to let go. To let the loved person choose. He has free will. Yet I could never have let Modi go. I'd have followed him to the ends of the night.'

She sat, quite forlorn, all the longings of the past stirring inside her. It was worth it, all the blackness, to have had just a moment of belonging to him. He was mine, I was his.

Jay had asked a question. 'What happens if Serge Marais leaves you?'

She answered rationally, 'I hope I don't have to find out.' And she remembered the first night, seeing him on television, and the feeling she had experienced. He was the only light in considerable darkness and she would have done anything to reach him. She had promised herself that. So that was ruthless. She had pursued him and got him. She may or may not have taken him from his wife – she believed you could only take someone if they were inclined to come.

'So, if I am ruthless, even though I don't know it, why am I fussing around, trying to do the right thing, trying to do good? I don't know myself. Do other people? I might as well be really bad and get something out of it.'

'D'you think he might leave?' asked Jay.

'You don't think he loves me?'

'Oddly, I think he does. But when the blaze of sexuality wears down who knows what will be left. Put some of the housekeeping cash to one side and keep all your options open. Don't turn down any jobs. It's a long time till April 6th.'

· *Forty-two* ·

Jeanne Hebuterne, born on April 6th 1898, was a Catholic and she fell in love with a drunken, debauched, Sephardic Jew, penniless and dying. Her parents were bourgeois, her father worked as a cashier in the perfume department of the Bon Marché store. Jeanne's brother, André, a couple of years older, went to art school and shortly afterwards Jeanne was allowed to join him. She became Modigliani's mistress at Easter time 1917, just before Simone Thiroux gave birth to the son he refused to acknowledge. He made love to Jeanne and painted her, in hotels and studios across Paris. Finally, her parents threw her out and she went to live with him.

In March 1918, to escape the Big Bertha bombing of Paris and to improve Modigliani's health, they went to Nice. The trip was arranged by Modi's dealer, Zbo, and he brought his wife, Hanka, and some other artists along. Jeanne's mother also accompanied them. Jeanne was pregnant. Modi nearly missed the train because he was in the station buffet buying enough bottles to last him the long journey.

In Nice trouble began between Jeanne's mother and Modi and soon he moved to Cagnes and stayed with various friends. Zbo could not sell his paintings in Nice and had to return, penniless, to Paris. Modi soon followed, leaving Jeanne behind, pregnant again. She arrived at the end of June interrupting his sojourn with Lunia. Jeanne and Modi spent their remaining days in the studio at the top of 8, Rue de la Grande Chaumière. Their baby daughter was sent to the country to be cared for by a nurse. Modi considered going to Italy as soon as the next child was born. He believed his mother could help him recover his health and in November, Lunia tried to persuade him to go with her to the Midi and try to get well but Jeanne did not want him to go. He stayed in Paris and, in the icy winter, courted death on the streets. He died of tubercular meningitis on January 24th, 1920. Jeanne was taken to the hospital where she kissed Modi goodbye and left, her eyes on his face, as though she never wished to see anything else. Then she went to the mortuary where she slapped Simone Thiroux who was also visiting her dead lover, and to Zborowski's flat, where she held Paulette's hand and said, 'Please don't leave me.' Paulette later said it seemed something terrible had happened to her in that last week. Jeanne was booked to have her baby in the Tarnier Clinic but it was decided her father would take her to the family home in Rue Amyot. A friend of hers, Stanislaw Fumet, saw her walking with her father past the Panthéon and said she looked as though she was sleep-walking. She was put in the servant's room on the fifth floor while her family argued about what was to be done with her. They could not allow her to stay in their care. She had brought shame and disgrace to their lives. She had nothing from the penniless painter, not even marriage. At four o'clock in the morning she took her life, throwing herself out of the window.

Vicky knew Jeanne had fallen backwards. Modi was familiar with old Greek, loved Greek temples, caryatids. He would have known the Greek customs and told her, when a Greek took his life, he fell backwards, so seeing what he was leaving and how far he had come. And she could see him say, 'Go backwards, towards me, and see what you're leaving behind.'

Vicky thought a great deal about the facts of Jeanne's life, which she had compiled from the available books and felt the information was not right. There was no chance that Jeanne would let Modigliani simply return to Paris, leaving her. He would have said he would go for a day or two to arrange a place to live and then come back and get her. Yes, that felt right. Yet she waited with the baby and the nurse in Nice, already feeling ill with the second pregnancy, and there he was, silent, in Paris. She knew, how she did, that Lunia was there. And he was fascinated by Lunia and didn't drink while with her. Finally, when he did not return, she had to send a telegram asking for her train fare and that of the nurse. Modi agreed to marry her, at least he wrote a declaration. How she could feel his sensuality, how it drew the women. He could have them for nothing.

Jeanne was trapped with the burden of pregnancy. Did he want the child? Either the first or the one to be born? She saw the studio where her body was finally laid. Women tidied it, collected the bottles, swept up the coal and the sardine tins. And his drawings, and hers, were all over the floor, and the uncashed cheque from Italy with his mother's last letter. She saw a priest waving a censer in the studio before her body was taken downstairs for burial and she knew his face. So often he had tried to reason with her about spiritual obligation and salvation. She should love God above a man and honour her family. She could not, a young Catholic, go off with a non-Catholic and fornicate and bear him children out of wedlock, not christened into the church. She knew it all. Oh, how she did. They had all tried to persuade her to give him up, but her wise heart stayed with the one she loved.

In one of the books, Idenaum said, 'Jeanne was always searching and then she found him, and the search was over. She loved him in a way that could only be acceptable to Modigliani. It was a love that was made for him. He, in turn, loved her because she was the unique woman for him. That is why she loved this impoverished, sick artist, past his best, obviously with the mark of death upon him. And he loved her, this young, not particularly extrovert girl, so unlike Beatrice Hastings or La Quique.'

Vicky thought, I loved him because I already knew him, as he did me. We had known each other in earlier lives. We had found each other again for a short time.

· Forty-three ·

Vicky's life was like a switchback in a fairground. High, low, excitement, exhaustion, she was always out of control. She was swept back and forth across the world as the Maestro made guest appearances, attended royal banquets, was awarded honours and prizes at crowded, incomprehensible ceremonies.

The bedroom was still their sanctuary and his appetite was insatiable. She was expected to buy the clothes he liked and wear them for the sexual act, be beautifully made-up at all times. She was to keep her jet-lag and exhaustion to herself, although she had yet to find a way to adjust her body clock to each new country through which she flitted. Once, at a banquet in the Far East, she had fallen asleep, head first, in her plate. Tireless, Serge slept only five hours a night whereas she needed eight.

The past caught her anywhere. Hurtling on and off planes, at the same time hurtling in and out of Paris boulevards between 1900 and 1920, the visions came in full colour without any sound. She could hear Jay say, 'Take Vitamins B and C for jet-lag in large doses. It's your circadian rhythm that's thrown out. I'll try and get you something out of the research lab.' And, in the same way, she could hear another voice, rasping, angry, sometimes soft, seductive, even full of tenderness. She understood the meaning, if not the words. Did her mind do a quick translation? Or maybe the spirit of this man, wherever he was, approached her in a language she understood. She tried to see him. She would recapture the hot room with the fly beating against the panes of glass, or the café terrace where she would go looking for him, and he would be passed out on a bench or in a yard. And she would see no more. She saw only what she was given.

They lay on the bed in the muggy January of Los Angeles, watching a young prize-winning pianist play Tchaikovsky. Serge was full of disdain, not at the pianist but at the choice of music. 'There are some things I couldn't touch. That is sentimental to the point of nausea. It's all so sugary, isn't it? What do you think?' He allowed a pause. 'What are you thinking, Vicky?'

'Thinking?' Asking the question again always gave her time to find an answer, he noticed.

'You were miles away.'

Years away. She had been back in the city where Modigliani appeared outlined against the sky. Trees around him were in blossom. He had the tricks of a tinker, the mind of a scholar, the imagination of a genius, but innocence too. People had made him cruel. He came towards her, smiling, and she knew she was loved. He had an elegance and charm, however bad he felt, even when dirty, tired, depressed. And her heart leaped like a young puppy as she reached out to join him. He untied his red scarf and knotted it around her neck and she could smell cigarette smoke and Pernod. He was so close he almost came through the frame to meet her.

Serge tapped her head and said something.

'Nice,' she said. 'I was thinking about Nice.'

'If you want, we can still go.'

She wanted never to go. If Paris was full of memories what would Nice be like?

'After all, we'll be in Paris soon, so –' he made a decisive gesture. 'I will take you wherever you want.'

She looked at him and gave a sweet smile, her eyes full of a dreamy love. It was not an expression he would associate with her. It belonged on a woman who knew she was mysterious and used it.

'I've asked the office in Paris to look for a house so we can make a new start. Because you don't like the city I'm quite happy to live in the provinces, say, twenty miles out. Paris brings out the best in me. I will do my best work there. I know now is the time for me really to find out what I can do. I've cut the performances after April, to ten a year at the most.'

'You love Paris, don't you, Serge?'

'I feel very happy there. I think you should try and overcome your bad reaction. It's only a place.'

But it was not. Its very beauty threatened her. As far as she was concerned it was Satanic material and her only weapon to fight it with was Serge's presence.

· *Forty-four* ·

Back in Los Angeles, up under the cedar trees, Vicky roamed the garden. Serge had gone with friends to the beach, chasing the last of the sun and sea before life began in wintry Paris. Vicky had just finished a breakdown for the documentary on Serge to be broadcast on Radio 3. She had listed the people she needed to interview, including friends still living in Romania. She wanted to get hold of material recorded when he had been working with Toscanini. She started a second list, the influences on Serge Marais' life, then felt tired, a deep tiredness that drew her into the house, into the bedroom. She closed the blinds and fell back across the king-size bed like a tree axed. Gradually, her body accepted the luxury of having to do nothing and her mind slowed. She could almost be asleep. But although she burned with tiredness she could not sleep.

She rolled over on the white and silver duvet onto her stomach, then onto her other side, and so rolled against his body. Her eyes were shut and she said, 'Don't tell me it's time for the plane already? I haven't slept at all.'

He did not speak. Had he come back from the beach to make love before the farewell dinner? She put an arm across his thighs and pressed her head down against his hip. She was in no mood for sex. There was not one piece of her alive enough for arousal, let alone orgasm. The jet-lag had finally taken its toll. 'I can't,' she said.

The material of the trousers was wrong: it was slightly ribbed. Then she smelt cigarette smoke, alcohol, paint, garlic, and a perfumed toilet water amongst it all. She could feel the texture of his shirt, of his trousers and the well-made thighs inside them.

She was terrified. How would he look, coming back from death? And then she felt his hand stroking her hair and all of it changed, became charged with energy and a desire that was almost agonizing in its intensity. She rolled to and fro against him and his hand slid under her skirt, between her thighs and finally he began to give her so much pleasure she cried out. It was all so familiar, so necessary. He kissed her breasts and that gave her an orgasm. She wanted to open her eyes and see him and, at the same time, was frightened of how he would look. She heard his clothes drop to the floor. Now he was on her, holding her backwards in an arched position so the penetration was total. He fucked her hard, brutally, and she was on her way to a very long, high climax.

'Now, say you want it. Do it.' His voice was quite sober. She knew exactly what he wanted. He clawed her thighs, they were hot, burning, and she had to hold back because she knew so well what he liked, how he wanted to climax. But she was coming and it felt like a huge tidal wave rolling in from a long way away. She kept him in her and clawed him and cried out, and coolly he said, 'Look at me. Come on.' He put his penis against her mouth and came over her face and hair. It ran into her mouth, and she closed her eyes tighter against the gush of warm, sticky liquid, the smell of it so strong.

'Look at me!' His voice was hoarse from cigarettes and he was stroking her cheek. Something about his voice was irresistible. 'Do what I say. You have to do what I tell you. You'd die with me if I asked you to. Open your eyes.'

She felt his body, satin-skinned, well-toned. He kissed her face, small fluttery kisses then a long one, drawing at her mouth, his tongue deep against hers, the fringe of his eyelashes brushing her cheek. She felt the waviness of his thick hair into which he combed eau de cologne like all Continentals. How she had longed for this closeness. All her life. It was a memory she was born with. No one had remotely satisfied this hunger. And her face creased slightly as she started to cry.

'Don't!'

She remembered that he hated her crying.

She felt downwards to his pubic hair, and with her hand on him she opened her eyes.

There was no one there.

She sat up, shocked. Her blouse was ripped and she was dishevelled. Had she experienced a dream in which she had had a sexual climax and torn her clothing? But she could smell the semen. It was on her skin. And there was a faint smell, ever decreasing, of sweat and alcohol. She leapt out of the bed and ran into the garden. She ran to the wild shrubbery beyond the trees.

And she screamed, 'Modi!'

She insisted Serge conduct Mozart. Why should he be trapped by a residual fear of not being good enough? 'Do it. And you don't need the Russian playing. You're good enough yourself.'

He was amused by her attempts to stimulate him and surprised she was so forceful. She certainly had a way with her about anything blocking him, which was odd because she did not know anything about music except that she liked it.

After Modi had been kicked out of the Rotonde, she found him in the Dôme, in the afternoon. He loved her exotic turban, influenced by the Russian ballet. Bakst was everywhere. And she insisted he use the colour red in his paintings. Bright red. Was he scared of it? 'Do it for me.'

He had said it was not a colour he used.

'Use it!' And the next time he painted her she wore a red skirt and made him enjoy it, the colour. And she made him enjoy taking the red clothes off her afterwards.

Serge was sitting at the piano, striking chords, faster, faster, and the sound jarred. He saw the panic in her eyes as Paris 1917 was shattered. The fear flickered, then was gone. He asked if she was alright and she smiled beautifully, a big smile with her teeth showing. And, quite casually, she said, 'I'm doomed.'

'That's a very big word for a little girl, no?' He played a Brahms melody very quietly and as his eyes watched her, he thought, yes, there is something short-lasting about her, as though she'll expire before her next breath. Is that why I love her? Because she can never come between me and what I need to do? Was that her great attraction, being transitory, like a marvellous flower with a short but intense life? And afterwards he could live off the memory of what they had shared and there would be no need to take another wife. What freedom!

Later he hated himself for what he had thought and blamed the unusual humidity of the weather. She was a marvellous companion, always there but not intrusive. Occasionally they spent half-an-hour on the radio documentary about his life. She asked questions about music which he enjoyed because it made it all seem fresh again for him. Serge was amused by her insistence.

'But Mozart is so perfect. You know what they say? Beethoven goes to heaven, Mozart comes from heaven.'

She persuaded him well enough to play some Mozart on the piano and after a while he agreed to honour their wedding by conducting 'The Marriage of Figaro'.

The move to Paris was halted because Vicky had some kind of collapse. Serge, in bed beside her, could feel the heat leaving her body. He sat up, alarmed. Why had he not realized something was wrong? He had been lying there aware for an hour that she was not as she should be. Her hands and feet were like ice and she was completely still, her face a bluish-white, lips blacked. Nothing his mother had taught him seemed suitable for such a moment. He piled the bed with blankets and duvets and tried to spoon hot, sweet tea into her mouth. He rubbed her hands and feet, added a hot water bottle. The maid brought in an electric blanket.

Vicky spoke with effort. 'If you lie on top of me you'll give me your warmth.' And her eyes closed.

The doctor had to make some sort of diagnosis, so called it exhaustion compounded by shock. He thought, but did not say, that the future Madame Marais seemed stoical about her condition, as thought it was not a surprise to her at all. He would have expected more reaction. But then, he was used to the women of Bel Air.

Serge instinctively knew she had been near a crisis and decided to stop work instantly to be with her. He tried everything to reassure her. 'Forget about Paris. We're not going. Try and sleep.'

But, as usual these days, it was to Paris that her mind was drawn. He was her fix. She walked along the dark path towards him, where he waited in even greater darkness. And she threw off self-restraint, self-containment, like an old coat, a heavy coat, unnecessary in this sweet, balmy night. He made love to her under the trees, fantastic love that made her cry out.

'So he likes it, that man. Likes to take what's mine.' His voice was sharp and piercing. 'How else did you know all that?' He slapped her face. 'What you do to him, I taught you. I brought it out of you.' He pulled at the locket, her engagement present from Serge. 'Take it off. Don't you remember what I gave you? That's the only jewellery you will ever wear. That's what you said.' Then he lay on his side, all anger gone, smiling at her with such sweetness.

'High, low, dark, light. That's what you are,' she said.

In the morning she wondered if she had dreamed the love-making with the Italian. But her locket was on the floor, its chain broken.

The day after the night of lost heat she could not get up and Serge suggested she stay in bed and sleep. In the afternoon, Jay sat with her. 'He's gone off to talk with the laboratory. He's worried to death,' said Jay.

'I'm not that bad.'

'About his compact recordings and videos. I've just told him some more bad news. He wants whatever he does to be eternal. How about you?'

'Did you just happen to pay a visit?'

'No, he called me. I think he thought you were like a compact disc too, about to erase. I told him it was probably some female thing. It's Paris, isn't it?'

She said, 'I think I understand what Paris means, now. It wasn't that I was bitterly sad because I'd been unhappy there and couldn't get over it. That's what I thought at first. But I was heart-broken because what I loved was no longer there on the streets, in the cafés. Would never be there again. It was gone forever, the much-loved.'

'There's no proof, Vicky. There are only your feelings and what you see. The psychics offer evidence that sounds credible and give explanations that come from indisputable sources, or that's how they make it sound. A priest would make it sound different. So would a psychiatrist.'

She said quite simply, 'I belong to him.'

And she did look different, softer, her eyes so alive. She looked like a woodland animal, and as vulnerable. Jay knew he had to fight for her.

'But you're here, in 1989, and you're meant to be living this life, Vicky, and be grateful for it. What you're doing is rejecting life. That's wrong. You're denying God's gift. In your worst hell you must still see God's glory.'

'How do you know all that, Jay?' She was surprised.

'I've always known it.' He, too, seemed surprised at his words.

She could see her situation was, in fact, a battle between passion, clinging, attachment and a going forward into a freer state where there was less elation and closeness but more wisdom.

'At least think about going to Paris, Vicky. Give it a try.'

Serge's favourite pianist was performing with the Los Angeles symphony orchestra the following week. 'And it's Mozart. So let's go,' he said. Afterwards, he wanted to arrange a celebration dinner. Would she be well enough?

She had refused to have medical tests. She had also told him she refused to go to Paris.

'I'll go to the concert, though. Does that make it better?'

'Vicky, Vicky,' he cried softly. 'I love you. Why make me an enemy?' Was that what she had done?

She was happy, but not completely. Something was missing. A wondrous delight, absent. She looked at this well-dressed man, admired, received, every prize, goblet, plaque bestowed on him.

But she had known better, wilder, dizzying, marvellous joy, and it came from a drunk in the gutter. In him, all the notes of the universe were played like a rainbow, some so high they were almost unheard. The range belonged to a poet, a genius. And as she laughed, she could see him smile with the broken tooth. 'Not long now, cara.'

The Maestro said, 'You look so young all of a sudden.' It sounded like a reproach. 'Why don't you trust me? I'll make our marriage work. Maybe the answer is to live in Italy or Germany and I'll fly to Paris for three or four days a week.'

'Maybe the answer is I'm holding you back. Why don't you just say I'm like my mother and shut me away?'

'Do you want to be like your mother? Try if you want, but you're not. Your mother suffered from clinical depression. It's *her* illness. I don't see why you should be so defensive and ashamed. Just trust me. I'm wiser than you and a lot older. I'm not going to turn away from you because of something in your past. That all goes to make up the you I love. Do you love me enough to trust me?'

She shrugged: it could have meant anything.

'I'm sure you could tell me all about Paris. I know you feel you've had a bad experience there. But you can't allow a past life, if that's what it is, to stop your freedom of choice. It's the same as my block about Mozart. We shared that, didn't we? What do you think you did in Paris?'

She would never talk to him about that. It made even her mother seem lightweight.

'Can't you tell me who you think you were?'

She could see he was very curious.

She said. 'Past lives should not be known, Serge.'

'Why?'

'Because God, in His mercy, lets us come back here with a clean sheet, innocent again.'

'But it is a past life problem, isn't it? Paris?'

'I've tried, but my modern life isn't strong enough to keep the previous one out.' And she thought, that earlier time was sublime, desperate, reviled, elated and there's nothing I can do in Paris except be overwhelmed by its memories and pay with suffering. She said, 'I will never go to Paris again.'

*

The lights went down and Mozart's divine music lifted up over the auditorium. Serge took her hand in both of his and she felt safe. He loved her enough to accept what she was. He had proved that. He had cut his professional life in half, in quarters, so as to spend his days with her. The marriage was a serious commitment. He had arranged to take a house in Northern Italy and to fly to Paris for three days a week. He would concentrate on his videos and get the product on the market.

And she, in turn, knew him now. He was not a fantasy figure, an escape offered on television. He was a disciplined, controlled man who knew life was short and would make the best of it. She respected him and loved him. The other recent experience, which she had no explanation for, had spoiled things for a while. Of course they had never occurred when she was living a low and unlucky life. They had started the minute she found a love she could live with and that was reciprocated. She decided this was ironical, and clung onto Lorraine's advice. 'If that one comes into your mind, kick him out!'

Serge went backstage in the interval and she stayed with the guests who would be coming to dinner. She talked about recording techniques and the theory that each colour had sound. On Serge's advice she stayed away from musical discussion.

Towards the end of the programme, the man behind her leaned forwards. She could feel his breath against her ear. She looked at Serge but, absorbed by the performance, he noticed nothing. The man's lips moved against her ear and her eyes closed in pleasure.

'Meet me at our usual place. Come to me there,' he said softly.

'Where?' she whispered urgently.

'Oh, don't tell me you've forgotten.' He laughed. It was not an altogether pleasant sound. 'Place Calvaire. I'll be there.'

· *Forty-five* ·

When Serge came back from the beach he was taken aback to see Jay and Vicky bent over a map of Paris.

Vicky was looking at the map and wondering what it was that so terrified her. The names? Jardin du Luxembourg, St Anne's Hospital, Rue du Bac, then the blackest, Père Lachaise. She could hear the Polish dealer say, 'We'll take him to Père Lachaise. His brother wants the very best for him so bury him like a prince. Cover him in flowers.' She knew he was holding a telegram from the brother in Italy, but did not want to see it. She thought of the quais along the river, Angelina's teashop near the Tuileries, the Medici fountains. It was all beautiful, yet it all hated her, because she had done the unforgivable, killed herself while carrying a child. It was against nature, so nature, in turn, would be against her.

She folded the map. The Place Calvaire was not in Montparnasse but at the top of Montmartre.

'What is this?' said Serge. He looked at Jay, then back at Vicky. 'You're going to Paris?'

They did not answer.

'That's wonderful. You will go for him, Vicky, but not for me. Wonderful.'

Which 'he' did he mean? thought Jay. Not knowing how much she had told Serge, he said, 'She's not going for me either.' And he looked at Vicky – more explanation would have to come from her.

'It's not a visit, Serge, but an expiation.' She had decided to lay a cross, thin and golden, in the place where Jeanne's body had fallen.

'I will take a very bad view of it if you go,' said Serge. 'For weeks we have argued over Paris and you won. I've lost quite a lot by not living there. So the least you could do is put away that map.'

Jay was watching him walk away to his rehearsal room.

'Vicky, he doesn't like you and me going to Paris.'

'We'll go, just for the day. I can't go alone. You know that.' And she thought of Place Calvaire, the way he had whispered the name. Then she gave Jay the secret notes locked away in the film reel case. She just tossed them casually onto the cushion beside him. 'In case I don't get to write my life story, you do it – with these.'

'Oh, Vicky, for Crissake, I love you.'

He probably did, but the Maestro did too and still none of it was enough.

She went upstairs and looked at the abundance of luxury clothes laid out on the bed, Serge's cufflinks and watches and tie pins. They amounted to one thing – wealth. And she saw a table in a room full of paintings and people. A man was playing an accordion, girls were dancing, and a thin, pale man was reciting a poem. There was half a loaf of bread and some cut sausage on the table, several bottles of wine. And a good-looking, friendly man, with a face she knew so well, said, 'It's not a feast.'

Oh, but it was. It was a feast of life. Everyone in the room was so rich. They had everything: adventure, courage, companionship, hope, the way to be different. They knew how to enjoy themselves. They could make something of the moment. They had everything except the burden of riches. And the sun may or may not have shone in the room but it felt to her as though it did, because he was there, at the corner of the table with the thin poet. He, too, was pale, but mysterious and alive and everyone watched him. You could never have enough of that face, the mercurial expressions. She felt, looking at him, that this was as rich as life could be.

Tears splashed onto the luxury objects on the bed. Serge added a pile of jewelled cigarette cases, presents from admirers.

'Yes, you can cry. You deceive me and you're caught out. I tell you, Vicky, that if you go to Paris you'll really have something to cry about.'

· *Forty-six* ·

The night was beautiful. A fresh breeze was blowing and everything conspired to bring a lover to the place of his longing. Even the Butte was deserted apart from the Place du Tertre where tourists stood about in groups. The Place Calvaire looked out across Paris. It was a small area with trees, a bench, rather secret and secluded. It felt kind. Vicky leaned against the wall and looked over the city. The view was little changed from the one he must have seen – the Eiffel Tower, a blur of buildings, then fields, now more buildings. It was all the same. The iron rail in the middle, the iron street lamp on each platform were still there. She imagined Modigliani climbing the steps with Utrillo, drunk after a night at the Lapin Agile, clinging to the centre railing. Utrillo would be flung out of bars for not paying, for bad behaviour, getting too noisy, and Modi would buy hash pellets from the dealers in the Rue Lepic. Of course they starved. It was a way of life. And they all drank, except Picasso – his was not the path to self-destruction, and she was sure he was no friend of Modigliani's. Now she thought she knew why she had always felt a dislike for Picasso. He had won the worldly acceptance Modigliani had craved. Eleven o'clock struck on a church clock and still he did not come.

She got up and checked the name on the wall. Place Calvaire. She felt nothing. He was not there. Here was only the present and a longing for the past. Around the corner was the Rue Norvins where Modigliani had lived with Beatrice Hastings and, during a particularly drunken party, had thrown her through a window. She had read in the books how they fought, how he would hide from her and she from him, how they were both sexually jealous. Below were the streets with names she dreaded, Rue des Martyrs, Place des Abbesses. And yet, it was beautiful down there.

Midnight, and the early spring wind filled the trees, already in leaf. Again, she looked over at the flight of steps. She was sure this was the way he would approach. It was quite peaceful and she was not at all afraid. She thought quite calmly about Jeanne's last week in the studio in the Grande Chaumière. Why had she not called for help? Was it some terrible revenge because he still thought of Lunia, had considered leaving with Lunia, or others? Had she killed him by allowing him to die? Her mind was obstinate, gave no clues. It was flat, functioning in its topsoil, the way it was when she worked in radio, did shopping, made choices about everyday things. She waited alone in the Place Calvaire for several hours. He did not come.

Jay waited in the all-night brasserie in Pigalle. Vicky arrived and said, 'As soon as it's light we'll go to the Rue Amyot, Number eight, where Jeanne lived with her parents and brother. That's where she jumped, from the fifth floor. I want to lay a gold cross there, in the street. I'll recognize the exact place.' She felt agitated, as she always did in Paris, as though something bad was about to happen. She wanted to flee. Her instincts were not wrong. Under her breath, she said a prayer. Jay looked at her anxious face and wished they had never left America.

'Vicky, I don't want to kill the fun or anything, but you do have a fiancé who might be waiting for a call. Why don't we walk over to the Gare du Nord and get on the first train out of here?'

She liked the idea. Everything in her was ready to go. And then she thought of the studio and the dying man and she had to go and see it. She had to know.

'I'm going back to the Place Calvaire. He might come as it's getting light. I bet that's when he did most of his walking – he could hardly afford a cab home. Come with me, Jay.'

Life, for all its dizzying speed and luxury, was a thin grey skin. Colour began with Modi.

*

The Rue Amyot lay in the same direction as she had seen it in her mind, while looking at the body lying, dying, in a winter dawn. It was short and narrow. What surprised her was the happiness she felt. She turned the corner from the Rue Mouffetard into bright sunlight. She believed she had known happiness and optimism in the area. There was no fear or dread. In fact, she felt quite differently from the way she did in the other parts of town.

She stood opposite Number 8 and looked up at the fifth floor. This was the house from which she had taken her life. She had promised herself she would not force a response. She would either feel something or she would not. But all she felt was doubt. This was not the house. She wanted to go to the next one on the corner of the street. 'I don't care if it's ten or twelve. That's the one.' And now she sensed a familiarity. Above the corner house was the number 8 Bis. She stood in the doorway and looked opposite at a courtyard with trees, then right and left along the road as she would have done in the years before 1920. She was greedy to go inside.

'But this is not Number eight,' said Jay. 'The research says eight.'

'Eight B,' she said. 'And she did not fall into the courtyard opposite either, as the books said. It was here, in the street.'

Standing in the sun she felt utterly light-hearted. She did not want to leave. The terrible night long ago was quite forgotten. She realized that Jeanne Hebuterne had been a young girl, happy and looking forward to things, not at all cut off and strange as described in the biographies.

A man carrying a loaf pressed the button for the concierge and let himself into 8B. Vicky followed. A red painted stairway spiralled upwards in the left corner and the hallway was dominated by letter boxes. The man with the loaf had alerted his father, an old man, who appeared, aggressive and inquisitive, expecting trouble.

Vicky was instantly charming and explained she was doing a book about Jeanne Hebuterne. The man was intrigued. 'That was years ago, Madame. The Hebuternes are not in the area now.'

'This was the house from which she killed herself. From the fifth floor, wasn't it?'

He was surprised. 'A lot of people thought it was Number eight. But you are right.'

'And she landed there, in the street.'

'You know more about it than most around here. My father said it was just outside. People over the years assumed it must be the courtyard opposite but she did not do that kind of – jump.'

Of course not. Vicky knew she had toppled out backwards.

'Logically, it should have been into that courtyard opposite that she fell, seeing as it's a narrow street. But she came straight down. A terrible business. Dreadful.'

But in the morning sunlight there was no feeling of sadness or distress.

'And she played the violin?'

The man thought about it. 'Yes, I believe she did. Her brother André was a painter. We've always lived here. My father knew the Hebuternes. A good Catholic family.'

'But they wouldn't take her body in. The workman who found it carried it upstairs.' She was angry but allowed no emotion in her voice.

'That I wouldn't know. She was the mistress of the painter Modigliani and he was given a big funeral. She got nothing. But it all comes to the same. I think, now you remind me, there had been a lot of trouble having her back here. She was pregnant. She already had one child, or was it two. She couldn't have stayed with her parents.'

'Why not?'

'It wouldn't have been right. Not in those days. The priest came round – I remember him. I do remember the violin. She used to go for lessons. And when I was a kid, the violin shop was still there. She must have got her violin there, new strings and maybe sheet music, and I think even her lessons in that shop. Fancy remembering that.'

'Where is it?' said Jay.

The old man looked left towards the Rue Mouffetard. 'One of those streets up there. I can't remember. It's been shut since the twenties.'

'Can I ask how old you are?' asked Vicky.

'Seventy-eight. Sometimes I think I remember that night. Or maybe it was just my parents talking about it. I was ten.'

'Why did she come back here when he died if her parents so disapproved of her?'

'Where else would she go?'

'But she must have had friends,' said Vicky.

Jay said in English, 'He wouldn't know that.' Jay was curious because the old man spoke as though it was a long time ago, and she, like it was yesterday.

It was time to go but she wanted to see the apartment. It was on the fourth and fifth floors.

'There's no point.' The man was hostile again in spite of himself. 'It's all changed up there.'

'I'd still like to look,' she said firmly. It was, for Vicky, a return. To him, she was a pushy stranger.

'Leave it,' said Jay, urging her away from her old home.

There were dozens of restaurants nearby. It was definitely an up and coming tourist area. She swooped into one on impulse and sat down.

'Why here?' said Jay.

'It's got a great atmosphere.'

But she had not known that when she was in the street. Her entrance had been almost automatic. Throughout the meal she was cheerful, even said, 'I feel good in here.' Jay did not find it particularly uplifting.

She paid for lunch and then called the proprietor over. 'What was this place before?'

'It's been empty for years.'

'And before.'

'A violin shop.'

She thought about leaving the gold cross in the Rue Amyot but there seemed no sense in it. Instead she mentally placed a long pale gold cross outside the door of Number 8B and some white flowers.

On the way to the studio at 8 Rue de La Grande Chaumière, Jay said, 'I feel I should tell you what I'm writing about at the moment. I'm doing a play about a victim – a spider caught in her own web. I had to tell you. Forgive me, Vicky.'

Vicky was not surprised. She knew about the detachment of artists. 'Artists are like spies. They can be friendly, but the exiled part watches and judges and creates and is quite cruel. I just want to know about the last week in the studio and then we can leave. So keep writing, Jay. This is your last chance.' She sounded bitter, in spite of her understanding.

They stopped the cab near the Rotonde and she got out and looked across at the terrace. The first time I saw him, when I was grown up, I knew joy. My heart lifted and the small prison in which I had lived could keep me no longer. His eyes glowed as he saw me, as though my arrival in his life pleased him. The prison had been of my own making to keep my wildness contained. And then I met the one my soul loved. He was the person who came into a room and made it radiant. He was born to be happy.

And she saw, too, how he would make his way from the bar along the narrow street, drunk, exhausted, ill. And of course he could not make love. He could hardly live. But she still wanted him, whatever his condition, however much or little he could give. And there were some days when he would rise up like a phoenix from the ashes, potent, and what they did made him forget all about – she knew the woman he most thought of was his mother. He wanted to be great for her, his love was so strong.

Jay said, 'How d'you feel about going in?' At Number 8 there was a small sign, Atelier Modigliani. She pushed a bell, the door clicked and opened. Inside, the stone hallway was much as it had been since the day it was built. She felt nervous, as though she had no right to be there.

Jay knocked on a door at the side of the hallway, then looked at the mailboxes. She was scared, now, that the memories she would encounter would overwhelm her, make her unbalanced. What if they held her and she could not escape back to the present? Yet she experienced no recollection and the building seemed to mean nothing to her. They went across the hallway to a glass-panelled door and down a flight of steps into a yard with plants, grass and a stone fountain with a tap. Children were playing on bikes. She recognized the tree. It had been reproduced in books, painted by Jeanne Hebuterne.

They had a choice: the hallway behind them offered a flight of steps. Across the yard was another building. Jay asked an old man wearing a beret if the Modigliani studio was open. He pointed to the further building. They crossed the yard.

Jay stopped at the tap. 'She'd have got her water from here. I don't think they had plumbing.'

The second building was older than the first and seemed more or less unchanged. A long, steep stairwell rose up with four flights of curving steps, wooden and well-worn. The metal bannister had a shiny wooden hand rail, also worn. The doors and bannisters were painted a powdery green. She was surprised by the height. High at the top was a skylight and that was where she had lived. There was a huge expanse of dirty white peeling wall. The entrance floor was tessellated and coloured grey, beige and white in a nineteenth-century design. On the first landing stood a strange shaped cupboard, like a coffin.

Vicky was bright, light, alive, energized. She was home. As she climbed the stairs she felt a unique sensation of pleasure – coming home. It was the best present she could ever have.

They stopped to get their breath on the third floor, where Ortiz de Zarate had lived and painted. He had carried up Jeanne's coal and her lover when drunk.

Vicky felt high, reborn. She was truly home. She said to Jay, 'I must have felt such happiness here. It all seems so full of hope.'

Before they started on the last flight, a woman came down from the Modigliani studio. She looked with hesitation at Vicky.

'Can we see upstairs, Madame?' said Jay.

'But it's empty,' said the woman. 'It's been empty for years. And it's locked.'

Jay said, 'Could we still go up? Just to get an idea.'

The woman said it would be better from the first building. If they went to the top landing they could look across at the windows of Modigliani's studio. But nothing more – there was nothing to see. They waited for her to continue down until she was out of sight, then went up to the top studio.

Two doors stood at right angles to each other, and in front was the frame of the original doorway. 'There was just one door,' said Jay. 'If no one's here, what was she doing?'

They looked through the keyhole of the facing door into bright red light which seemed to be part of a wall and a wooden floor. Jay felt cold. This was the place he had first seen in a dream and then in his waking mind, a place where hell began, where spiritual torment revealed itself to be worse than the physical variety. The door at right angles had a shopping basket in front of it. There was only darkness through that keyhole. 'She must live in there, that woman,' said Jay. 'Well, that's it, Vicky. We can't get in.' He pushed at the Yale lock on the first door.

Vicky crouched down in front of the door, looking up at the skylight, then down at the steep stairwell, feeling very young. The atmosphere seemed so happy. 'Did I really live here? Was this my home?'

At that moment the door behind made a noise as though being opened. It was being forced from the inside and the locks rattled and floorboards shook.

Vicky jumped up. Jay started down the stairs, reaching for her. Then they waited, but no one opened the door. Silence.

'Someone is in there.'

Jay went to the door and knocked loudly. Then he knocked at the side door, called out, shrugged. 'Well, whatever it is won't let us in so let's go and get a drink.'

She did not move. Jay went down to the studio below and knocked on the door. The painter working inside Ortiz de Zarate's studio confirmed there was no one living upstairs.

Vicky sat still, as though she would never move again. It was like living in another time. This was happiness. She almost cried with the sharpness of it. Nothing else was in her mind, her world.

Jay stayed downstairs. It was the first time in his life he had been frightened of something he could not see.

'Come and pick the lock for me,' she said. 'You've got a credit card and I'm sure you know all about breaking in, with your childhood.'

Jay did not move.

'I want to go in. I've not come all this way for nothing. I'm going in.' She kicked the main door, hard. Jay ran back up the stairs.

'Don't get boisterous, Vicky! They may be painters here, but they're still bourgeois.' He started to work with the credit card. Immediately footsteps, quite clear and firm, came to the door, heavy footsteps that made the floor shake.

They both leapt away. The footsteps stopped by the door, paused, then moved away again. Pacing footsteps, belonging to a solid person.

Jay did not have an answer for what was happening. There could be no scientific explanation. He hoped, how he hoped, that the woman had somehow returned while he was talking to the artist on the floor below. Except she was in the wrong room.

Vicky waited but there were no more sounds.

'I'm not going in, Vicky. Whoever is in there – well, I think we should ask permission. Why don't we go and find the guy who's put on all the locks?'

'You're scared, Jay. But it's all right because I'm not.' She knew who was in there. She even recognized the walk. She wanted Jay to leave. She wanted to sit outside the door alone.

Jay said, 'Do me a favour. Let's go in with a key and a landlord and –'

'And a protector.'

She followed him down the stairs. At the bottom, she stopped. She was looking at the tessellated floor, trying to recognize it. She sat on the lowest step. She did not want to leave the building. She could see through the window into the yard and could hear the children playing. Then she heard him coming towards her, whistling and singing, his footsteps fast and light, like no other footsteps in the world. And he came through the door, very fast, passed her and went up the stairs. He was real, solid. The only unreality was the speed at which he moved. Where was the sick, drunken person? But, of course, he was now in spirit, mended, cleansed. She called to him and said, 'I am so sorry, forgive me.' He did not notice her and was gone up the stairs. She started to cry, all the grief, the pain, the remorse, filling her chest, her mind. Jay had his arms around her.

'Come on, kid. Don't crack up now.'

Modigliani was alive, so life-loving, so full, so blessed by life. How could a woman compare with life? He would never love her as much. And she was jealous of the fact life loved him, gave him all its best gifts.

And she knew she had let him die.

Now she understood why she had suffered in this, her present life. How jealous she had been. Her possessiveness had been a prison around both of them. And now she comprehended the last week. She had not called a doctor as he lay ill. Deliberately, she had summoned no help.

Jay was asking her to leave with him. She was not even aware of him, as he had not been aware of Modigliani climbing the stairs.

Then the woman from upstairs returned. Vicky, very pale, put on dark glasses. When she spoke she sounded normal. She asked the woman who had the key to the studio.

'Monsieur George.' She took them to the first floor and knocked on a door but he was not in.

'It was all one studio upstairs, wasn't it?' said Vicky. 'You live in just one part of it.'

The woman agreed with that.

'Can I come up and see where you live?'

The woman was reluctant. 'It's all changed. Very different furnishings. You wouldn't find anything, Madame.'

'Do you ever hear any noises?' asked Jay. 'In the next room? Footsteps or –'

The woman laughed. She liked Jay but there was something about the girl she did not feel easy with.

Vicky asked if she knew what had happened there in Modigliani's last week. 'When they had only sardines and alcohol to live on and no one went near them.' Jeanne did not get help.

'It is logical to help someone if they are ill. And she was about to have a baby –'

'No one went near them, that's right,' said the woman. 'Of course, people justified it afterwards but – I think Ortiz de Zarate found them and got him to hospital. But you're right, it is logical to get help for someone who's dying.'

'Did she want him to die?' said Vicky. Her eyes were wild beneath the glasses. 'Was she jealous? Because of Lunia?'

'He had more women than just Lunia. He slept with lots of girls. Even her best friend. So it was said in the quartier.'

It was all Vicky could do not to give a stricken cry.

'Jeanne must have known and accepted it. They say she accepted him for what he was. And she did not try to change him. But something terrible happened in there that last week.' She pulled her coat around her, although it was not a cold day, and started up the stairs. Yet again, Vicky stopped her.

'Is there anyone alive now who knew them?'

'No, I don't think so. There was Roger Wild, the painter. But he died last year.'

'What about her brother, André Hebuterne?'

Monsieur George opened his door. 'André Hebuterne still lives in the area but he must be ninety-two or ninety-four. Come in.' George had been working and had not heard the woman knock. He was clear-eyed, with a wonderful smile and forceful manner. 'I don't think he or his wife will speak. They never have.' He indicated that the woman should come in, too. But she was looking at Vicky. She closed her coat tighter, shivered.

'You've got a chill,' said George. 'Come and have a drink.' Monsieur George had authority. The woman came in like an unwilling cat and sat on the chair furthest from Vicky. She looked terrible and looked at Vicky as though it was her fault.

The artist's room was full of a life's work, ordered, rich, harmonious. Vicky thought Serge would have liked it. She thought of him for the first time.

George said, 'My father owned the building. Modigliani never paid his rent. He always said, take a painting. It will be worth a thousand times the rent. If only my father had, I wouldn't be sitting here now. I'd be in the South Seas. But how could my father know? They all said they were geniuses. How did he know which one was going to come up trumps? He had a soft spot for Modi – everyone did. There was a place, the Crémerie, run by Rosalie. She was Italian and crazy about Modi. Threw him out twice a week because he was a noisy drunk. But he could charm the devils out of hell. He slept with her, too, of course.'

The woman gave a sickly gasp and tried to get up from her chair. She looked ravaged as though all the devils had been loosed from hell. George asked if she was alright and she nodded.

Vicky said to Jay in English, 'I don't think Paris suits her either. She looks worse than you.'

George tried to get the woman to have another drink. She was unable to say exactly what was wrong. Then she put her head in her hands and muttered some incomprehensible complaints.

'What?' said Jay.

'She says there are five people in the room. There should only be four.'

The woman looked once more at Vicky, one last, furtive, curious look as though Vicky was a plague victim. Then she ran from the room. Jay suggested going after her.

'No,' said George placidly. 'Neurotic. Now we are three, or is it four?' He laughed and poured more drink.

'There *is* a woman who would know stories from that time. She used to live in the quartier. Ginette de Fleury, who married a racehorse owner.'

Vicky was surprised at the name.

'Do you know anything about the last week?' she said.

'It's funny, because in this area we know everything. And I've lived here all my life. I was born in the first building as you come off the street. We can tell you any detail about something that happened a hundred years ago, but about that death upstairs and her suicide, we know nothing. Isn't that extraordinary? A hundred years ago, like yesterday. Ask me about Radiguet, Cocteau, Kiki the model –'

'Was there a flower stall opposite the Dôme? Or was it the

Rotonde?' She was no longer sure. She remembered the primroses and was sure they had been on a barrow. 'Years ago, when Modigliani was alive.' She described the exact spot and how you could see the terrace.

'No, that was a grocer's.'

Vicky was disappointed.

'Oh, but you mean Beaumont's. That was an enormous flower shop, very expensive. Yes, that's the one. How did you know about Beaumont's? But it was on the other side, where the Coupole is now.'

So she had got the position wrong. Or maybe it was not this shop but a simple barrow she had remembered. She recollected seeing Modi over the mound of primroses, fresh from the country.

'So, let's go up and see the studio.' And George took the keys. 'It's been empty for years. The present landlord wants to make it into an apartment for his grand-daughter. It needs a lot of work.'

Again, she felt so much light happiness climbing the stairs to the apartment. It was an innocent feeling, nothing could go wrong. There was no fear or compromise, just absolute joy. How she must have loved being with him.

George unlocked the door and, with difficulty, pushed it open. It was a dusty room with noisy floorboards. The windows, the doors, even the walls, made noise. The shape of the room was oblong with windows along one side. At the end, a small corridor led into another oblong room. In the corridor was the lavatory. In the second room, there were windows at one end that Vicky remembered opening. In her mind, how often she had opened those windows to get some relief from the summer heat. She checked the view from the window was correct. And there, below, was the tree.

She knew where the stove had been, the easel, the table. Where was the bed? She did not know. She thought it might have been moved according to the weather, near the stove in the cold.

'There are a lot of windows,' said George. 'They didn't have curtains, so he or she painted over the windows.'

Vicky said, 'In the books I've read it says Hanka and Lunia furnished this for Modigliani. It was his first home with Jeanne.'

Jay was quiet. It was the studio he had dreaded. He knew now he had to stop Vicky from pursuing the past life. It was his duty.

She was now looking at the lavatory. 'Of course, it would have been a hole in the floor. And that wall was orange. And that one red.'

George was amazed. 'How do you know?'

'From the paintings, naturally. He brought his models here sometimes. And the walls were background. But I think he did his nudes at the dealer's house. Not near Jeanne. He painted Jeanne Hebuterne, pregnant, by the main door.' She felt nothing in the studio.

Jay said, 'Let's get out of here.'

They took George for a drink at the Rotonde. He said, 'Jeanne used to climb all those stairs when she was pregnant. Have you any children?'

'No,' said Vicky.

'D'you want any?'

'No.'

George laughed. And Jay realized he was the first person in Paris to like Vicky.

Vicky looked at the photos of Modigliani on the café walls, and her heart leapt. She wanted to rip them down and hold them to her. They were hers.

· Forty-seven ·

She longed to know Modi. It consumed her. She no longer cared about food or rest. She stopped the taxi at the address of André Hebuterne. She could not remember when she had last slept.

'Oh, no,' said Jay. 'I'm shattered. I'm getting out of this city on the first thing that flies and I'm going to sleep.'

'But I have to go back to the Place Calvaire.' She told the cab to go. Jay told the driver to wait.

'You're in trouble, Vicky. I know that studio.' He told her about his recurring dream and how bad it felt.

She said, 'It's funny, because I did a drawing of it once, a sort of doodle, when I was still at the BBC. I saw it when I was last in there cleaning my desk. I drew it before I knew anything about Modigliani.'

She was full of a compulsive energy and wasn't worried by his feelings of foreboding.

'I'm going to try and see the Hebuternes. Jay, it's up to you. I'll understand if you have to go.'

He paid off the cab and wished he had some uppers. Once again, there were a lot of stairs to climb. Jay waited, one flight below. Terrified, Vicky knocked on the door on the top landing. Inside, was her brother, still alive. The very thought of it made her want to slump to the ground.

'Who is it?' said a woman. It was an old voice but lucid, clear. The door remained shut.

'I need to talk to you, Madame, about Jeanne.'

'No, no. Absolutely not. I have nothing whatsoever to say about that business. It all happened a long time ago.'

'I want to see André.'

'My husband is very old and I will not have him upset like this. I will not even mention your visit.'

So Vicky did something rare. She used Serge Marais' name. 'I am his wife.'

There was a pause.

'You have heard of him?'

'Of course I've heard of him. Who hasn't?'

'And Serge Marais would like to know about Jeanne.'

'Absolutely not, I regret. My husband knows nothing about that death. He was away at the war, the First World War. It was a long time ago.'

Vicky knew that Jeanne had died in 1920. She said, 'The War didn't last until 1920.'

'He knows nothing. Go away.'

Silence.

Vicky sat on the stairs. And then she heard André's voice, so old, almost musical, from another world. A nice voice. André said, 'Who was it?'

'It's all that business again. Does it never rest? She says she's Serge Marais' wife.'

'Serge Marais? Serge Marais? Where? Here?' The old man was incredulous. 'Serge Marais! Whatever does he want with me?' The voice was full of wonder.

'It's that affair all over again. Do they never stop?'

Silence.

Vicky went down the stairs and Jay took her arm. Coming towards them was an old woman with bright beady eyes. Vicky said, 'Good evening. I've been to visit André Hebuterne.'

'Ah, my brother-in-law.' She had an alert face which missed nothing.

'I'm writing a book about Jeanne Hebuterne. I want to know the truth about her death.'

'Bravo!' And the woman shook Vicky's hand, then Jay's. 'I wish you luck.'

Then she went into her apartment. Vicky, not wanting to lose her, held the door to stop it shutting. 'Madame, do you remember anything about Jeanne?'

The woman looked into her face, paused, and didn't like what she saw. She started to shut the door firmly. 'That dreadful, horrible business.'

Vicky said, 'I'm desperate. Please help me. I have to know.'

The woman's face held the same expression of furtive, greedy interest, a look into the unknown, that Vicky had seen earlier in the day. The disturbed woman in the Atelier Modigliani had looked at her in the same way.

The door shut decisively.

Jay coaxed her away from the building.

Again the breeze was soft and kind and full of the smell of early spring. Still, he didn't come. She wanted to spend the night there on the bench. 'Our place'. That sounded safe, better, far safer than a hotel.

Slow feet were coming up the steep steps with the central iron rail. Eagerly, she looked over the small wall. In the night it was hard to tell. The hair from above was the same. Then he looked up and she saw Jay's face. 'He wants you back.'

For a moment she was so pleased, then realized who he meant.

'Come down these stairs and phone him.'

'But I need to know.'

'Vicky, please don't hang around in this cold.'

'But it's not cold.'

'Vicky it's fucking winter. If you get ill again I'll be blamed and he's got a horrible temper, believe me. I can't climb any more of these terrible stairs. I'm going into the first hotel I find, to sleep.'

'It'll soon be over,' she said.

'Over?' He didn't like that.

'So leave me here.'

'What exactly will be over, Vicky?'

'The torment of it. I'll know what I've done and be free of it.'

In the end, cold drove her down and into the first hotel.

· *Forty-eight* ·

They stayed together in the small bed and Jay kept his arms around her. 'You sleep, Vicky, and I'll keep awake. Then, at first light we go to Munich. No, it's Italy now.'

She laughed. 'You make it sound as though we're in a war.'

'Please try and sleep. That's all I'm asking, right now.'

'They hate me here, don't they, Jay? I knock on a door, it opens a crack, I begin to speak and they can't wait to slam it in my face. "Go away, Madame." But their eyes are frightened. The door shuts. But they've seen it in my face. And they don't like me. I get nothing but closed doors. It's because of the other life, not this one.'

She closed her eyes and saw the studio all cluttered with drawings, books, tins of sardines opened, the oil spilt. A painting of a Greek musician was still on the easel, wet. The priest with the censer was saying prayers for her spirit. How like Jay he was! She could see his boots stained with snow, walking over the dusty, creaking floor, and the bottles rolled and the wind howled.

Through the valley of death, I will fear no evil because Thou art with me.

'Jay, what do you think about priests?'

'I think what a lot there is to learn. What a lot of repetition, ceremony. I'd rather go and discover the unknown, the new. I couldn't do the work myself.'

'D'you think you were one, in a past life?'

'Vicky, this is your trip. I do not believe in other lives.'

'But you can't prove they don't exist.'

'When we die, that's it. Dust.'

'You can't prove that either, Jay. You can't prove much.'

And, in spite of himself, he fell asleep.

And there was Modi, standing at the bottom of the bed as though he had been there all the time. He smiled a sarcastic smile. It was provocative, perhaps playful. They looked at each other with great love. And he said, 'Not long now.'

She did not even question what he meant.

The bedside table light was on. Had he switched it on? Jay was deeply asleep.

'Ask them about the pink bangle.' And he tapped his right wrist. She sat forward to see, her heart pounding. He stretched out his arm and she saw a pink bracelet decorated in lacquer, mauve, pink and dark green, and then he smiled, his eyes radiant, his expression brightening. She could have examined his face for an hour and always seen something different. His expression seemed to convey a victory.

There were so many things she wanted to ask. Where do you exist? Why are you here? What will happen? But his being there was such an overwhelming experience she couldn't say one thing.

'Ask for my niece.'

'Your niece?' Her voice shook.

'You need not be frightened of me. She has a beautiful soul. A very special way of seeing things. But she has it wrong, our story. Put it right.'

She felt freezing cold. 'Please don't go. Don't leave me.'

'How could I?' he whispered seductively, and blew her a kiss. Then he saw Jay sleeping. 'You're not wrong.' He mimed the action of a priest giving a blessing, and looked at her with a gaze more potent than a full sexual act could be with Serge Marais. 'You're mine.' His lips hardly moved. Every gesture, every move, excited her more. She had never been alive until this moment. She had to keep him, hold him, understand him. He was more real, more solid, than anything in the room, including her. Her body was icy, without life, but her thoughts were full of wanting, agonized, in a continuing consciousness like a physical pain.

Then he was gone.

The next day, almost fainting with exhaustion, she turned the taxi away from the airport road towards the Hebuternes' apartment. 'I saw him, Jay,' she said.

'Not possible. You slept. I sat up and watched over you all night.'

'I saw him.'

'Dreamed you saw him. Sorry, Vicky. It's not possible.'

'But does he come to me or do I go to him?'

While Vicky crept up the stairs to the Hebuternes' apartment, Jay phoned Monsieur George in the Rue de la Grande Chaumière, and asked about the woman in the upstairs studio. Was she alright?

'She's had a terrible night,' said Monsieur George. 'She said it was as though they were back. She could hear them arguing and then making love. She could hear his laugh, piercing and childish. Sarcastic, very sarcastic. So she said. And the fights were physical. Crashes, screams, things being broken. She blames it on your friend.'

'What has it got to do with her?' said Jay.

'Nothing. Except she came and then it all started. She's threatening to leave.'

'Why has the studio been empty for so long?' asked Jay.

'Maybe that's the reason. It isn't empty.'

Vicky expected the Hebuternes' door to remain shut. Like last time, the conversation was conducted from the landing. This time, André answered. He said, 'What do you want?'

She said she was Serge Marais' wife. He said, as though recognizing her, 'Jeanne, Jeanne.'

Then his wife came out of the lavatory and spoke against the door. 'I have told you, Madame, to go away. You disturb my husband.'

'I've come for the pink bracelet.'

'What bracelet?'

Vicky described it.

The woman tried to pretend it did not exist.

The old man said, 'But how could she possibly know about the bracelet?'

The wife said, 'Go on your way and leave us in peace.' She spoke as though to a ghost. 'That bracelet was lost years ago.' She murmured a prayer.

'Was it Jeanne's bracelet?'

'Of course it was. I don't know why you bring all this up. My husband wasn't there.'

'Couldn't they have stopped her from taking her life?'

'Madame, I wasn't there, was I?' she said angrily. 'It seems to me, she would have been better off without him.'

'Why?'

'Because he drank, Madame!' This time she did not leave the door. Worried, she said, 'Anyway, there's nothing to worry about. Their child was brought up very well by his family in Italy. She was well-educated.' It sounded as though Vicky had accused her of neglect.

'She died a drunk,' said Vicky.

'I didn't know that.' The woman was interested.

'Why don't you open the door and let me ask André something? I want to know what happened in the last week and why she died. He'd know that.'

'Go away!'

As she went downstairs Vicky heard André say, 'How could she have known? He gave her that bracelet years ago. Painted it himself.'

Vicky slumped against the taxi window. Jay was burning with tiredness, lightheaded. Yet Vicky insisted on going to Ginette de Fleury's house. She had no choice.

'Then you have to go home,' he said.

'Home?' Where was it? Germany? Italy? London?

'You risk losing your husband-to-be. I guess you know that.'

'I have to know. If I don't, I'll never have peace.' And the energy slid out of her body like sand through an egg-timer.

Ginette de Fleury had agreed to see Vicky only because she was now the fiancée of the great one. The house was in the sixteenth arrondissement. As the taxi crossed the Seine, Vicky peered out from between her fingers at the Eiffel Tower.

'I hate it. All of it. It fills me with dread. I knew what I was going to do, that's why I wanted to run. I couldn't exist without him, every street was unbearable. But I was terrified of killing myself. Get out, said my heart. Out!' Her mouth dry, she closed her eyes.

She could see him as he had been during his last winter, unshaven, pale, thin, his looks quite gone, false teeth, face grimacing. He looked haunted and knew he was near the end. He was in the street, in the grey light. He had been walking again, always up to Montmartre to the place where his dream was first challenged. It was like a pilgrimage, his walk across the river to the Rue Lepic. What did he hope to find? Was he trying to lose death, which he described as the man waiting in the hallway? Yet he was still beautiful. Nothing, not even disease, could lessen it. He possessed eternal love for life, enough to light up the whole city. He changed the chemistry of any room he entered. He made people alive, pleased to be themselves. He brought them grace.

She told Jay about the pink bangle.

'Pink, mauve and dark green. Sounds like art deco. Those were the colours.'

'It looked sort of hard, plastic. Is there something called lalique? It had dark green leaves. It could have been hand-painted. I think he did paint it. And I have to find his niece. Which niece? Where is she?'

'You'll be doing that alone. We'll both be asleep within the hour, or in a hospital.'

Ginette loved the way they looked. 'Ah, my darlings. You've been doing Paris the way I used to. All night, all day, drinking, dancing, clubs. Oh, my darlings, how I envy you.'

She insisted they have a good breakfast and brought it in on individual trays. Jay was trying to catch Vicky's eye but it would not be caught. Time was running out.

Vicky struck into the past. She wanted to know about Jeanne Hebuterne.

Madam de Fleury rose up like a serpent, her mouth a hard, lipsticked slit.

'Jeanne? What made you think of her?'

'Did your mother know Modigliani?'

'Know? Of course Maman knew Modi. He was one of her greatest friends. So that's why you come to see me.' She gave a barking laugh, not pleasant. 'So you come to pick my brains? Another little film, is it? I said when she phoned, the English girl, she is not coming to visit. She wants something. It is not to talk about music festivals and the Maestro, like she says. You are a wolf, chérie.'

Vicky, exhausted, waited for the attack to finish.

Jay cut in, 'Actually, I have an interest. I'm doing a project on Modigliani at Yale and –'

'You're a wolf come to strip me. I don't mind that.' She went on looking at Vicky.

Jay again tried to say that the idea of the interview was his. For Ginette, he did not exist.

Vicky asked her some questions.

Ginette said, 'Jeanne was the sacrificial lamb – she chose to die with him. She was his only friend. Always loyal. It was a Greek tragedy that shocked everyone. The whole of the community went to his funeral. He was the Prince of Montparnasse. His brother said, "Cover him with flowers, bury him like a prince." And they did. It would be impossible for you to understand.'

'Why?' Vicky was hostile.

'What it was like in those days. How could you know? A little modern girl. I came from the same place as Modi. He stayed in his milieu and died. I had to get out of it to survive. I married a very rich man but I never had children. Do you want children?' she asked carefully.

'I don't know.'

'I don't think so. I know these things.'

There was too much hostility. Jay said, 'Did you know Modigliani personally, Madame?'

'How old do you think I am, darling? Should I sue my plastic surgeon? Maman knew him.'

'Why did he die like that?' said Vicky. 'He could have gone back to his mother.'

'How could he let his mother see him like that? He wanted to die with his own kind, the artists, the street people who understood him. And there was no doubt he would die.'

'And Lunia? What was she like?'

'She lived with the Zborowskis in the Rue Joseph Bara. Modi used to go there to paint.'

'Did he have an affair with her?'

'My darling, you make it sound so urgent. It's not happening today. Lunia said not. I expect he did. Why make her an exception? He had everyone else. What did he care? He could get anyone. They fell into his bed. Maman said he never had time to work up an appetite because he never had to go after anyone. Except Lunia.'

'And Jeanne.'

'No, darling. She was obsessed by him.'

'What was she like?'

'She was a good artist. But she gave it up for him. She gave up her life for him. She would do anything for him because she thought that was the one way to keep him. He liked submissive types like –' Ginette realized she was sitting opposite one. 'A bit childish. He liked that.'

'Did he love Jeanne?'

'Not in the way she loved him. They all said she was the sacrificial lamb. Sacrificed for his genius. I remember, now, that Lunia was her rival or one of them. Lunia was mad for him because he was a fantastic lover. So Maman said, and she should know. But he could be violent. He beat his women. When he was drunk he was terrible. Sober, enchanting. He was not of this world. He was a ray of light, a poet. He had to die to become glorious. Maman said, for a long time after he died, she could see him in the street. He was still there for those he cared for. Other people felt his presence too. Maman said, when he was alive, he often used to throw a rose into her room. After his death she would come in and find a rose on the bed or the table. Who else would put it there?'

'Do you think he's here now?' asked Vicky.

'He's not at rest, darling.' She was suddenly quiet and her mouth swung downwards in a disapproving arc. She felt wrong talking about Modigliani, almost as if it were indecent.

Jay was so tired his face was as white as icing. Only Vicky looked as though she had any energy. She kept pecking at the past with questions, as though it was her own. Ginette sensed her proprietorial attitude and did not like it.

'You won't find out much about Modi, you won't capture him.' Ginette gathered the trays and stacked them for the maid.

Coldly, furious, Vicky said, 'Why? Have you an exclusive option on his past?'

'No, darling, but Maman knew him well so I know a great deal. I should write my own book on his life. Why should I tell you everything and get nothing?'

'So who was your mother?'

Jay had never heard Vicky sound so cold.

'She was the famous nude, La Quique.' The confession meant she must be over seventy.

'You look very young,' said Jay.

'Thank you, chéri. I do my best.'

Jay was thinking, she is trying to say she is Modigliani's love child. Dare she? Could she get away with it?

'Where is his niece?' said Vicky.

Ginette had to admit she did not know he had one. It lessened her position of authority. She decided to regain some ground by revealing a little more, although not too much.

'Maman told me many things about him. How they would eat at Rosalie's Hole in the Wall Café. He didn't belong to this earth at all. He lived amongst the stars, a child of the night. He was innocent, made you feel joyous. They all loved him and forgave him for everything.'

'Forgave?' said Vicky.

'He didn't behave well when he was drunk. He threw that English girl, Beatrice Hastings, through a window without opening it first.'

'She was South African,' said Vicky.

'But he had her under his skin. He liked her fire. That's what he admired in my mother. He either went for the fire and the challenge, although he wouldn't live with that kind, or he chose the submissive, yielding types he could abuse. Yes, he slept with everyone and that little Jeanne waited patiently for him to come home.'

Every time she mentioned Jeanne she knew she drew blood.

'I think he did love her,' said Vicky.

'Maybe, but not as she loved him. He was her god. She was not his goddess. He felt tender towards her. She had a sweetness and he was very protective. Soutine said he needed her because he thought perhaps her purity could save him. Give him life. He needed purity. Maybe Indenaum said that. He described her as a madonna.' She was quiet again. She started on another huge sandwich but thought better of finishing it.

Vicky was angry. Did Ginette think she owned Modigliani? She wanted to make out she knew more than anyone else and could withhold information.

In turn, Ginette loathed Vicky. She sensed she had a quality and that made her jealous and vengeful. It always had. It would never have occurred to her to want to injunct a tiny, unnoticed movie until she saw its creator on television. Ginette's eyes were now so hostile she had to hide them. She chose a pair of tinted glasses with rhinestone frames.

Jay said, 'Do you think Modigliani would have liked Vicky, Madame?'

So he had put into words the unspoken. Of course, there was something about this girl that stirred Ginette. She was as insulting as possible as she replied. 'Perhaps. In a cerebral way. But the women he really liked were –' She gestured fire. 'Or much younger than Miss Graham.'

'Yet your mother doesn't appear in the books,' said Vicky. 'There's a mere mention of their dancing together, naked, in Montmartre. She was a bull and he the bullfighter.'

'The books know nothing. What can they know? What people tell. And after that tragedy no one would tell the truth. I remember the people, chéri.' She stopped speaking.

The way the girl sat – of what did it remind her? And she knew, absolutely, it was jealousy and dislike that had made her suppress this girl's film, because around her she sensed a special love. Again, the girl pierced her with questions.

'Do you know why they were left alone to die?'

'Because, my darling, everyone abandoned them. He was impossible at the end. He was drunk, insolent, spiteful. Only Jeanne stayed. Yet, as they put him into the earth, his painting prices soared and the word genius was heard. Then everyone in Montparnasse began to say they were there during the end. At that rate, the studio must have been full for a week! And his last words were so many, even for a healthy man. I have never heard so many last words. "Cara, cara, Italy. I leave you, Soutine. I have made my last – whatever it was, with my wife."' Madame Fleury now arrived at the cause of her distress. Yes, the girl had been loved in a special way. But more, she could have easily what Ginette had always craved, and be careless about it, ungrateful. This girl could throw into a grave what Ginette most wanted. A child. Children.

'You know, darling, when I first saw you I thought, this girl can hold in her hand my dearest dreams and crush them into nothing and not even know it.'

Jay knew it was time to go and stood up.

Vicky said, 'But why didn't she get help for him? She needed nourishment –'

Ginette waved her hands around, resigned. 'I think they had gone, both of them, far beyond nourishment. I think they were in hell.'

· *Forty-nine* ·

Serge was furious with Jay. How could a responsible person deliver his fiancée to London instead of Italy, and looking so ill? They looked as though they had been on a perilous expedition into a little-known part of the planet. How could anyone go to Paris and have such a terrible time?

'I brought her back, didn't I?'

'Back!' said Serge.

Jay meant from a little further away than Paris. For a moment Serge doubted the American's account of events. 'So she just walked around the streets, night and day?'

Jay got up. 'I don't want to speak about it.' He wanted to be alone, to think. He felt light years away from the Maestro and the glitter of the modern world.

'Vicky's gone to the BBC?'

'Yeah,' said Jay. He went into the spare room of Vicky's Hampstead flat and lay on his back on the bed. Serge looked at his watch. 'I have work to do. I'll be at Claridges if Vicky wants to ring me.'

Vicky found the drawing of the studio in the Rue de la Grande Chaumière in her files which Micky Duke had kept.

'I'm going to be doing something on Serge Marais. A documentary. I want you to assist me, Micky.'

He was delighted.

She looked at the doodle. There was the lavatory, the stove, the windows, the two rooms and the small round shape hanging from the end window. She did not have to look at it for long to see it was the pink bangle.

*

When she got back to the Hampstead flat the phone was ringing. Kirsty Cobb said, 'Vicky, are you alright?'

Vicky said yes.

'I'm so relieved to hear your voice. I had an awful feeling you'd gone for good. Please don't go. I realized how much I needed you.'

Vicky laughed. 'What do you need me for?'

'Just to be around in my life. It's funny. When you're here, I don't value you. But gone, you're very important to me. You really understand my drinking and you're the only one I can talk to who doesn't start moralizing. It may or may not seem like much of a compliment. I miss the married guy. I find I really do go for him. Drink makes up the love deficit.'

'What does the healer say?'

'The healer is in North London. I'm in New York. What he does is great, but after a lapse I go back to my bad old ways. I love you, Vicky, so don't go.' She hung up.

The next call was not so loving. Serge said, 'So you're crazy about Paris all of a sudden?' He sounded dangerous. She thought, be careful.

'I'm not.'

'You spend enough time there.'

'Not pleasantly.'

'Well you obviously prefer to be with someone else.' A sarcastic pause. 'What am I supposed to say?' His voice was terrible.

Now she was frightened. A colossal crisis was in the air – wedding off, engagement ring back, Matisse back. He would go back to Anna and to the correct number of concerts each year, yet she had no desire to fight for herself. Everyday reality had begun to fade when she first saw Modi. All the yearning she had gone through for Serge Marais was as nothing compared with her craving for the painter.

'So, how was Paris?' He had not hung up. 'You tell me nothing.'

She said, 'Light and dark.'

And she heard Modi cough and say, just like a sketch, what else?

After a silence she said, 'I've taken the reels we taped into the BBC. I'll do the documentary on your life if you still want me to.'

'Perhaps it will give you an identity, going back to work. Being in my life certainly has not.' And he hung up.

She bit her bottom lip and took her time replacing the receiver. It was over. If she had not been so exhausted she would be appalled. But she had not slept since going to Paris. Was it four days? Five? She thought about her life, her marriage, her small affairs and her fairytale romance with the music king. It was obvious she had always belonged to someone else. Her life was a waiting room and she was patiently waiting, for what, she did not know.

Jay went to the healer in North London. He was feeling so ill he thought he might require the man's services himself. 'I need to talk about Vicky.'

'She mustn't go back. She keeps going back.'

Jay thought he meant Paris.

'Into the past. She's calling out for him.'

'Can she actually become the person she was?'

'No. That's over. She's another person now. That last life wasn't such a wonderful thing. She's not meant to be with the painter. That's why he's in the spirit world and she's here.'

'But I think that she's in love with him.'

'A remembered love, that takes her away again from life. She must never go to Paris again. She links into the past life there and she's not strong enough, especially at night. When her subconscious mind is loose she's in danger. I don't know how she got out of Paris this time without medical help.'

Jay described the footsteps in the studio.

'She caused that phenomenon by her own energy. The psychic activity she caused took too much of her energy and disturbed others.'

'Is he around? You know –' Jay felt silly asking the question.

'The pull between them is so strong she could bring him into the room.'

'Would I see him?'

'You'd feel very cold. So would she. To manifest itself a spirit takes energy from human beings. They work at a higher vibration than us. To show themselves they have to attune to a lower level.'

'But were they his footsteps?' Jay sounded scared.

'Memory. She stirred up the memories of her past, made them real. Her energy reproduced all sorts of things. It takes her very life force. No wonder she was exhausted.'

'So it's not him pacing the floor and shaking the locks?'

'Reactivated memory.'

'What can he do?' Jay was more terrified of him than of Serge Marais.

'If you have any influence on this girl, get her mind into the present. Their passion was intense, but what good does it bring to them or to anyone else?'

Jay noticed he had not answered the question.

Vicky's mother was well and wanted to conduct her own life. She had discharged herself from the clinic and moved into her flat. She made it clear that Vicky could telephone but it was for her own benefit. Her mother did not need her.

'D'you want me to come and see you?'

'If you want to. It's up to you.' No mention was made of her last illness. As far as she was concerned she was a widow who could handle her own affairs.

When Vicky got back to Hampstead Jay had cooked a huge dinner. He watched her eat and said, 'If you did have a past life I'm sure you must have starved. You certainly eat enough in this one. I've never seen anyone eat so much.'

She laughed, thinking of the French studio. That last week had been freezing, and only tins of sardines to eat. It was enough to make you hungry for an eternity.

The painter had not made any more appearances. She no longer slipped back into that other world which changed her brain's rhythm and gave her clear and unforgettable images. Her mind felt dull and flat. She had reflected a great deal on what had happened to her. It certainly had not been imagination.

That came from a different source and its images could not be recalled vividly and effortlessly. Imagination was, to her, like daydreaming. She had also given considerable thought to Modigliani and what he was like. She kept coming back to his mother.

'You'd think if he loved her he wouldn't have destroyed himself.'

Jay said, 'He was mother-attached. That was his problem. He couldn't get away from his mother.'

'But he did. Get away.'

'Geographically, he put space between them, but he was still attached, mother-fixed.'

'How can you tell?'

'By looking at his relationships and the women he went with. All quick, sexual affairs. He used them, got rid of them. I think it was difficult for him to make a lasting, close relationship with a woman. The first one, Beatrice Hastings, didn't happen until he was thirty. But she kept him. And she was liberated and an equal in many ways. Certainly intellectually. It wasn't a close, domestic relationship. I think as soon as it got too domestic, too close, it reminded him too much of his mother and he became uncomfortable. He could not maintain a domestic set-up with anyone. The Canadian girl, Simone Thiroux – that was a series of one-night-stands for him, whatever it was for her. I think he did try and live with Jeanne Hebuterne.'

'Try?' She did not like the sound of that. 'You don't think he succeeded?'

'No, I don't. I think he continued his life exactly as he always had. I'm sure he still had casual sex with all sorts of people and Jeanne was jealous and possessive. I know the books tell it like a romance but I'd be surprised. If he could have settled down with her she would not have been allowed to threaten his mother's position. He never had a home as such, did he?'

'But their relationship was very sexual.'

'Vicky, I'm not saying he didn't like sex. I'm talking about making a commitment. I can see he'd go after somebody, especially if they were hard to get, like Lunia. But he wouldn't stay with them. You'll never know the truth, Vicky. After the girl leapt from the window everyone felt guilty and found only the prettiest things to say. No one's going to remember the fights.'

'He slept with Jeanne.'

'But would he have married her? Why d'you think her family threw her out? Imagine the pressure put on him to draw up that funny little document where he spells her name wrong. All that about "I'll marry her when my papers come." Well, they came. And they still weren't married.'

'Well, you've certainly given it a lot of thought, Jay.' She felt upset as though she had been rejected.

'Vicky, I know this scene. I've been through it, don't you understand? The switch from whore to mother. You have to be one or the other.'

He did not like the way she was looking at him. Reproachful. No, as though he was her lover's best friend telling her the truth. He was, in fact, fighting to break the hold the past had, kick the romance out of it, give back to it the problems he knew it would have contained. 'I think the sex came from her. She was always on the boil. Couldn't get enough of it. Provided him with a canvas to paint his fantasies on to. Provoked him into all kinds of things. I bet she loved it. She was mad for him and he was turned on by that.'

'You're talking about yourself, Jay.'

'It takes one to see one. He was tied to his mother, I don't care how far apart they were. If it got too close he'd be uncomfortable. So he'd move around, play around and come back and she'd be waiting there. But no wedding bells.'

Vicky thought of Lunia, the one who played hard to get and wanted to take him away. She could imagine the rows and fights that would have caused. And there was that dream where she had plunged the woman's head through a glass window and screamed, 'You can't leave me! I'm pregnant!'

Lunia tried to secure him by not letting him have her, but he stayed with Jeanne. 'In spite of what you say, I know he loved her.'

She was sure that not every return to the studio had been a cause for celebration. He was moody, she knew it instinctively.

It was not always a radiant entrance, transforming a room. And he did not always want sex. Not at all. She might, but not him. The painting came first and last.

Jay made the coffee. 'In his serious relationships he'd go for the same type. Young, receptive, submissive, adoring. You go for the same type; he was sturdy, dark-eyed, Jewish, Mediterranean. You went for his type in that life and you continue to do so in this. Dean Tyrell was like that when he was young. Your idols as a kid. Your holiday encounters. And I fit into that type.' Then he realized Serge Marais was not that type and he had not telephoned.

She said, 'I came into this life remembering him, looking for him. I went for any man that even resembled him. Then I found him.' How she wished he would come into the room now.

Jay said, 'I expect Serge wanted to know a little more about your experiences in Paris than your aversion towards the Eiffel Tower.'

'I don't know, I haven't seen him.'

She felt guilty about Serge, but wrote, instead, to Kirsty Cobb.

> 'You are right, I am ruthless. I go after what I want, but only from great need. General, everyday things around me, I can take or leave. The other, my soul tracks down like a wolf in the night, to the death. There's no choice about it. I have to have what I love, no mattter what I have to do, or what suffering I cause others. And I disguise it with my quietness and modesty and submissive ways. But I love . . . love . . .'

Kirsty thought it was a slightly old-fashioned letter. More importantly, she knew Vicky was not referring to the Maestro.

· *Fifty* ·

Serge healed himself through music. There was no question of returning to Anna. He would rather live alone or have a series of young sexual partners. He assumed his sexual urges would fade with age and Vicky's disappearance from his life.

Back in London he paced the drawing room of his rented house in Chester Square. Vicky had sent no letter, there had been no phonecall. He could not understand how she could turn her back on what he had to offer – in the material, worldly sense. He would have given her a position as his wife, encouraged her to make films, improved her health, been a father to her. Then he asked himself, what had she done that had so upset him? She had gone to Paris, said it was an expiation. She accepted what he did. Why could he not accept her. And he wanted her there near him, in his sight. She was the erotic, rather mysterious, soft-centred female who had moments of wildness, provoked only by him. He could change her. While making love, her face, excited, became extremely beautiful. He held the key to that beauty and no other man was going to see it or have the pleasure of knowing what she truly was.

'She's done nothing wrong. She's young. I should look after her. In other words, I want her back.'

When she picked up the phone, he said, 'Come back. Tonight. Why make ourselves wait like this? Come on. I'll send the car to get you.'

The wedding was still fixed for April 6th. That, she realized, was Jeanne's birthday.

'Let's make it April 7th.'

Serge agreed and also changed the location of the wedding, from Siena to a country church in England. He cut the guest list so that only a few close friends would attend. They would stay on the country estate of Serge's aristocratic business partner who had shares in the CD video company. A dinner was arranged for the eve of the wedding. The following morning, they would walk informally across the fields for the simple ceremony in the fourteenth-century church. After a modest reception came the honeymoon in Greece. Serge believed spring was the best time to visit the islands because there was a special energy and vibrance there then, which he was looking forward to sharing with his wife. Then began his time of rehearsal for more public performances.

When Anna heard the wedding had been put back a day she said that it was a sign. 'What he's doing is wrong. After all, I know a scherzo when it's being taken too fast. He can't manage alone. He'll be back.'

During the days before the wedding Vicky spent a lot of time with friends. She wanted to share her good fortune. She would do the smallest or the biggest act to please them. Lorraine's baby was now overdue and she was so big she could hardly move.

For one impulsive moment, Jay had considered marrying her. 'I actually like the way she looks after me. She's the mother type. This time it might work – I don't love her, so I might grow to love her. With the others, I loved them and I grew not to love them.'

'Is your mother still alive?'

'No, sweetheart.' He laughed. 'But if you're mother-fixated it doesn't matter if they're on the moon. The results are the same. If you're attached, what's space?'

Vicky shivered. Where was he? The moments he would come to her were always of his choosing. Yet now, seeing she was committed to another man, had he simply turned his back? Did spirits sulk? She knew he had been with her from her first moment of consciousness: he was her charismatic friend who had kept her company in the garden in Hampshire. He had given her the ideas that people found so quaint. And helped her make scent, and ponds and cities of mud. His sleeves were soft velvet like the rose petals.

'I'm probably going to let Lo down, so look after her.'

Vicky loved the suggestion. These days, women clung together, understood each other, mopped up each other's tears. 'What about the baby?'

'I can't acknowledge the child if it's not mine.'

'Will one more make any difference? You've got so many,' she snapped.

'Why should I give my name to a kid that isn't mine? Anyway, she'll be a good mother. And she's very fond of you, Vicky. She wants you to be godmother. We all need you so you've got to be in one piece.'

'Aren't I?'

'I suppose so.' He did not know why he had said that.

Vicky visited her mother again. She was sitting quite calmly in the freshly-painted kitchen, peeling vegetables. Vicky wanted to give her some money but Ruby would not take it.

'But wouldn't you like a dog or a cat? You love animals, don't you?'

'How do I know when I'll be ill again? Who'll look after it then?'

The hospital had offered her pills to keep her stable. She would not take them. 'What if they make it worse?'

'I'd take them if it starts again. You seem fine now.' She did not seem fine, just resigned.

'It's not insanity, if that's what you think, Vicky. It's a depression, a cross I have to bear.'

Vicky asked what it was like.

'Chaos. A bad place. Bits of everything, the past, places I don't know, like in dreams. I'm terrified out of my mind most of the time. I just don't want it to get any worse so I try and hold myself together. That's why I don't want their pills.'

'When did it start?'

'It's a chemical imbalance. Being with your father didn't help.

Never marry an older man. You end up having to be their nurse. Of course, that's why they marry you.'

Before she left, Vicky asked again about the French names she had known as a child. 'There was Antoinette and perhaps Sophie? And there was a man. He was very good-looking. I must have had a name for him.'

Her mother's eyes narrowed. 'It's right, you did say French names.'

'How did I get them?'

'Out of your head. You were always good at inventing things. A world of your own, your dad would say. And you were very knowing. Not like a kid. You'd play with a girl in the village and then come running home to your real friend. You said he made you feel safe.'

'What was his name?'

Her mother shrugged. 'I wouldn't know it if I heard it. There was no French in our family. I never left England. Obviously, I wasn't meant to travel. And you weren't allowed to watch television. Your dad wasn't having that.'

'Did you want me, Mum?'

'Did I have a choice? The truth is, I never felt close to you.'

'Did Dad want me?'

'Who knows? I suppose so. I expect you feel angry with what I've told you.'

'No,' said Vicky calmly. 'I just feel I passed through you to be born here. My real people are not you or Dad. They're from another time.'

'Well, that's one way to deal with rejection, Vicky. But I wouldn't go around talking like that or you'll end up where I just came from.'

Vicky did not tell her about the wedding. It seemed unsuitable for her mother to come into her life now. It was over between them, settled, as though Vicky had paid an old debt. No one had to lie any more. Vicky's mother was just a vehicle to propel Vicky into life. After that, it was up to her.

When she had gone, Ruby sat at the table motionless and chewed her bottom lip. She felt guilty. She had not given Vicky enough love, enough of anything. The moment passed and she carried on peeling the vegetables.

For once, she was alone in bed, her old bed in the Hampstead flat. She turned from side to side, covers off, light on, but nothing in her would let sleep come. She felt naked, all bare bones. There was none of the voluptuous atmosphere Serge Marais created and absolutely no contact with any time other than the present. She was pared down to her essentials, as though a light bulb was shining, bright, unshaded, without flattery. Tonight she was Vicky, twenty-seven, in London alone and very much in her own life. This was reality. How odd that, now she was really alone, there were no memories or tokens from the previous time.

She had a few choices. She was not at all sure marrying Serge Marais in two weeks time was the right thing to do. What had there been in her life so far that fitted her for his world? Could she journey tirelessly across the globe giving enough stimulus and love to keep him on top form? There would not be any time for the occasional off day. One look at Anna had shown her that. Anna had dedicated her whole being to this public figure. She read all the newspapers so that, in a few concise sentences, she could sum up the world situation each morning. She was therapeutic when faced with Serge's sudden mood changes. She could deal with the customs of different countries. She was strong. Just thinking about Anna Marais made Vicky want to run to the nearest bus station and get on the first vehicle that moved.

Then the phone rang and Lorraine said, 'They want to induce the baby, but the healer said to wait. He says the baby needs to come in his own time.'

'Is Jay –'

'Oh, screw Jay! I don't need him.' And she sounded pleased with herself, almost smug. 'I know Jay doesn't go in for reincarnation or anything, but the healer told me who my son was.'

'Was?'

'In his last earth life. If I've got him, who needs Jay? Of course, I'm not allowed to say. It sounds like showing off.'

Vicky said she was glad anyway. She was terrified Lorraine was going to say the baby was a Second Coming.

'You sound as though you're alone.'

'Serge has flown to New York to see his children. In under two weeks I'll be Madame Marais. I take my hat off to her – Anna. She certainly did it in style. Never an off day.'

'He wouldn't allow her an off day,' said Lorraine. 'What about those other life experiences you were going through? Who was it with? Jay would never tell me. Did you find out why it happened?'

'No.'

'You don't want to talk about it, do you?'

'It's all over anyway, Lorraine. It doesn't happen any more. It was just something I went through. I can't explain it.'

'Did you know that, in some cases, the spirit does not attach itself to the foetus in the womb until the moment of birth?'

Vicky said she had not known that. But she was glad Lorraine was happy about the one she had got.

The next morning she bought Serge a black silk kimono and a new white silk scarf. She bought herself a white silk slip. Of the three, she thought he would like that present the best. She ordered a layette and other baby items to be sent to Lorraine. Then, as she looked into a side window of Harrods, she thought how she missed Jay. It was not desperate and there was no need to contact him. It was all easy and harmonious between them. Some people you met and would not see again and you did not even think about it. But with others, if you knew they were gone for ever, a life without them was unthinkable. And Modi? He had been absent recently, even from her thoughts. She supposed it was like recovering from an illness. In the last week she had felt nothing.

She was spending more money in the designer lingerie department when the thought of never seeing him again sent her hurtling out of the store and into the nearest church. She got onto her knees. She prayed to God, how she prayed, that she would see him again. Life without him would be unendurable. And here she knelt, feeling all the purgatorial misery of Paris in

1920, and yet she was in London in 1989.

When she left the church by a side door she saw the word 'Love' painted on a wall, and she realized she did love him. Modigliani. She sat on the steps, the trees with new leaves rustling in the wind. And she thought of a way to please him: she would find the niece he had mentioned, go and see her, and tell her that the story, as she had been told it, was not true.

She phoned every source of information, every person in the art world, but she could not track down the niece.

The healer gave her a tissue to dry her eyes. Vicky went on sobbing, so he gave her the whole box.

'But where is he?' she said. 'Can't you tell me anything? You're supposed to see things.' She considered trying another psychic but did not have time. There was a reception for Serge at the Royal Festival Hall that evening and she had to be there so they could make their entrance together. Afterwards, he would conduct the Mozart she had chosen.

'You're getting married and starting a new life. Didn't you say your house was in Italy?'

'Oh, don't go on. Please. You know I'm not here about that!'

'In the other life you were in cloud cuckoo land. Now you're in reality, and it hurts.'

'So I'm supposed to deny joy? Is that why I'm shown it?'

'You can't go back. You can't learn anything by repeating the past. That's not the point of being born.'

'But I saw him and I've heard him, even his voice.'

'He's not a settled spirit, he's unable to go to rest. He's very powerful, I think because he was psychic. He had the power but didn't use it.'

'So why does he come to me?'

'Because you've disturbed him. Obviously.'

'Upset him, you mean?'

'Get on with your own life.'

'But now I want him he doesn't come.'

'Because you've angered him by marrying. Why shouldn't

you? If he comes into your thoughts, tell him to go!' The healer slapped the couch.

'What I really want to do is go and live in the studio. I felt such a wondrous happiness there. Why shouldn't I be happy? I could see him as he entered the courtyard and ran up the stairs.'

'Memories. Vicky, you can only repeat the past. You cannot change it. You slip back there to see only the same things time after time and experience what you have already gone through. Don't you see? The past. You can't change it.'

· Fifty-one ·

Before she went into the Festival Hall she sat by the river.

'Please, please don't leave me.'

As she waited, she tried to recall the Parisian studio but saw only her father dying in the kitchen asking about Julius Caesar. And then he was dead, biscuit crumbs still stuck to his mouth. It had been a terrifying moment, his face drained and waxy. Nothing, though, was as terrifying as the things she had glimpsed from another time.

When she finally reached the right part of the Festival Hall, she met the impresario's wife, who said, 'You've got such a lovely life – you should be so grateful.'

She was surprised when Vicky snapped, 'Life? It's a joke!'

Vicky went off to the public lavatory to do something about her appearance. She stood by the sink, not knowing where to start. She could go to the dressing room, but did not want Serge to see her like this, so disarranged. Behind her, women queued for the lavatories. She would have to take herself in hand, keep her strength up, try to look good. So she had been abandoned. He never had done her much good. She crunched a minor sedative and washed her face.

The woman next to her passed some soap. 'It's mine. Please use it if you wish.' She had a lovely smile. The accent was French. She was old but ageless. 'It's so tiring, isn't it, travelling?'

Vicky agreed.

'But worth anything to hear Marais. He's giving up for good, they say. I'm glad that I did finally see him.'

The woman said she came from a village near Paris and,

although the Maestro conducted in France, she had never been able to get a ticket. 'Then, quite by chance, an English friend managed to get one but became ill, so I am here instead.'

Vicky agreed that was marvellous. And she realized what a great deal he did mean to his public. She combed her hair and put on some face cream and would have left. But there was something about this woman: she was enchanting, full of life and fun. Vicky, not used to talking to strangers, said, 'I can see you've had a happy life, Madame.'

The woman laughed. 'I am happy. Perhaps that's it.'

Still Vicky did not want to leave her. They walked together to the powder room exit.

'What makes you happy?'

'Maybe I was born that way.'

'Where?'

'My family come from Marseilles.' She laughed. 'It's not a family trait, being happy. I think if you're not too disturbed by things, you have a chance.' She started towards level B, and then she said, 'I had an uncle who should have been happy. But he *was* disturbed by things. Perhaps I learned a lesson from his life. Still, that's being an artist, I suppose.'

Afterwards, the niece could not have said why she mentioned her uncle, the artist. She was not in the habit of going around saying she was his niece. Vicky missed the reception because she stayed with the woman, taking her into a box to watch the performance. Afterwards, she brought her backstage to meet the Maestro. The line was long, so they waited in a dressing room. The questions began straight away.

'Was he going to marry Jeanne?'

'He wrote to his mother and said he would but he died too quickly. The family Hebuterne were devout Catholics. They could not understand why their daughter chose to lead that life. But nothing they could do would dissuade her.'

'Why didn't she get a doctor when he was so ill?'

'What could you do for TB in those days? There were no antibiotics.'

'But he died in great pain from tubercular meningitis. The TB had moved upwards.'

'Well, yes, they could give morphine. Perhaps Jeanne saw no point in getting him to hospital. I think she was completely at a loss. But I never met either of them. I was ten when my uncle died.'

And then the other possibility occurred again to Vicky. 'Perhaps he wanted to die. A week before his last illness he was wandering around in the freezing night without a coat, ill. Why do that?'

'Because he was drunk, that's why.' She said it quite brightly. Life, even tragedies, did not subdue her. 'Every sou the family sent he spent with his friends in bars. It wasn't true he was impoverished. His mother was always sending him money. He was her favourite. She adored him. She sent everything she could.'

'Do you know anything about Jeanne Hebuterne?'

'They say she was a little strange. One of her friends said she never heard Jeanne say a word. She just sat absorbing everything he said and did. I also heard she was intelligent and quite an artist. But she never got a chance.'

'Strange? You mean mad?'

The woman laughed. 'It was he who was mad. All the Garsins were. It was part of their charm. People who are too direct are no fun.'

Vicky gave her another drink. Talk to my niece, he had said. Tell her the truth about our story.

'He had quite a reputation with women, didn't he?' said Vicky.

'Certainly. He was generous with his heart, his money, his bed. He had a large generosity. My mother and father took the baby, the little Jeanne, after his death. They brought her back to Marseilles. She was fourteen months old and adorable. The nurse, out of respect because she was now an orphan, had dressed her completely in black. From head to foot. So my mother had to buy her new clothes in Paris. My father was a brother of Modigliani's mother. She was an exceptional woman, a grande dame. She made a rich marriage but her husband failed in business so she took over the family and ran a school.'

'Did she bring up the little girl?'

'No, Dedo's sister did. Dedo was his nickname. The French called him Modi. But the sister was very strict, you understand.' It was the first time the woman had looked sad. 'It wasn't a good thing for the child. I wish we could have kept her.'

'Is there anything mysterious about it all that you don't understand?'

'I could never understand why my mother and father, when they went to the studio, did not take one of his works away, even as a souvenir. They were lying about on the floor, everywhere, yet they did not take even one. Not even as a souvenir for the child. Nor his brother, Mene, the Deputy. My mother said, "Those horrors. I couldn't touch one." She was provincial. But the family could never understand why Mene, who was very cultured, did not choose a work.'

Vicky could see the queue was coming to an end. The Maestro only sounded charming. She would see the real mood later. The woman put down her glass and smiled delightfully. They had got on well, but it was time to go. She said, 'You seem very interested in Modigliani. You know a lot about his life. It's a shame he drank himself to death. All that talent wasted.'

'Oh, but he didn't,' said Vicky. 'Drink himself to death, I mean. He just gave up. What he did, no one wanted. There seemed no point in going on with it. Why fill canvasses that you couldn't even give away? No one appreciated what he gave his very soul to show.'

'That's a different way of looking at it. So much success came to him, sometimes you forget it happened after his death. Of course, he never saw any of it.'

'He wasn't some drunk, drinking himself to death. He just didn't want to go on living. He saw no future in what he knew he had been born to do.' She still could not let the woman go. There was something still not said.

'Why did Jeanne Hebuterne die?'

'Because she was too sad to live.' The woman was now finding Vicky far too direct. She would have preferred some of the mad charm of the Garsins.

'It wasn't remorse?' said Vicky. 'Because she was jealous and so she never sent for a doctor? She let him die. He had other women –'

'No, they were very much in love. She could not have gone on without him.' The niece believed in the family history as it had been selectively recorded.

'But she was having a baby. That's what I can't understand.'

'All the more reason to die. All the more.'

'What do you mean?' asked Vicky sharply.

'She already had one. How could she bring up two alone? She couldn't go through the bereavement and –'

And then Vicky saw it, the untruth. 'No, Madame. He wanted her to go with him because they weren't meant to be apart. He didn't want her to suffer. He loved her. It just wasn't the very best circumstance in which to be in love.'

The woman laughed. 'If that's what you want to believe, I won't dissuade you.'

Serge Marais had entered the room. Vicky was not alone so he could not show his rage. He shook the stranger's hand and allowed her to express her pleasure.

'Yes, well, Mozart is very demanding. Once you are on the podium you have to clear your mind. It's better to forget about a row you have had with your wife, a pain in the head, when it's Mozart. But my fiancée knows all about Mozart. She made me approach that perfection one more time. Did you hear it or were you off somewhere, as usual, darling?'

Vicky led her new friend out into the corridor.

'Come here, please, Vicky!' said Serge sternly. Vicky saw Micky Duke leaving with the last of the queue and asked him to find Modigliani's niece a taxi.

'He wanted her to go with him. Please believe me, she didn't just abandon those new lives.' And Vicky pressed the woman's hand, a gesture totally new and unexpected.

She went back into the dressing room and closed the door as a precaution. Serge was tugging off his white scarf and threw it to the floor. 'You're completely disloyal. Don't you know I have to go out there feeling tranquil? All rows must be forgotten when Mozart begins, you'd better believe that. The reception which you missed was to celebrate our getting married but I am stood up. It looks wonderful, doesn't it?' He tore at his jacket. 'You're the one who said, go back to Mozart, I love you, I am there for you. I am certainly not going to do "The Marriage of Figaro" tomorrow. I am going to cancel.'

Serge, something extraordinary happened. I met this woman in the powder room and she is Modigliani's niece.'

'Modigliani! Modigliani!' His eyes gleamed maliciously. 'That's a strange life he had. What a terrible life. Ugh.' He shuddered. 'And you spend all your time reading about him. All those books. I don't understand why you waste your thoughts on that – poseur.' He could not be contemptuous enough. 'What kind of indulgent show off was he?'

'A genius.'

'A genius!' That made him more outraged. 'So that destructive, womanizing, self-indulgent, overrated, irresponsible addict, who drank himself to death, was a genius!'

'That's right, darling.' She sounded sweet. 'They have poor lives, so you'd never notice them. They don't eat and they never get any applause and they have to struggle for everything, and they get dispirited and dejected and try and soothe themselves with artificial highs. They go through all the illness and weakness a body can conceivably endure and then they die. And, in that moment, their work soars free and people like you buy it.'

'Poverty, no recognition, dejection, bitterness, addiction. These are genius? So, you're telling me I'm not a genius?'

'Don't worry, Serge. You've got everything else. The luxury, the abundance, the fame, the respect, the power –'

He slapped her hard, twice.

'So it's not such a terrible thing, missing out on the genius.'

He slapped her harder.

'Mozart wrote it. You just play it. Now *he's* a genius.'

'And I'm not?' His voice was bitter and dangerous.

'You're an interpreter. The pay's better. She grabbed her bag and Serge tried to strangle her.

At that moment the impresario opened the door.

Serge said, 'Get out!'

The man left in an icy panic.

Serge turned on Vicky. 'You seem like one huge mess.'

'Fuck you, Serge. I'm organizing the wedding, programming your social life, waiting at airports, backstage, at society banquets, at recording studios, sympathizing over a disc dissolving, going to bed with you, and I'm trying to stay fucking sane.'

'Sane?' He picked up on that one.

She bit her bottom lip like a child. That was not smart. Never hint at the possibility of not being sane. 'The travelling doesn't suit me.'

'But you never stop. Paris, London, Paris. Do you need a doctor?'

She was frightened. She might lose him. She realized he was here in the flesh, loyal to her, wanting to share his life with her and she was almost idly putting it all at risk because she had met a French woman in the powder room. She would never, ever mention the name Modigliani again, even in her head.

'Do you know what you should do, since you hate my life, being in it? Be in yours. Go and do the radio documentary. I gave you the interviews and you have the recorded material from my friends.'

She didn't say anything.

'I mean, do the radio documentary on me.'

'Yes, that would get me back my identity,' she said sarcastically.

He reached across and pulled her dress straps down. 'Bed time,' he smiled. 'At least you still enjoy that.' And he locked the dressing-room door.

· *Fifty-two* ·

Micky Duke ran the tapes back again. 'There was something.'

'Oh, leave it,' she said, irritated. 'It's probably an echo.' She was meeting Serge in ten minutes so they could drive down to the country house together. She had apologized for her embittered outburst in the dressing-room and called it wedding nerves. But it was nerves of another kind. The endless search for Modigliani had worn her down. And her own life, not being lived, had become abandoned, its protagonists angry. It had all been too tough. She would give up this quest for a man half-seen. The documentary was put together speedily, as her wedding present to Serge.

Micky Duke was still busy at the grams. 'It's incredible that he's put Mozart into his répertoire.' Micky reversed the tapes. 'He'd vowed never to conduct Mozart again. What changed his mind?'

'Ego,' she said fiercely.

Micky laughed. 'Are you nervous? It's tomorrow, isn't it?'

She had no idea what their life together would be like. There would be a lot of violent musical clashes and cancellations which his fans were still happy to call temperament. But he was kind to her. After their quarrel he had pulled her into his arms, in tears because he had harmed her. He had never harmed a woman in his life. 'I just wish, Vicky, that I could be sure of you. When you go out of the door I never know if I'll see you again.'

Vicky gathered her pencils and notebook and bag together. Less than a year ago she had sat in this room dreaming of Serge Marais. Now she was marrying him.

'Here it is,' said Micky.

'Just erase it. I trust you. Hurry up!'

'No, it's a word. Listen.'

Serge Marais said, 'My life is music. Everything I do strives for its perfection. No, it is not a religion. I am not religious, not at all. I was as a child. From my mother's influence I became a Christian but then, later, I became a Buddhist because I am in tune with that –' Micky jerked forward onto the next tape. Serge said, 'How can you put music into words? Mozart is gold. Music begins where words cannot reach.'

A voice she would know anywhere said, 'Jeanne.' Silence. 'Jeanne. I cannot let you do it. It goes against us, everything that we are –'

Silence.

'Play it back.'

It was Modi's voice.

She sat down, shaken.

Micky said it must have got cut in from another production and she agreed. He took the reel. He wanted to erase the interloper.

'No,' she said. 'I'll take that.'

Later, in the pub, Micky Duke said, 'I'll really miss working with her. She was always so nice and modest.'

Another technician said, 'No airs and graces. She just did her job.'

They all talked about her as though she had gone forever.

If Serge had to sum up in one word why he stayed with Vicky, that word was loss. A particular evening always came to mind. They were in Bel Air and they had been making lists of guests for their wedding. They had played backgammon and after that, he had gone for a walk alone. He felt suddenly jaded and that he was tired of her. He wondered if it was worth all the change. She was becoming as habitual as Anna. Yes, he was getting tired of her.

When he got back home, a stranger was sitting in her place. She did not speak or even look at him. Her thoughts were far away. When he spoke, she answered mechanically. For the rest of the evening it was as though a fairy wand had spirited away his mistress. During the night she was distant, as though belonging to someone else, as though she had another lover. Terrified, he vowed he would never think of leaving her again. He blamed work pressure for his thoughts of disloyalty. In the days that followed, he needed her more than ever. Her very look said, 'Don't take me for granted.'

Vicky left the guests in the library. Serge was putting away the brandy. Jay had still not arrived. Vicky went into the bedroom to try on her dress of *eau de Nil* silk and a small veil covered in apple blossom. It was April 6th, Jeanne Hebuterne's birthday. Looking in the mirror, she said, 'Why don't I like my life? Because I feel so exhausted.' Twice she asked and each time came the same answer. She checked her make-up and heated rollers. Downstairs, the guests were growing noisy. The window flew open, as though pushed by a strong wind, and he, the painter, was there, silhouetted against a country sky full of stars. He held out his hand to her. He looked beautiful, healed, well.

'You cannot marry that man. He is everything I am not.' He was solid, with all the necessary dimensions to make him real.

'I have to,' she said.

'You don't love him.'

The healer had said, 'Tell him to go. Get him out of your thoughts. You cannot change the past. Only repeat it.' But she was slipping back, sliding fast into the other time, so much stronger, more vital than now, when she felt something she was not ashamed to call loving.

'I promised him.'

'You promised me.' He was angry. 'Don't you remember? We made a pact for eternity. You joined me. You must remember.' He tried to take off her veil. 'What are you doing? How can you give yourself to a man like that?' He sounded amazed. 'Hold my hand.' And he held out his, a hand that, with one confident line, could draw a face, or whatever was behind the face.

She did not take it.

'Come with me, Jeanne. I promise you better than what he can give. Joy. You know I give you that.'

She could see the stars, very bright, behind him, as though clustered around for his benefit. 'We can have what we agreed, for eternity. I've come for you, as I promised. Don't let us lose each other now. Now is all I have. Now I'm here, I'm with you. Join me.'

'Join you?' She was astounded.

'Come on. Hold my hand.'

Hypnotized by his eyes, she went towards him and touched his hand. It was real. It was warm. He let his fingers slide over hers until their hands were joined. Her blood tingled with happiness. He took off her engagement ring and threw it onto the bed. 'All the things I promised you, remember?' His voice was so seductive. He always said he could get anything out of a woman just by looking at her in a certain way. His voice alone could give total pleasure.

And then she remembered Jay saying, 'Modigliani can never commit himself to a woman. He's fixed on his mother.'

'But you weren't free,' she said. 'You were joined to your mother.'

'What if I was!' He was outraged. 'What difference does that make? You're mine.' And his eyes flared so his pupils expanded over the dark irises. He caressed her neck. 'We've been through the time of waiting. We've endured such distress and still you hesitate. I don't understand.' He touched her neck, where recently Serge's locket had hung. 'If you love me, there's no hesitation. I don't understand your distrust.' Then he held her and her body strained against his and her arms wound around his back, pulling him closer. And in that moment she felt he was all she had ever looked for or wanted. As she held him she saw the carnival dance where he had first touched her. And as she danced with him her friend, Julie, said, 'You look as though you're in a dream.'

'I'm an art student,' she had said.

'I've seen you,' he had said.

For how long she had seen him, wanted him.

'Be with me.' And he lifted back her wedding veil.

'How?'

'Just jump.' He made it sound so enticing.

'Jump?' And she remembered she was Vicky, that she was independent. She knew reality this time round. She was loved, needed. She wanted to be spiritually evolved. She had a certain self-respect, earned from passing through only bad experiences, and she knew who she was. She went to the window and he helped her onto the ledge. She said, 'I have a choice. I've chosen.'

'Oh, Jeanne,' he said, his voice so happy.

And she jumped.

Jeanne sat beside him in the studio and the sardines were withered and grey in their tin, past eating. He took the tin and she helped him get one into his mouth. Across the courtyard a violinist played Mozart. Modi gestured for the bottle and she gave it to him. He washed the sardine down, choking. The painting was still wet and shining on the easel. It depicted a musician he had met and had a drink with on New Year's Eve.

Still no one came up the stairs. He held onto her, his hands on her breasts. 'It will be alright,' he said.

The air was icy and the child kicked strongly inside her.

'They could still get you to Italy.'

'For what?' He closed his eyes. 'Why fill more canvasses that no one wants? I'm done for.' The smell of death, it was in the bed, sickly sweet. It had been there since the morning. 'Lie on me, Jeanne, and that will give me warmth.'

At last he was hers. No one else could come and take him away. And they lay together, she, he and the baby kicking inside her stomach. They drifted in and out of a grey sleep into a freezing January day. Then he lurched up from the bed, covered in sweat, feverish, and she thought he was going to try again to go out. 'Give me a drink.'

She gave him what there was.

'Say it. Now.'

'I can't.' And she remembered the priest.

'Then you will lose me and I you.'

Horrified, she said quickly, 'I give up all religion, all belief in

God, all faith, to be with you. I give up myself, my future. I've already given up my mother, father, brother, child. There will be no one else for me for eternity. Our souls are united. I have no other wish to be –'

He was looking at her, his mournful eyes heavy with fever. Even drunk, he knew exactly what he was doing. Dying made no difference. 'Do it, Jeanne. What I told you.'

And she promised, even cut their skin with a razor so their blood joined together. Yet she was terrified of God, of the punishment she would receive.

'You will be with me?' Her voice was full of fear.

'Always, always.' And he gestured the Greek way of dying. Backwards, still looking at the life that had gone.

She felt so broken by the pact she had just made, she could no longer speak.

Then the Chilean, Ortiz, pushed his way into the room. Now they were there, all of them, to take him away. 'Hold my hand, Jeanne.' His voice was hoarse, barely audible. And their hands joined in a clasp that the Chilean had difficulty breaking.

'Just leave him,' she said. 'He's almost gone anyway. You're always interfering, always taking him from me.'

As they carried him away he whispered, 'Jeanne, you know what you have to do.'

She watched them carry him down the stairs. From the window, she saw them run with him across the courtyard, past the tree. She scribbled on the wall, the awful truth, the worst of all. 'The past can only be repeated. You change nothing.'

And she took the bangle which hung in the end window, the one he had given her. She had watched him paint it. 'Who's that for?' she had asked.

He gave it to her. 'The only jewellery you will ever wear and be happy with.' Painted inside, 'To Jeanne, from Modi'. And then someone took her downstairs. She could not even think anymore. They took her to see him and then to Zbo's, then to a hotel. She knew the pains in his head were terrible. She could always feel whatever he did, they were so close. Then they took her to the mortuary and from there, past the Panthéon, to the apartment in Rue Amyot. Against the background of their terrible arguments, she went to the window. She was so exhausted, she had no energy left, nothing left, not one breath in her body. She was incapable of bringing this child into the world. She had not one jot of energy that could help her give birth, get her through all that pain. Of course, he was dead. And she was dead. She had seen her end a long time ago, long before they had made the pact. He was a psychic and he could influence her, he had said. He would come and get her. Where was he now? The room was empty, she was empty. He had not come. She opened the window and climbed on to the low railing outside and fell backwards. Just before toppling out she grasped hold of the bangle he had painted for her. She did not want it smashed. It was still half around her hand as she fell.

Vicky's mother, reading about the proposed marriage of her daughter, was waiting outside the house, hoping at least to catch one glimpse of this secretive daughter she had never been able to love. She was glad Vicky had made a good marriage. One glimpse and then she would go. She would not cause the girl any embarrassment. Ruby felt guilty that she had never been a proper mother. She could see posh people in evening clothes in the garden and more in a ground-floor room full of books. There was piano music, drunken laughter, the chink of glasses.

The glimpse she got of her daughter was not the one she had expected.

From a window at the top of the house a girl in a wedding veil came toppling down. Thinking it might be a return of her illness, Ruby left hurriedly.

Lorraine was in labour but did not want Jay to be with her. 'Vicky gave me a beautiful letter, written by a woman called Simone Thiroux. She had Modigliani's child but he wouldn't acknowledge it either.'

'OK, I got the either,' said Jay.

'Vicky said the painter would come rushing out of a place called Rosalie's screaming, Simone's child is not mine, I'll have nothing to do with it, or her. Vicky said he was angry because he felt he had been duped. Nothing changes much, does it? Vicky knows a lot about Modigliani. And is that a coincidence?'

'Why?' said Jay.

Lorraine looked smug.' Who needs you, Jay? I know who my baby is. He's the reincarnation of someone great – a painter,' she said simply. 'And when his spirit links into the baby, he will be born.'

Jay sat with the healer in North London. 'Vicky wants you to come to the wedding reception. It's tomorrow afternoon.'

The healer shook his head.

'D'you think the things she says she experienced are actual?'

'Of course,' said the healer.

'The thing she can't work out, and nor can I, is why Jeanne took her life with the baby about to be born? Why didn't she wait a day? Two days?'

'Have you any other questions?'

'Yes. Why didn't she get a doctor for Modigliani? She let him die.'

'Is this for your book?' asked the healer.

'The book has no validity, not without proof. If I could get that I'd have a best-seller. But Vicky's getting married tomorrow and I must go now and see her. They're giving a party tonight. Honeymoon in Greece. My book is useless but she's happy. Can you answer my questions at least?'

The healer sat very still and when he spoke his voice was slightly altered. It seemed as though he was speaking from another location.

'Vicky was Jeanne Hebuterne in a former life. She was in love with Modi – he was her whole life. She knew it would be difficult to keep him because other women, other people, were always trying to get him away from her. They were always interfering. She couldn't bear him to go. His model, Lunia, had tried to take him, to save him, because she, too, loved him. Jeanne was jealous and so he did not go. He loved her in his fashion, but he did not want her to be always in front of his face, looking at him, adoring him. He needed a certain freedom. In that last week that so bothers you, she did not deliberately keep him from medical help. She knew he was dying and he no longer wanted to live. She wanted those days, at least, to be spent with her. She wanted those last hours. But then they came and took him away and they took her also, but not directly to the house of her family. I feel she went somewhere else first.'

Jay said, 'To a hotel. They put her for one night into a hotel. But alone.'

The healer continued speaking, rhythmically, in a light trance. 'Then they came and took her to the hospital, then to someone's studio, then to the mortuary. Then her father took her to his house. She had nothing left inside her. She was exhausted, and she went to the window like an automaton. He was dead and so she had no reason to live. She had no energy to give birth to that child. I would say her death was inevitable. She had decided on her end some time before. It had always been decided. Before he died he made her swear something, to join him in the next world, to be his for eternity. When she fell into the street her spirit remained attached, just above her body. And she could still feel everything. She saw the futility of what she had done. She had committed that act and yet was still alive, conscious. She saw her body taken here, there, in the streets and buildings of Paris. It was unwanted. She didn't journey to the spirit world but remained in the ethera, waiting for him.'

'The ethera. She mentioned that. A grey place with nothing there. Was that a punishment?'

'A state of limbo where she waited because she remained attached to her past joy and passion. She couldn't let go. She waited for him to join her. Vicky was born into this life with the opportunity to put right some of the wrongs she'd done in her former life and so go forward. From his spirit state, he found her in this life and became linked with her again. As long as she was alone and not likely to be taken from him, he remained hidden. The moment she fell in love with Serge Marais he made himself known and claimed her back. I think you will be able to write your book and get the reward for it you ask.'

He saw Jay to the door. 'Paris was a terrible place for her. A purgatorial path. She knew spiritual misery there, the bereavement she could not bear, her suicide, and thus the death of her baby, and the afterdeath state which she could never lose. That's a spiritual pain worse than any physical suffering. Do you agree?'

Jay remembered the feeling he had got from the image of the dusty studio. It was a doorway into hell or, as the healer said, purgatory.

When he got to the party, Serge said Vicky was preparing for the following day. 'Have a drink. Toast my happiness. I never thought I'd get her.'

Jay heard the crash and reached her first. A crowd gathered and Serge knelt beside her. Jay said not to touch her.

Serge put his head to her chest, but Jay could see that Vicky was dead. Then he saw the bangle. It had slipped over her hand as though she had tried to take it off at the last minute. He looked at it, pink with a mauve and green decoration and eased it off gently. 'I have never seen that,' said Serge. 'Where did it come from? Why is it on her hand?'

Jay turned it around, then looked inside.

In black paint it said, 'To Jeanne, con tanto, tanto amore. Modi. Paris, 1919.'

Also available from Mandarin Paperbacks

JOAN DRUETT

Abigail

Born at sea in the 1830s. Abigail is the headstrong daughter of Captain Sherman, American vice-consul in Auckland, New Zealand.

As quick and supple as the natives with whom she grows, Abigail is sent to America on the *Erasmus* to stay with relatives and learn a decorum that chafes against her every instinct for freedom.

Shocked by the news of the murder of her father, she vows to trace both his killers and her inheritance, the brig *Pandora* on which she was born.

Defiantly returning to her first love the ocean, Abigail becomes embroiled with Seth Morgan, the whaler who is as wild and stormy as the seas he sails.

Richly embellished with vivid details of life on board the whaling ships of the last century, *Abigail* is the irresistible story of a most remarkable woman.

Love, Mutiny and Peril on the World's Most Lonely Ocean

KATE SAUNDERS

Storm In The Citadel

'A stinging portrayal of the intriguing, promiscuous, backbiting life of a theatrical company.'
Daily Telegraph

DRAMA CHAOS AND TRAGEDY OFF-STAGE

Cosmo Brady is the tortured Irish actor haunted by his loss of faith in God and his long-standing girlfriend, a different Faith, who has quietly married another man.

Grief gives him centre stage in the viper's nest of incestuous tensions and jealousies of the famous theatrical company for which he is the frequent butt of gossipy jokes. So no one could be more palpably grateful than he when he wins stupendously beautiful Hester Stretton, herself on the rebound from the villainously amorous Vinny with whom Cosmo shares his dressing room.

When Cosmo's love begins to reach unthinkable proportions Hester's hesitant favours finally give way to a rejection that betrays in Cosmo a shocking and unexpected twist of character and fate.

Kate Saunders has the wickedest sense of dark humour and a sharp eye for the pathos, desperation and farce to be found in the quicksilver quality of company life.

'Saunders writes about the incidental traumas of ordinary life with a cool, off-centre absorption . . . She can be very funny.' *Sunday Times*

'Excellent . . . toxically funny' *Guardian*